GOLDEN GIRL

"Why, Kate Holden, are you scared of me?"

"I suppose I am, a little. Mr. Talbott, you should know that with very little effort on your part, I could come to care for you." Her cheeks were on fire and her mouth was dry, but she forced herself to continue on. "In the past, you have been very kind to me. I am hoping that you could extend that kindness once again and not come calling at our boarding house."

"Let me make certain I know what you are asking, my golden girl. You do not wish for me to call on you, or take you on drives, or out to dinner, or on any other diversion which a young lady your age might find pleasant?" His blue gaze was unreadable.

"That is correct, sir. I wish to ask, at the risk of being rude once again, that you will simply stay away from me."

"It is a wise request, little scholar, but I'm not at all sure I can abide by it," Justin muttered under his breath. He stepped forward and pulled her into his arms.

GOLDEN DREAMS

ANNA DeFOREST

LEISURE BOOKS   NEW YORK CITY

For my father,
John B. Holyoke
Because this is the first, and because he always
knew and cared about my golden dreams.

A LEISURE BOOK®

February 1997

Published by

Dorchester Publishing Co., Inc.
276 Fifth Avenue
New York, NY 10001

The name "Leisure Books" and the stylized "L" with design are trademarks of Dorchester Publishing Co., Inc.

Printed in the United States of America.

ACKNOWLEDGMENTS

Pam Hopkins, my loyal agent, for sticking with me during four long, lean years.

Joanna Cagan, my editor, for having such excellent taste and being so easy to work with.

Julie Holyoke, my loving sister, for being my most insightful and helpful critic.

Jane Champ, my dear mother-in-law, for her terrific proofreading.

Laurie Kuelthau, for reading every one of my books and being so excited about all of them.

Cindy Gay, my very first reader, for saying, "This actually reads like a book!"

Jeanette Baker-Ramirez, my mentor, for her excellent critique and wise advice.

RWA Members of LARA, Orange County and San Diego chapters, for their ongoing support and encouragement.

Angie Ray and Sandy Chvostal, for just assuming I would make a sale someday soon.

Laura Peters, Billie Jo Johnston, Kristin Hanson, Jeanne Maas, Lynn Key, Susan Tweedy, and Patty Sorenson for reading my various manuscripts and helping to improve them.

Beth, Jill, Cynthia, K-Rae, Corinne, Jim, Denny, and Maureen, for being so supportive of my writing and making me feel so welcome in San Diego.

Meg Meis, for being the other best sister in the whole world, and a wonderful aunt into the bargain.

Beau, our quiet, loyal friend, for being the best companion a writer could have. Max and the rest of us miss you every day.

Edith Holyoke, my remarkable mother, for giving me the confidence that I could do or be anything I wanted.

Joseph and Sarah, my wonderful husband and daughter, for their endless patience, love and caring.

GOLDEN DREAMS

Prologue

June 8, 1892
Boston, Massachusetts

His debt was paid at last. Justin Talbott smiled grimly as he stepped out into the greenness of the formal garden. He never would be able to pay the old man back for all he truly owed him. The money was only part of it. More important was the faith Thomas Holden had always had in his abilities and his judgment.

Justin glanced back at the elegant brick mansion. Thomas's loan had made it possible for him to leave Boston and his father's shattered reputation behind. In the gold and silver camps of the West, Justin had done well for himself. He had taken Thomas's stake and multiplied it ten times over. In another few years Justin meant to be a millionaire.

Then he could show the bigoted citizens of Boston a thing or two. He would make the very men and women who had ostracized him rue their intolerance. He glanced down at his hands. They were clenched into fists. Deliberately he forced himself to relax. Perhaps by then he would have outgrown this provincial city. He had spent so much time in the clean, vast lands beyond the Mississippi that Boston already seemed dingier and smaller than he remembered. He turned and strode along the stone wall bordering the garden.

Suddenly he glimpsed a flash of white skirts and the glint of sun shining off dark brown curls. Ruefully he shook his head. He should have known the old fox was up to something when Thomas suggested that he take a quick stroll in the gardens before leaving. So the old man wanted to match him with one of his two daughters. He had thought that might have been

9

his play when Thomas was so insistent about his coming to their dinner tomorrow night. He supposed he should feel honored instead of annoyed by the old man's machinations. Considering the shadow still attached to the Talbott name, it was amazing that Thomas would let him near the two young women who were his pride and joy.

Justin turned about and walked toward the other end of the garden. He was not about to fall into Thomas's trap. He had lost his heart once to a pampered, well-bred Boston girl, and now he no longer possessed a heart to lose again. He moved quietly across the green lawn, having spent time in wild places out west where noisy tenderfeet and pilgrims never lived long. Still absorbed in his thoughts, he hardly noticed the beds of blue forget-me-nots, pink foxglove, and white candytuft blooming at his feet.

A few moments later he walked right past her. In fact he wouldn't have noticed her at all if she hadn't moved just then. He heard the rustle of cloth on cloth and spun about in surprise. Not twenty feet away a beautiful girl sat reading beneath a rose arbor. He paused, his eyebrows lifting in cynical appreciation. She had tucked her legs sideways on the little wooden bench, affording him a tantalizing glimpse of a slim ankle. The white skirts of her cotton frock had slipped off the bench onto the green grass beneath it. She had discarded her straw hat, which lay on the grass near her skirts. Her long, blond hair curled about her shoulders and flowed down to her waist. Her tresses glowed a brilliant gold where the sun touched them. She had her chin propped on her hand while she pored over the slim volume in her lap.

She made a lovely sight. Indeed, she looked so appealing that he was quite willing to wager that the clever minx had posed herself in the arbor just that way to catch his attention.

Unwilling to play games with a young miss just out of the schoolroom, he pivoted swiftly and walked away. He paused near an ash tree and glanced over his shoulder. He was curious to see what Thomas's daughter would do when she realized that her game had been foiled. To his surprise she did nothing. After several moments she turned a page of the book she was reading. He turned about to study her again, beginning to think he had been wrong. While he watched, her fine brows drew together in a frown, and her lips moved.

Abruptly he remembered where he was. Although he had little use for the rules of polite society, he felt bad for staring at his benefactor's daughter. He was about to slip away when she glanced up suddenly. Her expressive eyes were dreamy and unfocused, and she didn't seem to notice him at first. He was pleased to discover her eyes weren't the common blue color he was expecting. Instead they were a remarkable dark green, the color of fine jade, rimmed round with long dark lashes. They could have been the eyes of a siren or a temptress. Yet the innocent look in them told him clearly that this girl was neither.

When she finally noticed him standing beside the ash tree, her eyes widened. She snatched her skirts down over her ankles and jumped to her feet. Her book went tumbling out of her lap to fall unnoticed on the ground.

"Oh, hullo there." Her cheeks were blushing rosily, but she managed to offer him an apology with remarkable composure. "I'm sorry, I didn't mean to be rude. Papa always says I'm oblivious to the world when I'm reading."

"It was rude of me to startle you," Justin declared as he strode forward and leaned over to retrieve her book.

"You must be able to walk very quietly." She smiled at him when he stood upright again with her book in his hand. She cocked her head while she studied him with a frank look.

"You must be Justin Talbott. Papa has told us all about you. He admires you a great deal, you know. Since he is not here to do the formal honors, I think we will just have to introduce ourselves. My name is Kate," she finished in a friendly fashion and held out her hand.

"I'd heard that Thomas Holden's daughter was a beauty." He took her hand and held on to it longer than he meant to.

"Indeed, sir, you are very kind, but the daughter you most likely heard about is my sister Elizabeth," Kate corrected him cheerfully and pulled her hand back. "The newspapers all say she is the belle of the season."

"Are you envious?" The girl's frank manner encouraged him to ask a personal question.

She gave a surprised laugh. "Oh, no, sir. I am very pleased for my sister's social success. You see, Elizabeth wants to marry a kind, handsome husband more than anything. Now that she is a belle, she will have plenty of suitors to choose from.''

"And what do you want?" he asked, watching her curiously.

"Well, getting married someday might be fine if I have time for it, but first I want to go to college, and I would like to travel all about the Continent. And then there's something I want to do more than anything else, but I don't think I'll tell you what it is because you will think I'm being eccentric and quaint. Everyone else does, except Papa."

"What if I promise that I couldn't possibly believe your dream is quaint?" Justin surprised himself by saying gallantly. He wondered when the last time was that he had bothered to be gallant to a woman.

"Well, Papa says that you are a man of great honor, and so I will trust you to hold to your promise." She paused and drew in a deep breath. "I should very much like to be a professor of history at a women's college," she declared in a grand tone.

It took all of Justin's considerable self-control not to let his amusement show. Here one of the most lovely creatures he had ever seen was declaring she meant to spend her life mewed up in the dry, dusty halls of academia. Before she knew it, some passionate young man would sweep her off her feet and show her there was much more to life than history. But Justin knew what it was to love learning and to have ideals and dreams. He had possessed dreams of his own once, and he understood what it was like to have them laughed at and eventually crushed. And so he didn't laugh or even smile at her earnest declaration.

Instead he said simply, "I wish you the best of luck. But surely you have much studying to do to reach such a goal."

She sighed and nodded seriously. "It's true. Papa lets me work with a special tutor several times a week. I will be starting my first year at Wellesley College in the fall. But I'm not the least bit interesting to talk about. Please, could you tell me something about your travels in the west? Although I've read about the frontier, it's not the same as seeing a place with your own eyes."

"What would you like to know? The great West is a broad topic." At that moment he was wondering if she had already begun to learn how to use that green gaze of hers to bend men to her will, and so he spoke more sternly than he intended. His young listener, however, didn't seem the least bit intimidated by his tone.

"You are quite right. I should know better than to ask a vague question after all the logic I've been studying recently. I will ask instead, sir, have you seen any buffalo?"

"When I first went west fifteen years ago, the great, shaggy beasts were everywhere. Once, a train I was riding stopped for over an hour while a herd of thousands of buffalo drifted across the tracks. Since that time, though, the hide hunters have been reducing their numbers steadily."

"It must have been grand when they covered the prairie by the millions. I'm afraid there won't be any left by the time I have a chance to travel out west," she said pensively, and then she brightened. "Are the Rocky Mountains truly higher than our Adirondacks and the White Mountains?"

"The rugged young peaks rising from the western plains make our eastern mountains look like sedate old gentlemen," he replied warmly.

Her eyes danced with delight. "Why, sir, you have a fine gift for simile."

He stared down at her, amazed that she was actually laughing at him. "You begin to make me feel like a sedate old gentleman," he said with feeling.

She peered up at him. "Honestly, sir, I did not mean to. The way you appeared when I first saw you reminded me so of Papa when he is worrying about his business affairs. I meant only to tease you out of your doldrums."

"My dear, this dried-up old husk is not worth your efforts." He glanced away from her steady gaze, amazed at how much he suddenly wished he were ten years younger. So much hard and decadent living separated him from her and her buoyant outlook on life.

"Oh, so you see yourself as a dried-up husk at what, the ripe old age of thirty?" she scoffed at his words. "You certainly don't look old. Besides, I have it on good authority that no man can be dried up or a husk until he is at least forty."

Justin threw back his head and laughed aloud at her pronouncement, for it was delivered in such a sage, serious way.

"There, you see, you are looking younger now. You should
do that much more often," she said with a smile.

"I believe, little minx, that if I spent more time in your
company I would laugh much more often. Unfortunately I
must leave now for a business appointment, or I will be late.
Here is your book I rescued from the grass."

He glanced down at the title as he started to hand the volume back to her. He paused and raised an eyebrow at her. He
opened the first few pages to skim their contents.

"Very impressive. I don't believe I've ever known a female
who could read the *Iliad* in Greek."

"There are no biological precepts that state the female mind
cannot understand ancient languages," she said a little stiffly.

"There's no need to ruffle your feathers at me, young Kate.
I've never thought women were incapable of such intellectual
exercise. I simply have never met a female dedicated enough
to master the language before now. Will I see you at the dinner
your father is hosting here tomorrow night?"

"Why, yes, you will," she answered uncertainly, obviously
thrown off by his abrupt change of subject.

"If you have more questions about the frontier, I shall be
happy to answer them for you then," he said cordially. "And
now I must let you return to Homer and his battles."

"But sir, don't you have time to meet my sister? I know
she is here in the garden, and she would love to make your
acquaintance."

"For today, I'm happy to have shared the company of such
a lovely scholar. I can meet the belle of your family tomorrow
night." He tipped his hat to her and took himself off toward
the house.

Kate stared after the retreating figure of Justin Talbott for
several moments before dashing away to find her sister.

"Libby, Libby, where are you?" she called as she ran along
the garden paths.

"I'm over here on the seat by the peonies," Elizabeth replied calmly when Kate would have gone charging past her.
Kate came to a quick stop in a flurry of petticoats.

"I just met the most remarkable man," Kate managed to get out between pants.

Elizabeth glanced up at her young sister and immediately put her needlework aside. "He must have been remarkable to get you into such a tither. You are usually too busy with your books to notice much about gentlemen."

"I couldn't help but notice this one. Oh, Libby, he is so handsome. He's taller than your Edward Hollister and his shoulders are broader, too. He has this wonderful thick, black hair, and I think the western sun must have tanned him dark as an Indian. He has deep blue eyes that look right through you. And I told him I was going to be a professor, and he didn't even laugh at me."

"Ah, so you've met Justin Talbott. You know he is too old for you," Elizabeth said gently, reluctant to quench her sister's enthusiasm.

"I know. I think he was trying to point that out to me, too, in the nicest possible way." Kate sank down beside Elizabeth on the bench. "But that doesn't mean I can't enjoy thinking about him. He said he would come to the party tomorrow night, and I can ask him about life out west."

"That was kind of him," Elizabeth said in a carefully neutral tone.

"Libby, what do you know about him?" Kate asked in a rush. "Father talked all about his going west and making a fortune in the gold camps, but I think there must be a great deal more that he didn't tell us. Mr. Talbott looks so bitter and sad sometimes."

"I suppose he has good cause," Elizabeth said slowly.

"So you do know what happened to him. Please tell me," Kate pleaded and leaned forward on the seat.

"You were probably too young when the scandal took place to remember, but it was all anyone in Boston talked about for a long time. Justin's father, Brian Talbott, was a great friend of Father's. In fact he was our banker for many years. Mr. Talbott's wife was a beautiful woman, but Alicia Talbott had expensive tastes. She made her husband buy her a mansion here on Beacon Hill and another one in Newport. She always wore the finest fashions and entertained lavishly. Unfortunately she squandered his family's fortune, and Mr. Talbott couldn't support the life she wanted on his banker's salary. Because he loved her desperately, he did a terrible thing. He began taking money from the bank that wasn't his.''

Kate drew in a breath. "Did they catch him?"

"Eventually they did, and he was ruined. Alicia left him the moment she discovered her husband could no longer finance her extravagant lifestyle. Brian Talbott shot himself before they could bring him to trial for embezzlement.''

"Poor, poor Justin," Kate exclaimed in dismay. "How old was he when all this happened?"

"He was just starting his final year at Harvard. He was engaged to marry Lavinia Westford, the current Mrs. Peter Moore. Her family broke off the engagement the minute they heard about Mr. Talbott's problems at the bank. Father says Justin worked his way through his final year of college and then decided to go west to seek his fortune. Boston was just too small a city, and people here have long memories.''

"How could anyone possibly blame Justin for what his father did, or what his mother drove his father to do?"

"It's not fair at all," Elizabeth replied serenely, "but no one ever said the social leaders of this city were fair."

"So that's why there's something so hard about him," Kate said musingly.

"He hasn't exactly been pining for female companionship all this time, you know," Elizabeth said with some amusement. "Your Justin has gained quite a reputation as a ladies' man here in Boston and in New York whenever he comes east.''

"Well, I'm glad he's found some pleasure and entertainment with women after what that Lavinia did to him."

"Kate, when will you ever learn not to speak of such things? You know it isn't ladylike."

"I don't think Mr. Talbott cared that I wasn't ladylike," Kate said dreamily as she leaned back and stretched her arms above her head. "I introduced myself to him, and he didn't seem the least bit shocked."

"Kate, you shouldn't be so forward." Elizabeth sighed, knowing better than to press the matter. The intricate rules that bound the members of their polite society constantly chafed her high-spirited sister. Elizabeth decided it was time to change the subject.

"Justin Talbott certainly seems to have made an impression on you. I'm looking forward to meeting him tomorrow night," she stated as she picked up her embroidery hoop once more.

"He'll probably take one look at you and forget all about me," Kate predicted glumly. "When men catch a glimpse of your big brown eyes and porcelain-fine skin, they cease to remember there are any other females in the room."

"Oh, Kate, you silly goose. We've been through all this before. You could have gentlemen flocking all about you if you would just pay them a little mind. Men like to be listened to. You scare them off with all your talk about history, Latin, and Greek."

"I don't want men flocking all about me. I wouldn't have any idea what to do with them. Besides, we have too many of your suitors about the house as it is. I keep tripping over them in the hall and the parlor." Kate slanted a teasing glance at her sister. "And tomorrow night we'll have rooms full of them. When are you going to choose one and put the rest of the poor devils out of their misery?"

"When I find the right one," Elizabeth replied placidly and made a neat French knot with her lavender silk thread. When she finished, she glanced up at the sun.

"I suppose I had best go inside now. It's almost time for dinner." She gathered up her embroidery and placed it in her brocade sewing bag. "Are you coming?"

"No, you go ahead. I will be along in a few minutes," Kate replied absently.

Smiling and shaking her head, Elizabeth made her way toward the house. She was willing to wager her favorite thimble that for once Kate wasn't dreaming about her ancient Greeks.

Chapter One

May 14, 1894
Pikes Peak region

As the stagecoach wheels jolted over a particularly large rock, the entire conveyance swung wildly from side to side on its leather braces. Kate smothered a laugh and grasped the edge of the window beside her to steady herself. They had been on the road for several hours now, and the Florissant route to Cripple Creek was proving to be even rougher than the driver had described. It was also unbelievably lovely. Above green rolling hills dotted with ponderosa pines, the rocky shoulders and ridges of legendary Pikes Peak rose gray and jagged against the brilliantly blue Colorado sky.

After the stage coach resumed its normal bouncing and swaying, Kate hugged herself in excitement. For so many months now she had been dreaming of coming to Cripple Creek, the site of the newest gold rush in the country. Ever since she had heard Justin Talbott describe this colorful town where firemen, druggists, and cowboys had become rich overnight, she had wanted to see Cripple Creek and experience the excitement of a boomtown firsthand. She bit her lip at the thought of Justin. For the thousandth time she told herself she must not indulge in foolish daydreams. Even if by some chance their paths did cross in Cripple Creek, Justin would not want to be a part of her future now.

Kate stroked the plain gray folds of her traveling dress. If only dear Papa had lived. Everything would be so different. This spring she would be at college studying for her examinations and looking forward to the long summer holiday at her old home in Boston. Lifting her chin, she decided that she

18

simply had different challenges to face now, and she was lucky that they were so intriguing. She could hardly wait to begin her new life in Cripple Creek. Surely she would be able to find some sort of post there as a teacher, tutor, or governess.

The stagecoach suddenly lurched again, throwing its passengers sharply forward and then back.

"Christ almighty," the red-faced rancher sitting next to Kate in one of the unpopular middle seats swore aloud as his cowboy hat fell into his lap. Clapping the hat back on his head, the man ducked his head apologetically to Kate and turned even redder. "Beggin' your pardon, miss. I swear this road has gotten rougher than a hog's back since that last rain. Next time I have to come this way, I'm hiring me a horse."

She flashed the man a quick smile, but most of her attention was focused on Elizabeth, who was sitting across from her. Kate frowned when she saw this latest bump had jolted her sister awake.

"Stop worrying about me, Kate, dear. I'm fine," Elizabeth admonished Kate gently and nestled her head against Robert's shoulder. Kate sighed and wished fervently that Elizabeth's words were true, but her appearance alone contradicted them. Elizabeth's pale cheeks were flushed by the fever brought on by consumption, and her beautiful brown eyes looked bruised and tired. She had contracted tuberculosis during the horrible winter after their father's death when they had lived at Aunt Mildred's drafty old house in Marblehead.

Thank goodness Robert Townsend had come and taken Elizabeth away from all that. Kate grinned at her handsome, blond brother-in-law. Back in the days when Elizabeth had been the reigning belle of Boston, Kate had always liked him the best of Elizabeth's many beaux. He had been reluctant to press his suit, however, because his prospects were limited. After the Holdens' family shipping firm had failed and Papa died, Robert was the only one of her former suitors who came to call on Elizabeth in Marblehead. Even the knowledge that Elizabeth had weak lungs did not deter him in the end.

"Kate Holden, you look like you are about ready to jump out of this coach and run the rest of the way to Cripple Creek." Robert's teasing words roused Kate from her musings.

"I'm so eager to get there, I feel like I could outrace these horses. You two don't know how glad I am that you asked me to come with you."

"We are the ones who have cause to be grateful. I know Elizabeth is going to feel much more comfortable in this rough-and-ready mining town with you for company. Genteel womenfolk are supposed to be scarce in these parts. I only hope you won't regret giving up your post as a governess."

"I did grow very fond of little Edward and Emily, but I wasn't sorry to leave the Livingstons' household. Although I liked teaching, I found being a governess puts one in an awkward position. I wasn't quite a servant and I wasn't quite a member of the family."

She decided there was no point in telling Robert and Elizabeth about the terrible loneliness she had endured this past year. Today it was far more appropriate to be talking about their future and their new life in Cripple Creek.

"I honestly think," she added firmly, "that this was a good decision for all of us. The dry climate will do wonders for Elizabeth's lungs, and I know you will be a mining tycoon in no time."

The stagecoach, which had been climbing steadily for some time, now slowed to a stop. "That down thar is Cripple Creek, folks!" John Hundley, the driver, sang out.

Kate just had time to catch a glimpse of a large town sprawled across a wide green bowl surrounded by rolling hills before she heard the driver crack his whip again and again. The horses leaped into a gallop and the coach careened forward. The conveyance steadily gathered speed down the steep grade into town until the passengers inside were being bounced from side to side, and all were holding on for dear life.

"Good heavens, are there outlaws after us?" Elizabeth gasped in alarm as she clutched Robert's arm.

"No, ma'am." The rancher beside Kate had to shout to make himself heard over the rattling and rumblings of the coach. "This is just the ol' sidewinder's idea of fun. We'll all be safe enough, you'll see."

Sure enough, a lifetime later, it seemed to Kate, the driver pulled up in front of a frame building with a grand facade and sign that read, THE CONTINENTAL HOTEL. As Kate drew in a deep breath and made herself let go of the leather strap by her right shoulder, she looked out and saw that the street before the hotel was teeming with freighting wagons and commercial vehicles of every shape and description. The boardwalks were likewise thick with men striding along in a most businesslike fashion. The sound of Elizabeth's coughing abruptly drew Kate's attention away from the fascinating spectacle taking place outside the stage. When she glanced over at her sister, she saw Elizabeth was convulsed by a spasm of coughing, and Robert appeared furious enough to pound someone.

She shared Robert's anger that Mr. Hundley had scared Elizabeth so unnecessarily, but she could see the humor in what the man had done. What a way to introduce newcomers to Cripple Creek! When the driver, who looked much like a grizzled old bandit himself, helped her down from the coach, she gave him a dazzling smile and said, "What fine horses you have, Mr. Hundley. It's remarkable that they have so much energy left at the end of a long day."

Clearly delighted, the old man snatched off his battered black hat and grinned back at her, revealing more gaps than teeth.

"That they are, miss. I do believe you'll take to Cripple Creek, for yer a prime 'un yerself."

Laughing at this compliment, she turned about and waited while Robert helped Elizabeth from the stage. Soon he had both young women settled on a fine settee in the lobby of the Continental Hotel while he went to the front desk to inquire after rooms. Within moments Kate realized that every man in the lobby was staring at them. Some were watching her and Elizabeth openly, while others were more surreptitious in their glances, but there was no question that they were the center of every man's attention. Kate swallowed hard and tried to concentrate on what Elizabeth was saying about the cost of their rooms for the night.

Well, she had been warned that decent womenfolk were rare in this town, and now she was seeing proof of it firsthand. She was just going to have to become used to the notion that she was now an oddity of sorts, Kate told herself gamely. She was relieved when Robert returned to them, but her relief was short-lived. He explained that Cripple Creek had gotten so much publicity in recent months that the town was filled to the brim with eager gold-seekers. The sympathetic desk clerk had sent a boy running up Bennett Avenue to see if the El Dorado might have rooms for the weary travelers. In short order the boy returned with the news that the El Dorado could indeed accommodate the ladies.

Kate smiled to herself when four men stepped forward and offered to help Robert carry their bags and trunks. Their trip up Bennett Avenue to the next hotel turned into quite a procession. Each man they passed along the boardwalk tipped his hat and wished them good day. The third gentleman they encountered, a rather thin fellow with stooped shoulders and a drooping mustache, stopped dead in his tracks and looked at Elizabeth with such a stunned and worshipful expression on his face that Kate had to bite her lip to keep from giggling aloud.

When they came to the first side street they had to cross, Kate and Elizabeth exchanged worried looks. There was so much wagon traffic, Kate wondered if they and their luggage would possibly make it across the street in one piece. The moment Elizabeth and Kate stepped off the boardwalk, however, drivers hauled on the reins of their horses and their mules, and traffic came to an abrupt halt.

"I feel like Moses parting the Red Sea," Kate whispered to Elizabeth as they passed down a narrow lane between a remarkable variety of wagons and rigs.

"Kate, you mustn't be sacrilegious," Elizabeth replied automatically, but Kate saw Robert's lips twitch at her remark.

When their party reached the relative safety of the boardwalk, the traffic in the street resumed its normal hectic pace. Men continued to tip their hats to the young ladies, and some of the most exuberant fellows even called out compliments. One young Irish dray driver passing in the opposite direction snatched his cap off when he saw them on the boardwalk. With a charming smile he cried out, "Surely, Lord, you've sent two of your fairest angels to visit us right here in Cripple Creek."

And so it went as the two sisters made their way up Bennett Avenue. The comments the men made were all so good-natured and reverent that Kate could hardly take offense. Even ladylike Elizabeth, with her strong sense of propriety, was laughing and blushing by the time they reached the El Dorado.

After they were settled into their rooms and had washed away the worst of the dust from their journey, Robert came to Kate's door and suggested that she rest before supper. Now that she was finally here in Cripple Creek, resting was the last thing Kate wanted to do. She longed to suggest the two of them go for a walk, but she knew Robert would want to stay close to Elizabeth. Instead Kate contented herself with pacing up and down in front of her window, which had a fine view of Bennett Avenue, the main street of Cripple Creek. She soon forgot her restlessness in her fascination over the steady stream of people passing by the hotel.

As she settled herself on her window seat, she was amazed by the diversity of the men who had been drawn to this boomtown. There were elegantly dressed gentlemen with top hats and canes and grime-covered miners just off their shifts. She saw wiry old prospectors with bushy beards, and thin young men in ragged clothing who looked as if their search for a bonanza had been long, hard, and unsuccessful. As an hour passed, again and again she caught herself searching for a particular face in that river of humanity. She knew she was being absurd. Justin Talbott owned business ventures throughout the West, and he could easily be thousands of miles away from Cripple Creek right now. But for the past two years whenever she thought of the West, she pictured this place in her mind and the man who had described it to her with such enthusiasm.

Suddenly, just as she was about to stand up and turn away from the window, she saw him. He was striding along by himself, dressed in an elegant gray suit and top hat, disdaining the use of the walking canes that so many men affected. Cheeks burning, pulse racing, she simply sat there and watched him come closer and closer along the boardwalk. His dark brows were drawn together, as if he were concentrating hard on some problem. He still wore his thick black hair and sideburns longer than was truly fashionable.

Distance obscured the color of his eyes, but her memory

supplied that detail easily. They were a beautiful rich blue that seemed to lighten or darken according to his mood. His nose was aristocratically straight but not too thin, his lips were well shaped, and his jaw was strong. Altogether he looked just as heart-stoppingly handsome as she remembered. After he passed directly beneath her window, she watched his long-legged stride and his broad shoulders until the crowd swallowed him.

She leaned back against the wall and let go her pent-up breath. Somehow she had felt it, somehow she had known all along that she would see him if she came to Cripple Creek. It was no use trying to hold the memories back any longer. She closed her eyes and let the tide of images and emotions wash over her. She wondered weakly if she hadn't fallen in love with him the very first time they had met back in Boston. When she had looked up from her reading that day in the garden, she found a man more handsome than any Greek god she had ever imagined watching her.

Despite his charm, she had heard the cynicism in his tone and seen the world-weariness in his eyes. Deliberately she set out to make him laugh. He had seemed surprised that she had been so successful in amusing him, and he appeared reluctant to end their conversation. After he left, she clung to the knowledge that he was planning to attend the dinner party they were hosting the following evening.

The next afternoon Elizabeth gave in to her pleading and helped her dress up for the party. It was the first time she had ever truly cared about her appearance, for romance had held little interest for her before now. Dear Elizabeth had helped her shine, putting her hair up in a sophisticated coiffure and sewing silk roses onto her white satin dancing frock. All the time, however, Elizabeth had reminded her sternly that Justin Talbott had a well-deserved reputation as a ladies' man.

Kate spent that entire evening waiting for the moment when Justin would ask her to dance. When he came to stand before her, looking magnificent and distinguished in his dark evening clothes, she was so tongue-tied that she couldn't say a single thing to him. Instead she did her best to smile and held out her hand. He took it and led her directly to the center of the ballroom. When the musicians struck up the tune to a lively waltz, Justin swept her into his arms and whirled her away.

After a few minutes she realized she was gawking at him like a silly schoolgirl. She cleared her throat and asked the first question that popped into her mind.

"Mr. Talbott, is it true that the lands beyond the Mississippi enjoy a much sunnier climate than our own?"

He looked down at her with a lazy smile and shook his head. "I promise to tell you everything you wish about the great West when we finish this dance. For the moment, though, my golden girl, I want you to relax and let me guide you about."

She was happy to acquiesce to his request. She wasn't quite sure why it should be, but dancing with Justin felt completely different from dancing with anyone else. He was light on his feet and graceful for a man of his size. His shoulder was warm and hard beneath her hand. He was so tall, she had to tip her head back to see his face.

As they swirled about, a daring plan began to form in her mind. Waltzing with Justin felt so wonderful and right. Glancing up at him again, she decided he looked exactly like the sort of man who knew a great deal about kissing. Since meeting Justin Talbott two days ago, she had begun to wonder if she had been in error to spend so much time on her studies. Up until now she had simply ignored the young men who had shown an interest in her. It was beginning to dawn on her, though, that romance might be an interesting and pleasurable pastime, but she knew so little about it. If she wanted to find out what romance was all about, why not go to someone who was an expert on the topic?

Because tonight would probably be her last chance to spend any time with Justin, Kate resolved to put her plan into effect right away. When the waltz finished, she declared that she was feeling warm and suggested that they go out on the balcony. She thought she saw surprise in his eyes and a knowing look she didn't like at all, but he agreed to her suggestion readily enough.

She was annoyed to see he carefully stayed in the well-lit area right outside the French doors. Immediately she launched into a list of questions about the mining camps he had visited. In reply he began telling her about a new boomtown out west called Cripple Creek. Although it sounded like a fascinating place, she couldn't concentrate on his description, for she was frantically trying to remember the subtle ways Elizabeth managed her many suitors. Now that Kate had Justin out on the balcony, she wasn't at all sure how to go about getting him to kiss her.

To begin with, she thought she probably ought to stand a little closer to him. She screwed up her courage and inched nearer until her shoulder almost brushed his sleeve. After several minutes of steady conversation, it became clear that simple proximity wasn't enough to advance her cause. Gritting her teeth, she opened her green eyes a little wider, the way she had seen Elizabeth do a hundred times when she wanted to turn the head of one of her gentlemen. All the while Justin lounged back against the stone balustrade, his arms crossed over his chest as he gave her polite, dispassionate answers to the questions she asked.

At last she couldn't bear it any longer. She felt disgusted with herself. She wasn't at all comfortable with this indirect manner of going about getting what she wanted. When he paused after answering her last query about transportation routes into Cripple Creek, she decided to take the plunge.

"Mr. Talbott, I would like to ask you a great favor. I was hoping this would just happen between us, but I'm not very experienced in these matters, and I'm afraid I've already bungled things terribly."

He straightened up from the balustrade, a smile lurking in his blue eyes. "And just what sort of matters are you referring to, my little professor?" he asked in his deep voice.

Her cheeks began to warm, but she forced herself to meet his gaze. "I'm afraid that I know little about romantic matters between ladies and gentlemen, but it occurred to me that I ought to know more if I'm to make an informed decision. You see, I'm about to go off to college, where I'm going to be far too busy to indulge in any sort of romantic pursuits. My sister, Elizabeth, though, seems to enjoy the attentions of her many suitors."

"And you want to make certain that you aren't going to be missing out on an enjoyable pastime." Some of the warmth seemed to have vanished from his tone. But she refused to be diverted from her course now that she had ventured forth upon it.

"I should like to make a logical decision on the matter, but I have no experience to go by," she said steadily.

"And you would like me to help you gain some experience, is that it?" His voice had gone as cold as a winter wind.

Kate swallowed hard. This was definitely turning out to be more difficult than she expected. "You see, Elizabeth told me that you are a ladies man. Therefore, I thought that you might be very good at this romancing business."

Justin stepped forward until he was standing so close that she had to still an impulse to move back from him. "I'm afraid that in romantic matters, a man and a woman must first have a considerable interest in each other." His blue eyes were unreadable.

"Oh, dear," she said as she retreated a few steps back into the shadows behind the door. "I hadn't thought about that. I suppose it wouldn't be fair to ask you to kiss me then. I could see that if you weren't interested in me, it could prove to be quite a chore."

"I'm not sure any man in his right mind would consider kissing you a chore."

Puzzled by the humor she heard in his tone again, she protested, "But you just said that a gentleman must have considerable interest in a lady to want to pursue her romantically. I'm afraid I will just have to keep looking until I can find such a gentleman. I hope it doesn't take me too long. I only have three months before I go away to college."

"I never said I wasn't intrigued with you, little scholar. And if you are so determined to find a man to kiss you, I will be happy to oblige." Justin moved two steps closer and put a warm hand on her shoulder.

"Truly, you are very kind. I hope I'm not putting you out in any way." She was surprised to find that she was suddenly breathless.

"Kate, be quiet, will you?" The laughter was unmistakable in his tone now. "A gentleman can't do a proper job of kissing a young lady if she's clucking on like a hen."

She obediently closed her mouth. As an afterthought she also closed her eyes. She thought it might be helpful if she tipped her face up while she was at it. His breath warmed her face. He smelled of cedar, and brandy, and some nice male scent that seemed to be all his own.

And then his lips covered hers. They lingered there for a few seconds and withdrew. She kept her eyes closed for several moments more, waiting for the earth to tremble or for lightning to strike her.

"Is that all there is to it?" she asked disappointedly after opening her eyes again. "I meant no offense," she added hurriedly, for he was scowling like a thundercloud. "Your kiss was quite pleasant, but I can't imagine what all the fuss is about. I believe you've just done me a great favor. I can go off to college now and not worry any more about missing this."

She thought she heard him swear under his breath. The next moment his hands grasped her shoulders much more firmly than before and pulled her close. He slipped his left hand down to the small of her back and urged her body against his own. He slipped his right hand beneath her chin and tipped her face up to his once more. This time his lips didn't settle on her own. Slowly, oh so slowly, they traced the line of her right jaw, sending delicious little shivers skittering down her neck and back. Once again his scent enveloped her, and she became very conscious of the strong fingers splayed across her back.

As his warm, clever lips moved down toward her mouth, she shyly raised her arms and placed them about his neck. The material of his evening jacket felt cool and smooth beneath her fingers. Greatly daring, she reached one hand up and touched the thick, black hair curling at his nape. She was delighted to find it was silky soft. His lips began to nibble at the corner of her mouth, and she forgot all about the adventure her own hands were enjoying.

Dear heavens, I'm getting what I asked for now, she thought, before those warm lips covered hers again and all conscious thought spun away from her. This time he pressed his mouth against hers more firmly, coaxing and cajoling until her trembling lips kissed him back. His thumb and forefinger tugged gently at her chin. She opened her mouth, since he seemed to wish it. She was startled when she felt his tongue slide between her lips. Within moments she was lost in the velvet taste of him. He explored her mouth tentatively at first, but when she showed no fear he grew more bold. Dimly she realized that her breath was coming in gasps now.

Daringly she touched the tip of her tongue to his. She was startled when she heard him groan. He gathered her closer against his chest while his lips ranged feverishly over her cheekbones and eyelids. His right hand slipped from her chin to play with the lace edge of the bodice of her dress. His fingers left a burning trail against her skin just above her breasts. Slowly she became aware of a strange warmth growing in her, sending tingling sensations throughout her body. Feeling bereft without his lips covering hers, she framed his face with her hands and guided his mouth back to hers. This time he kissed her with such intensity that she could hardly breathe.

Suddenly Justin tensed. He broke off his kiss and leaned his forehead against her own. She was surprised to discover he was breathing almost as heavily as she. How could a simple kiss possibly have affected a man of his experience? she wondered dazedly.

"Oh, my sweet, sweet golden girl, you surprised me," she heard him murmur. He straightened up and firmly put her away from him. Kate leaned against the wall of the house, trying desperately to control the riotous sensations he had just aroused in her.

"I . . . I think I should thank you, sir. I understand a great deal more now," she managed to say weakly when she had got her breath back.

"I showed you far more than I should have." He spoke in such a harsh tone that she shivered.

"Why do you sound so angry at yourself? You've done nothing wrong."

"If your father horsewhipped me for what I just did, it would be no more than I deserve," he said bitterly as he swung away from her and looked out over the stone balustrade.

"Oh, for heaven's sake, you've hardly ruined me," she declared as she moved to stand beside him. "In fact I'm very grateful that you showed me what kissing is all about. I don't understand why you must see yourself in such a criminal light.''

"There are kisses, young Kate, and there are kisses. You are at the stage where you should be receiving chaste pecks on the cheek from blushing, innocent young men. I had no business kissing you that way just now.''

She fell silent for several moments, trying to think of a way to ease his guilt. It just wasn't fair that he blamed himself for something she had started. Perhaps it would help if he believed that earth-shattering kiss had meant less to her than it actually did. All at once she thought of just the right way to lighten his mood, and perhaps even make him laugh.

"Well, I for one am glad you did it," she said in a thoughtful tone. "You just helped me a great deal with my studies. I never could understand why Paris and the Greeks and the Trojans would start a whole war over Helen of Troy, no matter how beautiful she was. But if Paris enjoyed kissing Helen half as much as I liked kissing you, I begin to see why the man just had to carry her off.''

Justin stared at her as if he were thunderstruck while she delivered this little speech, and then his lips started to twitch. Suddenly he let go a deep laugh that made Kate smile in relief.

"Oh, my quaint, quaint little Kate," he said when he had finished laughing, "the things you say. But I must face the fact 'I wasted time and now time doth waste me,' " he quoted cryptically. "In two days I'm going back to my mining camps, and you are soon going to forget all about our kiss in your excitement over your new life at college. I promise handsome fellows will come flocking to your Wellesley campus, and you will have ample opportunity to enjoy sundry romances. And now, my golden girl, because I won't be able to keep my hands off you if we stay out here any longer, I suggest we return you to the safety of your father's well-lit ballroom.''

She decided it would be best to let him have his way for the moment. As he guided her back inside, she reflected that if Justin Talbott was truly a womanizer, he was a singularly kind and honorable one. There on the spot she promised herself that someday she would travel out to his gold camps and make him fall in love with her.

*   *   *

Kate sighed and opened her eyes. She had made those pledges back in the days when she had still been very wealthy, very young, and very naive. During the past two years she had learned a great deal more about human nature. It had been a shocking and painful experience to watch so many of her friends disappear with her loss of fortune and status. Although Justin had been kind to her, she was well aware of the fact that he was an ambitious and driven man. He had worked hard to regain the social standing and wealth he had lost so suddenly. She doubted he would have much interest in a young woman who could do nothing to help him reach his goals.

Kate stood up and began to pace about the hotel room. It would have been far easier, she realized now, if Elizabeth and Robert had chosen some other western town in which to make their start. Then again, Cripple Creek was obviously a large, bustling sort of a place. With any luck she could manage to avoid Justin Talbott. And if someday she did find herself face-to-face with the man, she knew she would simply have to cope with his surprise over her change in circumstances and be strong enough to survive his eventual rejection.

She returned to her window. For the first time she noticed that the sun was setting. The sky overhead had turned dusky violet, and the long, narrow clouds above the horizon blushed pink and rose. She sat for several minutes, letting the peace of the sunset become a part of her. The West was proving to be even more beautiful than she had imagined. She already loved its vast expanses and the clear skies that seemed to stretch forever. It was a good place to build a new life.

Surely she had the intelligence and the drive to succeed in a town where so many had made their golden dreams come true. After she found a place to live, she would start looking for employment. As always, making plans made her feel better. Her unruly emotions carefully reined in once more, Kate briskly set about getting ready to go down to supper.

Chapter Two

Justin Talbott peered down the mountainside into the deepening twilight. Jordan and his men were going to have to work quickly to get that last leg of the claim surveyed before dark. It was also possible that the old man could return at any time. Justin had told his surveying team to be careful not to set foot on Gunnar Carlson's land. The old Swede was famous for his short fuse and his quick trigger finger. At the same time, Justin was determined to know exactly where the borders of Carlson's claims ran. He was convinced one of the richest veins in the district ran under this side of Elk Mountain. If there was a legal way to get at that vein, he wanted to find it.

Sighing impatiently, Justin turned toward the west. The last rays of sun were silhouetting the rocky spires and towers of the formidable Sangre de Cristo range. It was a spectacular sight, but not an uncommon one here in the Colorado Rockies. These western peaks did make the eastern mountain ranges such as the Adirondacks look like sedate old gentlemen. He smiled as he remembered the words he had spoken to young Kate Holden two years ago in her father's garden.

He was surprised by how often he thought about Thomas Holden's daughter. On the whole, Justin considered himself a cold, calculating man. Life had stolen away his dreams and taught him love was for sentimental fools. Still, he cherished his memories of young Kate and her remarkable freshness, intelligence, and beauty. Somehow she had come to represent his image of ideal womanhood, a girl unsullied by greed or vanity. He enjoyed picturing her at college, poring over her classical books and texts. It was a sad business that she had to lose her father, but he knew Thomas Holden was the sort to provide well for the financial security of his family. Kate would be able to have or become anything she wanted in life.

The booming sound of a shotgun blast abruptly roused Justin from his musings. He looked down the mountainside in time to witness an entertaining spectacle. Jordan and his two young assistants were racing up the rocky hillside as fast as they could run, a tall, rangy old man with a shotgun hot on their heels. Even as Justin watched, Gunnar Carlson slowed, raised the gun to his shoulder, and let fly with the other barrel. Jordan and his team desperately redoubled their pace. The old Swede stopped and shook a fist at their swiftly retreating figures.

Justin smiled sardonically as his surveyors stumbled up the ridge to where he was standing. Running at this altitude was brutal work, and it was some time before any of them could get enough air into their burning lungs to say anything coherent.

"I swear that old coot came within inches of shooting my parts off," young Madden gasped.

"If he had wanted to nail them, you can rest assured you'd never be a father. Carlson was a mountain man, and the old fellow knows how to shoot," Justin said with a grin.

"We can't give you good news, Justin," Pete Jordan got out between breaths. "Carlson and his partner knew what they were doing when they staked their claims. There isn't a free inch of ground on that mountainside."

"Thanks, Pete. I guessed as much," Justin admitted, "but I had to make certain. I will replace the equipment you had to leave down there, and I will send around a bonus in the morning you can share with your boys. You can call it hazard pay."

Jordan chuckled and shook his head. "Hazardous is right. That old man is a holy terror. They just don't make 'em like that anymore."

"They probably broke the mold after Gunnar Carlson came along," Justin agreed dryly. "I just hope a claim jumper doesn't catch the old cuss napping and murder him in his sleep. I've done everything I can to make him see reason. I've tried to buy the damn claims from him, but he just slams his door in my face. The old fool doesn't have the resources to develop the mine on his own, but he's too damn stubborn to admit it.''

Shaking his head, Justin turned away from the surveyors and started down the other side of the ridge. Perhaps he should try talking to Carlson about a partnership. When all was said and done, he liked the cantankerous old man, and he would be glad to see him get a fair share of the profits.

When he reached the place where Ben and the horses were waiting, Justin lit a match, looked at his pocket watch, and grimaced. He was going to be late for his dinner with Miss LaMonte and her father. Ostensibly tonight was to be a social occasion, but Justin knew that Pierre LaMonte would be fencing with him all evening about purchasing shares in his new mining company. The canny Frenchman had made a fortune with his silver mines over in Leadville. Now, with the price of silver tumbling, LaMonte had his eye on Cripple Creek gold. He also had an eye on Justin's business interests and had all but said he would like Justin to become his son-in-law.

Justin sighed as he swung up into the saddle and pointed the sorrel toward Cripple Creek. Ben fell in silently behind him. Annette LaMonte was as beautiful in her cool, dark way as she was ambitious. At least she was direct about what she wanted. A month ago she had told him she wanted his fortune, his position, and him, in that order. He appreciated her honesty, and he expected nothing more but such venality in women. Annette would be an excellent hostess and a glittering social asset if he decided to move to Colorado Springs or to Denver. Although he knew he would have to marry someday, he was in no hurry to make a commitment to Annette or any other woman. Cool Miss LaMonte would just have to be patient while he made up his mind.

All unbidden, the image of a girl with golden hair and laughing green eyes flashed into his mind. Kate Holden, with her exuberance and unrestrained vitality, did make quite a contrast to the carefully controlled Annette. He found himself hoping strongly that the prediction he had made to Kate would come true. Some upright fellow would burst into her life, sweep Kate off her feet, and give her the happy home and family she deserved.

Telling himself Kate's future was none of his affair, Justin sternly pushed her image from his mind. It was time he started concentrating on more important matters, such as whether or not he wanted to purchase some of Pierre's mining shares. Frowning to himself, Justin urged the surefooted sorrel into a trot.

The morning after they arrived in Cripple Creek, Kate and Elizabeth decided that their first order of business was to leave their expensive hotel and find quarters in a good boarding-house. They told Robert, who was eager to start making inquiries about investments at the mining exchanges, that they would take care of looking for their new lodgings. The front desk clerk gladly wrote out a list for Kate and Elizabeth of the better boarding establishments, but the kindly man was less than optimistic about their chances of finding rooms in busy Cripple Creek.

Once they stepped outside the El Dorado, Kate couldn't stay worried by the clerk's pessimistic attitude for long. The sun was shining, the cloudless sky was the deep blue color of willowware china, and a light breeze brought with it the scent of pines. Even Elizabeth seemed invigorated by the cool, dry air, although she had to stop from time to time to catch her breath as they climbed up and down the steep streets above Bennett Avenue. What people had told them about Colorado and the high altitude here was true. The air was indeed thinner than it had been in Boston.

Kate, however, didn't mind the opportunities to stop and look around her. She had never seen so much construction. Commercial buildings and houses seemed to be going up everywhere. The whining of saws and the pounding of hammers served as a constant counterpoint to the clip-clop of horses' hooves and the rumble of wagons.

The two sisters soon discovered that what the desk clerk had told them was distressingly accurate. Every boardinghouse they visited was full, and many had long waiting lists. Toward the end of the morning, even Kate was beginning to feel discouraged. They agreed to try one more establishment before returning to the hotel for lunch. The sixth place on their list was a tidy white frame house with red roses growing in a garden out front and a black-and-white cow munching hay in a corral out back. When they knocked on the door, a big, red-haired Irishwoman greeted them cheerfully. Elly O'Connell, as she introduced herself, was so delighted to have female visitors that she insisted they both stay for lunch even though she had no rooms for them. Elly was even more excited when she discovered they were from Boston, for she had lived there several years before coming west.

She ushered them into her neat home, which was full of white lace doilies. As Kate and Elizabeth ate a hearty meal of soup, bread, and cheese in her dining room, Elly told them stories of how she and her husband Rory O'Connell had spent the last twenty years moving from mining town to mining town trying to make their fortune.

"This time we have the trick of it, you see," she finished with a smile. "There's just as much money to be made sup-portin' the mining and the miners as there is coming out of the ground itself. My man, he went broke again and again and ruined his back trying to get rich from worthless holes in the ground. Now he owns a fine freighting company with five wagons and teams. Since he has more business than he can handle, next year he's planning to buy two more wagons.

"With my girls grown and married, I decided to run this place, for I can't stand not to be doin', and I must admit I make a tidy sum meself from the lodgers we take in. But the stories I could be telling you about other mining camps would make the hair on your lovely heads curl. This Cripple Creek town may seem wild to you, but it's surely the tamest of the boomtowns I've ever lived in.

"And now," she said when she saw they both had finished eating, "I should be telling you two there is one small room I have up in the attic of this place that I suppose I could let to Kate here, but it's far too small for a couple. I'm so sorry I don't have any other rooms available."

Elizabeth shook her head regretfully. "Mrs. O'Connell, it's kind of you to offer it, but I'm not sure I'd feel comfortable if my husband and I had to live across town from Kate."

Kate was going to protest her sister's protectiveness, but at just that moment she noticed a well-dressed young man hes-itating in the hallway. When he saw Kate looking at him, he seemed to make up his mind about something and strode forward into the room. He had a nice, open face, his curly chestnut hair was carefully combed, and his mustache was neatly trimmed. As he came closer she could see his eyes were chocolate-colored, and when he glanced at her his admiration was obvious.

"Excuse me, Mrs. O'Connell, I didn't mean to eavesdrop, but I couldn't help but overhear these ladies' dilemma. I would be happy to give up my room and move in with Mr. Burton until someone else leaves your establishment."

"Well, Mr. Cooper, that would be a fine solution indeed to the problem." Elly O'Connell smiled widely. "Mrs. Townsend, Miss Holden, I would like you to meet Geoffrey Cooper, one of my favorite boarders and assistant superintendent of the Copper Kettle mine."

"Mr. Cooper, it's a pleasure to meet you. Surely you don't want to give up your room for us." Elizabeth looked at the young man with some dismay. She was unused to accepting favors from strangers, and Kate could tell the propriety of the situation was weighing on her.

Geoffrey Cooper reluctantly turned his attention from Kate to address Elizabeth. "Mrs. Townsend, I can assure you I would not be inconvenienced by the move. And if I may be so bold as to say it, I think this is the only way you and your sister will be able to stay together. Cripple Creek is bursting at its seams these days, and you will be lucky to find one room, much less two, in any decent boardinghouse in the district."

"He's right, you know," Elly chimed in. "Please do be accepting his offer. It would be a rare treat for me to have womenfolk around. I do get lonely now me girls are gone."

Elizabeth glanced over at Kate, who gave her an enthusiastic nod to show her approval of the plan. Geoffrey Cooper hardly looked the sort to take advantage of the favor he was granting them, and Kate already felt very comfortable with Elly O'Connell and her home.

"Very well," Elizabeth gave in gracefully, "we accept your kind offer."

It was agreed that their little party would move into Elly's boardinghouse the following day. Clearly delighted by the way things had turned out, Elly O'Connell showed Kate and Elizabeth to her door. As soon as they returned to the hotel, Elizabeth decided she wanted to lie down for a while. Kate, however, could not face an entire afternoon cooped up in her hotel room. After Elizabeth went to sleep, Kate decided there was no time like the present to begin her job-hunting. After changing into her gray silk shirtwaist and matching skirt, which was her most businesslike outfit, she essayed forth on her own.

The afternoon desk clerk at the El Dorado had given Kate the address of the building where Mr. Josiah Murdoch, the president of the newly elected board of education, had his place of business. Mr. Murdoch proved to be a rather fat man who slicked his thinning gray hair across the top of his head in an unsuccessful effort to hide his bald spot. Unfortunately, early on in their interview it became clear that Mr. Murdoch was mostly interested in boasting about the two new schools the board of education had just built and the fine instructors they had hired. After asking briefly about Kate's credentials, he wrote her name down on a slip of paper.

"I will keep you in mind if any positions come open," he said, heaving himself to his feet.

"I could also tutor advanced students in Latin or Greek," Kate offered quickly.

"A young woman who can tutor in Latin and Greek, my, how remarkable. Now I'm afraid I need to get back to my own affairs here. Good day, Miss Holden," he said as he escorted her to the door. For all his politeness, she received the strong impression Mr. Josiah Murdoch hadn't taken her seriously from the moment their interview began.

Fighting down her anger and disappointment, Kate strode away from Mr. Murdoch's business. Blind to her surroundings, she was slow to realize she must have taken a wrong turn. She blinked and looked around her when she noticed that the sound of laughter and piano music was growing louder. She was standing just a block off Myers Avenue. Elly O'Connell had told them yesterday that every mining town sported a street like this one, lined entirely with saloons and brothels.

Curious, Kate decided to take a quick look before turning

around. It was amazing to see the street below her was almost as busy as Bennett Avenue. Her cheeks warmed when she spotted several scantily clad women hanging out the windows of the brothels, calling shrill invitations to the men passing below. Between the larger wood saloons there were several small cabins and canvas tents. Her face began to burn when she noticed the older, slovenly prostitutes lounging in front of the one-woman cribs. When she saw a man come up and start fondling a prostitute right there in broad daylight, Kate whirled about. It was time to beat a hasty retreat back to the hotel.

The next morning Rory O'Connell left a message at the hotel desk that their rooms were ready. That afternoon Kate, Elizabeth, and Robert moved into their new lodgings. The newlyweds' room was far smaller than the one Elizabeth had as a girl, but the young couple were content with it. Kate's little nook up in the attic barely had space for a small white iron bed, an oak dresser, a pine wardrobe, and a washstand. She did have a wonderful view out her window, though, toward the northern ridges and hills surrounding Cripple Creek. Once she spread a few pictures and knickknacks about the tiny chamber, Kate, too, was happy with her new accommodations.

For the rest of the week Robert continued to haunt the mining exchanges, looking for the right investments to start building his nest egg. Elizabeth rested, sewed, and went on long walks. Kate made the rounds of sundry legal and mining offices, looking for a job as a clerk or as a secretary. Although the owners of these businesses were invariably polite to her, again and again she was turned down or given vague promises that she might be contacted later. Clearly employers were not taking her seriously.

They did, however, seem very interested in her, much to her chagrin. She found herself politely but firmly turning down invitations to dinner, some issued by men two and three times her twenty years.

By the end of the second week she was growing tired and discouraged. At last she asked Elly what other sorts of decent employment might be open to a young woman. They were sitting at Elly's kitchen table after supper when the Irishwoman explained Kate's other options.

"Well, now, you can always do work as a laundress or as a seamstress. The miners, especially the single fellows, will pay good money to have their clothing washed and mended. If this work doesn't suit you, you can surely find a job as a waitress. With your looks, any restaurant owner in town will hire you in a moment."

As she walked up the stairs to her room that night, Kate couldn't decide whether she should be horrified or amused to think she could be hired as a waitress for such a reason.

At the end of the third week she finally decided to throw in the towel. Her meager savings were disappearing at an alarming rate because everything was dreadfully expensive in Cripple Creek. In the long run waitressing seemed like a much more interesting occupation than doing laundry or sewing.

On Monday morning of the fourth week she donned a simple shirtwaist and skirt and presented herself at the Golden Spike. This was an unpretentious but well-run eatery right on Bennett Avenue. Elly O'Connell had recommended that Kate try this establishment first, for the owner was known to be a fair and honest man.

A hush fell over the busy restaurant the moment Kate walked in the door. Luckily she was beginning to get used to this reaction to her appearance, and so the abrupt silence didn't throw her off balance too much. When a blushing young man with a blond cowlick hurried over and asked if she wanted a table, she told him quietly that she was looking for a job as a waitress. He gazed at her in amazement, and then a wide grin flashed across his homely face.

"I'll fetch Mr. Gregory. You just wait right there, miss," he said over his shoulder as he rushed off toward the back.

Kate spent her time while she was waiting studying the restaurant itself. The tables were covered with blue checked cloths, and the walls were decorated with a simple cream wallpaper. Large windows along two sides of the restaurant let in plenty of light. The place was clean, cheerful, and bright. It also appeared to be incredibly busy. She could spot only one empty table in the entire eatery. The young man who had greeted her was now hustling from table to table, and a young waitress with striking dark hair and eyes was also hurrying about.

A few minutes later a short, plump man sporting a tremendous set of gray side-whiskers came bustling up to Kate. He had his shirtsleeves rolled up to his elbows, and he wore an apron tied about his round middle. His face was red and shiny with perspiration, and his blue eyes studied her keenly.

"So you're the one wanting a job. What's your name?" he asked quickly in a precise English accent.

"My name is Kate Holden. I was hoping you might have a waitressing position open. Elly O'Connell said I should try your establishment first."

"Elly O'Connell sent you, eh? Well, come on into the kitchen while I go back to frying eggs."

The Englishman spun about and headed toward the rear of the restaurant, never once looking over his shoulder to see if Kate was following him. He led her directly into the kitchen, where various pots and frying pans were heating over two enormous stoves. A large woman with her hair caught back in a tight bun nodded to Kate and made room for Mr. Gregory beside her at one of the stoves. Immediately he began picking up eggs and cracking them neatly into a skillet while he proceeded to shoot questions at Kate.

"Tell me, have you ever done any waitressing work before?"

"No, sir, I have not." Kate met his gaze as directly as she could.

"Hmph, I'd rather guessed you hadn't. Well, Miss Holden, did anyone tell you that waiting tables is hard work? At the end of the day your arms and your feet will be aching. People will shout at you. I will probably shout at you, and crying isn't going to do you the least bit of good."

"I am young and strong, and I am not the sort who cries easily," she responded evenly.

"Hmph, yes, so you say. Waitressing isn't exactly ladylike, you know. I expect my customers to treat my staff decently, but you're going to overhear some rough language out there and some less than delicate conversations."

"I do realize that, Mr. Gregory. I'm hardly going to faint at the sound of profanity." Kate decided it was time to show he wasn't the only one who could be blunt.

"I see. Well, you're in luck, Kate Holden, who's never

waitressed before. One of my lads didn't show up for work today. Tie on one of those smocks, and Mrs. Gregory here will tell you the basics. We'll try you for one week. Do your best not to drop anything, for we have a devil of a time getting new china to match the old.''

And so her first day waitressing at the Golden Spike began. After Kate took off her hat and tied on a smock, Mrs. Gregory did indeed explain the basics as she deftly made toast and fried bacon. When the pretty young waitress dashed into the kitchen with an order, Mrs. Gregory introduced Mary McPherson to Kate. The Scottish girl seemed delighted to learn that Kate would be working at the Golden Spike. The homely young man with the cowlick that refused to stay slicked down was named Tom, and he, too, seemed pleased that Kate had been hired.

She had no time to get to know her fellow workers, however, for the breakfast rush was on, and Mr. Gregory made it clear that he wanted Kate to start pulling her weight right away. The first table she sallied forth to wait upon was occupied by a trio of young prospectors. She soon forgot her own nervousness when one of the young men appeared to be so overwhelmed by her that he could hardly stutter out his order. She was still chuckling over the way his companions had teased him so unmercifully when she went on to her next table. Suddenly there was no time for laughing, for her next customer was demanding to know where the breakfast was that he had ordered a half hour ago, and she found herself hustling back and forth to the kitchen along with the rest.

It seemed the breakfast rush was just over, and they had barely finished re-laying all the tables when the lunch rush began. At the height of it she was almost running on her trips to the kitchen. The worst moment came when she realized she had completely switched the orders for two tables of four men. The game fellows never said a word to her and ate whole meals they hadn't ordered.

As soon as she realized her mistake, her cheeks blazed and her stomach tightened. She went right over to the two tables and apologized to their occupants. They smiled at her and said such mistakes were to be expected during her first day on the job. She was amazed when they didn't complain to Mr. Gregory and left her generous tips into the bargain.

Her oddest customer of the day was an old prospector who came in after most of the lunch patrons had left. He had such a thick white mane of hair and beard that she could hardly see his face. He sat there most of the afternoon, asking only that she refill his coffee cup from time to time.

He rose to leave just as she approached his table a final time. "I don't suppose you'd marry me, would you, girlie?"

"I beg your pardon, sir?"

"I'm asking, will you marry me, girlie?"

She stared at him in appalled amazement for several moments before her sense of humor came to her rescue. Her lips were quivering, but she managed to say with a relatively straight face, "I am honored by your proposal, sir, but I do not believe that I am interested in marrying anyone at this time."

"Guessed not, but thought I'd ask just the same. You let me know if you change your mind. My name's Ben Doward, and I have a fine claim up toward Battle Mountain." He nodded to her, clapped his battered hat on his head, and wandered out of the restaurant.

Kate managed to keep her composure until the door closed behind him. She glanced over and saw from Mary McPherson's dancing eyes that the Scottish girl had overheard the entire conversation. They both let go peals of laughter at the same moment.

"Och, Kate, that's the first time I've ever heard him say a word besides placing his order," Mary managed to say after she regained some of her composure. "You surely must have made an impression on him."

"And he on me. I do believe this is the first time a man has ever proposed to me." Kate dissolved into helpless laughter once again. When Mr. Gregory emerged from the kitchen to see what was happening, Mary hastily explained the situation.

Shaking a finger at Kate, he said in a fierce tone, "If you marry that man, I just want you to know you're fired." At first she thought her employer was serious, but the glint in his blue eyes gave him away. With a loud sigh Mr. Gregory turned and stomped back to his kitchen, muttering that his waitresses were always getting married as fast as he could hire them.

By the time she left the restaurant that afternoon, Kate's feet were aching and her arms were quivering from the unaccustomed strain of carrying heavy trays. Her pocket was full of tips, however, and a small bag of gold dust that Ben Doward had left for her on his table. She was pleased she had survived her first day with only one major mix-up, and her story of old Ben's marriage proposal had Robert and Elizabeth in stitches that night. By the end of the week Kate was no longer mixing up orders, and she had become much more comfortable with her job. She still felt pleased and relieved on Friday, however, when Mr. Gregory informed her in his polite and formal way that she now had a permanent position at the Golden Spike.

Because she was so busy with her new work, Kate found the days began to fly by. When the Fourth of July arrived, she was delighted to discover that the inhabitants of Cripple Creek celebrated the nation's birthday with true frontier flair and enthusiasm. Someone fired off a booming cannon promptly at six o'clock. After breakfast, Kate went with Robert, Elizabeth, and the O'Connells to watch a colorful parade march down Bennett Avenue. Four bands participated, two of which could actually carry a tune. Kate's favorite entry in the parade was a transfer wagon bearing several pretty little girls who represented different states in the Union.

That afternoon, Robert, Elizabeth, Geoffrey Cooper, and Kate all attended the town barbecue together. Robert and Geoffrey had become firm friends during the past few months, and Geoffrey had made it very clear he wanted to be friends with Kate as well. Although she liked Geoffrey, she rarely accepted his frequent invitations to dinner and social gatherings, for she feared the earnest young man was seriously interested in her. Today, however, his mood was light and genial. He teased and coaxed her into trying deer, elk, and bear meat. Afterward they had a wonderful time watching horse-cart competitions, drilling contests, and bicycle races. That night they attended a lively square dance and watched a brilliant fireworks display.

Kate walked back to the boardinghouse alone with Geoffrey

because Elizabeth had been tired out by the exciting day and returned with Robert earlier. Kate was actually thinking about Justin Talbott and how relieved she had been not to bump into him today when Geoffrey suddenly stopped dead in his tracks. As she turned to look at her companion puzzledly in the moonlight, she found herself being pulled into his arms.

"Geoffrey, what are you doing?"

"Trying to steal a kiss from the prettiest gal in Cripple Creek," he confessed with a disarming smile.

"I think you had a little too much punch to drink at the square dance tonight." She shook her head at him.

"Or had just enough to get my nerve up. Kate, I've been wanting to tell you this for weeks now. I think you are the smartest, spunkiest girl I have ever met. I surely hope we might be able to spend more time together. I think if you got to know me better, you'd see I'm not such a bad sort myself."

"I'm sorry, Geoffrey. I do think you are a wonderful fellow, but I . . . I would truly prefer that we remain friends."

His hands tightened on her shoulders as he searched her face in the dim light. She met his gaze candidly, willing him to see the truth. She did care for Geoffrey as a friend, but somehow she could feel nothing more for him.

"Friends it will be, then," he said quietly and let his hands drop.

The rest of their walk back to the boardinghouse was silent and strained. When they paused in Elly's front hallway, Geoffrey made a game effort to smile at Kate and thanked her for accompanying him to the square dance. Kate returned his thanks and hastened up the stairs, for the crestfallen look on his face wrenched her heart.

While changing for bed, she hoped she hadn't hurt Geoffrey too much. It was better that they set things straight between them now. As she knelt beside her attic window and opened it wide, she wondered wistfully why she couldn't feel something more for Geoffrey. He was a wonderful young man. He had a good sense of humor, he was intelligent, and he was obviously a hard worker.

When he had come to eat at the restaurant, Mary McPherson had told her she thought Geoffrey was quite handsome. Kate, however, found herself preferring black hair to chestnut, blue eyes to brown. She couldn't help thinking that Geoffrey seemed so young and callow to her. She bit her lip and chided herself when she realized what she was doing. Few men would ever be able to compare to Justin Talbott's blazing good looks and intense personality. She was going to become a wizened old maid if she continued to hold up her potential suitors to his impossible standard.

The crackle of a string of firecrackers brought her thoughts back to the present. People had been setting off guns and firecrackers since early this morning. She hugged herself as she happily reviewed the day's events in her mind. She reveled in the enthusiasm and spirit these westerners put into their Independence Day celebrations. She grinned to herself at the thought. Horses and dogs didn't enjoy the Fourth of July much in Cripple Creek, but the human folk had a fine time.

By mid-July it was clear to Kate that Elizabeth's health was steadily improving. Plenty of rest, lots of Elly O'Connell's simple food, and long walks in the mountain air seemed to have arrested the course of Elizabeth's disease. Robert was excited because the first mining stocks he had purchased had already doubled in value. And life was settling into a routine for the three of them.

On Saturday afternoons, Kate often went to the hospital, where she read to injured miners and wrote letters for them. On Sundays, Kate, Robert, and Elizabeth all went to church together, and slowly their circle of acquaintances in Cripple Creek widened.

For all she had settled comfortably into her new life in Cripple Creek, Kate still worried about meeting Justin Talbott again. She did her best not to look for Justin when she strolled about town, and she tried not to think about him. It was difficult, though, for she overheard his name spoken often at the restaurant, and she read about him frequently in the newspapers. She was hardly surprised that she hadn't ever seen him at the Golden Spike. He and the other Upper Tens, as the affluent mine owners and mine managers were called in Cripple Creek, were much more apt to patronize places like the fashionable Clarendon Hotel.

She had quite a shock, therefore, on one busy Tuesday

morning in early August. It was one of those hectic days when every table was full, and a line was beginning to form by the door. She hurried over to take an order from a gentleman sitting with his back to her. When she glanced down at him, she found herself looking into a pair of stormy blue eyes. From far away, it seemed, she heard a voice she hadn't heard in over two years growl, "Kate Holden, what the hell are you doing in Cripple Creek?"

Chapter Three

For several frozen moments she just stared at him. Finally her deeply ingrained manners came to her rescue.

"Good morning, Mr. Talbott," she managed to say, "it's a pleasure to see you again. As you can see, I am working as a waitress these days. I came out here to Cripple Creek with my sister Elizabeth and her husband two months ago."

Even as she spoke, she gazed at him, drinking in every detail of his appearance. His eyes were the same wonderful color she remembered, more vivid than the royal blue of the gingham cloths covering the tables. His nose was elegantly straight, his jaw rugged, and his cheekbones strong. His thick black hair waved back from his face, and his sideburns gave him a slightly rakish look. His fine gray suit fit his broad shoulders perfectly.

He looked like a confident, polished man-about-town, and the force of his physical presence was almost overwhelming. A part of her blessed the fact that he was seated. If he had been standing and towering over her, she would have lost what little hold she had on her composure.

"I thought you would be in college now," he said in an accusing tone.

"Actually, it's the time of the summer holidays," she pointed out brightly. As she watched him try to assimilate her answer, it occurred to her for the first time that she had a strategic advantage in this meeting. She, at least, had known for two months now that there was a chance she would encounter Justin Talbott again. Whereas for him, seeing her in a Cripple Creek restaurant must be a complete and total shock. His next question confirmed this notion.

"Why the devil are you working here of all places?"

"That is rather a long story, Mr. Talbott, and I do have other customers waiting right now. Could I please take your order? I can recommend the fried eggs and donuts this morning. We also have a fresh batch of bearsign that Mrs. Gregory just made up."

"Very well, I'll take the damn eggs, and one of those fresh biscuits, but I warn you, we aren't done with this conversation."

He sounded so disgruntled and baffled that she almost burst out laughing. As she hurried back to the kitchen with his order, she decided it was just as well that she could find some humor in this awful situation, for her heart felt as if it were breaking. Soon he would find out the truth about her loss of fortune, and she could only hope she could bear it when he wanted nothing more to do with her.

After she left the kitchen and hurried about waiting on her other tables, Kate was keenly aware of his brooding gaze. Regretfully she decided the only way to protect herself from further hurt was by continuing to act as if their meeting again meant nothing more to her than a pleasant coincidence. He certainly must never know she had been silly enough to fall in love with him.

For a moment she halted in her tracks when a horrible thought occurred to her. Could he possibly think she had followed him out here? Her cheeks began to burn, and she forced herself to keep walking toward the kitchen. She simply couldn't stand it if he came to believe she was a fortune-hunter. She would have to make it very clear that Robert was the one who had chosen to come to Cripple Creek.

When Kate entered the kitchen, Mary McPherson pounced on her at once. "You know who that man is, don't you?"

Sighing inwardly, Kate decided she would be better off telling her friend and the others at least a portion of the truth. "If you mean the gentleman in the gray suit, I do know that he is Justin Talbott. We met once a long time ago back in Boston."

"You sound mighty cool about having one of the richest and most handsome men in all of Cripple Creek sitting at your table." Mary crossed her arms and looked disappointed.

"I expect he needs to eat just like the rest of us," Mr.

Gregory put in mildly. "And speaking of eating, I might be reminding a certain Scottish lassie in my employ that there are close to fifty hungry men out there who would like to be fed as well."

Mary McPherson tossed her head and huffed out the door. As Kate calmly recited Justin's order to Mr. Gregory, she knew he was studying her.

"I've heard Talbott is a hard but honest man," the Englishman said almost meditatively as he flipped eggs and flapjacks in the skillets before him. "I've also heard that he has quite an eye for the ladies, and he runs with a fast and powerful crowd. Such a man might be drawn to a lovely young woman, but I doubt he would stay long with a penniless one. But I expect you probably already know that about him, since you met him before."

"I expect I do," Kate said woodenly.

"Ah, well, here's the gentleman's order then," Mr. Gregory said as he handed her Justin's plate. The fury blazing inside her quickly died when she saw the real concern in her employer's eyes.

"You needn't worry," she told him quickly. "He was a good friend of my father's, and I will make certain he knows the penniless part at once."

"I'm glad to hear that. Now, we don't want one of the richest men in the district to eat cold eggs in my restaurant, do we?" With that Mr. Gregory waved her out of the kitchen.

As she approached Justin's table, she found to her intense irritation that her heart was starting to race again. When she placed the food on the table before him, she couldn't help but notice that his surprise had worn off. Instead his blue eyes were watchful and measuring. It was impossible to tell what he was thinking. She immediately decided she liked it better when he was puzzled and off balance.

"I was sorry to hear about your father's death. He was a good man, and a good friend," he said in his deep voice.

"Thank you. My sister and I still miss him very much." That much she could say to him with real sincerity.

"I would like to call upon you soon, and offer my condolences to your sister. Where are you staying?"

She found herself reciting the address to Elly O'Connell's

boarding establishment before she had time to wonder if it was a good idea for him to know where she lived.

"And when is your next afternoon off?"

She bristled at the implication that she would, of course, be available to receive him that afternoon. Briefly she considered telling him that she already had made plans for that day, but she knew there was no use in putting off his visit. With a mental sigh, she told Justin she and Elizabeth could receive him that Thursday afternoon.

"You may expect me at three o'clock."

Gritting her teeth at what sounded remarkably like a royal dismissal, Kate whirled away from his table.

"Wait, please, Kate."

She stopped and looked back over her shoulder when she heard a softer note in his voice. "I just wanted to ask, have you been keeping up with your studies?"

She thought of the neglected crate of books beneath her bed and winced inwardly. "I study when I can," she replied honestly enough.

"I'm glad to hear that," he said, the warm smile she remembered only too well lighting his glorious eyes.

She hurried off to her next table, thinking Justin Talbott looked entirely too attractive when he smiled. Fortunately for her peace of mind, she was too busy for the next half hour to spend much time sneaking peeks at Justin or worrying about him. He left when she was in the kitchen. When she cleared his table, she found he had left her a dollar as a tip and a penciled note that said in bold, flowing script, "It was good to see you again, little scholar."

Kate spent the next two days trying not to think about Justin Talbott, which was a frustrating and fruitless endeavor for many reasons. Elizabeth, who worked herself into a tizzy once she heard he was planning to call, could talk of little else. She vacillated between worrying over what dresses they should wear to warning Kate that she shouldn't read too much into this visit. Of course, Elizabeth knew or had guessed that Kate had fallen for Justin two years ago. In exasperation, Kate finally told her sister that she was no longer a naive, silly girl. She was quite aware that an ambitious man like Justin would not have any serious interest in her now.

When Elly discovered Justin Talbott was coming to visit, she promptly tore her parlor apart and scrubbed and polished every inch of it. At dinnertime when all the boarders sat about the dining room table, they discussed Justin Talbott, his mines, and his social life until Kate was ready to pull out her hair. All in all, it was a relief when Thursday afternoon finally arrived.

At one o'clock when her shift at the Golden Spike was finished, Kate hurried back to the boardinghouse. Out of pride and a strong need to bolster her confidence, she proceeded to take great care with her appearance. She pulled her hair back into a sleek chignon and curled her bangs in imitation of the latest styles in *Harper's Bazaar.* Unfortunately, she only had two day dresses left from her old life in Boston, and already their bustles and sleeves were hopelessly out of fashion. She chose the more complimentary of the two, a jade green dress of summer wool trimmed with green satin ribbons.

As she gazed at herself in the mirror, she wondered if Justin would notice the changes in her. Over the past two years her face had grown thinner, but her body had filled out considerably in the appropriate feminine places. Still, her figure would never be stylishly plump and rounded. She had always been slim, and her long days at the Golden Spike ensured that Elly O'Connell's best efforts to fatten her up came to no avail. After making an exasperated face at herself, Kate marched to the door.

When she went down to the second floor, she met her sister in the hallway. Elizabeth, of course, looked lovely in a brown tea gown of India silk trimmed with lace. Her cheeks were flushed with healthy color as she bustled downstairs in front of Kate to the parlor. There they found Elly wringing her hands and worrying whether or not Mr. Talbott would like her china tea set and freshly baked macaroons.

Justin Talbott's carriage pulled up in front of the boardinghouse promptly at three o'clock. Kate and Elizabeth let Elly open the door for him because the Irishwoman was so excited about having one of Cripple Creek's most famous citizens come calling at her house. Kate was pleased when Justin proceeded to compliment Elly on her comfortable home.

While they sat drinking tea in Elly's gleaming parlor, he also charmed Elizabeth, asking sympathetically about the dark days after Thomas Holden's death. Admitting that he hadn't heard about the demise of the Holden shipping firm, he asked how and why the company had failed. Kate bit her lip and tried to sit regally still as Elizabeth told Justin all about the string of lost ships and poor investments that had toppled their father's empire. To Kate's mortification, Elizabeth even told him about the forced sale of their family home to cover the last of the debts incurred by the firm.

Although he looked at Kate from time to time, he never once spoke to her directly. She wondered how Elizabeth could be so relaxed with him. Lounging there in Elly's walnut gentleman's chair, he reminded her of a sleek panther just waiting to pounce. The worst moment came when Elizabeth admitted that Kate had been forced to give up her college plans.

"I know it was a great disappointment for her, but I was so proud of the way Kate rallied. She went right out and found a post as a governess instead. And her young charges loved her from the start."

While Elizabeth went on about Kate's work, Justin shot Kate a quizzical look. She returned it defiantly. After all, she hadn't actually told him she had gone to college.

She was heartily relieved when Justin finally rose to his feet and thanked Elizabeth for the visit. Kate's relief was short-lived, for Justin added a surprising request to his thanks.

"Mrs. Townsend, do I have your permission to take your sister out for a drive? It is a beautiful afternoon, and after working so hard at the Golden Spike, surely Kate deserves a little relaxation in the out-of-doors."

Elizabeth stood and gave Justin her hand. Looking at him steadily, she said, "Papa always said you were a gentleman. I know you will take good care of our Kate, Mr. Talbott."

"That I can promise you, Mrs. Townsend," he replied with a gallant smile.

"I'm sorry, Mr. Talbott," Kate interrupted hastily before the situation got any more out of hand. The last thing she wanted to do was spend any time alone with Justin Talbott. Just sitting across the room from him for this past hour had been an excruciatingly sweet and terrible torture. She relished looking at him and hearing the rich timbre of his deep voice again, but it was too painful knowing she could never mean anything to him now.

"I do appreciate your kind invitation, but I promised Elizabeth that I would go for a walk with her this afternoon."

"Kate, I must admit the excitement of Mr. Talbott's visit has worn me out. I think I will go and lie down for a bit," Elizabeth claimed with a smile in her dark eyes.

"Then perhaps I should stay with you," Kate offered desperately.

"Oh, no, I refuse to keep you from such a treat. Mr. Talbott, it was truly a pleasure to see you again." With a gracious nod to their guest, Elizabeth left the parlor, abandoning a smoldering Kate to her fate. Promising herself a long talk later with her traitorous sister, she turned to face their caller.

"It must be nice to have such a knack for managing and manipulating people," she told him sweetly.

"It's a gift that has its uses," he admitted as he tilted his head and studied her. "You know, I don't believe I've ever seen you in a temper before, and I surely don't remember there being such a sharp edge to your tongue."

"I don't remember you being so arrogant and overbearing. Since the period of our acquaintance was so brief, there's probably quite a bit we don't know about each other."

"That is a situation I would definitely like to remedy," he surprised and panicked her by saying.

"Frankly I can see little point in it, Mr. Talbott. It was very kind of you to call on us today. I know Elizabeth enjoyed talking with you about our father. But now I really must refuse your invitation. I only have one afternoon off a week, and there's a great deal I need to get done today."

She tried to shepherd him toward the front hallway, but he was too large and too stubborn to give way. Instead he crossed his arms and raised one dark eyebrow at her.

"Kate Holden, I think you're actually scared of coming on a carriage ride with me. The girl I met two years ago was made of sterner stuff."

"The girl you met two years ago no longer exists," she told him stiffly. "I am older and wiser now, and I have more sense than to accept silly dares."

"Ah, the general in me is sensing it is time to try a different tactic. Please, Miss Holden, will you come for a drive with me? It's a lovely afternoon, I've been shut up in my house for the past two days reading dry assay reports, and I would greatly appreciate your company."

As she looked up into his warm, compelling eyes, her resolve began to melt. The problem was, she desperately did want to go for a drive and prolong this bittersweet time with him. It was so tempting to ignore the stern warnings of her mind and give in to the mad longings of her heart.

"From what I've heard and read about you, I can't imagine you ever lack for company, particularly of the female sort," she said in a last-ditch effort to resist him.

"You know better than to believe everything you read, little scholar."

She tried to ignore the intense pleasure that went shooting through her when he called her by that nickname. "But even if half of it is true, you hardly need me to accompany you this afternoon."

"What if I feel a sudden urge to conjugate Latin verbs or recite Cicero? You are the only female I know who could appreciate such erudite behavior. My coachman will think I'm mad if I start spouting Greek poetry to the hills and trees around us."

Her lips quivered for a moment, and then she let go the laughter she had been trying valiantly to hold back. "You are too absurd, sir. Very well, I will go along on this drive, and I promise to be impressed rather than alarmed if you begin reciting Cicero."

"Thank you, my dear," he responded instantly and sent her a smile that did strange things to her pulse. He gave her time to fetch a hat, shawl, and gloves before he escorted her out the door. His carriage was a beautifully sprung landau, with plush golden velvet upholstery. Handing her up into the vehicle, Justin introduced her to Ben Gallagher, his coachman. Although Ben tipped his hat to her politely, she decided with an inward chuckle that the fellow hardly looked like a coachman. He was a big bear of a man with long dark hair, a black eye patch, a battered black Stetson, and a well-oiled six-shooter tied low on his right thigh.

Justin gave her a lazy smile. "Ben and I go back a long way. I met him in the midst of a barroom brawl in San Francisco. At the end of it all, we were the only two left standing. Rather than try to take him on, I hired him on the spot. He's been with me ever since."

"I'm sure you feel much more comfortable with such a competent and imposing gentleman about," Kate said, her eyes dancing with laughter.

As they started off through town, Justin pointed out the houses of some of Cripple Creek's most famous residents and regaled her with stories about the town's early days. He told her of old Bob Womack, the stubborn cowpuncher who had always believed there was gold in this area. It took Bob over twenty years to convince other folk there was a bonanza located in the hills behind Pikes Peak. When his ore samples finally caught the attention of mining engineers, Bob launched one of the richest gold strikes in the history of the country. After people started flocking to Cripple Creek, Bob traded his rich El Paso claim for five hundred dollars and a case of whiskey. He then proceeded to give away five hundred one-dollar bills to children passing by on the street. When his money was gone, he wandered about helping others stake fine claims in the district.

Kate in turn told Justin amusing stories about some of the odd characters she had encountered at the Golden Spike. She was pleased to see that when she wanted to, she still could make Justin laugh. Yet all the time they talked, she was painfully aware of the handsome, elegant man lounging right beside her. At one point, a particularly large rut in the road jolted the landau. She was thrown against Justin, her heart racing. For one brief, delicious moment their shoulders touched, and she felt a lock of his hair brush against her cheek. She eased away from him and plunged on with the story she was telling, hoping Justin wouldn't guess how flustered she was feeling.

In the meantime Justin's fine team pulled the landau steadily up the Ute Pass road north out of Cripple Creek. Occasionally Ben reined the horses over to the side of the road as big freighting wagons came rumbling down the hill. When the team had climbed to the top of the northern ridge surrounding the Cripple Creek valley, Ben turned the landau onto a lane which led away from the main road. After another mile or so, they reached a clearing with a wonderful view out over the town. On Justin's orders, there Ben pulled the horses to a stop.

"Miss Holden, would you care to go for a walk with me?" Justin asked her with exaggerated courtesy.

She smiled and nodded her agreement and let him help her down from the landau. She was grateful he had kept the conversation light so far. He could easily steer their talk into more personal and dangerous channels, though, once they were out of earshot of Ben Gallagher. She decided that price was probably worth paying for the pleasure of spending the past hour with Justin. It would be better, too, if they could settle matters between them. She was alarmed by this new interest he seemed to have in her. Because she was so susceptible to this man, she was determined to harden her heart against him.

They strolled quietly side by side through a lovely aspen grove. The green grass made a thick, lush carpet beneath their feet. Wild geraniums and delicate blue and white columbines grew in profusion throughout the grove. The cool mountain breezes brought with them the fresh, sweet scent of wild roses and aspen bark. On the far side of the grove the trees fell away, and a magnificent view opened up toward Cripple Creek and cone-shaped Mount Pisgah beyond it. Kate stood there for several moments enjoying the scenery and trying to ignore the fact that Justin was watching her.

"Why did you give me the impression the other day that you had gone to college?" he asked suddenly.

She squared her shoulders and swung about to face him. "Because I didn't want your pity."

"You must have known I would find out sooner or later."

"I knew no such thing. At the time I was hoping that we could say hello and good-bye at the Golden Spike and leave matters at that."

"I doubt you truly mean that."

"Oh, but I do, Mr. Talbott," she said, struggling to keep her soaring temper in check. "I most surely do. I wonder if you know what it's like to see your best and oldest friends turn away from you simply because you no longer possess a fortune? I wonder if you can imagine what it feels like to see dreams you have worked toward for years suddenly turn to dust?''

Even as she spoke the words in anger, she saw his face change, and suddenly she remembered. Of course he could imagine what it was like. Of all the people she had ever known, he was the one person who might be able to understand what the past two years had been like for her. Fervently she wished she could take her thoughtless words back, but it was too late. The last thing she wanted to do was make him think about his painful past. "*Non ingara mali*—because I am no stranger to misfortune myself," he translated the Latin phrase with a self-deprecating smile, "I might be able to imagine what your life has been like since your father died. I am sorry you had to endure such a painful time."

"I am the one who should apologize. You of all people could understand. I should have thought before I spoke, as always."

"That, my dear, is part of your charm." He smiled at her again, and then his eyes grew serious. "Please don't let the difficult experiences of the last two years harden you."

"I don't think I have let them, not really." Taking a deep breath, she added, "I've been so horribly rude to you simply because I wanted to push you away before you had a chance to turn away from me."

"And what makes you think I would want to turn away from you, my golden girl?"

She looked up at him, her green eyes candid. "I have learned more about the world in the last two years, Mr. Talbott, and I have learned a good deal about people. Once I might have been able to help you reach what you have worked so hard to regain for yourself since leaving Boston, but there is little now I can offer you in the way of social standing or wealth."

"Such worldly wisdom in one so young," he mocked her gently. "You might be right about me and what I have been striving for, but then again, you could be wrong."

"It's been known to happen once or twice." She did her best to give him a pert smile. "On the off chance I am correct, I think this should be our last carriage drive together."

"Why, Kate Holden, are you scared of me?"

Briefly she considered lying and protecting her pride a while longer, and then she decided honesty at this point would be far the wiser course. She was gambling that his own instincts as a gentleman and his regard for her father would keep him from taking advantage of the declaration she was about to make.

"I suppose I am, a little. Mr. Talbott, you should know that with very little effort on your part, I could come to care for you." Her cheeks were on fire and her mouth was dry, but she forced herself to continue on. "In the past you have been very kind to me. I am hoping that you could extend that kindness once again and not come calling at our boardinghouse."

"Let me make certain I know what you are asking, my golden girl. You do not wish for me to call on you, or take you on drives, or out to dinner, or on any other diversion that a young lady your age might find pleasant?" His blue gaze was unreadable.

"That is correct, sir. I wish to ask, at the risk of being rude once again, that you will simply stay away from me."

"It is a wise request, little scholar, but I'm not at all sure I can abide by it," he muttered under his breath. He stepped forward and pulled her into his arms.

She gasped as his hands circled her waist. Instinctively she put her palms against his chest to steady herself. The material of his lapels was cool beneath her fingers. The spicy scent of cedar enveloped her, and within moments she was transported back to the time of their first kiss. But this was entirely different. From the start he was more bold. His right arm urged her toward him until her body fit snugly against his own. Suddenly she was intensely aware of the hardness of his legs, and an odd sensation began to kindle in the pit of her stomach. His left hand came up to caress the line of her jaw and linger at her neck, where it sent delightful shivers tracing down her back.

She watched, barely daring to breathe, as his head descended toward her. She noticed how long and dark his lashes were. The warm light she saw in his eyes made her head swim. When his lips came down to cover hers, she remembered the lesson he had taught her before. She parted her lips willingly and let his mouth take possession of her own. Within moments he was kissing her so thoroughly that she could hardly breathe. Her hands crept upward to cling to his shoulders. After another long, drugging kiss she finally wrapped her arms tightly about his neck.

She told herself, This is madness, I must not allow him to take such liberties. Yet a wild part of her was delighted that he wanted to kiss her in this way. She would never have the chance to be with him again. Surely she deserved this little piece of heaven he was offering her. Her sweet memories of this moment could help her through a lifetime without him.

Vaguely she was aware that his left hand was now tugging at her chignon. Suddenly her long hair came tumbling down about her shoulders. He ceased kissing her just long enough to thread his hands through her hair, spreading and smoothing it until it fell in a golden curtain down to her waist.

"This is much better, little pagan. This is the way I remember you when you were reading that afternoon in the garden, your hair cascading down in golden waves," he murmured hoarsely. She could only stare at him, and then he was kissing her again with even greater passion than before. Gradually she became aware that his right hand was massaging her waist, creating the oddest tingling sensations that seemed to flow all the way down to the warmth growing in the pit of her stomach. Slowly his hand moved up her rib cage, still generating those wonderful, peculiar feelings. He stopped kissing her and watched her with hooded eyes as his hand moved to gently cup her breast.

She gasped as waves of sensation went flooding through her. Her legs would have buckled, but his left hand moved quickly to cup her buttocks and pull her more tightly against his hardness. That only made the strange warmth in her lower body kindle into a blazing flame. As he gently touched and stroked her through her dress front, she closed her eyes against his gaze and leaned her head weakly against his chest.

It was that gesture of trust that abruptly brought Justin to his senses. Swearing under his breath, he loosened his hold on her trembling body. He gathered her gently into his arms and rested his chin on the top of her shining head.

As he waited for her trembling and his own to ease, he cursed himself inwardly. What was it about this slip of a girl that could drive him to the brink of insanity? In another moment he would have pulled her to the ground and taken her right there on the grass. And yet he was no seducer of innocent virgins. Despite her passionate response to him, he knew Kate Holden was exactly that. Glancing down at her flushed cheeks and exquisite features, he felt a surge of protectiveness sweep through him. Tempted as he was to see her again, he knew now that he would never be able to keep his hands off her. Yet he could only behave honorably toward Thomas Holden's daughter; surely he owed his benefactor that. Sighing inwardly, he decided Kate had been right from the outset.

"Can you stand on your own now?" He surprised himself with the tenderness he heard in his voice.

She nodded mutely.

"Very well then, turn around, little one, and we will see what we can do about your hair." When she was slow to respond, he placed his hands on her shoulders and gently turned her about. Fortunately a handful of pins remained caught in her thick tresses. Relishing the feel of her silken hair between his fingers, he retrieved what pins he could.

Deftly he caught her hair back and fashioned a chignon much like the one she had worn earlier. One of his former mistresses had liked him to brush her hair, and from that woman he had learned the rudiments of female hairstyling. He frowned at himself for remembering Sally Volker at this moment. Somehow her very memory seemed to sully the presence of the lovely girl before him.

When he had finished with his task, he pressed a quick kiss on the back of her neck and turned her about to face him once more. He was relieved to see the dazed look had begun to leave her eyes, but her cheeks were still flushed with color.

"I owe you an apology for what just happened here, little scholar. I am entirely to blame. I think your suggestion earlier was probably a wise one. Since you seem to have such a heady effect on me, it would be much better if I did not see you again."

She looked up at him, her green eyes grave. "I was right then. You could never come to care for me, for I have so little to offer you now."

"That's not true, young Kate." Justin paused. He had best

be clear. "You have a world of wonderful qualities that the man who eventually wins your heart will treasure. I, however, will never be able to care for any woman in the way you mean. I am a hard man with little love or sentiment left in me. If I ever do marry, it will be for convenience and social standing just as you predicted. You deserve a marriage full of love, tenderness, and caring. Because I can never offer you these things, it is better that we do not see each other again."

"I believe, Mr. Talbott, that you are very wrong about yourself," she replied in a low voice. "You have shown me such kindness and gentleness since the start. I accept that you can never care for me, but I pray you will not condemn yourself to a loveless marriage. You, too, have a great deal to offer, and the woman who wins your heart will discover a magnificent treasure trove inside it."

With that she turned away from him. Head and shoulders proudly erect, she walked back toward the carriage. He let Kate go on ahead of him, only catching up with her in time to help her up into the landau.

Their drive back to the boardinghouse was a silent one. He glanced over at her from time to time, memorizing the beauty of her features. It gave him a bleak sort of pleasure to see that she had grown only more lovely over the past two years. Her fair skin was flawless, her lips were perfectly shaped, and her fine cheekbones and nose would have delighted the ancient Greeks whom she loved to study. The deep green color of her eyes never ceased to surprise and please him. Surely some upright young man would come along soon, fall head over heels in love with her, and take her away from the drudgery of her work at the Golden Spike.

Throughout the drive she never cried, but her face was pale and set. He wondered uneasily if what she had told him earlier was true. She said she could come to care for him with very little effort on his part. Ruefully he had to acknowledge that he often had this effect on women, although he did little to encourage their affections. It pained him in this case, though, to think the harmless flirtation he had allowed to happen between them two years ago might have meant something to her.

To his amazement, she never did take him to task for his forwardness in the aspen grove. Instead, after Justin helped her alight, she gave Ben Gallagher a warm smile and thanked him for his driving. She turned back to Justin and said simply, "Thank you for the carriage ride, Mr. Talbott, and thank you for coming to call on my sister. Your visit meant a great deal to us both."

"It was my pleasure." He was startled by the urge he felt to slip an arm about her shoulder and kiss her in farewell. "I wish you well, little scholar, and I promise never to trouble you again."

"You could never trouble me, Justin," she said softly, using his given name for the very first time. *"Vade in pace."* She spoke the ancient Roman farewell "go in peace." Afterward she turned and hurried toward the boardinghouse.

Justin was left standing in the street, wondering if he had just let a golden opportunity slip away.

Chapter Four

Somehow Kate managed to get through the next few days. It helped, of course, that she was so busy at work. The Sunday after Justin's visit, however, seemed to drag on forever. No matter how hard she tried, she couldn't seem to concentrate on Reverend Elwood's sermon in church. Later that afternoon she went for a long walk by herself up to the Mount Pisgah cemetery. It seemed an appropriate place to visit, for a part of her felt as though she were in mourning.

As she stared down at the lambs and flowers carved on the little white marble headstones of small children, she realized her personal tragedy was not so important in the great scale of things. She told herself firmly that it was time to put her girlish dreams aside once and for all, but it was a sad and painful business saying good-bye to them just the same.

Fortunately Elizabeth, who was always sensitive to her moods, never spoke about Justin's visit. Elly, too, eventually stopped mentioning the proud moment when Justin Talbott came to her home. The time Kate came to dread the most was at night when she lay in her bed in her tiny attic room hoping to drift off to sleep right away. Instead memories, newer and therefore all the more vivid, came to haunt her. She could remember everything Justin had said to her during the carriage ride. He had been so funny and charming that afternoon. She also could not forget everything he had said and done in the aspen grove. She was still astonished by the way her own body had come alive with sensations she never dreamed she could feel.

What hurt the most was what he had said after he kissed her. He would not court her because he thought he would be too hard and uncaring a husband. She knew he was wrong, and her heart ached because now she would never have a chance to persuade him otherwise.

When two weeks had passed, she at last decided she couldn't bear moping in her attic room any longer. When Geoffrey asked her out to a concert, she accepted his invitation. Since the night she had told Geoffrey she wanted to be friends, he had made it clear he still liked spending time with her. To her surprise she enjoyed the concert greatly. From that evening on she did her best to forget Justin Talbott and to enjoy the great adventure she was living. Cripple Creek was such a fascinating parade of colorful people and personalities, she didn't want to miss out on another moment of it.

On a sunny afternoon in August, Kate entered the apothecary shop on Bennett Avenue to make some purchases for Elizabeth. Immediately she noticed an auburn-haired woman dressed in a scarlet satin gown arguing with Mr. Puckett, the shop's owner. As she drew closer Kate saw the woman was quite handsome in a dramatic sort of way. Even if she had wanted to, Kate could not have avoided hearing the heated words the two were exchanging.

"Madame De Vere, I must insist that you leave this shop immediately. I have told you before that I will only allow you and your girls to do business on these premises on Tuesday mornings. You know we both could be fined if the sheriff sees you here."

Kate's eyes widened when she realized the woman at the counter was one of the most famous madams in Cripple Creek. Of course, the boarders at Elly's house never spoke of such matters in Kate's presence, but she often overheard colorful snippets of conversations at the Golden Spike. Pearl De Vere ran the most expensive and exclusive brothel down on Myers Avenue. Kate had never seen the woman before because a city ordinance had been passed decreeing prostitutes could go shopping on Bennett Avenue only on Tuesday mornings. That way decent women could be spared the embarrassment of encountering these "soiled doves." Surely the matter must be urgent for Pearl De Vere to defy the ordinance. The madam's next words confirmed Kate's guess.

"I cannot and will not wait five days to buy cough syrup

for young Bessie, just because of this town's hypocritical rules,'' the woman replied angrily. "Half the men who sit on our town council visit Myers Avenue on a regular basis.''

"I am not going to debate town politics with you. I suggest you try Dr. Bogart or Dr. J. A. Smith. Either one of them may well have a supply of the medicine you need.''

"I already told you, both doctors are out on calls right now, and my girl needs something for her cough immediately.''

"You will simply have to wait until one of the two doctors return. Good day, madam.'' Kate thought the druggist relished putting special emphasis on that final word.

"I'm sure the good Lord will be impressed by your truly Christian attitude, Mr. Puckett,'' the madam said bitterly as she turned and strode away from the counter. Because Kate was standing near the main aisle of the shop, she caught a good glimpse of Pearl De Vere's face as she came storming by. The real worry and concern she saw in the woman's deep blue eyes prompted Kate to act. She followed the madam right out the door of the shop onto the boardwalk.

"Excuse me, ma'am,'' Kate called before the woman could stride away. Pearl De Vere swung about to look at her, anger and resentment still smoldering in her gaze.

"If you will tell me what medicine it is you need, I would be happy to purchase it for you,'' Kate offered.

The madam looked startled, and proceeded to eye her curiously. "It's good of you to offer, miss,'' she said shortly. "Here's a dollar, and I wanted to buy whatever Mr. Puckett recommends to ease a severe chest cough.''

Kate reached out and took the coin Pearl De Vere handed her. "I will be right back,'' she assured the woman and went inside to make her purchases. Mr. Puckett pursed his thin lips and looked quite disapproving when she requested cough syrup along with the other items on her list. Clearly the man had seen her talking with the madam, but Kate was relieved when he didn't mention the subject. Five minutes later she was back outside, handing the brown parcel containing the cough syrup over to Pearl.

"Well, young lady, it's a kind deed you've done today, and you have my thanks for it. My name is Pearl De Vere, but I'm guessing you know who and what I am already.''

"You are a rather famous person in this town, Mrs. De Vere." Deciding she would be intolerably rude if she didn't return the introduction, Kate added, "My name is Kate Holden, and it was truly no trouble to purchase the medicine. I only hope it helps your girl." She was pleased when she managed not to falter over that last term.

"It's Miss De Vere, actually. When you see as many married men as I do frequenting my place, you learn to mistrust the entire institution of marriage," the older woman declared with an ironic smile. "Listen, Miss Holden, I've no wish to be offensive after the good turn you just did me, but you should know this can be a difficult and cruel town for females down on their luck."

Under the madam's shrewd gaze, Kate was suddenly very aware of the fact that she was wearing one of her oldest skirts and a shabby bonnet. Her wages and tips at the Golden Spike covered her lodging and food comfortably, with a few dollars left over each week. She had been delaying buying new clothes for herself, however, until she built up her meager savings at the bank.

"If you ever need help, feel free to come down and see me during the day. And keep in mind, a beautiful girl can have a gold mine of her own working at the Old Homestead or a place like it."

"Thank you, Miss De Vere," Kate managed to reply, even though her cheeks were beginning to burn. The madam's offer was well intentioned, and she would be a puritanical goose to take it any other way.

"And now, I'd best be on my way before that old rascal Sheriff Peabody catches me here. You'd think with all the free time I've given him with my girls, he would go easy on these ridiculous fines."

With that parting comment, the remarkable woman marched over to a handsome black phaeton with bright red wheels. Settling herself on the driving seat, Pearl flipped a coin to the boy holding the horses' heads. After the madam competently gathered up the reins, the boy let go his hold, and the horses set off at a spanking trot. As she watched the rig turn at the corner toward Myers Avenue, only gradually did Kate realize her cheeks were still on fire. It wasn't every day she conversed with a notorious madam and was given an invitation to work as a prostitute.

As she walked back toward Elly's, Kate decided the entire situation was quite humorous. She supposed she ought to feel more shocked, but from her study of history she knew prostitution had always been a part of human societies. Even though she could accept this encounter with some equanimity, she decided this was one adventure she wasn't going to share with her ladylike sister.

In September Robert began frequenting the lobby of the Clarendon Hotel. Kate worried about him, for she knew swindlers and bunco men gathered at the hotel to sell worthless schemes and mines to tenderfeet. One night Robert insisted on taking both Elizabeth and Kate out to dine at the elegant Wolfe Hotel.

With great ceremony he informed them that he had just cashed in all of his stocks to purchase a mine of his own. Raising his glass, he toasted the Elizabeth, the claim he had just renamed in honor of his beautiful wife. As he talked excitedly about his hopes for the mine's future, Kate watched him with a sinking heart. A mining claim could indeed be the way to great riches, but she knew only too well from the stories she heard at work how risky mining could be.

Within two weeks assay reports proved the mine to be worthless. Crestfallen and concerned, Robert started job-hunting, for he had spent almost all of his savings on the Elizabeth. Unfortunately it was a difficult time to be looking for work. The country as a whole had been in a depression for two years now. Since the government had repealed the Sherman Silver Purchase Act in the fall of 1893, silver mines all over the state had started closing. Out-of-work miners, mine managers, and shopkeepers had been flocking to the rich gold town of Cripple Creek.

In desperation Robert finally took a job as a lowly mucker in a mine. For eight hours a day, six days a week he had to shovel tons of ore into mine carts. At night he returned to Elly's boardinghouse exhausted and filthy. Around the dinner table he did his best to tell amusing stories about the men he worked with and the odd happenings that took place down in the tunnels. Kate heard the hollow ring in his voice, though, and guessed at the charade he was putting on for Elizabeth's benefit.

Elizabeth was no fool, and she could fill in for herself the gaps in Robert's stories. The *Cripple Creek Register* was full of descriptions of blasting and drilling accidents which maimed and killed miners almost daily. To make matters worse, with the return of cold, damp weather, Elizabeth's health started to deteriorate again. Her coughing bouts grew longer, and she had less and less energy. Kate guessed the stress of worrying about Robert and their finances was also taking its toll.

One Sunday afternoon when Elizabeth felt too tired to go for a walk, Kate practically dragged Robert away from the boardinghouse. As they strolled along a lane on the eastern edge of town, Kate told him gently, "Elizabeth worries all the time about you down in that mine."

"I realize it bothers her more than she lets on," he replied wearily, "but it's only a temporary situation. I'm trying to save up enough money for us to move to Colorado Springs. I will have a better chance of finding clerical work of one kind or another there, and the climate will still be better for Elizabeth than moving back east. I can't believe I gambled everything on that mine. I was such a reckless, brainless idiot."

"You're hardly the first to succumb to gold fever," Kate countered, thinking of all the disillusioned young men she had waited on at the Golden Spike.

"I'm not the first, but I'm one who surely should have known better. Elizabeth is paying for my stupidity now."

Kate winced at the bitterness and regret she saw in his earnest blue eyes. "I've managed to save up some money from my tips. You could use a part of it to pay for the fare to the Springs and for a room there."

"I'm not going to touch a penny of your money, Kate. You've worked so hard to save what you have, and a young woman alone in the world needs her financial security," he said with a stubborn look on his face.

"You could consider it a loan, then," she replied evenly. "I'm not alone in the world. I have a wonderful sister, and you are not the only one who loves her. Worrying about you is wearing her down every day. And I worry about you, too. You are my favorite brother-in-law, after all,'' she finished on a lighter note.

''I'm your only brother-in-law.'' He grinned at her and squeezed her arm affectionately. ''I appreciate your offer, and I promise to consider it. Now tell me, have any of your patrons proposed to you this week?'' With that he turned their conversation onto other channels. Sighing inwardly, she decided to follow his lead. She had planted the seed, and she would just have to wait to see if it bore fruit.

A month later she desperately wished she had pushed Robert much harder that afternoon to accept her offer. On a dreary Thursday in mid-November, a boy sent by Elly O'Connell came running to fetch Kate from the restaurant. The news he brought was a cruel, brutal blow. Robert had been crushed and killed by a falling drill platform.

The next few days were terrible for both sisters. Elizabeth was beside herself with grief. Kate had little time for her own sorrow because the burden of making all the funeral arrangements fell upon her shoulders. Geoffrey Cooper was a great help throughout this nightmare period. He was the one who found a carpenter to make a casket, he hired the grave diggers, and he made arrangements for a hired rig to take them out to the Mount Pisgah cemetery the morning of the funeral service.

Later, as she watched him help Elizabeth walk away from the grave site, Kate wondered dully why she couldn't fall in love with a dependable, caring man like him. That night as she lay sobbing in her attic bed, she longed for Justin more fiercely than ever before. She would have given almost anything to feel his strong, warm arms about her.

Two weeks later she returned to her work at the Golden Spike. She dearly wanted to spend more time with Elizabeth, but their financial situation was grim. Even dying in Cripple Creek proved to be an expensive business. When she had finished paying all the bills, she found she had used up the last of the young couple's funds. To save money on their lodgings, she moved into Elizabeth's room. To pay the cost of Elizabeth's food and medicines, Kate started taking in laundry and washing it in Elly's kitchen after work.

It was hard for Kate to find the energy to do this extra labor after hustling about all day at the Golden Spike, but single miners were willing to pay good money to have their clothing washed. Her hands soon turned red and puffy from working with lye soap every night. Her fingers became crisscrossed with little burns, for she was clumsy with the heavy sadirons she heated on Elly's stove. Elly, at least, kept her distracted and amused as she worked, for the Irishwoman loved to talk, and she told wonderful stories as she prepared supper for her boarders and washed the dishes afterward.

Because Elizabeth rarely left her bed anymore, Kate also had to carry meals up to her sister in their room. To please Kate, Elizabeth did her best to eat, but she had little appetite or energy. Kate didn't nag her too much about not going on the walks that Elizabeth's doctors had recommended. She knew her sister needed time to grieve, but it hurt her to see Elizabeth so listless and apathetic.

As if she didn't have enough troubles, one day when she was at work, Kate spotted Justin Talbott walking down the other side of Bennett Avenue with a ravishing brunette on his arm. Mary McPherson, who made a hobby out of knowing all about the rich and famous in the district, noticed Kate watching the couple through the window.

"That's Annette LaMonte," Mary told her quietly. "Rumor has it that Justin Talbott will be announcing his engagement to her any day. She's the daughter of Pierre LaMonte, the Leadville mining baron. They make a striking couple, don't they?"

"They certainly do," Kate managed to murmur. Her eyes burning, she turned away from the window and hurried to wait on another customer. She hoped that Justin had found a woman he could love, but from the haughty, cool expression she had seen on Miss LaMonte's face, she guessed sadly that Justin was about to make his marriage of convenience.

One afternoon in December when Kate came home a little early from work, Elizabeth was sleeping soundly. As Kate tiptoed about, tidying up their room, she found a handkerchief lying by her sister's bedside. She froze when she saw the brown dots of blood on it. Elizabeth was hemorrhaging again, and she hadn't said a word about it. Kate whirled about and went to fetch a doctor. The kindly young physician whom Elly had recommended spent over an hour examining Elizabeth and listening to her lungs.

Dr. Sprague's face was grim when he came down to speak with Kate in the parlor. "If you want to save her, she needs to be admitted to a good sanatorium at once. There are several fine ones over in Colorado Springs that offer the most up-to-date treatments for tuberculosis."

"How much would such a place cost?" Kate asked falteringly.

"I'm afraid a year's treatment at a good institution will run you three to four hundred dollars," he replied soberly. "It's quite conceivable, however, that she could need to stay there for two or three years, if she survives the next few months. I fear, Miss Holden, that your sister is very ill. She needs the kind of care these facilities can provide as soon as possible."

He took a slip of paper from his satchel and handed it to Kate. "I took the liberty of writing down the names of the four sanatoriums with the best reputations."

"I promise I will have her admitted to one of those places shortly." Even as Kate said the words, she felt her stomach twist. She was only vaguely aware of thanking the doctor, paying his fee, and seeing him out the door as she thought furiously. She had only fifty-four dollars in her account at the bank. Where or how could she get hold of three or four hundred dollars, much less a thousand?

As she stood staring blankly at Elly's front door, Kate's stomach tightened even further. There was only one person she knew in the district with that kind of money. It was time for her to go calling on Justin Talbott.

Chapter Five

Kate hurried home from work the following afternoon to tidy her hair and change her clothes. From her bed Elizabeth watched Kate's preparations gravely. The evening before they had argued for a long time over Kate's going to Justin Talbott for help. Elizabeth had been adamantly opposed to the idea at first, but eventually she came to see Kate's point. They truly had no one else to turn to.

For her part, Kate had been greatly relieved to see Elizabeth was willing to be admitted to a sanatorium. Elizabeth had been so despondent after Robert's death that Kate had begun to wonder if her sister was giving up on life. The fact that Elizabeth was eager to undertake the lengthy fight against her illness was wonderful news.

Elizabeth even helped Kate dress her hair and loaned her their mother's cameo brooch to wear with her gray-and-maroon plaid dress. After inspecting both of their black woolen winter jackets, they decided that the fur trim on Elizabeth's made hers appear more elegant. Kate wore her own gray bonnet, which looked much more jaunty since Elizabeth had sewn on it some ostrich feathers taken from one of her old hats that very afternoon.

"How do I look?" Kate asked as she pirouetted about for Elizabeth's inspection.

"You look lovely, dear. I don't see how that man could refuse you anything."

"I hope you're right. I'm off then." Kate kissed Elizabeth on the forehead and bustled from the room. She paused in the doorway and glanced back over her shoulder. Elizabeth appeared so pale and frail lying there in bed. She looked like a shadow of her former vibrant self. Justin Talbott just had to help them.

Walking up the hill in the frosty dusk, Kate kept rehearsing what she planned to say to him. She was going to ask that he lend her the money to pay for Elizabeth's first year in the sanatorium. Somehow in the course of the next twelve months, she would find a way to pay him back, and to pay for future years of Elizabeth's treatment.

Although it was going to be difficult for her to ask this favor, she guessed Justin would probably grant it at once. His regard for her father was very real, and he certainly could afford to lend the money. Just last week the newspapers had announced that Justin's miners up on Battle Mountain had struck another rich vein of gold. He also planned to donate a thousand dollars to build an addition to the Cripple Creek hospital.

She paused when she reached the wrought-iron fence surrounding his home. Because she had been afraid of bumping into Justin, she had never strolled along this block before. Now she walked slower and let herself take in all the details of his house. It was one of the few brick homes in town, grand in scale and built in the French mansard style. He must have had mature trees transplanted just after the house was built, for five handsome maples grew about the yard's perimeter, and several good-sized shrubs softened the bold outlines of the house. It looked like a wonderful yard for children. Wistfully she imagined Justin's black-haired, blue-eyed sons and daughters running and playing beneath those trees.

Telling herself that she was stalling, she took a deep breath and walked up the path to the front porch. A thin woman with her iron gray hair pulled back in a tight bun answered Kate's knock on the door.

"Is Mr. Talbott in?" she asked, even as her cheeks began to flush under the woman's disapproving gaze. Kate knew it was highly irregular for a single lady to come calling on a gentleman, particularly at this time of day, but she hardly had any choice in the matter.

"No, miss, he is not. He has gone back east for the holidays."

She felt as though the earth were caving in beneath her.

Justin just couldn't be gone. What a silly fool she had been to assume he would be here, simply because she needed him.

"Please, could you tell me when you expect him back?" she gathered enough wits to ask.

"Not till February. Good evening." The curt woman promptly shut the door.

Kate was left staring at the heavy wooden panels before her, trying to come to terms with what she had just learned. Justin was gone, and he wouldn't be back for at least a month, perhaps two. But Elizabeth's treatment couldn't wait that long. The young doctor had been clear enough about that. Taking another deep breath, Kate rang the doorbell again. This time when Justin's housekeeper opened the door, she positively glowered.

"Ma'am, I am very sorry to trouble you again," Kate said hastily, "but it's terribly important that I contact Mr. Talbott. Did he leave an address where he can be reached?"

"Well, you certainly are a bold piece." the woman sneered. "In my day a young lady never would come to a gentleman's home unchaperoned. Even if Mr. Talbott had left an address with me, I certainly wouldn't be giving it to the likes of you." With that the woman slammed the door in Kate's face once again.

Kate gasped in outrage. She had never been treated so rudely in all her life. She thought about ringing the bell and telling the housekeeper that Justin would be furious when he found out about this incident. After a few moments, she changed her mind and turned away. There was a good chance the woman simply wouldn't open the door again. Besides, there was nothing to be gained by enduring her hostility once more. The older woman had all but admitted that she didn't have an address for her employer.

As Kate walked back toward Elly's boardinghouse, she racked her brain for ideas. She knew from her efforts to find employment six months ago that Justin did not keep a separate office in Cripple Creek. He conducted all his business affairs out of his home. Slowly she came to the frightening conclusion that she had no way of reaching Justin until he returned to the district.

If she couldn't borrow the money from Justin, where in the

world could she find three hundred dollars? There was no one else who could possibly loan her such a sum. Here she was, living in a town where simple carpenters, druggists, and firemen had become rich overnight. If only she had a gold mine of her own. And then she remembered what Pearl De Vere had told her that fateful afternoon back in August.

There was a way that destitute, beautiful young women could make hundreds of dollars in Cripple Creek. Kate came to an abrupt halt while shivers that had nothing to do with the deepening cold went racing down her back. Could she possibly do this? Could she possibly sell herself to raise the money to save Elizabeth? Kate was revolted by the very thought, but a pragmatic, rational side of her demanded that she at least consider the notion. For thousands of years desperate women had chosen prostitution as a means to survive.

It meant, of course, that she would have to give up all hopes of ever having a family of her own. She could hardly let a decent man marry her after she had worked in a brothel. But a cold, logical voice inside her insisted she could move away from the district when she had saved enough money to pay for Elizabeth's treatment. She could still have a fulfilling life without a husband, perhaps even teach school someday in a town where the people had no knowledge of her past.

She shook her head and started walking again. It was all very well to contemplate the vague future, but facing the immediate reality of what she would have to do working at the Old Homestead or a place like it was beyond her. She loved Elizabeth dearly, but she wasn't brave enough to make this great a sacrifice for her. She simply would have to pray that Elizabeth's condition wouldn't worsen before Justin came back to Cripple Creek.

When Kate returned to the boardinghouse, Elizabeth was awake and waiting for her, her pale cheeks flushed with strain and excitement.

"What did Mr. Talbott say?" she asked eagerly.

"Mr. Talbott wasn't home, but I did obtain his address back east." Kate found herself blurting out the lie before she could stop herself. "I will wire him in the morning and ask him for a loan to pay for your treatment."

It was the first time since she was a little child that she had lied to her sister. Yet Elizabeth seemed so eager and hopeful about what the sanatorium could do for her, Kate didn't have the heart to tell her she would have to wait another two months to travel to Colorado Springs. At least the falsehood had bought Kate a little more time to decide what to do.

She went downstairs to the kitchen to pick at the meal Elly had saved for her. Kate was surprised when Elly generously offered to lend her fifty dollars to pay for Elizabeth's treatment.

"I'm so sorry we don't have more spare cash we can loan you. All our savings are tied up in Rory's freighting teams, you see," the Irishwoman explained apologetically.

"Elly, you are very kind to offer us a loan, but we can't take your money. I'm just going to cross my fingers and hope Mr. Talbott comes through for us."

When Kate trudged up the stairs to her room an hour later, her heart was heavy. She hated lying to both Elizabeth and Elly, and she still could think of no way to raise the money for Elizabeth's treatment.

That night Elizabeth's hacking cough kept both sisters awake for hours. Around two o'clock in the morning, Kate rose to fetch Elizabeth a glass of water and helped her take the medicine Dr. Sprague had prescribed. She moistened Elizabeth's feverish cheeks and forehead with a damp cloth and straightened her bedding.

"Dear Kate," Elizabeth said softly, "I am so sorry that all these burdens have fallen on your shoulders. I think Papa would be very proud of you."

Kate's eyes filled with tears, but she managed to keep her voice even as she urged, "Sh, now, don't talk. You should try to sleep."

The medicine seemed to help, or perhaps Elizabeth was so worn out from the long coughing fits that her body at last succumbed to sleep. But Kate was left wide awake, staring up into the darkness, wondering how much longer Elizabeth could possibly survive more nights like this one.

What if Elizabeth died before Justin returned? What if her lungs worsened in the next two months to such a degree there was nothing the doctors at the sanatorium could do to help her? Once again Kate forced herself to look at the situation

logically, the way her tutors had taught her to do when she
was studying to enter college.

Objectively the choice seemed obvious. Letting men use her
body for two or three months was not such a great a price to
pay to save Elizabeth's life. Surely the experience would only
scar her as much as she let it. She thought back to their childhood together in Boston. Since their mother died, Elizabeth
had always looked after her. Certainly it was her turn to do
all she could to take care of Elizabeth.

In the end she knew she would never forgive herself if Elizabeth died, and she hadn't done everything she could to help
her. That last was the point Kate could not refute or ignore,
and it was the point that finally decided her. Tomorrow after
work she would go talk to Pearl De Vere.

It was four o'clock in the afternoon when Kate left the
Golden Spike. She walked a block away from the restaurant
down Bennett Avenue before turning toward Cripple Creek's
red-light district. She had purposely worn the only hat she
owned with heavy netting. This she pulled down beneath her
chin as she neared Myers Avenue. The gesture was silly, she
told herself bracingly, if she was about to become one of
Pearl's girls at the Old Homestead. She kept the netting in
place just the same.

The street seemed much quieter than it had been the day
she had seen it last summer. The cold weather appeared to be
keeping the prostitutes inside. Several men walked along the
street muffled in heavy jackets and caps, and there were many
horses tied at the hitching rails before the larger saloons. Fortunately she found the Old Homestead almost at once. Her
courage might have failed her if she had had to wander up
and down the street peering into saloons and parlor houses.
Pearl's place was easy to spot, though, for with its grand facade it did indeed look like the most elegant and prosperous
brothel on the street.

When Kate rang the doorbell, an older colored woman in a
maid's uniform opened the door. After Kate gave her name
and explained that she had come to see Pearl De Vere, the
woman silently ushered her inside and gestured that she should
have a seat in the front hallway. Kate was terribly relieved to

see there were no male customers waiting.

Pushing up the netting on her hat, she decided she was glad to have a little time alone to collect her thoughts and look about her. After the first few stunned moments, she realized that she had only seen such opulence in the finest homes back east. The floors were covered with fine Oriental rugs, and the windows were hung with rich green velvet curtains. Across from her opened up a large room full of elegant walnut settees and chairs upholstered in more green velvet. Even the light fixtures were extravagant affairs made of crystal and brass.

She looked away from the remarkable room when she heard Pearl De Vere coming down the stairs. The madam was wearing a white silk kimono embroidered with scarlet and golden chrysanthemums. Her long auburn hair cascaded down her back in a loose ponytail, and her striking features were devoid of any makeup.

"Ah, you are the young lady who was kind enough to purchase the cough syrup for Bessie," Pearl said in her rich contralto voice. She stopped at the base of the steps and watched Kate measuringly.

"I'm sorry I couldn't come in the middle of the day, Miss De Vere. I hope this time isn't inconvenient for you."

"It's early yet. We won't see much business here for another few hours. And call me Pearl. No one has called me Miss De Vere for a very long time," the madam said with a wry twist to her lips. "Well, Miss Holden, why don't you take your coat off. You can come back to the dining room, and we'll have a cup of tea while we talk about why you've come to see me in this den of iniquity."

Kate thanked Pearl quietly and gave her coat and gloves to the maid, who was hovering nearby. Kate followed the madam down the hallway that ran along one side of the house. They passed a second ornate room furnished with green card tables and a grand piano. Pearl halted when they came to the equally elegant dining room and gestured for Kate to have a seat while she pulled a chair out for herself. The maid came by quietly and vanished through a side door that Kate assumed led into the kitchen.

"Maddie will have our tea ready in a moment. Now tell me why you're here."

Kate found herself appreciating the madam's direct approach. Taking a deep breath, she decided to plunge right in. "You said I could come to you if I ever needed a favor. I'm afraid I need more than that, however. I'm looking for work, either here or at a place like it."

The madam listened quietly, her blue eyes sympathetic and nonjudgmental as Kate proceeded to explain why she needed to earn hundreds of dollars in a short period of time. In the midst of Kate's tale, Maddie returned with a tea tray and silently served them both before withdrawing to the kitchen again. When Kate had finished, Pearl cocked her head and eyed her shrewdly.

"It's true enough that you could earn a thousand dollars or more here in the next few months, and I would be willing to lend you the money to set your sister up right away at the best sanatorium you can find. But there are some things you should know before I agree to take you on, and I want to be certain you've thought this thing all the way through."

Pearl idly traced the rim of her china teacup with her fingertips as she spoke. "First of all, you should understand that just being lovely is not going to make you a success in this place. All my girls are young and attractive. Time and time again I find homelier girls in this business can be in greater demand if they have the right attitude toward their occupation. Since it's obvious that events are forcing you into this, you must consider how good an actress you can be. Sorrowful harlots don't make money.

"I've also noticed over the years that it can be more difficult for young women from the upper class to abandon their deeply ingrained notions about what is proper and ladylike behavior. Prissy harlots also don't make money. And you mustn't forget what this choice will cost you. You will be shunned by polite society. Proper women will cross the street just to avoid being contaminated by your presence."

Pearl sighed and looked up from the teacup, her blue gaze serious. "If you ever do decide to marry, what you have been and done will haunt you. If you are honest enough to confess it to your man, he may very well up and leave you, even though he himself may have frequented a hundred bawdy houses in his time. If you do not tell him, the knowledge will prey upon your mind, and you will have an awkward time of it on your wedding night explaining why you are not a virgin.

"If you move away from Cripple Creek and try to build a new, respectable life for yourself, you will always have to worry about discovery. Your greatest fear will be coming face-to-face with a stranger on the street whom you serviced in your former life. If he tells the folk of your town what you were, the new life you have built will come crashing down about you."

Kate nodded slowly when Pearl had finished speaking. "I do appreciate your telling me all this. In fact, you do a fine job of persuading someone not to work for you." She smiled sadly. "You still haven't told me anything I hadn't already figured out for myself."

"I'm not done with you yet, young lady," Pearl said grimly. "Now you need to come upstairs with me." Something in the woman's face warned Kate that further trials awaited her. Telling herself she was strong enough to face anything Pearl was about to show her, Kate followed the madam toward the front of the house and up the stairs.

Her heart was beating faster and her stomach had tied itself in a nasty knot by the time they reached the top. As she glanced about, Kate saw a long hallway that stretched toward the back of the house. Several small rooms opened off of it. Their doors all had rectangular brass holders with name cards in them. Three rooms were open, and Kate saw they were all prettily furnished bedchambers. She even caught glimpses of two lovely young women sitting at their dressing tables. The blond-haired one ignored Kate, but the brunette smiled at her in a friendly fashion.

"I think you should hear what a typical night is like in this place."

When the madam spoke, Kate focused her attention back on Pearl at once. "The gentlemen"—Pearl said this word with real irony—"begin arriving around six o'clock. Most are mine owners and businessmen. No one else can afford our prices. Often they wish to drink, talk, eat supper, and smoke before coming upstairs. Therefore our job early in the evening is to make these men feel welcome and comfortable. We often drink with our customers and watch them play card games if they wish it.''

Pearl moved forward along the hall until they stood before a door with a clear pane of glass in it. Beyond the door was a closetlike room. ''If a gentleman is a new customer and therefore unfamiliar with our girls, he can request that all of them disrobe for him, one at a time, in this viewing room. After he makes his selection for the evening, the two will retire to the girl's bedroom. We expect all our clients to wash themselves with a mild carbolic solution. Disease is always a concern in this business, and we do everything we can to keep our girls and our clientele healthy.''

Kate was doing her best to keep her features calm and composed, but it was a real battle. If Pearl had meant to shock and horrify her, she was doing a good job of it.

''Here at the Old Homestead we charge by either the trick or by the hour,'' Pearl continued on ruthlessly. ''I take sixty percent and the girl takes forty. If the gentleman is quite wealthy, he may elect to stay with one girl for the entire evening, but it will cost him two hundred dollars. Sometimes the entire house, and all of us, will be hired for a private party.''

''How many clients will a girl entertain in a given evening?'' Kate wanted to show that she was not completely flummoxed by Pearl's bald recital.

''Anywhere from one to seven or eight. That number is quite low, by the way, compared to the number you would be servicing in any other brothel in this town. And the money you would be making per trick is the highest in town.''

''I see,'' Kate said quietly. ''So I would be lucky if you decided to take me on here.''

''You would indeed. We also make certain that none of our girls are ever hurt or mistreated by our customers. Lower-class establishments are not so particular about their clientele or the way they behave.''

''Is there anything else you think I should know?''

For the first time Pearl seemed to relax. ''There's quite a bit more I would expect a young miss like you to know before I would let you entertain a gentleman under my roof,'' she said with a dry smile, ''but that kind of training can wait till later. Well, have I succeeded in scaring you off yet? I usually have the proper ones in tears by now.''

Kate decided she was very glad that she had made such an effort to keep control of her reactions and emotions during Pearl's introduction to her business. ''No, you haven't, although I'm grateful for your honesty and frankness. In some ways it's almost easier now that I know more about what working here would be like, and in some ways it's harder.'' She tried not to glance toward the viewing room as she spoke.

Pearl crossed her arms and eyed her a final time. ''Normally I would consider a young woman of your background too great a risk, but I think you've got enough grit to see this through. You showed me that the first day we met. Your sister is very lucky that you care this much about her. I have a sister, too, whom I love very much. I have not seen or heard from her in years,'' she admitted in a softer tone. Her eyes grew distant, as if she were picturing an entirely different place and time.

Suddenly Pearl seemed to remember herself and returned to her former businesslike tone. ''All right, Kate Holden, you have a job. Come on back to my room, and I will count out three hundred and fifty dollars for you in advance wages. That should help you travel to the Springs in style, and pay for a good sanatorium for your sister.''

Kate followed her back to a large, tastefully furnished bedroom. She watched in some bemusement as Pearl took hundreds of dollars in greenbacks from a wooden box on her bureau.

''This is so generous of you,'' Kate said as the madam started counting out bills. ''How can you possibly know that I won't just run off with your money?''

''One thing this business teaches you is how to read people.'' Pearl glanced up with a glint in her eye. ''You're the sort to pay her debts. Now, you come here right after Christmas, and we'll start showing you the ropes. One of my girls is planning to leave after the first of the year, so we'll have a room for you by then.'' Pearl handed her a large wad of bills that Kate had to struggle to fold and tuck into her reticule.

''And unless you want to run into some of our customers before you're ready for 'em, I recommend you be on your way. I need to get my face on and get these lazy girls of mine prettied up and ready to do business,'' Pearl said in a louder voice that carried up and down the hall.

After thanking Pearl sincerely for the loan, Kate made her way downstairs. She had just finished buttoning her coat and pulling the hat net over her face when the front doorbell rang. Blushing furiously, she slipped past two well-dressed gentlemen on the doorstep. She walked hurriedly away from Myers Avenue toward the more respectable parts of town. She only relaxed once she had regained Bennett Avenue once more.

Passing a group of carolers singing on a street corner, she blinked back tears as she listened to them sing. There would be no joy for her this holiday season, but she did feel a deep, abiding relief now that she knew Elizabeth could be properly cared for. She had a sense this awful step she was about to take was right, and she could only hope that conviction would help her through what was to come.

Fortunately Kate was too busy during the next few weeks to dwell on the bitter choice she had made. She quit her job at the Golden Spike after explaining to Mary McPherson and the Gregorys about her sister's illness. She told them and the rest of her friends in the district that she was moving to Colorado Springs to be closer to Elizabeth. Kate was deeply touched when her employers held a farewell party for her on her last day at work. Mrs. Gregory even baked a cake, and Mr. Gregory led the rest in making toasts with sarsaparilla to Kate's happiness and future.

The morning after she talked with Pearl, Kate told Elizabeth that Justin had agreed to give them a loan. His money would pay for their trip to Colorado Springs and the first year's fee at a sanatorium. It was a tense moment for Kate because she was terribly afraid that Elizabeth would sense that she was lying. Elizabeth was feeling so ill and tired, though, that she accepted Kate's explanation about the money, and she never once questioned it during the days that followed.

Thanks to Pearl's generosity, Kate was indeed able to take Elizabeth to Colorado Springs in style and comfort. After touring all the institutions on Dr. Sprague's list, Kate and Elizabeth chose the Brentwood Sanatorium. The staff was cheerful and professional, and Elizabeth liked the private rooms there. Kate spent almost two weeks with Elizabeth, celebrating

Christmas and New Year's quietly and helping her settle in.

And then Kate returned to the district and told Elly O'Connell the truth. Kate could not bear to lie to the woman who had been such a loyal friend. The Irishwoman listened in growing surprise and dismay as Kate explained that Mr. Talbott had not provided the funds for Elizabeth's treatment. She would be earning them soon down at the Old Homestead. When Kate finished with her explanation, Elly immediately embraced her in a tearful hug.

"You aren't angry with me?" Kate asked falteringly.

"Oh, I'm angry, all right, but not at you." Elly spun away and began to pace up and down her kitchen. "I'm angry at this cruel world we live in that gives young women so few real ways to make money. Females can only sew, teach, clean, or lie on their backs for a man's pleasure. And you know the only one of the four that can bring in big money.

"Many's the time I've wondered what I would do if I'd lost my Rory in the mines like your sister lost her man. There's no way a widow woman can support her brood in a costly mining town like this one. I told myself back then that I'd become a lightskirt in a moment to feed my little ones. It's a damn shame, but I understand just why you are doing this. Katie-girl, you are very brave, and I want you to know that you will always be welcome in our home."

That night as Kate packed up her belongings, she was warmed by the knowledge that she had shared her terrible secret with another woman, and dear, practical Elly hadn't spurned her. Going down to the Old Homestead tomorrow was going to be just a little easier because she had one friend who understood the choice she had made.

The next day just before noon, Rory O'Connell dropped Kate and her trunks off at the Old Homestead. Pearl greeted her at the front door and showed her up to a small bedroom at the back of the house.

The other girls soon appeared, curious about the newcomer in their midst. Jennie, the brunette who had smiled at Kate during her last visit to the Old Homestead, was a friendly, easygoing girl. Kate soon learned that Jennie spent every dollar she earned on fancy clothing. Violet, a beautiful young woman with raven-black hair and pansy-brown eyes, was much more ambitious. She never spoke much about her background, but she was clear about her goals. She was determined to make so much money at the Old Homestead that someday she could move to another town and live in comfort and security for the rest of her days. Lola, the last of Pearl's girls, was a flaxen-haired beauty with big blue eyes. She was hostile toward Kate from the start.

"That's because Lola's used to being the only blond gal working at the Old Homestead," Jennie told Kate after Lola left the room. "She's just afraid you'll steal some of her regulars away. Don't let her bother you none."

"Is there competition between the girls here?" Kate asked uneasily.

"No reason for it," Jennie said in her lazy way. "There's plenty of gents to go around. You'll see." Jennie meant her words comfortingly, but they made Kate shudder.

She was relieved to learn that Pearl did not mean for her to start working right away. Pearl had a whole series of lessons she wanted Kate to learn, from how to play poker downstairs to how to entertain a man in her room upstairs. Kate also needed a proper wardrobe before she would be presented to the Old Homestead's patrons. A seamstress came and took Kate's measurements that afternoon. Afterward Pearl took Kate aside for the first of several talks about entertaining gentlemen that left her blushing and amazed.

The next four days were a strange, dreamlike time for her. She existed in a kind of limbo, trying not to think about the evening when she would have to fulfill her part of the bargain she had made with Pearl. Part of her sense of unreality stemmed from the Old Homestead itself. The heavy opulence of the house began to weigh on her. The hours that the houses' inmates kept were peculiar and artificial. Because of the lateness of the evenings that Pearl and her girls worked, they rarely rose before noon. Kate spent many quiet hours reading in her little room. Although she longed to go for walks she never did, for she was too afraid of running into former acquaintances who thought she was working over in Colorado Springs now.

At last the day she had been dreading arrived. The seamstress came to the house with Kate's two new gowns and a large collection of risqué lingerie. Jennie was impressed by the two dresses, but Kate could only be grimly thankful that they weren't worse. The first was a sleeveless emerald green affair made of green taffeta and silk. The second was made with burgundy satin, chiffon sleeves, and lace. The colors were complimentary on her, but both gowns were far more dramatic and low-cut than any dress she would have chosen for herself.

She took a long bath that afternoon. She had hoped the bath would help her relax, but as the day wore on, the tight coil of misery in her stomach seemed only to tighten. Violet came to her room at five o'clock. While Violet shaped Kate's hair into elaborate ringlets with curling irons, Jennie came in and sat on Kate's bed. The two girls kept up a constant stream of chatter. Although she couldn't seem to concentrate on their words, she appreciated the effort they were making to distract her. When Violet had finished with her hair, Jennie took over and applied the makeup Pearl expected them all to wear. Then she helped Kate into the emerald green gown.

Kate stared in horrified fascination at the mirror. Her eyes looked large and exotic. Her pale cheeks had been stained with rouge and her lips outlined with red paint. Unwilling to hurt the girls' feelings, Kate swallowed hard and turned away from the tawdry stranger in her mirror.

"Thank you both for helping me get ready," she said, doing her best to smile at them.

"You'll break hearts down there tonight, Daisy." Jennie called her by the professional name Pearl had decided to give her newest girl. "Just wait till Lola sees you. She's gonna bust her shirt. I think you're the prettiest girl there's ever been on Myers Avenue. The first time's the hardest, I know, but there's nothin' to it after that." Jennie squeezed her shoulder before she swished out the door.

"Just remember why you're a-doing this," Violet offered before she left. "Sometimes when I'm with a gent, I lie there and think about how I'm going to decorate my front parlor. I start with them Oriental rugs, and go to the chairs and pictures and all. You just think about that sister of yours and how happy you're gonna be when she's all well again, and your first time will be over before you know it."

Pearl, too, stopped by to have a final word with her before

going downstairs. Kate knew she wasn't supposed to make her own appearance until later in the evening. With her shrewd eye for drama, Pearl didn't want to present her new girl until the front parlor was full of male guests.

"Now, Kate, you try to remember everything I taught you. I promise I'll do my best to find you a decent man for your first trick tonight, and with any luck he'll keep you for most of the evening. You'd best be finding that actress you said you had inside you. Right now you look like you're going to a funeral, and you know how well that's going to play downstairs. If you can just get through tonight, my girl, you'll be well on your way to earning that thousand dollars you need."

Kate spent the next hour trying not to look in her mirror. She kept reminding herself what Pearl had told her. Sorrowful harlots did not make money. Pearl was right. Somehow she had to find a way to get through this first evening.

It was actually a relief of sorts when Pearl finally came and tapped on her door. Cold and numb, Kate rose to her feet and obediently followed Pearl down the hall. Kate averted her eyes as they walked past the viewing room. She paused at the head of the stairs while Pearl bustled down to make her dramatic announcement about her beautiful new girl, Daisy. And then Pearl was gesturing for her to come downstairs. Somehow Kate forced her wooden legs forward.

She kept her eyes on the steps before her and reached out a hand to the wooden banister to steady herself. Her limbs felt so shaky she was afraid she might fall. When she reached the bottom step, she squared her shoulders, took in a deep breath, and turned to face the room full of gentlemen guests. Her gaze skipped warily around the parlor and came to rest on a tall, black-haired man bending over to hear something Lola was saying. As he slowly straightened up, Kate shook her head in disbelief. The awful dream she was living had just turned into a nightmare. That man was Justin Talbott.

Chapter Six

She saw clearly his shock, dismay, and anger following one upon the other in quick progression. She simply stood there on the bottom step, wishing the earth would open up and swallow her. He's not supposed to be here, a part of her kept thinking dazedly. Another part of her realized the Old Homestead was exactly the sort of place a man like Justin Talbott would frequent. How foolish she had been not to consider this possibility.

He must have decided to return early from his trip east. If only she had known he was going to come back right after the first of the year, she might have been able to put off Elizabeth's treatment for another month. Wildly she considered throwing herself on his mercy, explaining exactly why she was here and how she had gone to his house in December for help.

As she watched his disdain and fury grow, she guessed it was already too late to ask him for anything. Already she was a whore in his eyes. While his insolent gaze wandered up and down her body, her own anger began to rise. How dare he judge her? Did his fiancée know he frequented places like this? She wondered what the lovely Miss LaMonte would think if she could see Justin now and the company he was keeping.

Clenching her hands, Kate looked away from his insulting gaze and stared straight ahead over the heads of the other gentlemen who were eyeing her appreciatively. She was still very aware, however, when Justin turned and went to speak quietly with Pearl. The madam had been watching the silent interchange between them with great interest. After a few moments Pearl nodded and smiled. Justin left her and came striding toward the base of the steps.

''Well, Daisy''—he said her name with ironic emphasis

while his blue eyes bored into hers—"I've just agreed to purchase your services for the entire evening. Shall we retire upstairs?"

"Wouldn't you rather have a few drinks or play some cards first?" she suggested faintly.

"On second thought, that is an excellent idea, my dear," he agreed in a silky tone. He slipped one arm around her waist and urged her none too gently toward the gaming room. Although she knew he meant his touch to be another insult, she was actually grateful for his support. Her legs were shaking so badly that she was afraid she might stumble. At last they reached the gaming room, and Justin pulled a chair out from a table for her with elaborate politeness.

"Wouldn't you rather play cards with another gentleman?" she asked when he beckoned Clyde, the colored waiter and piano player, over to fetch them poker chips and cards.

"No, I think it would be more amusing to test your skill at this game before I test your talents and abilities in other areas."

Her cheeks warmed at his deliberate innuendo.

"Tsk, tsk, you're blushing, my dear." He raised a dark brow at her. "That is a reflex I would have thought you would lose quite quickly in this place. I almost begin to believe Pearl's claim that this is your first evening as a harlot. Would you like to deal?"

Again her temper flared, and she decided for once not to try to restrain it. If she was feeling furious at him, she wasn't quite so aware that a part of her was dying inside.

"You may deal." She was pleased when her voice came out sounding remarkably cool and composed.

"The dealer chooses five-card stud. You may name the stakes."

Kate automatically recited the amounts Pearl preferred her girls to gamble. When gentlemen wanted to play with them, they always used the house's funds. Pearl was not happy, however, if her girls lost too much to guests. Despite the tumult going on inside her, she would have to play well.

Picking up the cards Justin had dealt her, she blessed the hours she had spent with Violet and Jennie playing poker. Her mind was racing so wildly it was hard to concentrate on the cards before her, but it was obvious she should discard all but the pair of tens in her hand.

"Ah, but you're not drinking, my dear, and you could use some more color besides that rouge on your cheeks. A gentleman never likes to drink alone."

"That shouldn't trouble you, then," she shot back without thinking. He tipped his head back and let go his first honest laugh of the evening. "I forgot my golden rose had thorns. Clyde"—he beckoned the waiter over once more—"I will take a whiskey and my lovely companion here will have . . ."

"A sherry, thank you," Kate replied grimly. Perhaps having a drink or two wasn't such a bad idea. She was hoping a little liquor might make sitting here enduring his taunts easier.

She glanced at Justin as she slipped the three new cards he had dealt her into her hand. The tight set to his jaw warned her he was still enraged. Even in a temper Justin was the most splendid-looking man here tonight. The other girls were probably jealous. What none of them would understand was that she would give anything to be able to run away from him, this horrible place, and the reckless bargain she had made with Pearl. But of course she couldn't, and so she simply sat there wondering at the whims of fate which had brought him here to the Old Homestead on this night of all nights.

She glanced down and saw she had drawn another ten. Three of a kind was a strong hand, especially with only two players in the game. Suddenly eager to best him at this, perhaps because she knew he owned her for the rest of the evening, she pretended to hesitate over her bet. He promptly met her wager and doubled it. Again simulating confusion, she at last called his bet. She was delighted to see her three of a kind beat his pair of jacks. While she raked the pile of chips toward her, Clyde brought their drinks.

"To your victory in this first round," Justin raised his glass in a toast.

Kate tossed off her drink in a single swallow. She watched his gaze follow her glass as she set it back down on the table. Wondering if it was a flash of disapproval she saw in his eyes, she recklessly signaled Clyde for another. This next drink she would consume more slowly, for she needed to keep her wits about her. As she pondered her discards, it occurred to her that fate was actually being kind to her. She had feared this evening so, to have her first time be with some stranger. Although Justin was hurting her now with his angry remarks, at least the idea of sharing her body with him was not revolting or repugnant.

Her gaze traveled to his lips, and within moments she was remembering the feel of them on her own. She almost laughed at her naivete of only a few weeks ago. In her most daring moments these past two years, she had longed for Justin and wondered in her innocent way what it might be like to share marital intimacies with him. Now she knew so much more, she could guess he would be an accomplished and skillful lover. She could imagine in much more graphic detail what it would be like to make love with him. Glancing upward, she found he was studying her coldly again, and she shuddered inwardly. She doubted he would show her his tenderness or his skill tonight. He was too furious with her for that.

To her surprise she won her second hand with a pair of nines, and her third with a pair of kings. How ironic it was that the luck of the cards seemed to be running her way. She knew, though, that Pearl wouldn't want her to win too many hands in a row, for gentlemen guests enjoyed winning. Thus when Kate drew a pair of aces, she still decided to fold. As she started to lower her cards, Justin's hand flashed out across the table and gripped her wrist. He forced her to turn her cards over before she placed them on the table.

"Ah, humoring the gentleman, I see," he said coolly. "That would probably be a shrewd choice in most cases, but not in mine. My dear Daisy, you should know that you never need to let me win at anything."

"I will do my best to remember that in the future, Mr. Talbott," she said with icy politeness. "And now I should like to have my wrist back before you bruise it any further."

"My apologies if I've hurt you," he said quickly and raised her hand to his lips. To her surprise he turned it gently at the last moment and pressed a kiss on her wrist.

"Although I should like to remind you that your hand, your wrist, and the rest of your delectable body belong to me for the evening," he added in a cold voice as he proceeded to kiss each of her fingertips.

To her intense irritation, she felt her cheeks flame again. She also could not ignore the strange shivers racing down her neck or the odd feeling in the pit of her stomach caused by the sensation of his warm lips on her skin.

"That is something I can hardly forget," she muttered as she pulled her hand back and stared down at the green felt of the table before her. She was aware he was watching her again, but she refused to look up until her blush had faded.

"Pearl boasted to us that you were a fine musician," he said after a few moments. "I've grown bored of our game here. Now I would like to be entertained by your angelic voice and playing."

Incensed, Kate looked up from the table. He knew, of course, just how humiliating it would be for her to perform before him and the rest. It would be a cruel parody of the way young women at proper parties were often coaxed to demonstrate their ladylike accomplishments. As his blue gaze met her own, she sighed. She had no choice in this matter, either. As she rose to her feet and made her way to the piano, an idea occurred to her. If he didn't like her drinking, she might as well try to shock him with the most appropriate of the naughty songs Pearl had asked her to learn.

As she settled herself on the piano bench, he came to lean against a nearby wall. She sent him a challenging smile and launched into a spirited rendition of "Ta-ra-ra Boom-de-ay":

A smart and stylish girl you see, Belle of good society;
Not too strict, but rather free, yet as right as right can be!
Never forward, never bold—not too hot and not too cold,
But the very thing, I'm told,
That in your arms you'd like to hold!

Ta-ra-ra Boom-de-ay!   Ta-ra-ra Boom-de-ay!
Ta-ra-ra Boom-de-ay!   Ta-ra-ra Boom-de-ay!
Ta-ra-ra Boom-de-ay!   Ta-ra-ra Boom-de-ay!

I'm not extravagantly shy,
And when a nice young man is nigh,
For his heart I have a try—

And faint away with a tearful cry!
When the good young man, in haste,
Will support me around the waist;
I don't come to while thus embraced,
Till of my lips he steals a taste!

I'm a timid flow'r of innocence,
Pa says that I have no sense
I'm one eternal big expense;
But men say that I'm just immense!
Ere my verses I conclude, I'd like known and understood,
Tho' free as air, I'm never rude—
I'm not too bad and not too good!

Justin raised one eyebrow when he recognized the opening
lines of the popular saloon song. For a moment she wondered
if she didn't see a flash of amusement and admiration in his
eyes. Violet came and joined in during the second verse. Their
voices combined well, and Violet put real zest into the comic
lines. When Kate brought the song to a rollicking finale, the
seven gentlemen who had clustered about the piano applauded
their efforts enthusiastically and demanded an encore. Kate
made a great point of looking to Justin for permission. He had,
after all, declared that he owned her for the evening. After a
few moments he nodded to show she could continue.

As she stared down at the ivory keys, a sudden wave of
nostalgia rose up inside her. This Steinway reminded her so
much of the piano they had had in the music room back at
her family home in Boston. Remembering the happy hours she
had spent practicing in that room, she suddenly thought of a
song she wanted to sing. In defiance of Pearl, the hedonistic
opulence of the Old Homestead, and the brooding man watching her, Kate decided to play a sentimental piece with a message. In a way, it was her affirmation of the fact that these
people, these surroundings, and what would happen to her
body later this evening could not touch the person inside her.

She played the sad opening notes and began to sing,

Two drummers sat at dinner, in a grand hotel one day.
While dining they were chatting in a jolly sort of way.

And when a pretty waitress brought them a tray of food,
They spoke to her familiarly in a manner rather rude;
At first she did not notice them or make the least reply,
But one remark was passed that brought
The teardrops to her eye.
And facing her tormentor, with cheeks now burning red,
She looked a perfect picture as appealingly she said,

"My mother was a lady like yours, you will allow,
And you may have a sister, who needs protection now.
I've come to this great city to find a brother dear,
And you wouldn't dare insult me, sir,
If Jack were only here."

It's one true touch of nature,
it makes the whole world kin,
And every word she uttered
Seemed to touch their hearts within,
They sat there stunned and silent,
until one cried in shame,
"Forgive me, miss! I meant no harm,
Pray tell me what's your name?"
She told him what and he cried again,
"I know your brother too.
Why we've been friends for many years,
And he often speaks of you.
He'll be so glad to see you, and if you'll only wed,
I'll take you to him as my wife,
for I love you since you said,

"My mother was a lady . . ."

When she finished the final lines of the chorus, there was a
long silence. She glanced up in time to see that Jennie was
actually wiping her eyes. Pearl grimaced at her and shook her
head. Moments later she was motioning Clyde to take Kate's
place at the piano. Kate stood and walked toward the man
who had purchased her for the evening. On Pearl's whispered
request, Clyde started pounding out a lively dance tune that
quickly dispelled the pensive mood Kate's music had created.

"That was very touching," Justin said ironically as she came to stand beside him, "if a bit out of place. I did not know you could play or sing so well."

"As I told you before, there is quite a bit you do not know about me, Mr. Talbott."

"Indeed, this evening has certainly proved that." The harshness was back in his tone. "Well, Daisy, I believe you have entertained me well enough downstairs. It's time to show me your upstairs talents."

Her stomach tightened again. She told herself that there was no use in putting this off any longer. "If it be not now, yet it will come." The line from *Hamlet* had never seemed so appropriate. In fact it kept repeating itself in her mind like a somber litany as he took her cold hand in his and drew her up the stairs. Her heart was in her mouth when he paused in front of the viewing room and turned to face her.

Holding her head high, she asked before he could suggest it, "Do you wish to make certain in advance that your purchase will please you?"

She could not meet his eyes, no matter how hard she tried. Instead she looked over his right shoulder, praying that he would not order her to enter that room and disrobe for him. After a few moments he cleared his throat and said gruffly, "That won't be necessary."

She nodded and hoped he didn't notice the shudder of relief that went through her. He pulled her on down the hall, reading the name cards on each of the doors they passed. He came to a stop when he found hers. "I see they've put you in the smallest room here in the back. I suppose you have to work your way up the pecking order to graduate to a larger one."

"I expect you are familiar with all these rooms," she said scornfully.

"I expect I am." His lips twitched. "And I expect it's not particularly good business for Pearl's girls to insult their customers."

Kate bit her lip and looked away from his mocking gaze. She reached past him and twisted the doorknob. She now believed the sooner they got this over with the better.

"Eager, are we now? I commend your enthusiasm for your work."

She shot him a speaking glance as she pushed past him into the room. She was brought up short at the sight of her bed. Suddenly the reality of what she was about to do hit home with a vengeance. Only vaguely was she aware that he had entered the room and closed the door behind him.

"Before we move on to more pleasurable matters, we have a few things to discuss." The iron was back in his tone again.

"Indeed, Mr. Talbott. I do not think there is anything at all we need to discuss," she said bitterly as she turned to face him.

"I suppose I should ask why you are working here of all places, just like the last time I was surprised to see you in Cripple Creek." His blue eyes were the color of a frozen lake. "This time I know the answer to the question. Waitressing was hard work, wasn't it? You grew tired of the long hours and not having enough money to spend on pretty gowns and fripperies. This looked like an easier way to get what you wanted, didn't it? I thought you were different from the other women I've known, but now I know you are just as greedy, shallow, and frivolous as the rest."

She stared at him, too stunned and hurt to protest his accusations. Any impulse she might have had to tell him the truth died then, and her anger kindled once more.

"What I am and what I have chosen to be is none of your business, Mr. Talbott," she told him with frosty dignity.

"I believe my friendship with your father at least gives me the right to express some concern over your new career choice," he countered sarcastically. "Thank God Thomas will never know his youngest daughter became a whore when honest ways of earning a living became too tedious for her."

"You leave my father out of this," she replied fiercely. "I know in my heart of hearts he would have understood the choice I made and forgiven me for it."

Justin stepped forward and grabbed her shoulders. "If you truly believe that, you can convince yourself of anything." As he gazed down at her, the furious light in his eyes began to change to something else. "Well, Miss Holden, since you seem to be feeling so little shame or remorse over what you've become, I might as well start getting my money's worth this evening. Turn around, Daisy dear, and I will help you out of this remarkable gown you're wearing.''

She clenched her teeth when he returned to his former mocking tone. She turned around so that he could unhook her dress. She was startled when he instead lifted her heavy ringlets aside and began to press warm kisses down the side and back of her neck. She was just beginning to cope with the riotous sensations his lips were causing when his hands closed about her waist and pulled her back until she was leaning against the full hard length of him. His left hand slipped around her front and splayed across her stomach. His right traveled up to lightly massage the base of her neck, and he started to nibble on her right earlobe.

She drew in a deep breath. She never dreamed she could be so sensitive in these places. She began to tremble when his right hand left her neck and slipped beneath her arm. Slowly, oh so slowly, his hand came up to cup her left breast through her dress front. She started at the electric contact that sent pulses shooting all through her, but his left hand only pulled her against him more snugly.

From beneath lowered lids she glanced at him and saw he was staring down over her shoulder. They both watched as his right hand slipped inside her bodice and caressed her breast through her thin chemise. Again a wave of intense sensation went rushing through her body as the smooth cloth and his agile fingers pressed against her. With a helpless moan she tilted her head back and let it rest against his shoulder.

''I'm glad to see you can enjoy your work so thoroughly, but I believe it's time you began performing your share of your duties.''

His voice sounded like dull thunder while she leaned against his chest. Only gradually did his words register as he withdrew his hands and quickly unhooked the back of her dress. Dazedly she watched as her gown slipped forward and collapsed into a ring of emerald fabric at her feet.

His hands closed on her shoulders and turned her around to face him. ''You must work on your powers of concentration, my dear. Pearl is going to expect you to be much more efficient than this if you are to see to the needs of several gentlemen each evening. Now it's time you helped me out of my clothes.''

Trying to keep her hands from trembling, she reached out and pushed his jacket from his shoulders. How could he make her feel like this with just a few touches? Some of her inner tumult began to ease as her irritation grew over his unhelpfulness. He simply stood there as she pulled the jacket down his arms and placed it on a nearby chair. His tie and starched collar were easier, although she was painfully aware of his bright gaze following her every movement. She fumbled when she came to the top button on his shirt, for she could feel his warm breath on the back of her hand.

"Remember efficiency and speed," he murmured, his eyes full of deviltry as he caught her hand and placed a kiss on her palm.

"You're not helping matters any," she muttered as she pulled her hand back and resolutely returned to undoing his shirt buttons. "Besides, I thought you bought me for the entire evening. Why are you in such a hurry?"

She glanced up and saw he had raised an eyebrow at her question. When she saw the gleam in his eyes, she realized she had left herself wide open for any number of embarrassing responses. Hastily she added, "Please don't answer that. I will hurry if you want me to."

"I stand corrected, my dear. You are quite right. There is no reason for us to hurry over something so pleasurable. Please take your time."

She gritted her teeth and finished with the last of the buttons, including the links fastening his cuffs. She forgot her irritation when she pushed his shirt back off his shoulders and saw his bare chest for the first time. He looked just like engravings she had seen of Greek sculptures. His build certainly would have made a Grecian athlete proud. His shoulders and arms were well muscled, and his rib cage was lean. A rift of fine dark hair trailed down to his waist. She started to reach out and touch him, but when she looked up and saw his knowing smile, she caught her hand back and stooped to pick up his shirt instead. Fighting for composure, she turned aside and laid that garment over the chair arm as well.

"It's my turn again," he declared before she could face him once more. His nimble fingers made quick work of her corset strings. While she slipped the corset down over her hips, she felt his hands plucking the pins from her hair. Suddenly it came tumbling down in a golden tangle of ringlets. He plunged his hands into the silken mass, spreading her hair out until it lay like a rippling golden curtain about her shoulders.

He turned her about to face him once more. She saw his gaze go to the top of her chemise. His beautiful blue eyes darkened. The distant sound of piano music drifted up the stairs. Otherwise the small room suddenly seemed very quiet. He reached forward slowly and tugged at the bow tying the gathered top of the garment closed. She wanted to shut her eyes, but she didn't want him to think she was being cowardly. And so she watched his face as the chemise fell in a soft linen cloud about her hips, and he saw her for the first time.

"Dear lord, you are more lovely than I dreamed you would be," he said in a thick voice.

Before she could retreat from him, he stepped forward and swung her into his arms. Moments later she found herself lying on her back in the middle of her bed. When she saw he was stripping off his shoes, socks, and trousers impatiently, she quickly looked away. She longed to slip under the bedclothes, but she knew he would only taunt her for her bashfulness.

All too soon the mattress dipped and he came to lie beside her. Refusing to look at him, she stared up at the ceiling. She was miserably aware that her cheeks were flaming again. How could she possibly have thought she could go through with this? A man, Justin Talbott, was lying next to her stark naked. She knew only too well the sorts of things she was supposed to do for and with him now, but she could not summon the courage to begin them. If she couldn't please her first patron, she reminded herself desperately, Pearl would throw her out and expect her money back.

"Daisy, it's going to be difficult for you to perform your job tonight if you aren't going to look at me."

His words were mocking, but she heard real humor in his tone for the first time. She forced herself to turn her head, and instantly she was lost in his warm blue gaze. He reached out and traced the outline of her lips with his fingers. Wondering at his gentleness, she tried not to shiver as his fingertips skimmed across her shoulder, down her arm, and lingered on her hip. While he did nothing more for several moments, she searched his gaze puzzledly for a clue as to what he was thinking. Now more than ever she wished she could read his moods better.

She would have been surprised to know the depths of confusion and fury raging inside him. He wanted to hate her. He wanted to punish her for betraying him. She was just like his faithless mother and fiancée, trading her body and her honor for material possessions and an easy life. From the first moment he had seen Kate downstairs and realized what she had become, he had meant to make her pay for destroying his delightful illusion that she at least had been different. His lip curled when he thought how he had so nobly chosen to stay away from her. Now that she was willing to let any man have her, he had no qualms about being the first of them.

He had meant to make her play the role she had chosen for herself, but when he had looked into her green eyes just now and saw her fear and despair, his resolve had been sorely shaken. So Kate had been foolish and vain, and had sacrificed her honor for so little. Surely he had punished her enough this evening with his taunts.

They both would enjoy greater pleasure if he aroused her passions. Taking a cold, frightened virgin held no appeal. He raised himself up on his elbow so that he could see her better. She was exquisite. Her body was small but perfectly formed, and far more womanly than he had imagined. Her white skin was softer than velvet, and her hair was spread out in shimmering golden waves about her head and shoulders. She was the most delectable woman he had ever seen, and, he reminded himself, she was his for the evening.

His facial expression never changed, but Kate saw that smoldering look flare in his eyes once more as he dipped his head and took possession of her mouth. His tongue plunged between her lips, exploring and tasting her in a bold, sensual rhythm she could not resist. Suddenly his warm hands seemed to be everywhere, touching, smoothing, arousing her, making all that had gone on between them before seem like a spring shower compared to this thunderstorm of sensation.

She gasped when he cupped her breasts, teasing and massaging their peaks. Bolts of desire streaked through her, warming the pit of her stomach and making her restlessly long for something more. Shyly she brought her hands up to his neck and ran her fingers through his soft, thick hair as his mouth continued to plunder her own.

Suddenly he raised his head and started to rain burning kisses down the line of her jaw to her neck and then across her collarbone. She heard herself moan as he bent and kissed the tip of one rosy breast and then the other. As his clever mouth teased, licked, and tasted her, she began to tremble. With all that Pearl had told her, she never guessed her body could feel like this, feel as if it were on fire, feel as if she were drowning in a hot sea of sensation.

As he moved lower, kissing the smooth skin of her sides and stomach, his soft, feathery hair brushed against the lower sides of her breasts and sent little shivers everywhere. When he moved even lower, her breath caught. What was he going to do to her? she wondered wildly and clenched her hands in the covers.

He paused when he came to the top of her drawers. She closed her eyes when she felt him undo the top button and thoroughly kiss the area of skin around her navel. Slowly, button by button, he undid the rest, lavishing the same care on the skin he exposed while the heat in the pit of her stomach grew. When he reached the last button, he paused again and sent his hands tracing lightly over the insides of her thighs. In one quick motion he slipped his arm under her lower back, lifted her hips, and skimmed the drawers off her.

When his warm hands began to caress her thighs again, Kate instinctively clamped her legs together. In some dim recess of her mind she was aware that she should be letting him do whatever he wished. She should be feeling grateful for the fact that he had chosen to take the initiative when her own resolve had failed so completely. Yet now she felt too exposed and vulnerable, overwhelmed by the flood of sensations he called forth so effortlessly from within her.

He twisted about and came to lie beside her again. His left hand caressed her breasts while he spoke gently in her ear. "No, my golden girl, you must trust me. If you let me ready you, the first time will be much easier."

She could not find the strength to answer him, but this time when his hand slipped lower, she did not move to stop him.

As his fingertips traced the outline of her curls, she moaned. When he moved closer to the center of her femininity, the flame inside her transformed into a raging fire of need. Gently, slowly, his fingers entered her, releasing a flood of warmth. She clenched the bedclothes again as her body tightened, and wave after wave of sensation exploded through her.

As he watched her pleasure crest, Justin fought for control. She was so lovely in her passion. He longed to take her now, but there was more he wanted to show her. He raised himself up on his elbow so that he could watch her expression as she came back down to earth. The dazed look in her green eyes gradually turned to one of wonder. He saw the questions forming there, and took possession of her mouth once more before she could speak. He stroked her everywhere, readying her and building her need swiftly.

This time, when she was quivering again beneath his hands, he raised himself over her. He nudged her legs apart with his knees. He was dimly aware of his own low moan as he entered her. He felt resistance almost at once—confirming that it was her first time. He had come to believe it during the course of the past hour, but he had originally doubted Pearl's assertion that her Daisy was still innocent. Madams often claimed their girls were virgins to titillate the tastes of their jaded clients.

There would have to be pain for young Kate. There was no avoiding it. He looked down and saw she was watching him with apprehension growing now in those jade green eyes. Knowing prolonging her suspense would only make it harder for her, he leaned down and nipped at her lower lip. At the same moment he thrust forward and in. She tensed in pain and surprise as he breached her maidenhead.

He could not reassure her at first because he was struggling to rein in his own desire. She was so moist and tight, he longed to plunge into her with wild abandon. With shock he realized she had him trembling once more.

"Sh, now, that's the worst of it," he managed to whisper to her. "It only gets better from here, golden girl." As soon as he had his own body firmly under control, he shifted inside her.

She tensed, obviously expecting further pain. He murmured more reassurances and began to rock gently. The fear in her eyes dissipated, to be replaced by surprise and growing desire. She learned to match his rhythm almost too swiftly. He had intended to go slowly, but with her rising to meet his every thrust, he could not help but quicken his pace. He had meant to lead her, but she was fast urging him higher and deeper than he had ever gone before. When she wrapped her legs around him, he groaned mindlessly. Her head was thrown back, her green eyes closed, her slim, perfect body agile and twisting beneath his.

He closed his eyes as well and surrendered to what was building between them. He forgot where he was, he forgot his anger toward her, he forgot everything but their race upward toward the peak. Their climb was a breathless ascent, each pulling and pushing the other onward. He felt her reach the summit just moments before he was ready, and the shudders of her body sent him over the top.

At the moment when limitless heights of pleasure engulfed him, he was only dimly aware that she had called out his name. Stunned and gasping, he collapsed briefly on top of her, burying his face in the soft waves of her hair. Afraid he might be too heavy, he withdrew from her and lay upon his side. He gathered her gently into his arms as they drifted back down from the heights together.

Chapter Seven

When Kate awoke the next morning, it took her several moments to remember why her bedding was in such a tangle. As her memories of the night before came flooding back, she groaned. She rolled over on her stomach and buried her face in her pillow. Justin had made love to her two more times before he had finally left her. Each experience had been more tumultuous than the last. But had he been pleased and satisfied? Those second two times he had again had to take the initiative when she had faltered out of shyness. Pearl was going to be very angry and disappointed if she learned how poorly her new girl had performed last night.

Kate sat up and slipped out of bed. So now she was a fallen woman, she reflected as she put on a robe over her nightgown. Last night after Justin left she had washed away the signs of her ruin. She had also douched carefully with vinegar water the way Pearl had taught her to prevent conception.

She made a face at herself in the mirror and stretched her arms over her head. Most proper young women would probably be in hysterics right now, but for the life of her she couldn't see what good tears would do her. She was shocked over the way her body had responded to Justin. Perhaps she had been meant to be a harlot. It seemed more likely, though, that her ardent reactions last night were largely the result of Justin's skillful lovemaking.

As she padded back to her bed, another disturbing notion occurred to her. Perhaps she had responded so fervently because she was susceptible to this particular man. She told herself firmly that any love she still felt for him died the moment he informed Pearl that he wanted to purchase Daisy for the evening. Pain lanced the heart of her to think he could have

105

cheapened whatever had been between them in this way.

For a few naive moments last night, she had hoped he might try to change her mind, or protect her, or even take her away from the Old Homestead. Instead he had, with little remorse or compunction, set out to enjoy her. Sadly she realized she should have put romantic innocence and ideals aside the day she decided to work for Pearl.

Kate sat down cross-legged on her bed and rested her chin on her hands. She was still left with a puzzle. Why had Justin taken so much care to arouse her last evening? She was just beginning to ponder this question when a firm rap sounded on her door. Pearl poked her head in the doorway moments later.

"Good, I'm glad to see you're up." She sailed in bearing a large breakfast tray, which she deposited on the bed. When she noticed Kate's quizzical look, the madam explained with a wide smile, "The morning after, I always try to give special treatment to successful first-timers like yourself."

"Was I successful then?" Kate murmured as she eyed the breakfast feast spread out before her. She might be a fallen woman, but suddenly she felt ravenous. She pulled the tray closer to her and started eating.

"I should say so. You and I, young woman, have some important business to discuss."

Kate glanced up from the food and noticed for the first time that Pearl looked pleased and excited. The madam settled herself in the rocking chair while Kate made inroads on her breakfast.

"It seems Mr. Talbott was quite impressed with you. I was surprised, by the way, to learn you two were acquainted."

"You couldn't have been more surprised than I was when I saw him downstairs last night," Kate said feelingly.

"You should have seen the look on your face." Pearl shook her head and chuckled. "You shouldn't have been so shocked, though. Mr. Talbott has been a generous patron of this establishment for some time."

"I should have figured that out on my own," Kate said with a wry shake of her head.

"What may be more surprising to you is that Mr. Talbott has offered to purchase your services for the next two months."

Kate dropped her fork and stared at Pearl. "Are you joking?"

"I never joke when it comes to business. Mr. Talbott has offered to pay two thousand dollars for the pleasure of your company during the next two months. He does expect you to move into his home rather than remain here. I, of course, will receive a quarter of that fee as my commission for your introduction. In theory I'm entitled to half, but I wouldn't feel right taking it. Because you would be living under his roof, you won't be costing me a cent. At the end of the two months, you would have fifteen hundred dollars, which should cover the costs of your sister's treatment well into the foreseeable future."

" 'The pleasure of my company,' " Kate mimicked Pearl's phrasing bitterly. "What you really mean is that he wants me to be his mistress. He wants me in his home so that I will be conveniently at his beck and call. Well, I won't do it. I won't become his private plaything."

"It's your choice, of course," Pearl said in an even tone, "but I think you should consider his offer carefully." The madam rose and went to look out the window.

"Kate, I was right to believe you had the determination to see this thing through, but it will be very, very hard for you." Pearl turned from the window and held her gaze. "Remember how you felt right before going downstairs last night? Tonight you will have to go downstairs again, and this time you may have to please seven or eight gentlemen, all strangers to you. And it will be that way night after night for the next two months. Wouldn't it be better to have to share your body with only one man? I don't know what there is or was between you and Justin Talbott, but surely facing that would be better than staying here."

Kate stared blindly at her coverlet. Pearl was right, of course. Just the thought of letting another man do what Justin had done made her shudder. And she hadn't played her part at all. Last evening had proved to her that she didn't have the determination to see this business through, at least not in the sense Pearl meant. She could not be a whore to the men who patronized this place. It would be better to be a whore for one man, no matter how susceptible or vulnerable she would be to

him. And she knew Justin was not going to make this easy
for her.

It was obvious that she had disappointed and hurt him. In-
advertently she had confirmed his already dark picture of the
female gender. She winced when she realized he must have
been referring in part to his mother last night. He probably
had been thinking about his faithless fiancée as well. Both
must have wounded him deeply. Now he was determined to
punish her for acting like those women who had betrayed him.
She sighed at the thought of enduring more insults and in-
nuendos of the kind he had fired her way last night. Still,
enduring his searing words and his enmity would be easier
than letting Pearl's clientele have their way with her, and she
would be foolish to think otherwise.

"You're right, of course." She pushed the breakfast tray
away from her, for she had just lost her appetite. "I'll start
packing."

Right at noon Ben Gallagher rang the doorbell of the Old
Homestead. While he was fetching her trunk from upstairs,
Kate said her final farewells. She hugged both Jennie and Vi-
olet, who told her to come visit if she became lonely up in
Mr. Talbott's mansion. When Kate turned to Pearl, she found
her throat had suddenly gone tight.

"I want to thank you for helping my sister and me. I still
can't believe you trusted me to go off to the Springs with so
much of your money."

"Thank me all you want, but remember I'm a business-
woman first, and my instincts were right on this one. We are
both going to end up making a nice profit, thanks to Mr. Talbott," Pearl said in her dry way before she added seriously,
"I know you have some misgivings about this, but you are
making the right decision. Remember, your situation with him
will be what you make it. Men are simple creatures compared
to us womenfolk, and easily managed when all is said and
done. Make your Mr. Talbott happy, and your two months
with him won't be difficult at all."

Kate shook her head inwardly at these words. Justin Talbott
was hardly a simple man, nor was he the sort to be easily
managed. Rather than contradict Pearl, Kate simply thanked

the madam again and promised she would remember her advice. Because Ben Gallagher was waiting in the hall now, Kate left the parlor and followed him out the front door.

She was surprised and pleased when he politely commented on the sunny weather as he handed her up into Justin's fine, covered landau. She had been afraid Ben Gallagher might be disapproving and unfriendly because of her dubious new position in his employer's household. The large man, who looked even more like a desperado than she remembered, seemed quite accepting of the situation. As they drove off toward Justin's home, she worried about her first encounter with Justin's housekeeper. It seemed unlikely that the stern woman she had seen back in December was going to make Justin Talbott's new mistress feel welcome.

Her concerns proved to be well founded just a few minutes later. After Ben escorted Kate up to the front door of Justin's home, the housekeeper didn't answer Ben's ring. At last, when he grew tired of waiting, Ben picked up Kate's trunk, opened the door himself, and ushered Kate inside.

The tight-lipped woman stalked into the front hall moments later. She looked even more lean and angular and gray than Kate had remembered. Her pale blue eyes burned with scorn as she looked Kate up and down. "You may put her things in the guest bedroom upstairs." Somehow the housekeeper managed to heap a world of scorn into the words *her* and *guest*. She turned about and marched back the way she had come.

Kate was left staring after her, wondering how she was going to cope with such venom on a daily basis. Ben must have seen her stricken expression, for he spoke up kindly, "Now, missee, don't you mind Mrs. Drury any. She's just a dried-up old prune. I'm real happy to have you here, and so is Mr. Talbott."

When Ben turned away and led the way up the ornate mahogany staircase, Kate grimaced over his latter comment. If Mr. Talbott was so thrilled by his mistress's arrival, why wasn't he here to greet her? Actually, she felt more relieved than peeved that Justin hadn't put in an appearance yet. She needed more time to think about what had happened between them last night, and to get used to the notion that she would actually be living under his roof for the next two months.

On the way upstairs she couldn't help but admire the handsome cream-and-gold camel-hair wallpaper and the elegant crystal chandelier illuminating the front hall. The guest bedroom proved to be a lovely corner chamber with windows facing south and east. It was papered with a pretty white, pink, and blue floral wallpaper, and the pine flooring was covered by a bright Oriental rug. The windows were hung with blue brocade curtains, and both had charming window seats upholstered with the same fabric. The bed was a graceful fourposter made of cherry wood and covered with a white satin spread. Against one inside wall there was a large walnut wardrobe and a matching dressing table and mirror. Along the other inside wall was a cherry dresser, a rocking chair, a bookshelf, and a small writing table. All in all it was a comfortable room, much larger than the one she had shared with Elizabeth at Elly O'Connell's, and much more cheerful.

Ben deposited her trunk near the foot of the bed. After asking if she needed anything else, he smiled, tipped his hat, and left her to her privacy. It took her only an hour to unpack and settle her things about the room. Feeling sleepy after so little rest the night before, she decided to take a nap. When she awoke a few hours later, she discovered her stomach was growling. She had eaten little of her breakfast this morning, and she had left the Old Homestead before lunch.

After straightening her hair and dressing in a simple skirt and blouse, Kate checked the little brass clock on the dresser. She groaned when she saw it was only three o'clock. Dinner might not be served until seven or eight o'clock in this household. She was going to get even more hungry between now and then. Briefly she considered tackling Mrs. Drury and asking her for tea and a light meal. But she just couldn't brave another unpleasant confrontation.

Telling herself she would face Mrs. Drury tomorrow, Kate picked up *Life on the Mississippi*, which she had purchased during her trip to Colorado Springs. Resolutely ignoring her hunger pangs, she settled herself on the southern window seat. Hopefully some of Mr. Twain's humor would lighten her mood.

Three hours later she was lost in her reading when Justin

opened the door to her room and came striding in. To hide
her consternation over his abrupt arrival, she looked up at him
and said tartly, "I don't suppose you could do me the courtesy
of knocking?"

"I've been looking for you all over this damned house.
Why are you hiding yourself up here?"

Justin was feeling irritated because he had just searched
every room on the first floor for her. Memories of last night
had haunted him all day. He had been inordinately pleased
when Pearl had sent word Kate had said yes to his proposal.
He had not truly believed she could say no, for he had purposely made his proposal too generous for her mercenary side
to refuse.

This afternoon while he negotiated the terms for buying a
new mine, he found himself remembering smoldering moments from the evening before. Shy young Kate had surprised
and pleased him no end. He had hurried home from his meeting, telling himself he was eager to enjoy the beautiful body
of the young woman he had purchased for his pleasure these
next two months.

Now here she was dressed in a demure blouse and skirt,
and she still looked so lovely that she made his body ache.
When he first had seen her reading moments ago, he had been
reminded strongly of their meeting in the garden two years
back. But she was no longer the innocent girl who had intrigued and entertained him in Boston. Had the sweet image
of that girl, which he had cherished for so long, ever been
real? He would never forgive her for destroying his illusions.
Here was the real Kate Holden, complete with the foolish,
venal flaws of her gender. Yet she appeared even more exquisite and womanly than she had been before. Briefly he considered taking her right now. Her next words, however,
distracted him from that pleasurable intention.

"I wasn't hiding. I simply did not know where in this house
I would be welcome."

"You're welcome to the whole place. I just don't want you
in my office when I'm working."

"I will remember that in the future, sir," she replied politely.

Angered by the ridiculously formal barriers she seemed

determined to erect between them, he paused while he considered a suitably scathing comment. It was absurd that she was acting so prim and ladylike when they had spent most of last night naked in each other's arms. Suddenly he heard a rather loud intestinal rumble emanating from her direction. Her face went so scarlet, his lips twitched. Raising an eyebrow at her, he asked "Hungry, are we? Just when did you eat last?"

She ducked her head. "I . . . I had no lunch today, and I didn't wish to trouble your housekeeper."

"There's no reason for you to go hungry while you're under my roof," he said gruffly. "I don't exactly overwork Mrs. Drury or her staff. When you want anything, just ring for someone."

Sighing aloud, he plucked his pocket watch from his vest. There was no use proceeding with what he had in mind. A rumbling stomach would distract them both, and she would need her stamina. Ah, well, the very best things in life were often worth waiting for, he told himself with an inward smile. In the meantime he would tell Madame Dupuy to move their meal forward an hour.

"Dinner will be served downstairs at seven. I trust you will dress suitably." With that he nodded to her curtly, turned, and left the room.

Kate was left staring after him, amazed and appalled that he thought he could control even her dressing now. Only the great respect she had for books kept her from flinging the volume in her hand at the door.

At precisely seven o'clock, Kate took one last look at herself in the mirror before she started downstairs. She had chosen to wear the second dress Pearl had ordered for her, the burgundy satin. She hoped this was what Justin had meant when he said she should dress suitably for dinner. Now that she was his mistress, this outfit certainly seemed the sort of gown a demimondaine should wear.

She was painfully aware of the way the shimmering material clung to her, emphasizing her waist and curves. The bodice definitely exposed more of her bosom than any dress she had ever worn before. Remembering his disparaging comment about her rouge last night, she decided not to wear the makeup

Pearl had insisted that she take with her. The cut of the gown and its color was bold enough. She did take the time to pile her hair atop her head. It made her look older and more sophisticated. She also hoped it would make her appear in control of a situation in which she was feeling more than a little lost.

When she sallied forth from her room, she was almost as tense as she had been last night. It was going to be a long two months, she told herself bracingly, if she didn't become accustomed soon to this life she had chosen for herself. Right now her stomach was tied in such tight knots she couldn't imagine eating a bite of supper. It was absurd to be so nervous.

She knew so much more now about what to expect. Last night had hardly been painful in a physical sense, thanks to Justin's expertise. But in her heart of hearts, she knew it was Justin himself who was making her nervous. She told herself she was strong enough to endure his scorn and anger, but a part of her wondered if that was true.

When she reached the front hallway she looked about and spotted him. Justin was standing by the fireplace in the library, staring down into the flames of a crackling fire. As she rustled toward him he glanced at her. Her heart rate quickened as his eyes widened and he scanned her from head to toe. Was he pleased or dismayed by her gown? she wondered uneasily, and wished for the thousandth time she could read him better. His deep blue gaze never left her as he tossed off his drink and placed the glass on the mantel. And then he was striding toward her. Moments later his arms closed around her, and she found herself being thoroughly kissed.

At first she was too startled to participate. His hold about her waist tightened while he slipped his tongue between her lips. She decided ruefully that her appearance must have pleased him. She closed her eyes and tried to control her own fiery response to his caresses. There was no question but Justin Talbott was sinfully skilled at this business. How right she had been two years ago to think he knew a great deal about kissing. Her skin warmed when she reminded herself he indeed knew about kissing and so much more.

Remembering her failures last night, she wondered if this might be a safe time to try a little harder to please him. She

could easily disappoint him later this evening. Perhaps she
should do what she could now. Tentatively she pulled back
from him and framed his face with her gloved hands. Looking
into his eyes, she traced the outline of his lips with the tip of
her own tongue. After just a few seconds he groaned and
pulled her so tightly against him she couldn't help but be
aware of his arousal. He kissed her with such ferocity all conscious thought flowed away from her, until her only reality
was his clever lips and the desire kindling inside her.

She was gasping for breath by the time he raised his head.
"You make it very difficult to hold to my resolve to feed you
some of Madame Dupuy's fine coq au vin before we go upstairs," he growled in her ear.

The very mention of food made her hunger return with a
rush. Much to Kate's mortification her stomach gave out another very audible grumble. She sighed with relief when Justin
simply laughed and shook his head. He let her go, picked up
his glass, and went to pour himself another drink. By the time
he returned to where she was standing, she had herself back
in hand again. She was startled when he held out his arm to
escort her to dinner. Although she was suspicious that he
might be mocking her with such a polite gesture, she laid her
right arm atop his and let him lead her down the hall.

She blinked when she saw his magnificent dining room for
the first time. The ceiling was hand-painted with intricate,
swirling designs in gold, blue, green, and red. The fireplace
along the far wall was crowned with an elegant gray marble
mantelpiece, which clearly had been imported from Europe.
The long Chippendale table was set with a linen cloth, silver
candlesticks, and crystal wineglasses. The fine bone china was
rimmed with deep blue enamel and gold leaf, and the silver
flatware was etched with lovely Renaissance figures. Justin
Talbott clearly believed in surrounding himself with beautiful
things, she reflected as he pulled back her chair and seated
her. Was she just another pretty possession to him now? The
question haunted her.

She had been worried that dinner would be a tense, unpleasant affair. She had been particularly afraid he might torment
her with more barbs and taunts. He had been so furious when
he first saw her at the Old Homestead, and such intense emo-

tion could not simply vanish overnight. She was surprised and relieved when Justin instead began to play the part of a charming dinner companion. She did her best to follow his lead, but it was difficult to become involved in the conversation when a part of her was still shocked by the notion that she was dining alone in a man's house. This was her first night as his mistress, and that fact seemed to weigh more and more heavily upon her as the evening progressed.

Still, there was one topic he introduced that did provoke a strong response from her. She was working her way through Madame Dupuy's mouthwatering coq au vin with real enthusiasm when Justin asked her in a rather disdainful tone, "I suppose, Miss Holden, that you are all in favor of granting women the vote?"

She rose to the bait, and a spirited discussion of women's suffrage ensued. She was appalled when Justin proceeded to trot out every one of the preposterous arguments men had been using to deny her sex the vote for years. One by one she did her best to counter the absurd and illogical points he made. As her crowning argument she cited the example of Wyoming.

"They granted their pioneering women the vote, and that territory has yet to suffer any of the terrible consequences you've been predicting. In fact many of their towns are run better than our own here in Colorado. I think you men are being ridiculously inflexible and old-fashioned to deny my gender the vote any longer."

"Enough, my girl." He held up his hands laughingly. "You may be surprised to hear I agree with you. I do believe your sex deserves the vote."

Flabbergasted, she stared at him. "You, sir, should have been a lawyer," she said with disgust when she realized he had been leading her on simply to enjoy a good argument.

"I will admit to being one of the best debaters on my college debating team," he said with a gleam in his eye. Before she could make a retort, he added smoothly, "and now I should like for us both to retire to the library. I believe Ben has kept a fire going in there, and we will find it quite pleasant and warm."

"Am I to enjoy brandy and a cigar as well?" She couldn't keep the bitterness from her tone, for his suggestion had sounded suspiciously like a command.

"Only if you wish it. I have plenty to spare."

"That doesn't surprise me in the least," she said darkly while he came about the table to stand beside her chair. As she rose to her feet and laid her napkin upon the table, she smiled sadly at her memory of the one and only time she had tried both brandy and cigars.

"What are you thinking about, little scholar?" he asked in a curiously gentle voice.

"That I have little interest in either brandy or cigars for a good reason," she said, lifting her gaze to meet his. "When Elizabeth and I were little girls, we sneaked into Papa's study one night while he was away on business. We were both quite intrigued with cigars and brandy because they seemed like part of a forbidden, secret ritual to us. Papa and his friends were always disappearing into his study after dinner and closing the door behind them. I think we believed all sorts of wonderful, magical things happened behind those doors. And so, of course, we had to find out for ourselves."

"I gather wonderful and magical things did not happen?"

"No, not exactly. We ruined one of Papa's fine Cuban cigars and almost burned the study down trying to light it. Both the smoke and the brandy made us quite ill. Even though we did everything we could think of to hide the signs of our trespassing, he must have found out what we had done. The very next evening after supper, he invited us into his study. Wearing a perfectly straight face, he offered us both cigars and brandy. Elizabeth and I turned pea green and confessed our sins at once."

"That sounds just like your father," Justin said warmly. "What I want to know is who thought up the notion of sneaking into his study in the first place?"

"I rather expect I suggested it, now that I think about it," she admitted as they left the dining room and started down the hall.

"Somehow that news doesn't surprise me," he commented. "Elizabeth seems far too ladylike to think up such a lark."

"Indeed, Elizabeth was always much better behaved than I was," Kate agreed, remembering all at once that she was now anything but a lady in his eyes.

He arched an eyebrow at her cool tone, but he didn't say anything more until they reached the library. There he gestured that she should take a seat on the handsome mahogany sofa before the fire. When he asked if she wanted anything to drink, she politely refused. Although she longed for a way to make the rest of this evening easier, she decided that getting tipsy was a cowardly solution. Besides, she needed to keep her wits about her, for she still wasn't the least bit comfortable around Justin Talbott.

After he finished pouring a drink for himself, he came to stand before the fire. "I haven't told you," he said suddenly, "that I heard just recently about Robert Townsend's death. I'm sorry for your loss. It must have come as a great blow to your sister, and to you." His words were comforting, but the inscrutable look on his face made her wary.

"Thank you," she replied cautiously. "It was much harder for Elizabeth, of course. She adored him. I'm not sure she will ever get over losing Robert."

"I'm certain you were a great comfort to her in the difficult time following his death. I've been meaning to ask, where is Elizabeth now, and does she know that her younger sister has become a harlot?"

She drew in a breath. There it was, the question she had been expecting and dreading. She supposed she ought to tell him the truth now about why she had gone to the Old Homestead, but she was too incensed about the cruel way he had phrased his question. Let him continue to think she was greedy and shallow and frivolous. Let him continue to believe all women were selfish, venal creatures. She didn't care in the least for the regard or the respect of a man who could be so callous.

"Elizabeth moved back east to live with our Aunt Mildred." Kate struggled to keep her voice even. She was determined not to let him see how his harsh words had hurt her. "She had no wish to remain in Cripple Creek after losing Robert. And no, she has no idea what I am doing now."

"You had no interest in returning with her?"

"There's nothing for me in the east anymore. Most of our friends disappeared with our fortune—I told you that before.

During the short time I've been here I've come to love the West.''

Justin spun away and strode to the cabinet where he kept his brandy, stunned by the strength of the rage rising inside him. How could she speak so dispassionately of her own ruin? Why hadn't she left Cripple Creek with her sister? If they had remained together, surely Elizabeth Townsend could have kept her younger sister from plunging so heedlessly into an occupation that led only to degradation.

Justin took a deep breath as he poured himself another brandy. He paused when he had finished and gazed at his lovely new mistress. She was staring into the fire now, her chin raised, her color high from their recent exchange of words.

The bold dress Pearl obviously had chosen for her should have made Kate look cheap and tawdry. Instead the wine red shade of the satin emphasized the deep jade color of her eyes and the translucent beauty of her skin. The dancing flames of the fire silhouetted her delicate profile and shone off the golden coils of her hair.

What was she thinking about now? Despite Kate's insouciant manner, the vulnerable set to her mouth made him wonder if she did regret her decision to work for Pearl. He reminded himself that what Kate was feeling or thinking was none of his affair. The girl had made her choice, and now she had to learn to live with it. She was, after all, extremely fortunate that he had decided to install her in his household. It had been a long time since he had been so taken with a woman to go to this extreme. Kate Holden could still be down at the Old Homestead, entertaining several gentlemen this evening. For some reason that thought only made him angrier.

He strode forward out of the shadows, resolved that young Kate should start earning her keep at once. Just then, however, Ben appeared discreetly in the doorway. His face expressionless, he came forward and added three chunks of wood to the fire.

"That will be all for the evening, Ben," Justin informed him curtly.

Kate watched apprehensively as Ben walked across the room and shut the door to the library behind him. She and

Justin were alone now. Slowly she turned about to face him. He was standing by the mantelpiece, and he was watching her with that smoldering look she was coming to know only too well.

"Kate Holden," he said in a deep voice, "I want you to come here."

Chapter Eight

She willed herself to go to him, but the first step she took would be admitting too clearly what she had become. Logically, rationally, she knew that he had purchased her, that he had every right to command her actions and her body for the next two months. Emotionally she loathed every order he gave her. And beneath it all was the growing fear that she might actually enjoy whatever he had in mind. It frightened her the way he had made her lose control of herself last night. She did not want that to happen again. Cheeks burning, she ducked her head and looked at her lap.

"Very well," he said softly, "I shall come to you." The sofa dipped as he sat down just inches away from her. "I wonder how long it will take you to lose these missish airs of yours? I tolerate them for the moment because they amuse me."

Still unable to face him, she looked up from her lap and stared at the fire. She was, however, achingly aware of him. His long muscular legs stretched out before her. Desperately she tried to forget how they had felt entwined with her own last night. His masculine cedar scent enveloped her, and she fancied she could feel the warmth of his body next to hers. Wildly she wondered if she could ever grow used to having a man, this man, so close to her.

He reached out with his hand and gently traced the line of her cheek. At the same time he began to weave a spell with his rich voice.

"Do you have any idea how lovely your skin is? It reminds me of fine porcelain, but to the touch it is softer than rose petals."

She closed her eyes and tried not to shy away from him as

his lips slowly traced the path his fingertips had just taken along her cheek. She did not resist him when he turned her head so that she was facing him now. She shivered when he went on to skim his thumbs down her high cheekbones.

"These make me wonder if there is Slavic blood in you, my dear, some generations back. And this stubborn little jawline is one of your most telling features. It betrays the willfulness that, I imagine, has gotten you into all sorts of scrapes over the years."

Kate swallowed hard as he bent his head and kissed her jawline as well, sending delicious little shivers racing down her neck and back.

"We mustn't forget your hair, young Kate," he declared as he came to study her once more. " 'For 'tis one of her greatest glories,' " he quoted softly as he reached up. With unerring skill he found and removed her hairpins, which brought her tresses tumbling down about her shoulders. She opened her eyes again, just in time to see him lean forward and pick up one long lock of her hair. He pressed it slowly to his lips, his burning blue gaze never leaving her own.

"Your eyes are remarkable. Their color reminds me of a jade krater I saw once in China. The piece was the greatest treasure in a warlord's fortress. Men had killed for it, my fierce host assured me." She closed her eyes again, for his hypnotic blue stare was already becoming too much for her to bear. She felt his fingertips brush each of her eyelids, and then his breath was warm on her face as he lightly kissed again where his fingers had passed.

"To sum it up, 'There's language in her eye, her cheek, her lip,' " he quoted Shakespeare softly, "but I prefer the language I use to converse with your pretty lips most of all."

As he outlined her lips gently, Kate was dismayed to discover she was quivering. How could he have such power to do this to her with just a few brief touches and some softly spoken words? Even as she struggled to find her equilibrium and poise, his lips captured her own, and the effort she was making to regain control of herself and her senses dissolved into nothingness. All there existed in the world was the taste of him, the intoxicating nearness of his body, and the feel of his strong shoulders beneath her hands.

Suddenly Justin broke off the kiss. "Turn around," he ordered gruffly. When she was slow to obey him, he placed his hands on her shoulders and turned her on the sofa until her back was facing him. She bit her lip when she felt him begin to undo the fastenings to her gown. He pressed his warm lips to the side of her neck, sending another wave of shivers racing down her backbone. Rapidly he released more fastenings until her dress began to slip down over her shoulders. With no maid to help her dress, she had chosen not to wear a corset this evening. And so when he eased his hands inside her dress, only her thin chemise lay between his touch and the sensitive skin of her back and rib cage.

Despite the devastating siege he was laying to her senses, it was impossible for Kate to ignore his intentions any longer. Even though the notion shocked her, she was beginning to think Justin meant to take her right here, in this very room. And if she didn't say something soon, she desperately feared that she wouldn't want to stop him. Once again he was taking control of her body in a way that both amazed and frightened her.

"Please, not here," she managed to get out. It just seemed so indecent to make love in a library on a sofa. Surely husbands and wives only performed the marital act in a proper bed in their proper bedrooms.

"Oh, yes, here, and anyplace else in my house that I've a mind to," he told her remorselessly as he rose to his feet. He leaned down and caught both of her hands.

"But you needn't worry that we will be disturbed," he added in a more gentle tone. "Not a person on my staff would dare knock on the door to this room right now."

Before she realized what he was about, Justin pulled her to her feet and slipped the gown off her shoulders. The burgundy dress fell in a soft heap about her knees. And then she was standing before him clad only in her fine linen chemise, petticoats, and drawers, the fire outlining the curves of her body and shining off the wild golden waves of her hair.

Justin groaned inwardly. He had been aroused from the moment he had brought her into this room. Now he longed to tumble her back on the sofa and take her at once. He was aware, however, of the apprehensive look in her green eyes.

He wanted to repeat and surpass last night's experiences if he could. Yet it was very clear she was not quite as ready as he was to embark immediately on such a sensual adventure. He reminded himself once again that the best things were worth working and waiting for. As he looked at the beautiful young woman trembling before him, he had to admit that readying Kate for what he had in mind was hardly going to be a chore.

He stepped forward and gently kissed the smooth white skin of her collarbone. Pleased by her quick intake of breath, he reached around her and deftly undid the ties holding up her petticoats. They, too, fell away in a soft rustle of cloth. He moved back from her and took her hands in his own. He raised them to his bow tie. Wordlessly she did as he wanted, undoing the tie and tugging his stiff collar free. When she hesitated, he guided her hands to the top button of his shirt. Shooting him a speaking glance, she proceeded to undo these fastenings as well.

He smiled at her obvious irritation as she tugged his shirt off less than smoothly. His smile faded when he saw the look of temper in her eyes change to something else entirely as she gazed wordlessly at his chest. Deeply pleased by her reaction to him, again he took her hands and spread them out with their palms against his chest. Almost of their own volition, her hands sifted through the fine drift of dark hair she found there, her green eyes wide and wondering. When her fingers moved lower, tracing the hard muscles of his stomach, his breath caught and his loins tightened painfully.

"You don't begin to realize the power you have over me," he muttered. He tugged her chemise free of her drawers and pulled it up over her head. Catching her up in his arms, he laid her down upon the sofa. It took him just moments to divest himself of the rest of his clothing, and then he knelt beside her, ready to worship her body with his own. Indeed, the way she lay back against the sofa, her golden hair spread across the cushions, she looked like some pagan offering to the gods. He spared a half moment to wonder ironically at himself and the way Kate Holden was bringing out the young, romantic scholar in him, a part of his personality that he assumed had died long ago with his dreams and his innocence.

His eyes focused on her lovely breasts. Slowly he reached

out and began to massage and tease those rosy buds until they hardened beneath his hands. She closed her eyes and turned her head away from him. Smiling at her shyness, he bent his head and thoroughly kissed the buds he had just fondled.

This time he wrung a small groan from her, and her hands came to clench his shoulders. He moved lower, kissing the soft white skin of her stomach until he came to the edge of her drawers. There he paused, nipping and tasting in a line across her belly while he quickly unfastened the buttons. When the drawers were undone, he lifted her hips and slid the undergarments off her. Kate moved instinctively to cover herself. He gently took her hands and laid them by her sides.

"No, my lovely girl, let me look at you," he said softly. She was simply exquisite. Her waist was trim, her hips rounded, and her slim white thighs were perfectly formed. Once again he conquered the wild urge to enter her immediately. Wanting at the very least to be closer to her, he came to lie beside her on the wide sofa. He bent his head and took possession of her lips once more. As his tongue plundered her mouth, his hand trailed across her midsection to the downy area between her legs. Once again she shook her head in protest and moved to stop him, and once again he gently pushed her hands aside.

The moment he slipped his fingers inside her, he felt her tense. Raising himself up on his elbow, he watched as he pressed just a little further. When he saw the real flash of pain in her eyes, he withdrew his hand at once. She had been a virgin last night, and he had taken her three times with real enthusiasm. No wonder she was tender. After thinking for several moments, he decided to change his plans. There was no reason to rush matters. He had two months to enjoy her delectable body, after all. And tonight there were still ways they both could achieve pleasure.

"Sh now," he said as he kissed her on the forehead. "I won't hurt you again, I promise. We can enjoy each other in a different fashion." Before she could begin to wonder or worry about what his words meant, he began kissing her everywhere, artfully stoking and building her passion again. This time when his hand slipped lower, his fingers did not enter her. Instead he found her secret place and teased and stroked her until she was writhing beneath his touch. He was surprised and pleased to see it did not take long before she was lifting her hips in rhythm with his movements.

When he sensed she was close, he raised his head from kissing her breasts to watch her. The sight of her almost proved to be his undoing. Her head was thrown back, her cheeks flushed, her pale chest rising in quick pants. No longer did she seem the sacrifice to him, but a goddess glorious in her passion. Just then her hips lifted again, her fists closed upon the sofa cushions, and a low cry was torn from her lips. As her pleasure peaked, he almost went with her to the top. He longed to bury himself inside her, but a part of him managed to hold to his resolve not to hurt her tender flesh any further this evening. Instead he waited impatiently for her to return from the dizzying heights she had just ascended.

"You must help me go where you just went," he told her hoarsely when he could wait no longer. He saw understanding dawn in her green eyes, and then blushing assent. As soon as he placed her trembling hand about him, deep, intense waves of pleasure engulfed him and carried him away to the dark and fiery place she had just visited. Surprised by his body's reaction to her innocent touch, he gathered her into his arms. They lay side by side on the sofa while their breathing and racing hearts gradually slowed.

"I can't believe I gave you much pleasure tonight. Once again you did most all the work for me," Kate confessed shyly into his shoulder after a long while.

"I'm a little amazed myself, but you may rest assured I enjoyed myself this evening," he said, smoothing a silky lock of her hair between his fingers.

"I'm glad to hear it." She finally raised her head to peek at him. At that very moment a huge yawn seized her. She tried, rather unsuccessfully, to hide it behind her palm. "I'm afraid you may have gotten a poor bargain in me when all is said and done," she admitted sleepily and yawned again.

"I was just thinking the opposite. And now, we had best go upstairs before you fall asleep on me, young woman."

Her unintelligible reply told him he was already too late. Briefly he considered rousing her. Carrying her upstairs in her current state, however, would bring its own rewards. After he knelt by the sofa and pulled her into his arms, she snuggled her head closer against his shoulder. He smiled to himself. If she were wide awake, he knew young Kate would hardly be so accommodating or so friendly.

As he stood up and settled her more comfortably in his arms, he glanced at the pieces of clothing that lay strewn about the floor like so many huddled casualties of war. He decided to leave the clothing right where it was. It was getting too damned chilly to come back downstairs for it, and proper Mrs. Drury could survive a shock or two.

When he reached the top of the stairs, Justin hesitated while he contemplated where he should deposit his sleeping burden. He wouldn't mind sharing his own bed with her for the evening, but he was afraid that he might not be able to leave her alone. Even as he considered the matter, the silken caress of her hair against his chest and the feel of her soft breast pressing against his forearm made his body stiffen once more. Definitely, it would be easier to hold to his good intentions if she were tucked up safely in her own bed.

That decision made, he walked down the hall to her room and opened the door. He laid her gently on the far side of her bed while he tugged the bedclothes down. His lips twitched as he picked her up and placed her on the sheets. She hardly stirred. Kate Holden was surely one of the soundest sleepers he had ever come across. He smiled as he pulled the covers up about her shoulders. He hardly expected to be tucking his mistress into her own bed the first evening of her stay in his home.

He turned to leave her, but the sight of the moonlight shining down on her made him pause. She looked so young and innocent lying there with her hair all tousled about her shoulders. A sharp pang of remorse seized him for the way he had used her and planned to continue using her. Grimly he reminded himself that someone else would have been enjoying her glorious body tonight if he hadn't purchased her for himself. Chances were those other nameless men would not have been as considerate as he had been. That line of reasoning still did not erase the guilt he felt. No longer smiling, he turned about and left the room.

*   *   *

When Kate awoke the next morning she found herself lying naked and quite alone under the covers of her own bed. As her memories of the night before came back to her, she blinked and sighed. Rolling over on her side, she stared out at the bright blue sky she could see between the curtains of her window. Once again Justin Talbott had surprised her. Considering the weighty sum he had paid for her services, it was remarkable how much restraint he had practiced last night. She could only guess that he had refrained from making love in the same manner he had their first night together because he had been aware of how sore she was. She hoped he had meant what he had said, that he had been pleased with his experiences last evening anyway.

There was no question that he had once again pleasured her fully. When she remembered just how fully, she made a face at her treacherous body lying stretched out beneath the covers. How could someone who prided herself on her logic and self-control turn to such total jelly in a man's arms? Although she longed to make light of the situation, deep down inside she knew the matter wasn't humorous at all.

She was afraid of this power Justin had over the sensual side of her nature, a side she didn't even know she possessed until two days ago. Some night she feared he might take more from her than she was willing to give, but the alternative of returning to the Old Homestead was simply too difficult for her to face.

She was roused from her musings by a sharp rap on the door. Before Kate could call for her visitor to enter, Mrs. Drury stormed into the room with the burgundy gown and a mound of white undergarments in her arms. She dropped the clothing onto a chair just inside the door as if it had dirtied her hands.

"You left these items down in the library," the gray-haired woman declared in an icy tone. "And I have far too much work to do about this household to spend my valuable time picking up after a lazy little hussy."

Kate stared at the woman in disbelief. A wave of anger surged through her, leaving her coldly furious. "I left my clothing in the library because our mutual employer gave me little choice in the matter," she informed the housekeeper in an equally frigid and polite tone. "If you are upset about this matter, I recommend you talk to Mr. Talbott about it. And in the meantime, I believe I would like to take breakfast in my room this morning. A boiled egg and some toast would be fine. After my meal I should like some clean towels brought upstairs for my bath."

"Why, you, you—"

"That will be all, Mrs. Drury," Kate interrupted the stuttering woman calmly.

At that dismissal, Mrs. Drury shot her a fulminating look and shut the door none too gently behind her. Kate let go a quavering breath and stifled an urge to bury her head under her pillow. Well, she'd done it; she had faced the woman down. It had not been too difficult after all. Then again, it had not been a particularly pleasant experience either, and she guessed she would probably have words with the housekeeper again sometime soon.

Kate sighed at the thought, but then she grinned when she remembered how startled Mrs. Drury had been. For a moment there, she had looked just like the goldfish Elizabeth used to keep in a bowl in her bedroom when they were children. That silly thought raised Kate's spirits considerably and sent her bouncing out of bed.

She had donned her dressing gown and had just finished brushing her hair when another knock came on her door. Hoping strongly this heralded the arrival of her breakfast, she nerved herself for another unpleasant confrontation with Justin's housekeeper. This time, however, the door was opened by a plump, short, dark-haired woman wearing a white apron. With a warm smile, she introduced herself in a thick French accent as Madame Dupuy, Mr. Talbott's cook.

Kate set her brush down immediately and rose to greet her guest. "*Votre coq au vin est magnifique, Madame. Monsieur Talbott est un homme très fortuné d'avoir vous dans son emploi.*"

The Frenchwoman's face lit up with a wide smile, and her dark brown eyes sparkled. "*Merci de compliment.* You speak my language very well, mademoiselle."

"I would welcome a chance to practice my accent. I have always wanted to travel to your country," Kate admitted shyly. "Where in France are you from?"

"From the area of the Dordogne, in southern France. It is a region most beautiful. But I do not wish for your food to grow cold, mademoiselle. Please, you must sit and eat."

"Very well, you may set the tray down over here on the writing table. Can you possibly stay for a bit and chat with me while I eat?"

As soon as she had issued the invitation, Kate could have kicked herself. If Madame Dupuy was of Mrs. Drury's mindset, she had just given the cook an excellent opportunity to give Mr. Talbott's new mistress a set-down.

But her fears proved to be unfounded. The Frenchwoman smiled and said she would be delighted to stay for a while. She came and settled herself comfortably in the rocker while Kate set to work on her breakfast. In no time the two of them were getting along famously. Kate learned that Madame Dupuy had emigrated to the United States twenty years ago with her husband and her brother and his family.

"My brother homesteaded a farm in Nebraska, but my *cher* Gaston and I found the life there too bleak and hard for us. We moved to Denver and opened a restaurant. This business kept us well for many years. But the typhoid fever carried off my *pauvre* Gaston five years ago, and I found the restaurant was too much to run on my own. I soon obtained work as a cook. Positions were easy to come by, you understand"—this Madame Dupuy admitted with a droll wink—"for rich Americans are eager to have a French cook in their household. They think it adds to their status, *n'est-ce pas?*"

By the time Kate had finished her breakfast, Madame Dupuy's frank and friendly manner had put Kate completely at her ease. She even ventured to bring up the issue that had been puzzling her ever since her visitor had arrived.

"Mrs. Drury has made it clear she is not pleased to have me join this household, but you don't seem to mind."

Madame Dupuy shrugged her shoulders in a very Gallic fashion. "*A vrai dire*, I do not mind at all. We French tend to be much more realistic about these matters than you Americans. This is a difficult and uncertain world, and there are few ways a woman can support herself and provide for her old age. When my Gaston died and left me alone, I might have chosen your path. But I was too old, and my looks were going. And I was very lucky to have my skill in the kitchen to keep me.

"You must try to ignore that old witch. Monsieur Gallagher and I are most pleased to have you with us. This house is a quiet place, for Monsieur Talbott works hard and is often gone. *Enfin*, your young presence will be a blessing. And now I must be getting back to my kitchen." Madame Dupuy heaved her plump self out of the rocker.

"Enjoy your bath, *mignonne*, and know you are most welcome to visit me in my kitchen anytime," the Frenchwoman declared as she picked up Kate's tray, smiled, and left the room.

Kate did enjoy her bath, greatly pleased by the notion she now had a friend and ally in Justin Talbott's household. She was also highly entertained by Justin's bathing room, which she discovered just down the hall. Clearly her employer believed in enjoying his creature comforts. His house was one of the few in Cripple Creek that had hot running water. His bathtub was an elegant porcelain affair, rimmed round with varnished cherry wood. It was also the biggest bathtub she had ever bathed in, for it was easily six feet in length.

Kate started to picture her dynamic employer taking the time to soak and relax in this tub, but her imaginings began to betray her. All too vividly she could remember the way he had looked last night after she had taken his shirt off, the firelight playing across the well-developed muscles in his chest and arms, his blue gaze dark and intense. The memory made an odd warmth begin to kindle in the bottom of her stomach. She swallowed hard and decided it would be far better if she thought about something else.

As she washed her hair and scrubbed herself clean, she wondered if Justin's fiancée knew he kept mistresses. The proud beauty she had seen on Justin's arm that day back in November hardly seemed the sort to put up with her fiancé's consorting with other women. Yet such arrangements were often common in upper-class marriages. In the long run, she supposed it really wasn't any of her business. It certainly wasn't the sort of topic she was going to bring up with Justin anytime soon, she concluded with a sigh.

An hour later she went downstairs and set about exploring the rest of Justin's home. Across the front hall from the library she discovered an elegant front parlor with a fine Oriental carpet, royal blue velvet drapes, and embossed wallpaper in a stylized Oriental design. The room was furnished with gilded classical revival chairs and sofas upholstered in blue French silk. Two end tables bore exquisite Tiffany lamps. She frowned when she saw the fine layer of dust covering both the tables and the lamps. In fact, now that she thought about it, much of the house did not seem particularly clean. She could not help wondering if Mrs. Drury truly worked diligently at her job.

Kate discovered the parlor led to a well-appointed music room, with a fine grand piano situated near the bay window. She wondered if Justin played the piano as she leafed through the large supply of sheet music lying in its rack. There was so much she didn't know about him, so much she probably never would know about the complex and contradictory man who was keeping her.

Across the hall from the music room she discovered a short corridor that led to an imposing set of double doors. This, she guessed, must be the way to Justin's office. Madame Dupuy had already explained to her that the office had a second outside entrance that Justin's business associates usually used. Was Justin in his office now, working on mining transactions? Although she was curious how he spent his day, she had no intention of going through those doors uninvited.

From the corridor she wandered through the dining room and knocked tentatively on the swinging door into the kitchen. Madame Dupuy's cheery voice invited her inside at once. Kate was charmed by the Frenchwoman's domain. It was a bright, sunny room filled with the scent of baking. The walls of the kitchen were painted white, and bright blue checked curtains hung by the windows. A colorful braided rug covered much of the wooden floor, and a modern blue, silver, and white stove took up much of the eastern wall of the room.

"This," Madame Dupuy informed Kate with a flourish, "is the pièce de résistance in my kitchen. Monsieur Talbott had this beautiful stove hauled into the district just so that I can bake him the French pastries he likes so well."

Smiling at the notion that Justin had a sweet tooth, Kate let the Frenchwoman settle her at the table with a cup of tea. While she was chatting with the cook, Ben Gallagher arrived to eat his lunch and took a seat at the table across from Kate.

"You gauche blackguard, have you washed your hands before sitting at my clean table?" Madame Dupuy asked with such fierceness that Kate was taken aback until she saw the laughing light in the cook's eyes.

"Why, yes, ma'am, I surely have," Ben Gallagher said with remarkable meekness as he held his large hands up for her inspection. Kate hid a smile as the plump Frenchwoman made a great show of examining Ben's hands for cleanliness. His knuckles were still pink from the vigorous washing he had just given them.

"Very well, then, I will let you have lunch. Myself, I do not understand why you wish to eat my fine French cooking. I thought bandits liked only cold beans, bacon, and biscuits."

"Well, ma'am, I'm not just sure myself. I expect it's probably because it's part of my pay and all."

"Ah, so you finally admit it. You only like to eat here because it costs you nothing. I should 'ave known." Even as the cook was shaking her head, she was putting together a heaping plate of food for Ben.

For all his pretended indifference to Madame Dupuy's cooking, Kate was amused to see that Ben proceeded to put away most of a cheese soufflé himself, along with a loaf of French bread and two bowls of tasty cream of chicken soup. The meal smelled so delicious, Kate was quickly persuaded to join Ben at his repast. During the meal Ben and Madame Dupuy flirted and teased each other outrageously. Halfway through, Mrs. Drury poked her head in the door. When she saw the three of them laughing as they sat about the table, she sent Kate a disdainful look and quickly withdrew. Ben and Madame Dupuy swiftly resumed their banter in a diplomatic effort, Kate guessed, to distract her from the obvious insult. By and large their efforts were successful. Her sides were sore from laughing by the end of the meal.

"For Frenchie food, this here souffler warn't half bad, ma'am," Ben drawled when he finally pushed his empty plate away from him.

"It is called a soufflé, you hopeless cretin. How many times must I tell you this?"

"Well, now, I guess until I get the hang of saying it right, you'll just have to keep making it." Ben sent Kate a wink with his one good eye as he clapped his battered hat on his head and strolled out the back door.

After helping Madame Dupuy wash up, Kate left the kitchen as well. While she made her way upstairs to read, she was still chuckling over her luncheon companions' behavior. Was there any serious sentiment under all that bluster? she wondered. What a wonderful, unlikely couple those two would make. It pleased her to think in a world that seemed stark, harsh, and unsentimental to her these days, there still might be some real romance.

She settled herself with her Mark Twain novel on the window seat and read for several hours. Although she became caught up in the story, she still found the afternoon crawled by. Her work at the Golden Spike had accustomed her to keeping physically busy and active most of the day.

When she finished the book, her restlessness finally got the best of her. She strode downstairs and hesitated in the hallway, trying to decide if she wanted to go for a walk, play the piano, or pick a new book from the library.

"There's no use waiting about down here hoping to see Mr. Talbott," Mrs. Drury said coldly from someplace behind her. "He told me first thing this morning that he was planning to go out this evening."

Kate whirled about to face the housekeeper, who was standing near the foot of the stairs. "It would seem your charms are already beginning to pall," Mrs. Drury added with a malicious smile.

Kate decided she wouldn't dignify the woman's taunt with a reply. Instead she turned her back on Mrs. Drury and stalked across the hall into the parlor. There she stared blindly at the carved white marble mantelpiece before her, wondering if what the housekeeper had said could possibly be true. One would think a man like Justin Talbott, if he were truly pleased with his new mistress, would want to stay home to enjoy her services. Could that have been why they had not truly made love last night? Kate bit her lip as she wandered into the music room. Despite all that Pearl had taught her, there was so much she didn't know about her new occupation. Even if in her naïveté and innocence she had failed to please her employer, she hoped he would give her another chance before terminating their arrangement. Justin just didn't seem the type to renege on his deal without talking to her first.

She crossed the room and settled herself on the piano bench. She leafed through the sheet music, looking for pieces she didn't know. But the sick, tight feeling in her stomach did not go away. What if Justin did decide to send her back to the Old Homestead? She closed her eyes and shuddered. She could not imagine letting another man touch her the way Justin had touched her last night. But she had to be strong enough to return to the Old Homestead when and if that time came. Elizabeth's treatment and perhaps her very life was at stake. Trying to ignore her fears for the moment, Kate opened her eyes again, selected a piece, and began to play softly.

When she finished the popular song, she went on to perform Beethoven's *Hammerklavier* Sonata, which was much more suited to her mood. Soon she lost herself in the crashing, dramatic chords, finally finding an outlet for some of the tumultuous emotions churning inside her.

She had just finished the second movement when some small sound, or a sixth sense perhaps, prompted her to glance over her shoulder. Justin was standing there, lounging in the doorway behind her with his arms folded across his chest. She drew in a deep breath and turned about on the piano bench to face him. Perhaps now she would learn if Mrs. Drury was right. Perhaps now she would learn if she should be packing her trunk to return to the Old Homestead.

Chapter Nine

"I'm sorry to keep you waiting," Kate said stiffly. "You should have said something if you wanted to talk with me."

"So we're back to being polite acquaintances, are we?" He raised a black eyebrow at her as he strolled forward into the room. This afternoon he was clad in gray trousers and a white shirt he wore open at the neck. His thick, black hair looked tousled, as if he had been running his hands through it. Perhaps he had been working hard back in his office. She tried to ignore the fact that he looked devastatingly handsome and much younger in his informal attire.

"I don't understand what you mean." Surely he wasn't going to bring up the topic of how she had behaved last night. She would be just mortified to have such matters discussed in broad daylight.

"You know exactly what I mean, but I won't call your bluff for the moment. I just wanted to say you do play well, with more talent and feeling than the usual drawing room miss."

"Thank you," she said, thawing just a bit. "I did not rebel against my piano lessons nearly as hard as I fought doing needlework and going to dancing school. I should also probably inform you that my sketching is hopeless."

"You may rest assured you won't have to perform any watercolors or sketches while you are under my roof."

She thought he meant the comment humorously, but his reference to her position here somehow cooled any warmth she had been beginning to feel toward him. It also revived all her fears about the precariousness of her situation. "No, I suppose not," she said quietly.

"I also wanted to let you know that I will be dining out

this evening,'' he said when it became obvious she wasn't going to say anything further.

"I hope you have a pleasant dinner. Should I . . . would you like me to wait up?" She was pleased that she had only stumbled a little over the question. She truly dreaded the notion of waiting up for hours, wondering whether or not he planned to come to her.

"That won't be necessary."

"Very good, sir. Again, I wish you a pleasant evening." She stood up from the piano bench, planning to beat a hasty retreat upstairs. She was happy to have made it through another conversation with him relatively unscathed, and she found she didn't have the nerve to ask him outright if he was considering terminating their arrangement.

"For God's sake"—his voice broke in on her thoughts— "you are not a servant in this household, so don't start acting like one."

She glanced up at him, startled by the sharpness of his tone. "I have never been in this position before," she replied slowly, "and therefore I am uncertain how I am supposed to act."

"Just be yourself. Just be the girl I found so charming and appealing two years ago in the garden at your father's house in Boston."

A wave of sadness washed through her. She thought about telling him that innocent girl no longer existed, thanks to the whims of fate and his own actions. She thought about telling him this entire situation made her feel like a stranger to herself, as if she were an actress playing a part in some melodramatic play. But of course she could not share these thoughts with him, and so she simply said, "I will do my best."

"That will please me greatly."

"Will it? I'm not sure I've managed to please you so far," she blurted out her main concern of the moment.

He cocked his head and studied her curiously. "What makes you think that?"

"Mrs. Drury told me this afternoon that you would not be going out for the evening if . . . if you knew you would be well entertained at home." Kate's cheeks began to burn. She longed to have the sophistication to discuss these matters with ease, but here she was blushing like a gauche schoolgirl. It was probably just this lack of polish and worldliness he found tiresome.

"Mrs. Drury should mind her own damn business," he said in such a curt tone that Kate drew in a breath and stared hard at her feet. Cursing her unruly tongue, she wished she had never brought the subject up. Then she heard him sigh and saw him step closer. He reached out and tipped her head up, his fingers gentle beneath her chin.

"Kate, you don't need to worry about my being happy with our little arrangement. The problem is quite the opposite, in fact." He dropped his hand and shoved it into his trouser pocket. "I'm going out this evening because I believe you need a little more time after what happened between us two nights ago. To put it more bluntly, I'm afraid that if I stay here for supper, I won't be able to keep my hands off you."

She must have let her disbelief show, for Justin let go a rather strained laugh and clasped her shoulders.

"You don't believe me, do you, my golden girl? But perhaps you will believe this," he said under his breath right before he bent his head and pulled her hard against him.

She was so startled and off balance, she had to put her hands out against his chest to steady herself. As his lips took possession of her own, she was conscious of the feel of the fine linen of his shirt and the hard warm muscles of his chest beneath that fabric.

Does any other man in the world kiss like this? she just had time to wonder, and then she was only feeling, not thinking at all. His warm lips roamed across her face and neck, sending shivers skittering down her back. His hands tugged her head back until his tongue could explore and stroke her mouth more easily. Shyly she slipped her hands about his neck. There her fingers could take delicious liberties of their own, touching his thick, silky hair.

A part of her longed to be even closer to him. As if he had read her mind, one of his hands slipped from her head to her waist and pulled her tighter against him. Through her skirts she now could feel his hard legs against her own. Down deep in the pit of her stomach, a fire begin to kindle. As the heat from that fire spread throughout her, she forgot it was midafternoon, forgot she was standing in the middle of the music room; she forgot everything but the incredible sensation of standing in his arms and being kissed like this.

At last Justin raised his head from hers, his blue eyes blazing. It came as some small consolation when she realized he was breathing just as hard as she was.

"Now you can believe me when I say it would be far better for you if I went out tonight." He cupped her face between his hands, pressed one last hard kiss on her lips, and left the room.

She stood there for a long time hoping some measure of her self-control and poise would come back to her. At last she started walking toward the stairs, wondering at how odd and heavy her body felt. Somehow it ached and tingled all at once, and Justin had brought to this state with just a few kisses. She shook her head at herself. Then the good news dawned on her. At least now she knew that Mrs. Drury was very wrong.

That night Kate shared a pleasant dinner with Madame Dupuy. Because she knew Justin would not come to her that evening, Kate slept soundly. After another one of Madame Dupuy's fine breakfasts, Kate decided to go for a walk. When she returned to the house, feeling much more lively and cheerful, she picked out a new novel from Justin's library and retired to her room to read. She shared another amusing lunch with Ben and Madame Dupuy and afterward went back to her reading. By midafternoon, once again she was ready to climb the walls of Justin's home. Knowing more physical activity was what she needed, she came up with a new notion. If Mrs. Drury didn't want to do her housework, perhaps she wouldn't mind if she had some help.

And so Kate set off to find Justin's prickly housekeeper. As Kate came down the steps, she spotted the woman crossing the front hall.

"Oh, Mrs. Drury, I was just coming to find you. You mentioned how busy you were, and I was wondering if you had any chores that needed doing about the place. I'm getting a little bored because I'm so used to keeping myself busy. I was hoping—"

"How dare you? How dare you even speak to a decent

woman like myself?'' Mrs. Drury shrilly interrupted Kate's carefully worded request.

"Mrs. Drury"—Kate did her best to hold on to her soaring temper—''like it or not, we are going to be living under the same roof for the next two months. I, for one, see no point in stalking around this place glaring at each other. Surely we can reach a truce of some sort.''

"That's easy for you to say. Your very presence in this household is an affront to me. You shame me, you shame all womankind by selling yourself for a man's pleasure. I don't know how you can hold your head up in public, knowing what you've done.''

Kate bowed her head before the housekeeper's wrath while her heart twisted inside her. Although she knew the woman's words were born of anger and intolerance, Kate couldn't help but wonder if a portion of what she was saying was true.

"It doesn't surprise me in the least that you are bored here. I'm sure a slut like you becomes bored with only one man to please. Why don't you go back to your brothel—''

"That's enough, Mrs. Drury." A cold male voice cut short the woman's tirade.

Kate looked up in dismay to find Justin standing in the hallway. One look at his glittering blue eyes told her he was furious. She swallowed hard and hoped fervently his anger wasn't directed at her.

His next words hardly reassured her on that score. "I did not realize Miss Holden's presence in this household constituted such a problem for you.''

"It does indeed, an overwhelming problem, in fact. I should tell you, sir, that I have been seriously considering handing in my notice. A decent woman like myself has her reputation to consider. It comes to this. Either that woman goes or I go.''

"Very well, Mrs. Drury, if that is the way you feel about this situation, you may pack your things and leave this afternoon. If you will come to my office shortly, I will have your next two weeks' wages waiting for you.''

Kate winced when she saw the stunned, sick look in Mrs. Drury's eyes. Obviously the housekeeper had overplayed her hand, and now she could hardly believe that she had just lost a prime position in the process. Working in almost any other household in the district would seem like a step down after being the housekeeper in Justin's elegant home. Kate wondered what chance Mrs. Drury had of finding employment now. So many had come to Cripple Creek in the past year that there were few jobs to be had anywhere.

"But, sir—" Mrs. Drury managed to stutter out the start of a protest.

"That will be all, Mrs. Drury. You have already made your feelings on this topic quite clear."

His dismissal was so firm and final, the expression on his face so stern, the older woman must have realized it was pointless to try arguing with him. As she marched up the stairs, Mrs. Drury sent Kate a venomous look. Kate waited until she heard the woman slam the door to her room on the third floor. Then Kate walked down the remaining three steps and went to stand in front of her employer.

"Mr. Talbott," she said after taking a deep breath, "would you please reconsider your decision?"

"What's this, young Kate, compassion for the enemy?" He cocked his head and studied her, an odd expression she couldn't quite read lurking in his eyes.

"I feel bad that Mrs. Drury just lost her position because of me. Surely you realize most decent women would feel exactly as she does about having to live in the same household with me."

"Well then, we may have to do without the services of a housekeeper for the next two months. The place may get dusty, but we will be having such a fine time together that we'll hardly notice."

How could he make light of this situation? She felt like stamping her foot at him. Instead she said as calmly as she could, "Mr. Talbott, although you do not seem to realize it, this is hardly a laughing matter either for Mrs. Drury or for myself."

"Call me Justin," he interrupted her quickly. "If you mean to plead the woman's case, you shouldn't aggravate me right at the start."

"Very well, Justin," she got out between gritted teeth, "firing Mrs. Drury hardly seems fair, given the circumstances."

"She is not being fired. She had a choice to stay or go, and she chose to go."

"It was choice she couldn't possibly accept, and you knew it."

"I would remind you that she was the one who voiced this ultimatum, not I. And the alternative she gave me was to let you go, and that is something I am not willing to do. I wonder if you are making such a protest to get out of our arrangement." His black brows drew together in a fierce frown. "I warn you, Kate Holden, I am not going to let you wriggle out of our agreement. A deal's a deal."

"I am not trying to get out of anything," she fired back indignantly. "I am simply trying to make you see that you've just turned an older woman out, and it could be very hard for her to find another position in the district."

He was silent for several moments as he studied her face broodingly. What he saw there must have convinced him, for at last his frown smoothed away. "If her fate concerns you all that much, I promise I will write her a decent reference, although in all honesty the woman hardly deserves one. In fact, if it makes your conscience any lighter, you should know I've been planning to sack her for some time. The woman is both lazy and incompetent."

"You knew that?" Kate asked in some surprise.

"Kate, I may be busy, but I'm not blind," he replied wryly.

"Then why haven't you fired her before?"

"I haven't had the time to get around to it."

"That's not it at all. You didn't want to face her down either," Kate guessed shrewdly.

"Well, now, she is a rather formidable woman, you must admit." He ran a hand through his hair and looked sheepish. Kate was delighted. The arrogant, confident Justin Talbott she knew hardly ever appeared this way. Although she wanted to tease him further, she decided she would be wise not to push her luck.

"Is it true, what she said about your being bored here?" he asked suddenly.

She swallowed hard, her amusement fading. She looked past his shoulder, wondering miserably how much of their conversation he had just overheard. How was she going to get out of this without offending him? "Your home is quite pleasant, of course," she began carefully, "and my room couldn't be more comfortable. It's just that . . ."

"Yes?" he prompted her when her voice trailed off.

"It's just that I am used to keeping busy all day long," she admitted in a rush. "I didn't realize how accustomed I was to being active all day at the Golden Spike. Sometimes I do feel a bit cooped up in here. I did go for a walk this morning, and when I got the fidgets again this afternoon I should have simply gone for another stroll."

"You are most welcome to go visit with friends, you know," he said after a few moments. "There's no need for you to be a hermit."

"I . . . I didn't know how you would feel about my going calling. But truly there is just one person I would want to see. Mrs. O'Connell is the only friend who knows what I am doing now." Kate sighed inwardly when she felt her cheeks start to heat once again. One of these days she was going to be able to refer to her new position in Justin Talbott's household without blushing. "The rest think I've left," she finished awkwardly.

"What if you could go for a drive from time to time? You could take one of the carriages when I won't be needing Ben."

"Going out for a drive occasionally would be wonderful, if you are certain I wouldn't be making more work for Mr. Gallagher."

"I think it would please Ben no end. He is quite taken with you, and he would enjoy more opportunities to show off his teams and rigs. In fact I've no plans to go anywhere this afternoon. Why don't you ask him to take you out now?"

Puzzled by what seemed to be real concern for her on Justin's part, she looked at him, really looked at him for the first time this afternoon. Just like yesterday he was clad simply in a white shirt and dark trousers. His face was pale, his eyes weary, and his hair rumpled. In short, he looked as if he had been working hard again. She could only imagine the kinds of hours he must have labored to create his fortune in such a short time. Now she was seeing firsthand the dues he paid to build and run his mining empire.

"Very well, I will ask him, but only if you will come along, too," she said impulsively.

"What's this? Be careful, Kate. I might think you are actually interested in sharing my company."

"You may think what you like." She tossed her head. "I just know a drive would do you a world of good as well. It doesn't take a medical genius to guess you've been working too hard back in that office of yours."

"I didn't hire you to act like a mother hen," he declared and crossed his arms across his chest.

"Believe me, sir, I can hardly escape the reason why you hired me, since any reference to it seems to make me turn redder than a sugar beet," she said so ruefully that he tipped his head back and let go a belly laugh.

She smiled to herself. It was good to know she could still amuse him when she put her mind to it.

"Do come." She decided to press her advantage. "It could be great fun. You can tell me more stories about the district and point out some of the mines you've bought. I won't ask you to show every one to me, for if what the folk at the Golden Spike said about your owning half of Cripple Creek is true, it would take us weeks to see them all."

At first she thought he was going to say no, but as he looked down at her his expression seemed to change.

"Very well, little scholar. I can't remember the last time I did anything you might call 'great fun.' I would be happy to go for a drive with you. Why don't you go fetch a coat, and I will speak with Ben about hitching up a team."

Flustered by the warm look in his blue eyes, she nodded and turned away. She had just started up the steps when he cleared his throat and said, "I'm sorry for the things Mrs. Drury said to you just now. You mustn't let them bother you."

She paused and looked back over her shoulder. "Thank you, Justin, I won't," she replied. It was a fib, of course, but just the fact that he had thought to apologize for his housekeeper helped ease the hurt considerably.

A half hour later they were both comfortably ensconced in the back of Justin's landau. At Kate's request they had put the top down. A warm buffalo robe lay across their laps, but the afternoon sun was so warm they hardly needed the covering.

"And where would you like to go? You should choose our destination, since this expedition was your idea."

Justin lounged back against the carriage seat, looking every inch an affluent Upper Ten. His top hat shone as if he had purchased it yesterday, and his elegant gray topcoat was cut in the height of fashion. Surreptitiously Kate twisted a mended spot on her own shabby coat sleeve away from him, hoping he wouldn't notice how old her garment looked in the merciless light of the winter sun.

"Driving to a place with a good view would be nice," she replied diffidently.

"How about it, Ben? Where can we go to find the young lady a good view?"

"To my mind there's nothing like the view from the top of Elk Mountain," the coachman suggested. "You can see the Sangre de Cristos from there and the back spires of Pikes Peak."

"To the top of Elk Mountain, then, if you think your nags are up to it," Justin said with a straight face.

Ben shot his employer a speaking look with his one good eye and sent the team off at such a sharp clip that both Justin and Kate were thrown back against the plush upholstery. Kate couldn't help letting go a merry laugh as Justin straightened his top hat, which had fallen forward over his eyes.

"That will teach you not to insult his horses," she said when she had got her breath back.

"I should have known better," he replied with a lazy grin. As he stared down at her, the burning look she was coming to recognize only too well kindled in his eyes. He dipped his head toward her, clearly intending to kiss her. She was agonizingly aware, however, that they were still passing through the northern edges of town. Horsemen, wagon drivers, and people in their yards could see into the back of the landau easily. Justin rarely gave her a quick kiss, and she rebelled at the notion of his declaring her shameful position so publicly with a long one.

"Please, Justin, not here. A hundred people could see us."

"Very well," he said in a cool tone and straightened up at once. As she watched, the bored, arrogant mask she was coming to hate stole over his features. She bit her lip and looked away. Had she ruined the entire drive for them both? Now that they were sitting side by side in his carriage, she was regretting her impulsive suggestion that he join her. Justin was just such an overwhelming presence, and she had succeeded in irritating him only five minutes into the drive. What could they possibly talk about for the next hour?

As the landau bowled up Shelf Road, which led south out of town, she saw two young miners resting wearily next to a large ore bucket by the head frame on their claim. She wondered if they had struck pay dirt yet for all the hours of back-breaking labor they were putting into their hole in the ground.

"Would you mind telling me how you got started in the mining business?" she asked him shyly after several minutes.

"I wouldn't mind telling you"—he gave her a skeptical look—"but are you sure that you want to hear such a long and tedious tale?"

"Oh, yes. Back at the Golden Spike I used to see these poor, worn-out, hungry young men come in and wolf down two or three breakfasts at a time. You could tell chasing their dreams of gold had turned out to be an exhausting, discouraging business, and I often wondered if you had hungry times when you were getting started."

"I surely did, and at one point I would have gone home with my tail between my legs if your father hadn't wired me a grubstake when I needed it most."

Encouraged that he seemed willing to talk, she asked quickly, "How did you get interested in mining in the first place?"

"A good friend of my father's back in Boston was a rock hound. He had wandered the world over indulging in his hobby. He traveled to the goldfields in California in the fifties and to Colorado in the sixties. When I was a young and impressionable twelve-year-old, I was fascinated by the glittering rock samples in his collection and I often went to visit him. He told me several times that he was amazed at how little real science and geology western miners knew. Since he had inherited a sizable fortune, he had no interest in using his knowledge to strike it rich, but he was convinced that a trained geologist could make a killing out west."

"I heard the two druggists who staked the pharmacist simply threw a hat on the ground and began digging where their hat landed," she offered.

"That is a true story. It certainly was a lucky toss, for that mine is producing ten thousand a month now. But for all the lucky men in the stories that you hear, there are a hundred more like those two young tenderfeet you saw back there. They are breaking their backs and using up their grubstake digging in one of the least likely spots, geologically speaking, in the entire district."

"Where did you start learning about geology?" She was careful not to ask why or when, for she did not want to remind him about the painful scandal that had driven him away from Boston.

His face lit up with a smile. "I think I traveled to just about every major gold and silver strike in the west, from California and Nevada to North Dakota and Colorado. When I wasn't pestering old-timers to tell me about rock formations and vein structures, I was reading everything I could find about the geology of precious metals. I quickly found out that what my father's friend had told me was true. So many prospectors, even experienced mining men, were searching for gold and silver with no real knowledge of the forces that formed the surface of the earth."

He leaned forward just then and said in a louder voice, "Ben, take us by the old Sadie Sue on the way up to Elk Mountain, will you?" The coachman nodded and took a right-hand turn at the next crossroads they encountered.

"It's amazing old Bob Womack ever found gold in this region," Justin continued after he settled back against the seat. "I've talked to him about it on a number of occasions, and I still can't figure why he was so certain the gold was here. The rolling hills, meadows, and ridges of Cripple Creek just don't look like any other goldfield in the West. This district lies in the heart of an ancient volcano. Elk Mountain, in fact, is one remaining side of the volcano's rim. This area is truly a unique formation in which to find gold, but once one knows a bit about the way volcanoes form, locating gold veins and outcroppings can definitely become easier. Ah, here's the Sadie Sue."

The landau rolled to a stop, and Justin gestured down toward the cluster of mine buildings on the hillside below the road. Kate watched with interest as a steam-generated hoist pulled a bucket of ore up the main shaft, and two men dumped its contents. The load of rock landed with a rumbling crash in a waiting mine cart.

"This claim is a good example of how a little knowledge can save a great deal of time. When I staked the Sadie Sue, I had only been in the district for three days, and I was the only one working in this area. All sorts of fellows stopped by to tell me they thought I was crazy, but I hit good color within a week and sold the claim two days later for six hundred dollars. Within a month every piece of ground on this hillside had been claimed."

"I thought you said you still owned this mine," she pointed out perplexedly.

"I won it back in a poker game just three months after I sold it." He sent her a smug look.

"And just who," she was emboldened to ask because of that look, "was Sadie Sue?"

"My first dog," he told her with a perfectly straight face. "She was a black labrador with the most wonderful chocolate brown eyes."

"Your first dog?" Kate didn't know whether to laugh or to shake a finger at him. "Justin Talbott, don't you have an ounce of romance in you?"

She regretted her comment almost as soon as she uttered it, for his face changed at once. He looked her up and down with such disdain, she was forcibly reminded of the way he had looked at her that first night at the Old Homestead. She had been a fool to forget for even a moment his terrible anger. He had hidden it behind his easy charm these past few days, but she had been right to think it had never truly gone away.

In a cool, mocking tone he assured her, "Not a single ounce of romance remains in me, my dear, for Sadie Sue was the one and only female who was faithful to me. I told you once before that I am a hard man with little softness or sentimentality left in me. You would do well to remember that."

"I promise I will never forget it again," she replied with real feeling and turned away from him. After a few moments

Justin called out to Ben that they could go on.

It was a quiet carriage ride after that. Kate kept herself busy watching the scenery and trying to ignore the large man sitting right beside her. It was a difficult task, however, for every time the wheels of the landau rolled over a rough spot in the road, the well-sprung vehicle swayed from side to side. No matter how stiffly she held herself, her shoulder and leg frequently brushed against his own, causing her own body to warm and tingle in a most frustrating fashion. She chose not to initiate any more conversation, for she was resolved not to leave herself open to any more of his scorn.

She was relieved when they reached the top of the rough road up Elk Mountain. After he pulled the horses to a stop, Ben tied up the reins and came and undid the door and folding steps of the landau. He handed her down with such a gentlemanly flourish, she could not help smiling as she thanked him.

"This is just breathtaking, Mr. Gallagher. You were right about the view." She clasped her hands together while she looked around her. In every direction it seemed as if she could see forever. In the foreground, Cripple Creek's rival town of Victor was spread out below them with head frames and tailing piles poking up right between businesses and houses. The hills all around were pockmarked with exploration holes dug by thousands of miners. The view to the horizon in each direction was magnificent. She spent a long time looking at the brown craggy cliffs on the backside of Pikes Peak. The majestic summit of the mountain itself was crowned with brilliant white snow.

She deliberately kept her back to Justin while she asked Ben about the rugged chain of peaks she could see off to the southwest silhouetted against the brilliant blue sky. He told her that was the Sangre de Cristo range, which had been named by early Spanish explorers in this area. She said the name under her breath, savoring its poetic flavor. *Sangre de Cristo* meant blood of Christ in English. Looking at the jagged crests and peaks of the range in the bright winter sun, she decided the Spanish had chosen a fine name indeed for these peaks.

At last, however, Justin must have sent Ben a signal of some sort, for suddenly the coachman cleared his throat, apologized to Kate, and said he had to see to his horses. She tensed as

Justin moved to stand beside her.

"It's appropriate that we came up here after what we were discussing earlier," Justin said in an offhand tone, as if their terse exchange a half hour earlier had never happened. "I'm convinced we are standing on top of one of the richest gold deposits in the district. My mines on the backside of this mountain have become steady producers, but from the way the veins have been running, I believe the mother lode is located beneath this southern side."

"Why haven't you started mining over here?" She decided to follow his lead, for she doubted he would tolerate her ignoring him much longer. Besides, she was intrigued by what he was telling her. As she peered down the rocky side of the mountain, all she could see was a shack and a cabin and some small tailing piles.

"For the simple reason that I don't own the land on this side of the mountain. An old Swede named Gunnar Carlson and his partner staked out claims here and bought two others right after the rush started to the district. Carlson's partner was killed in a barroom brawl six months ago. In his will he left his claims to Carlson. In effect, that old man controls most of this side of Elk Mountain."

"If this is such a likely area, why isn't he doing any mining?"

"It takes capital to develop a mine, particularly in a spot this remote, and Carlson doesn't have enough resources to do it on his own. The old devil knows it, but he's too stubborn and suspicious to deal with me. I would like to go partners with him, which means we both could see some handsome profits, but the old man won't even meet with me. Some night a claim jumper is going to kill the old fool, or, if Carlson doesn't move soon, lawyers are going to tie his claims into such knots in the courts, he'll lose everything."

"You sound as if developing a mine here is important to you." She risked glancing up at him for the first time.

Justin sighed. "I suppose it is at that. I've done well in the mining business, but I have yet to locate a big strike. All my gold mines are good producers, and I make steady profits from them by running each one efficiently. But I still haven't made the big find, a true bonanza which would give me the resources to develop it and the rest of my mines to their fullest potential.''

"Justin Talbott, you sound just like a man with gold fever," she blurted before she realized once again she had given him an opportunity to give her a scorching set-down.

But he was nodding his head thoughtfully. "You are probably right, little scholar. For all I like to think I go about the business of finding and purchasing mines more scientifically than the rest, deep down inside I suppose I'm not so different from all the gold-hunting, gold-dreaming fools digging like frantic gophers about this place."

He grimaced and swung away from her. He folded his arms across his chest and stared down at the buildings below them.

"I've tried just about everything to reach that old man. I've sent lawyers, businessmen, and even old sourdoughs he mined with over in Aspen and Leadville to talk with him. He chased my lawyers off the property with a shotgun, he told the businessmen to go to hell, and he got drunk with all the sourdoughs. When I tried myself, the old man just slammed his door shut in my face."

"Surely he will come to see reason sooner or later."

"I'm not so sure about that anymore." Justin rubbed his hand across his face and turned back to her.

"If he doesn't," she forged on gamely, "you can use your knowledge of vein structures and volcanoes and the earth's crust to go find your bonanza on some other hilltop in this district."

"Are you trying to comfort me now?" He tilted his head as he studied her. "What a surprising young woman you are proving to be, sweet Kate. What's even more surprising is that I told you any of this. Those green eyes of yours can make a man lose his wits. I thought that the very first afternoon I saw you. And now . . ." His voice trailed off and a wicked gleam came into his eyes. "There's comfort of a different sort you could offer me."

She blinked as he took a step closer, and she began to understand his meaning. "How misguided of me." She took a step back and tried to ward him off with sarcasm. "Of course, the mighty Justin Talbott doesn't need comfort or sympathy from anyone."

"Ah, so sweet Kate just vanished, and prickly Miss Holden just took her place. I shall have to phrase this differently. Miss Holden, it would please me if you came over here and kissed me." He put unmistakable emphasis on the word *please*.

As she glanced around self-consciously, he added in a sardonic tone, "You can't use the convenient excuse that someone might see us. Ben is busy with his beloved horses, Carlson doesn't have a window on the back side of his cabin, and there's not another soul on this side of the mountain. To date, I have been the one to initiate all our lovemaking. I want you to kiss me for a change."

It did seem like a fair request, for he was echoing one of her secret fears. A mistress was supposed to lead and seduce, and so far she had managed to do precious little of either. It seemed so brazen, though, to kiss him here, on an open, barren mountaintop in broad daylight. She peeked at him through her lashes and saw he was staring down at her, a taunting smile on his well-formed lips.

He's enjoying this, she realized suddenly, and her anger at that notion gave her the courage to step forward, reach up, and brush her lips against his own. Unnerved by even that brief contact, she stepped back again as soon as she had finished.

"I'd hardly call that peck a kiss. Surely you can do better than that."

She shot him a fulminating look before she stepped forward once more. Placing her hands on his shoulders, she pressed her lips against his own. This time she lingered for several moments, enjoying the smooth feel of his mouth. His overcoat was softer than lamb's wool beneath her fingers, and his breath was warm on her cheek. Gradually she became aware of the fact that he was just standing there like a block of wood while she was putting considerable effort and energy into the kiss. Fighting down her temper, she drew back and put both hands on her hips. He just looked at her, one black brow raised in inquiry.

"It's not fair if you don't kiss me back," she said indignantly.

"You're supposed to make me want to kiss you back," he

retorted, laughter making his eyes look as blue as the distant peaks.

"Very well then, Mr. Talbott, you asked for it," she said under her breath. This time when she stepped forward she slipped her hands inside his topcoat and under his jacket until her palms were pressing against his fine linen shirt. Drawing on what he had already taught her about kissing, she decided to see if any of the devastating things he did to her would have some effect on him. Standing on tiptoe, she ignored his lips completely and kissed the right side of his chin instead. From there she moved her lips along the line of his jaw. Impatient when she couldn't quite reach his ear, she moved one hand to the back of his neck and tugged his head lower. When she touched her tongue to his earlobe, she heard him draw in a quick breath. She smiled to herself in satisfaction.

Massaging both his chest and the skin at the back of his neck, she began nibbling enticingly at the corners of his mouth. When he turned to capture her lips with his own, she evaded him with a soft laugh and went on to press moist kisses on the side of his neck just above his collar. His muscles beneath her fingers had tensed, and he was breathing much more quickly now. Yet still his arms hung at his sides, and he made no move to touch her. Her own body was beginning to react to what she was doing in the most peculiar way. How could that strange warmth he usually kindled in her be starting again? This time she was doing the touching.

At last she moved to kiss his lips once more. Intending to taste him the way he so often had tasted her, she slipped her tongue between his lips. She had just begun to explore the contours of his mouth when suddenly he groaned. He caught her waist with both his hands and pulled her hard against him. All at once his lips seemed to be everywhere, ranging across her face and neck while his fingers plucked feverishly at the fastenings to her coat and blouse. Soon he had her shirt open almost to her waist. As his mouth took possession of hers, he began to cup and caress her breasts through her chemise. She told herself she should start wearing a corset again, if only to give herself another layer of protection against incursions like these. Soon she was lost in a tide of sensation as his fingers teased the tip of her right nipple until it hardened.

His tongue began plunging into her mouth in a heady rhythm as his right hand moved to torment her other breast. He was doing such a fine job of distracting all her senses, only slowly did she come to realize his left hand was raising the front of her skirt and her petticoats to her waist. Before she could protest such boldness, he had wedged his right leg between her knees and slipped his hands under her buttocks. She moaned aloud, half in dismay, half in desire as he lifted her up until she was straddling his thigh and he held her tight against him. To keep her balance, she had to lock her hands around his neck. Through the thin fabric of her drawers and his trousers she could not help but feel his arousal pressing against her right leg.

She soon understood the reason he had lifted her to this position when he bent his head and began to kiss the exposed skin of her neck and chin. She drew in a breath when he moved lower and started kissing her breasts through her chemise. Running her hands through his cool, soft hair, she kissed the side of his face and his neck. She gasped when he began to rock against her in a slow, rhythmic fashion. Instantly the fire in the pit of her stomach leaped into a real conflagration. As the flames of sensation went shooting throughout her, her treacherous body learned his rhythm swiftly and matched it.

Suddenly he stilled. "Don't move," he said in a thick voice and wrapped his arms around her shoulders. He rested his forehead against her own as he drew in deep, shuddering breaths.

After a few moments, Kate realized bemusedly she was doing just the same. When he finally picked her up and gently put her away from him, she was afraid her legs wouldn't hold her up. The last thing she wanted to do was go sprawling on this mountaintop before him, and so she willed her legs to hold. It was hard, however, to think about much else. Her lower body throbbed almost painfully, and a heavy, tingling lethargy held the rest of her.

He seemed to understand what she was feeling, for he stepped closer, and with real regret in his eyes he said, "I'm sorry, my golden girl. I did not mean for that to happen to either of us."

He reached out and carefully fastened all the buttons on her blouse and coat that he had undone so swiftly minutes earlier. When he had finished, he put an arm around her shoulder and urged her toward the landau. He helped her up the steps into the vehicle himself, and once he had settled her in the seat, he tucked the buffalo robe around her tenderly.

"Ben, take us home, and let those nags of yours show us whatever speed they've got," he ordered his coachman.

If she had thought the carriage ride up the mountain had been quiet, the ride back was positively silent. Justin only spoke to her once, and that was when the landau rolled to a stop in front of his home.

"I swore to myself I'd give you one more night," he said, looking straight ahead of him. "If you want me to hold to this resolution, I recommend that you stay out of my sight for the next few hours." With that he stood up and climbed down out of the landau, leaving Kate to follow more slowly after.

Chapter Ten

Kate did exactly as her employer had recommended. Still shaken by what had passed between them on the mountain, she thought it would be extremely wise to stay out of his sight. After she walked in the front door she went straight to her room and remained there until she heard Justin leave for the evening. That night she ate a quiet meal with Madame Dupuy in the kitchen.

After she went to bed Kate tossed and turned for several hours. Although she did not want to think about what had happened that afternoon, her body would not let her forget. Hours after Justin had let her go, she still ached with need. She continued to be amazed by this sensual part of her nature. It was appalling to think she had almost let Justin make love to her right there in broad daylight on an open mountaintop.

She thought about lighting a lamp and reading until she grew sleepy, but she was afraid Justin might see her light when he returned and reconsider his resolution. She was still wide awake when she heard him open the front door and say good night to Ben. She held her breath as he climbed the steps and started down the hall toward her room. She heard him hesitate in front of her door before he went on down the hall. She only let go that breath after she heard him close the door to his own bedroom. As she looked up into the darkness, she had to face the disturbing fact that a treacherous part of her was disappointed that he had not come to her. It was a long time before she finally fell asleep that night.

The next morning she awoke to a quiet tap on her door. Madame Dupuy bustled in with a sumptuous omelette and a freshly baked roll on a tray. When Kate had finished eating and dressing she went down to the library, determined to find more serious reading for herself. In the midst of her restless night she had decided she could at least use the next two months to improve her mind.

The few minutes she meant to stay in the library soon turned into an hour and then two. She was having a wonderful time skimming titles and sampling first chapters of volumes in Justin's remarkable history collection. As her pile of possible reading material grew next to the sofa, she wondered if she should ask her employer first before carrying these treasures up to her bedroom. Every time she considered bearding him in his office, her memories of what he had said and done the afternoon before stopped her. All things considered, she thought it would be a much better idea if today Justin were to seek her out rather than vice versa.

As she prowled about his library, she also discovered several shelves devoted entirely to Greek and Roman classics. These she was sorely tempted to browse as well, but she wanted her own dictionaries, texts, and notes before she tackled the fascinating job of translating these works. Wistfully she thought of her crate of books in Elly's attic and wondered if she could find some way to get it transported here.

At one end of the library Kate found a large, handsome Indian basket full of newspapers. The top issue was this morning's edition of the *Cripple Creek Register*. Beneath it lay a week-old copy of the *New York Times*. Intrigued by the headlines, she caught up both papers and went straight to the nearest sofa. After she opened the Cripple Creek newspaper to the employment section, she scanned the list of women seeking positions as housekeepers and domestics. Wondering if Justin truly meant to do without help for the next two months, she paused when a familiar name caught her eye.

Mrs. William Parslow was seeking a live-in position as a housekeeper. Kate pursed her lips as she read the notice carefully. She remembered Mrs. Parslow well. The middle-aged woman and her husband had been members of the First Episcopal Church. The couple had been both friendly and kind when she and Robert and Elizabeth had joined their congregation. A month ago Kate had been saddened to hear that Mr. William Parslow had died from a sudden seizure. She wondered how Mrs. Parslow was getting on, for the couple had no children and had been devoted to each other. An energetic, cheerful woman of good family, Mrs. Parslow seemed just the sort who would work hard and could fit well into Justin's household. Of course, she might feel the same way as Mrs. Drury had about living under the same roof with a "kept woman."

Sighing, Kate turned back to the front page of the paper. Somehow she doubted Mrs. Parslow could possibly be as malicious as Mrs. Drury had been. If there was any way she could help Mrs. Parslow, she was determined to do it. When Justin was in one of his more approachable moods, she would ask him to consider hiring the widow.

Justin found Kate there in the library around noontime, deeply engrossed in his *New York Times*. He paused in the doorway, struck anew by her remarkable beauty. It was not just the classic perfection of her features that made her so lovely. She possessed a vibrancy and a vitality that made her unique among all the women he had ever known. Then, too, there was a surprisingly passionate side to her that he had only begun to explore. All and all, Miss Holden was a heady package.

He wasn't going to be able to stay away from her much longer. In fact, as he gazed at her, he decided to end his wait tonight. He made a mental note to ask Madame Dupuy to fix something special for dinner this evening. He considered telling Kate about his intentions, but he decided she was probably better off wondering rather than knowing when he meant to have her again.

Suddenly she seemed to sense his presence and looked up from her reading. A spontaneous smile lit her features when she saw him standing by the doorway. That smile, however, quickly faded to a more guarded look. Her smile pleased him. To his surprise, her wariness did not.

After what had happened yesterday, he could hardly blame her. When he had challenged her to kiss him, he had only meant to start a light, pleasant diversion for them both. He had been stunned by how suddenly passion had flamed between them. When he had broken off their embrace, he had been moments away from pulling her to the ground and taking her right there on the mountainside. This kind of gut-wrenching desire was new to him. In the past he had been able to keep his flirtations light and pleasurable. He was not at all comfortable with the notion that this slip of a girl could drive him to such dark, burning need so swiftly.

Realizing she was watching him curiously, he thrust his hands into his trouser pockets and strolled into the room. "Raiding my library, eh?" he asked as he surveyed the pile of books by her feet. "And doing a thorough job of it, from the looks of things."

She glanced at the pile guiltily. "I was going to put most of them back. I . . . I did want to ask your permission to take a few of them up to my room, but you had said that you did not wish me to disturb you in your office."

"I said it before: you are welcome to make yourself at home everywhere in my household, and that includes this library."

"Thank you. You have a fine collection here."

"Unfortunately it is neglected. I have little time to read history these days, and these books were meant to be used. Please feel free to borrow anything you like."

He wandered over to the mantelpiece and leaned one elbow on it as he studied her. It hadn't occurred to him she might be reluctant to approach him when she wanted something. He had always been generous to the other women he had kept, and they had always been straightforward about their demands and wishes. Perhaps Kate was different. But then, he reminded himself bitterly, the fact she had been willing to sell herself in the first place meant she was no different from the rest.

"Is there anything else you need to make yourself comfortable in my home?" He decided to see just how bold and venal she could be when given the opportunity.

"Well, there are two things I've been hoping I could ask you." She hesitated as if she weren't sure how seriously she should take his offer. "I would like to resume my studies, but my classical dictionaries and texts are packed away in a crate in Mrs. O'Connell's attic. Do you suppose Mr. Gallagher would mind stopping by there someday and picking up my books?"

Justin's lips twitched. He had been expecting to be importuned for fine dresses, furs, jewels, or money, and here his little scholar wanted access to her books.

"I'll send him over there as soon as he has a few hours free. What is your second request?"

She looked down at her lap and plucked nervously at the folds of her skirt. He smiled cynically, thinking now she was about to voice a request for something expensive and more material.

"I know this is none of my business, but I was wondering if you had started looking for someone to fill Mrs. Drury's position. I read a notice in the paper that Mrs. William Parslow is looking for work as a housekeeper. We used to attend the same church. I know she comes from a genteel background, but her husband's recent death no doubt left her in straitened circumstances. I am sure she would work hard and keep your household running smoothly if you were to hire her."

His knowing smile disappeared halfway through her request. Could it be Kate was too naive to understand what he had been offering her? "I will keep her name in mind," he told her curtly. "Are you sure there is nothing else you need to make your stay here more comfortable? I'm used to sparing no expense when it comes to making certain my mistresses are content."

"I'm sure you are," she replied in an odd tone. Her cheeks flushed with color, a dead giveaway that he had either embarrassed her or made her angry again. He couldn't remember the last time he had spent time with a woman who could blush.

"No," she continued steadily, "I can't think of a single thing except my books. You have been most accommodating. And now, I hate to keep you from your work." She glanced longingly at the newspaper in her lap. So she was hoping he would leave her. That was a unique sensation in itself. He was used to women vying for his attention and showing their obvious preference for his company. The fact that young Kate clearly did not do either was entertaining. Instead of leaving, he leaned back against the wall beside the fireplace, crossed his arms, and looked at her musingly.

"You know, I like coming around corners in this house and finding you in odd places," he said suddenly. "I would enjoy it even more, however, if you didn't always dress during the daytime like a spinsterish old schoolmarm. That coat you had on yesterday is ready for the rubbish heap.''

She folded the newspaper in her lap with a sharp snap. ''I'm sorry if my dress offends you.''

''Tsk, tsk, there's that temper again. Your dress does not offend me, young woman, but it is hardly pleasing. I believe we had an interesting discussion about your pleasing me just two days ago. I'm curious, don't you have any pretty day dresses, or are you afraid of catching my eye and exciting my interest?''

Color stained her cheeks once more, and he smiled inwardly at the visible effort she was making to control her temper.

''I'm afraid the day dresses I own are in much the same state as my winter coat. The only new dresses I have are the two Pearl De Vere had made up for me. If you wish, I could wear those during the day.''

''Good God, if I saw you wearing one of those remarkable things, I'd never get any work done.''

''Pearl had them made. I never would have chosen them for myself,'' she declared hotly.

''I guessed as much.'' He sighed and reached into his jacket pocket and pulled out a long wallet. He removed a wad of greenbacks and counted out several bills. These he tossed on the sofa next to Kate.

She stared at the pile of money sitting next to her. ''What am I supposed to do with this?'' she asked faintly.

''Go shopping, of course. I won't be needing the carriage this afternoon, and I'm certain Ben would love to parade the grays up and down Bennett Avenue.''

''You wish to pay for my clothing now?''

He simply nodded his head in answer.

Kate felt her blood begin to pound in her ears. The very idea that he would own the clothes on her back was galling. Worse was the more immediate consequences of what he was expecting her to do. Surely he knew prostitutes could be fined and arrested if they were caught on Bennett Avenue. But if he made her explain this to him, she thought she would drop dead from mortification on the spot.

''I'm afraid I won't be able to go shopping this afternoon,'' she got out after several moments.

"I don't understand why not," he said in that cool tone that warned her she had irritated him. "Perhaps you have a more pressing engagement?"

"No, it's hardly that," she told him bitterly. "I already told you there's only one person in this entire town who would possibly receive me."

"Then why won't you go to Bennett Avenue this afternoon? I thought all women loved to shop," he said silkily.

"Actually, I've always thought it a rather tedious pastime." She drew in a deep breath and decided it would be better to get the humiliation over with. "It's simply this. I'm registered with the city as one of Pearl's girls now, and I can't go shopping on Bennett Avenue except on Tuesday mornings."

There, she had said it, and now she wished the floor would open up and swallow her. She was miserably aware that he was studying her again. A part of her felt like dissolving into tears, and a part of her was furious that he had made her admit this. Deciding she would much rather be angry, she continued on in a hard little voice she barely recognized as her own.

"Of course, if upgrading my wardrobe is of such immediate concern to you, I could try going to Bennett Avenue this afternoon anyway. Perhaps I won't be fined or thrown into jail."

"That won't be necessary," he said after a long silence. "I will send for a seamstress to come to the house." And then he left her.

"But Mr. Talbott, your young *cousine* is ravishing! It will be a delight to fit her for her trousseau." The tiny French seamstress whom Madame Dupuy had recommended bustled into Kate's bedroom. It was now four o'clock in the afternoon. Such was the power of Justin Talbott's name in this town that Madame Sophie had offered to come the very day she had been contacted by him.

Kate sent him a quizzical look. Why he had bothered to tell the woman such a fib? He shrugged his shoulders and glanced away. Could it be he had meant to save her the humiliation of explaining her position in his household? Whatever his reasons, she found she was very grateful for the lie as the seamstress and her young female assistant began spreading out samples of material across the bed.

Her feelings of gratitude soon dissolved into disbelief and exasperation. She had hoped Justin would just go away, but instead he remained in the room, lounging in the rocking chair and watching as they took her measurements. When Madame Sophie started showing Kate sketches and discussing specific dresses, he stood and began taking an active role. In fact he soon was doing all the talking with Madame Sophie while Kate simply watched. She quickly learned that Justin knew more about the new trends in women's fashion than she did. He also had very strong feelings about the color and the style of the gowns he wanted the Frenchwoman to make up for his "*cousine.*"

Kate grew appalled when she realized the large number of garments Justin was ordering. From day dresses to evening gowns, from lacy undergarments to fine silk stockings, he wanted Madame Sophie to provide them all. It was no wonder the Frenchwoman thought she was working on a full trousseau, and a generous one at that.

When Madame Sophie crossed to the far side of the room to look at her assistant's notes, Kate quickly beckoned Justin to her side. Afraid the French seamstress might hear her, Kate could only whisper her protest to him.

"Justin, this is absurd. I'm only going to be here for two months. No woman needs seven day dresses, and I can't imagine why I would possibly have any use for more than two or three evening gowns."

"Why, Kate Holden, you do your thrifty Yankee heritage proud," he taunted her in a low voice.

"You may laugh all you want, but it's positively obscene to have all these garments made up for me when I will only wear them a few times."

"It will please me to see you wearing these dresses," he said flatly. "Besides, you can keep the clothing when you leave."

"I don't want to keep any of it when I leave here," she hissed at him.

He raised an eyebrow at her, making it all too clear that he didn't believe her, and then he returned to his seat in the rocker. She closed her eyes and remembered his hateful words at the Old Homestead. He had accused her then of selling her body simply to pay for pretty gowns. She remembered, too, what he had said about her being just like the other shallow, greedy women he had known. She guessed he had meant his own mother, among others. It would be useless to try to change his opinion when it had been so warped and hardened by his own bitter experiences. Instead she held her tongue and promised herself that when it came time to leave his home, she would not take a single piece of the clothing he was ordering today.

At last Madame Sophie and her assistant departed, promising to send two day dresses they had ready-made in their shop to the house on the morrow. Kate let go a deep sigh of relief when Justin escorted the two women downstairs. Closing her bedroom door behind them all, she began to pace about the room. She told herself it was ridiculous to let him keep hurting her feelings, but no matter how hard she tried, she couldn't seem to ignore his barbs and taunts.

Even more important, she was afraid the time when he would want to make love to her again was fast approaching. Telling herself that worrying about it wasn't going to change anything, she sat down on her window seat and tried to read. When she realized that she had just read the same paragraph for the fourth time in a row, resignedly she put her book aside. She had to find out what Justin had in mind for tonight. Knowing would be better than wondering about his intentions. But when Kate marched downstairs, Madame Dupuy informed her that Justin had been called out on urgent business in Victor that would keep him away overnight.

"Between you and me, *enfant*, I do not think he was at all pleased. His eyebrows were like this when he told me." Madame Dupuy did a fine imitation of what Kate had come to think of as Justin's thundercloud look. "I think he would have much preferred to spend the evening here with you, *n'est-ce pas?*"

Kate shared an excellent dinner of stuffed capons with Madame Dupuy. During their meal the Frenchwoman told Kate that their employer had called Mrs. Parslow up to the house and hired her to be the new housekeeper. Kate couldn't help feeling pleased that Justin had trusted her recommendation and acted so swiftly upon it.

Knowing her employer was ten miles away, she slept well that night and rose feeling refreshed the next morning. At nine o'clock Madame Sophie's assistant arrived at the house with two of the new day dresses. Both, Kate was pleased to see, were in excellent taste. One was a lovely gown of green-and-white winter wool trimmed with silk braiding. The other was a charming affair in pale blue china silk finished with blue velvet ribbons.

When she tried them on, each fit perfectly. She continued to wear the blue silk, for she wasn't sure when Justin would be returning, and she did not want to give him an opportunity to take exception to her worn skirts and blouses again. As she walked Madame Sophie's assistant to the door, Kate caught herself touching and smoothing the shimmering fabric of her skirt. After she closed the front door, Kate made a wry face at herself in the hall mirror and went back upstairs. Papa used to give her a dozen new gowns at a time. Now it was a treat simply to wear one new dress. Except, of course, that she couldn't escape the fact that Justin Talbott's money had purchased it.

When she returned to her room she settled in to read more of her history book. Just before noon she grew restless and headed downstairs. She went to the music room and settled herself on the piano bench. She played a lively piece of sheet music, and then performed the "Arabeske," by Schumann.

"That's a lovely piece," a cultured female voice spoke from behind her when Kate had finished. "My mother used to play that when I was a little girl."

Kate turned about on the piano bench to find Mrs. Parslow standing in the doorway. Her first reaction was surprise over the widow's appearance. When she had last seen her the woman had been quite plump. Now her black dress seemed to hang on her thin frame, her beaky nose appeared more prominent, and her hair seemed a great deal grayer. But there was a light in her coffee brown eyes and a determined look about her that made Kate think Mrs. Parslow was hardly giving up on life even though her beloved William had passed away.

As Kate searched for something to say, the enormity of what she had done and what she had become loomed before her.

Mrs. Parslow was a decent woman. She enjoyed all the respect and status in respectable society Kate could no longer claim. Mrs. Parslow had never set foot in a sordid place like the Old Homestead, and yet she had sat in the same pew with Kate at church. Kate found her cheeks were burning, and no matter how she tried, she couldn't think of a single thing to bridge the awkward silence stretching between them.

"I understand you were the one who suggested me for this position, and I wanted to thank you," Mrs. Parslow continued on gamely after a few moments.

"There's no need to thank me." Because she didn't want the woman to go on feeling beholden to her, Kate found her tongue at last. "I knew you would be perfect for the position. I wanted to tell you, too, I was very sorry to hear about Mr. Parslow. He was a fine man, and you both were so kind to Elizabeth, Robert, and myself when we first moved here."

"You've paid back that kindness tenfold. I was just about at my wit's end when the boy came with the message from Mr. Talbott. I was thinking I might have to live with my niece, Sarah, in Chicago. That arrangement wouldn't have suited her husband or me in the least. I much prefer to support myself, and I wanted to stay near my friends here in the district, but it's hard these days to find work in this town. Obtaining a position in a home this elegant with good wages into the bargain is more than I had prayed for."

"I'm glad. I hope you will like it here." Kate found a little of her embarrassment was beginning to ease the longer they talked together.

"I'm sure I will, but I can see there is plenty of work to be done. I can't imagine how that Stella Drury let this lovely house get into such a sorry state."

"I know you will have it set to rights in no time. In fact, I was wondering if you might like a little help. Sometimes time hangs heavy on my hands, and doing some housework could help me work off my fidgets. . . ." Her voice trailed off when she remembered how Mrs. Drury had responded to a similar plea.

"Anytime you feel like picking up a feather duster, you just tell me," Mrs. Parslow said with a firm nod. "I would

welcome an extra hand. And now, I came to tell you that
Louise has our lunch ready.''

Louise, was it already? Kate hid a smile as she stood up
from the piano bench. She had thought the two widows might
have a great deal in common. It was nice to know that Justin's
housekeeper and his cook were going to get along well. It was
even nicer to know Mrs. Parslow wasn't going to stomp
around the place glaring at Mr. Talbott's mistress the way Mrs.
Drury had done.

Kate glanced up from her history book to look at the little
clock on the dresser. It was three-thirty. Surely she deserved
a respite. After donning her oldest blouse and skirt, she tied a
kerchief about her hair. Thus prepared to do household chores,
she went in search of Mrs. Parslow. She found the widow
busily scrubbing the floor in the dining room. Once she was
convinced Kate honestly wanted to do housework, she gave
her a feather duster and told her the front parlor needed dusting. That chore Kate finished all too quickly. Since the floor
and rugs obviously needed a good cleaning as well, she tackled
them next. Humming under her breath, she dragged each of
the three heavy rugs through the kitchen and flung them over
the fence in the backyard.

As she beat the dust out of each one, she decided she was
grateful to Aunt Mildred for teaching her how to keep house.
When they first arrived in Marblehead, Aunt Mildred had been
horrified to learn her nieces were completely ignorant of the
household arts. Under Aunt Mildred's stern tutelage, they both
had learned how to scrub floors, wash clothing, beat rugs, and
polish furniture, along with a host of other domestic chores.
Looking down at the little white scars on her hands, Kate
grimaced. She never had gotten the hang of ironing.

When she finished with the rugs, she dragged each one back
inside and left them neatly rolled up in the music room. She
had moved all of the furniture to one side of the parlor and
was in the midst of scrubbing the floor on her hands and knees
when a deep, accusing voice interrupted her labors.

''Just what do you think you are doing?''

She glanced up from the floor to see Justin standing in the

doorway, his hands on his hips and his thundercloud look very much in evidence.

At first she was dismayed by his expression, but then her sense of humor came to her rescue. It was, after all, rather obvious what she was doing. There was a small sea of soap suds all around her.

"Why, I do believe I'm scrubbing the floor, now that I think about it," she told him cheekily.

"I can see that," he said between gritted teeth. "Perhaps I should have asked, Why are you scrubbing the floor in my front parlor? I told you once before, you are not a servant in my household."

"Indeed you did, but you also told me I was free to do whatever I wished to keep myself entertained, and at this moment I am enjoying washing a floor that very much needs cleaning."

His face was a picture. She had to bite her lip to keep from laughing out loud. It wasn't often that she had a chance to throw him off balance, and she had to relish the moments when it happened.

"Why aren't you wearing one of your new dresses? I understand Madame Sophie's assistant came by this morning. That outfit, while rather fetching in a peasant wench sort of way, is even more ready for the rag bin than that tired old coat you had on the other day." He obviously was looking for a legitimate reason to voice his irritation with her. She was equally determined to make it difficult for him to find one.

Rising to her feet, she tilted her head and placed her hands on her hips in a conscious imitation of his own stance. "Mr. Talbott, if I were wearing one of my new dresses, it would be looking worse than any of my old dresses before this afternoon was over. You may know a great deal about mines and volcanoes and vein formations, but you obviously don't know much about housekeeping."

At first she thought he was going to say something horrible, and then the look on his face changed. Suddenly he burst out laughing. She smiled at the masculine sound. She heard it too rarely, which was a sad thing, she decided all at once. Justin Talbott was so driven and so serious, he rarely stopped to laugh at the simple things in life.

When he had got his breath back, he shook his head and smiled at her. "You certainly are a bold piece this afternoon, Miss Holden."

"I expect it's the physical exercise. Are you sure you wouldn't like to join me? I'm sure Mrs. Parslow has another scrub brush she could loan you." Kate gestured to the wet floor all about her.

"Why, yes, I believe I would, now that I think about it," he said with a devilish smile, and walked straight forward through a small wave of soap suds.

"Justin," she said helplessly as he splashed closer, "your shoes are getting all wet. You're going to ruin them."

"So what if I do? I've got four more pairs just like 'em upstairs. Right now I see a saucy young wench in front of me who deserves a thorough kissing." He stopped right before her and gave the kerchief about her hair a little tug. "In fact," he said as he gazed down at her, "I have a much better idea of what to do with such a comely wench, now that I think about it."

He stepped back, and before she could anticipate what he was up to, he had taken her right hand and tugged her toward him. Moments later she found herself tossed over his right shoulder, just like a sack of grain.

"Justin Talbott, you put me down this instant!"

"If you dress like a wench in my household, you can expect to be treated like one."

"Oh, for heaven's sake, I didn't dress like a wench on purpose. Where are you taking me?"

"Up to my pirate lair, of course," he said as he headed for the front stairs. "What else is a red-blooded man to do with a wench he captures in his front parlor?"

"Have you gone mad? You can't do this. I left dirty water all over the parlor floor. Oh dear, what is Mrs. Parslow going to think of me?" Kate wailed as he started up the steps.

"I don't give a damn about what Mrs. Parslow thinks."

"But don't you understand? I do. I have to see her every day. Please Justin, don't do this to me."

At last the concern in her voice seemed to get through to him. "Very well," he said simply and turned about on the landing. She hoped fervently he was about to put her down, but instead, once he reached the bottom of the stairs he headed back toward the dining room. There they found the widow industriously washing windows.

"Mrs. Parslow," he announced in an extremely polite and proper tone, "I am terribly sorry, but Miss Holden won't be able to finish scrubbing the front parlor. I just wanted you to know that this dereliction of duty is entirely my fault."

To her credit, the widow only blushed a little as she replied, "Very good, sir."

Kate groaned inwardly and covered her face with her hands. She was just as glad when Justin turned around and left the room. She couldn't face Mrs. Parslow right now for the life of her. As Justin carried her swiftly up the front stairs, it finally occurred to Kate. Instead of being consumed with embarrassment, she should probably start worrying about what was going to happen to her when they reached Justin's self-proclaimed pirate's lair.

Chapter Eleven

After Justin entered his bedchamber he kicked the door shut behind him. With little ceremony he deposited Kate on his bed. While she sat up a bit dizzily, he was proceeding to rid himself of his collar and his shoes with disturbing speed and efficiency. Although she was curious about his bedroom, she couldn't spare the time to study it when Justin was shrugging out of his shirt not three feet away from her. She did take in the fact that his bed was a massively long and wide affair he must have had specially built. It was crowned by a beautifully carved walnut headboard in the Renaissance revival style. Then she saw Justin had his shirt off completely, and she forgot all about his bed.

It was the first time she had seen him in the daylight. He was truly magnificent. Again she thought of the classical sculptures she had seen of Greek soldiers and athletes. His shoulders were wide and his arms well muscled. His lean torso tapered down to his narrow waist. Fine dark hair dusted his forearms and chest. And then she met his eyes and forgot all about Greek athletes and started thinking about pirates instead. With his wicked smile and long black hair, he looked just like a Caribbean buccaneer about to plunder and take what he wanted.

With a hard swallow she reminded herself that she was the one about to be plundered. He sat down beside her on the edge of the bed, wearing only his trousers. She looked straight ahead, for she was afraid he would catch her staring at him if she looked his way. As he leaned closer, she found she was having trouble breathing. He was just so big, and so male. He reached out and traced her cheekbone gently back toward her hairline. She blinked when he kissed the side of her chin and pulled her kerchief off at the same time. Recognizing his diversionary tactics, she wondered again where and when he had become so accomplished at lovemaking. His clever fingers started finding the pins in her hair and removing them one by one. "But it's still daytime," was the only thing she could think to say as her hair spilled down about her.

"So it is, my perceptive wench, so it is." He was busy running his hands through her hair, combing out the tangles until it flowed in a smooth golden river over her shoulders and back.

"But we can't—People don't do this; it's only five o'clock in the afternoon," she stuttered in protest.

"Sometimes I wonder if you learned anything down at the Old Homestead." Out of the corner of her eye she could see he had a quizzical gleam in his eye. "For your information, my dear, people throughout history have enjoyed making love at every hour of the day and night. I have been waiting for this moment for over four days, young woman, and I have no intention of waiting any longer."

"Oh," was all she managed to say in response. No logical argument to counteract his first assertion popped into her mind. In fact she had a terrible time thinking any logical thoughts at all when he was sitting so close to her, that devastating half smile of his playing on his beautifully shaped mouth. Certainly he knew more about this topic than she did, historically speaking and otherwise. She concentrated instead on something she had been wanting to tell him for several days now.

"I did want to thank you for waiting." She definitely couldn't look at him when she was coming so close to discussing "The Act" directly. "It was very kind of you to give me more time."

"You may think it was kindness on my part, but I was actually being self-serving and selfish as always. I was waiting to make certain that when I had you in my bed, it would be as remarkable as our first night together at the Old Homestead. And that could only happen if we both were ready."

She peeked at him skeptically through her lashes. If he were truly selfish, he wouldn't have cared in the least about her own pleasure. She started to open her mouth to argue this point when he leaned over suddenly and kissed her soundly.

"I am finished with this discussion," he informed her between soul-drugging kisses.

"What—what discussion were you referring to?" she asked confusedly and heard him give a soft, exultant laugh. He pushed her gently onto her back and came to lie beside her on the bed. She glanced over and saw a vast expanse of wonderful male chest. Blushing furiously, she twisted her head about and stared up at the ceiling.

"No, my golden girl, it's time you started getting over this delightful shyness of yours. I want you to look at me. I want you to start touching me the way I've enjoyed touching you."

He took her hand and placed it over his heart. She soon forgot her bashfulness in her fascination over the different textures she discovered there. His skin was smooth, but the muscles beneath it were firm and hard. The dark hair curling across the center of his chest was soft and springy. When she traced the line of his ribs, she felt his muscles contract beneath her hands. When she trailed her fingertips lower, across his sides and belly, she heard him draw in his breath. Ah, so he had places he was vulnerable just as she did. That knowledge was welcome and heady news.

Never daring to look at his face, she decided to try kissing that very spot where he seemed to be so sensitive. As she leaned across him, her hair spilled over his chest. She pressed just one lingering kiss on his side, and he gave a low groan. Then he was lying on top of her, kissing her face and neck in that all-consuming, fiery way he had. He tugged her old blouse open so roughly that two buttons went flying. And then he was kissing and caressing her breasts through her thin chemise. She moaned aloud as her body came alive with overwhelming sensations.

He paused long enough to pull her into a sitting position. He moved around behind her, until she was between his knees. Her legs dangled off the side of the bed and her back leaned against his warm, bare chest. He skimmed her blouse and her chemise off completely. He proceeded to tease and toy with the rosy tips of her breasts until she could only rest her head against his shoulder and whimper helplessly. Pressing warm kisses on the sides of her neck and shoulders, he undid the fastenings to her skirt and slipped it over her hips. Her petti-coats quickly followed. As he leaned forward and began to trace delicate patterns with his fingers on the insides of her thighs through her cotton drawers, she gradually became aware of a hardness pressing against her lower back. The knowledge that he wanted her sent a wave of desire pulsing from her loins.

Slowly, teasingly, he moved to undo each of the buttons down the center of her drawers. Tension began to build in the pit of her belly as his hands moved lower. She was conscious of his cool, silky hair brushing against her cheek, and the musky male scent of him all around her. The room was alto-gether silent except for the sound of their breathing and the occasional hiss from embers settling in the fire.

After he finished with the last button, he slipped his hand inside her drawers. When he pressed his fingertips gently against her, she gasped. Warmth seemed to flood between her legs. As he started to massage her gently, the warmth spread everywhere. Afraid of the tide of feeling rising so swiftly in-side her, she reached out and clutched his hard legs as if they were lifelines. She was only vaguely aware of the way he tensed beneath her touch.

When his right hand came up to cup her breast again, the tide boiled up too high. Frightened she would be whirled away and drowned in the black sea of desire surging inside her, she cried out his name.

"Sh, just go with it, my golden girl; let it take you," he whispered in her ear, and his fingers gently entered her.

As the floodgates loosed, Kate arched against his hands. From a long way away, it seemed, she could hear her own voice crying out as her tidal wave of pleasure crested.

At last, when the climactic feelings ebbed, she collapsed against him, panting and spent. He held her, whispering sooth-ing words and stroking her hair. Just when she had gotten her breath back, he began to caress her again. The tiny part of her that was still capable of rational thought was amazed by how quickly he brought her right to the edge again.

With quick, practiced movements he drew her drawers off and then his own trousers. He pushed her back on the bed, none too gently this time. As she gazed up at him, she realized the pirate had returned, determined to take his own pleasure now. As he spread her legs wide, his blazing blue gaze scorched her. She thought he would only drive toward his own satisfaction, but as soon as he entered her, he seemed determined that she go with him. He thrust deep and slowly at first, until she gasped and met his movements. They went together, this time, as the tides of desire swept them away to the plunging shores of delight.

They lay together silently as the winter dusk outside deepened. It was the most remarkable sensation, lying beside a man like this, Kate decided, her arms and legs intertwined with his. She felt so safe and protected. How much more wonderful it would be, she thought wistfully, if real sentiment existed between them. When Justin leaned forward and kissed her neck and started to play with a lock of her hair, it was all too easy to imagine he truly cared for her.

At last, when the room had grown quite dark, he sat up. She felt him lean over toward the bedside table. She heard the scratch of a match, and the clink of glass as he removed the chimney on the lamp. When the wick flared and brightened she instinctively raised the sheet and blankets to cover herself.

"Don't," he said quietly and took the covers back down again while she bit her lip and stared at the ceiling. "I've waited four days to see you like this again."

He was silent for a long time. It felt as if every single part of her were blushing beneath his prolonged scrutiny. She thought of Lola and her lush curves and wondered if Justin was sorry his mistress was so scrawny.

"Kate Holden, you are exquisite," he said in a husky voice.

She was startled into meeting his smoky blue gaze directly. "I'm sorry to inform you, sir, that either you are fibbing, or your tastes are quite out of step with current fashions. I'm far too thin to be beautiful."

He looked at her bemusedly, and then he let go a great gust of laughter and buried his face in the pillow beside her. "Oh, Kate, the things you say and the way you say them," he said when he raised his head again.

She couldn't help smiling when he looked at her that way, the fun she saw all too rarely lighting his glorious blue eyes.

His thick black hair was tousled from their lovemaking. One lock fell across his forehead, giving him a much younger and rather rakish look.

"Well, you seem to know so much about female fashion, I thought surely you knew beautiful women are, um, more well-rounded than I am."

He raised himself on one elbow as he looked down at her curiously. "You honestly do not think your body is beautiful, do you?"

Her treacherous face began to heat again. When would she ever learn to discuss these intimate matters with his kind of aplomb?

"People seem to think my face is well enough," she allowed after several moments, "although I cannot see anything remarkable in it. I know for certain I will never look like the ladies in *Harper's Bazaar*. I keep trying to gain weight, but it seems to be a hopeless endeavor. I'm afraid I will always be skinny as a rail."

"Kate, I'll tell you this just once. You are not skinny as a rail. You have just the right amount of curves in just the right places. A man would have to be out of his mind not to want you." As he stared down at her, the laughing light in his eyes changed to that warm look that did the strangest things to her pulse.

"In fact, I think I will just have to show you how lovely you are," he growled in her ear before he began pressing warm kisses down her neck and across her collarbone.

This time the pace he set was deliciously, maddeningly slow. He lavished and caressed her body until she was writhing beneath him. While he murmured soft words of praise, he found places like the backs of her knees and the undersides of her arms where she never dreamed she could be so sensitive. She was desperate for release by the time he entered her, but even that pace he kept deliberately slow at first. Impatient now, she used what she had learned from Pearl to build his need to a state that matched her own. Feverishly her hands roamed his back and shoulders, urging him on and pulling him closer. When she pushed her hips up to meet his thrusts, he groaned and pulled her legs upward until they were wrapped around him. Together they drove faster and faster, forgetting all but the hot, burning pleasure they gave each other.

When she finally peaked, the sensation seemed to go on and on forever. And yet she was very aware of the moment he joined her. A hoarse, wordless cry was torn from him right at the last, and then he flooded her with his warmth. Afterward he collapsed on top of her, his head resting partly on the pillow, partly on her shoulder.

He lay there for several moments, his breath coming in ragged gasps just like her own. Even in the midst of the warm velvet daze that enveloped her, she wondered why she didn't feel crushed or trapped beneath his weight. Somehow it seemed the most natural thing in the world to have him lying right where he was, still joined with her.

All of a sudden, into the quiet, Kate's stomach gave a loud growl. She groaned and tried to hide her face in his shoulder while Justin propped himself up on his elbows. He laughed at her, a bass, rumbling sound coming from deep inside his chest.

"I believe your stomach is trying to tell me it's time I fed you," he said as he withdrew and came to lie beside her. "In fact I'm hungry, too. Stay put, and I will go find some dinner for us both." He pressed a quick kiss on her shoulder and left her.

She spent part of the time he was gone wondering if she should go fetch her dressing gown. She simply couldn't face the notion of eating supper with him stark naked. Yet she somehow doubted he would be pleased if she put on her cleaning clothes again. The rest of the time she couldn't help thinking about what he had just said and done to her. Did he honestly think she was beautiful? Perhaps Justin's tastes were simply out of step with current fashions. It was all very curious. But for the moment there was no question that he thought she was desirable, and that notion gave her a surprising amount of satisfaction.

When he returned she saw with great relief that he had brought both a nightgown from her bedroom and her dressing gown. He himself was clad in a handsome royal blue dressing gown and a pair of dark trousers. As she shyly donned her garments under his warm gaze, he informed her that Madame Dupuy would be bringing their supper upstairs shortly.

Sitting in comfortable leather chairs, they dined on a sump-

tuous meal of veal marsala and glazed carrots in front of the
fire. While they ate, she entertained him with more stories of
the odd characters she had served at the Golden Spike, and he
in turn told her about some of his wild adventures in the mining camps. As they talked and laughed, she decided she had
never seen him so relaxed. She much preferred this charming
Justin to the hard, driven, bitter man she had encountered too
many times already.

When they came to Madame Dupuy's delicious brandy-and-
cream mousse, Justin insisted that Kate eat her portion from
his spoon. At first she thought he was being quite odd. He
drew his own chair close until it was right beside her own. As
he leaned over to feed her, his knee brushed hers and his
breath was warm on her cheek. The mousse he fed her bite
by bite was sweet and creamy. She could feel the brandy in
it warming her insides all the way down to her stomach. When
he brought each spoonful close to her mouth, she found herself
watching the way the dancing flames in the fireplace cast shadows across the rugged planes of his face. In the dim light his
eyes seemed dark and heavy lidded as they watched her.

As he wiped her lips gently with his own napkin and let the
smooth, cool linen touch the base of her throat, it dawned on
her. He was trying to seduce her again. She was surprised and
somehow amused that he would make such an effort with his
mistress. He doesn't even know, she thought ruefully to herself. All he has to do is look at me in that certain way he has,
and my heart begins to race.

She started when she felt him dab something cool on the
right side of her neck. He leaned forward and nibbled at the
cool place. Wondering what he was doing to her now, she
watched this time as he dipped a finger into the dessert. With
a little smile playing on his lips, he reached out and placed
the creamy mousse on her right earlobe.

Her pulse started to beat faster and a strange lassitude stole
over her limbs when he rested his right hand lightly on her
thigh and began nibbling at her earlobe. After the cream was
long gone, he remained, tracing her hairline with his tongue,
kissing her ear, nipping at her neck before he withdrew.

Next he gently pushed the top of her dressing gown aside
and placed a dollop of cream on the white skin above her right

breast. She gasped when he kissed and tasted her there, her
nipples hardening and aching for his touch. But he moved on,
placing mousse on her left collarbone. When he bent close
again, she longed to reach up and run her hands through his
thick, curling hair that brushed and tickled her as he kissed
and tasted, but somehow her arms had no strength, and the
slow throbbing in her loins intensified.

She was lost in a sensual haze by the time he leaned over
and placed a final drop on her lower lip. At first he nibbled
and sucked on that place playfully, but then his mood seemed
to change. His kiss swiftly intensified as he claimed her mouth
with his own. When he thrust his tongue between her lips, she
moaned softly. Sweeping her into his arms he carried her back
to bed. He proceeded to make love to her again with fierce
abandon. They fell sound asleep afterward cradled in each other's arms.

The next morning when Kate awoke Justin was gone, but
his cedar scent still clung to the pillow beside her. She groaned
as she sat up on one elbow and remembered the night before.
She never dreamed there was such a hedonist inside her. The
phrase *sins of the flesh* was coming to take on a whole new
meaning.

She could not, would not see the conjugal act as something
evil itself. She was coming to understand that if these intimacies were shared by two people in love, the entire experience could attain spiritual heights. It was much harder now
that she realized that she and Justin were degrading something
so wonderful. Pushing herself out of bed, she vowed that she
must never forget he was paying for what they shared.

She scrambled into the nightgown and robe Justin had
peeled off so swiftly last night. Then she lingered, taking advantage of the opportunity to study his bedroom. Perhaps she
could learn something more here about the enigmatic man who
was keeping her.

Prowling about, she found few clues of the sort she was
looking for. She liked his bedroom, but she guessed he spent
relatively little time here. A thick Oriental rug that was very
soft beneath her bare feet covered most of the wooden floor.
Dark green velvet drapes hung on brass rods at the windows.

A large mahogany wardrobe took up all of the inside corner of the room. The huge bed with its majestic arching headboard definitely dominated the bedchamber. Although the bed was handsome and elegant, she guessed Justin had had it made as much for its comfort as for its grandness.

She paused when she found the little watercolor of a sunset hanging beside the walnut washstand. The picture's frame was a delicate gilded affair that set off the golden colors in the scene beautifully. Looking more closely, she discovered the initials *MLT* painted in the corner. She found another pretty watercolor hanging beside his wardrobe signed by the same artist. Both paintings were obviously placed where he could see them frequently. She looked at them for a long time, wondering who had painted those delicate watercolors and why Justin seemed to cherish them. At last, with a sigh, she left the room and went to draw her bath.

She had bathed and finished eating breakfast in her room when someone knocked on her door. Kate opened it to find Ben standing out in the hall, a wooden crate balanced on his shoulder.

"I've brought your books, little missee," he declared with a wide smile. After he settled the crate next to her desk, he handed her two letters that Elly O'Connell had given him. One was a note from Elly asking Kate to come visit her soon, and the other was a thick missive from Elizabeth. After thanking Ben enthusiastically for bringing her books over from the boardinghouse, Kate settled down to read Elizabeth's letter.

She was struck at once by its cheerful tone. Elizabeth said she was feeling stronger. She even claimed she was eating and sleeping better, and the doctors were pleased with her improvement. She was also enjoying getting to know the staff and her fellow patients.

When she finished reading the letter, Kate stood and walked over to the nearest window. As she stared out at the brown hills and gray winter sky, she decided Elizabeth's letter couldn't have come at a better time. It helped her focus on the reason why she was here. She could accept and endure whatever happened between her and Justin in these next seven weeks. To know Elizabeth was well again was worth any price.

Feeling much cheerier than she had earlier, Kate decided to tackle the crate Ben had brought her. Soon she had her books unpacked and organized in the bookcase by her desk. She spent most of the day happily studying. Late in the afternoon she bundled herself up in her warmest clothing and went to call on Elly.

It turned out to be a wonderful visit. There were a few awkward moments right at the start, but Elly was so matter-of-fact about Kate's new occupation, they soon were talking together like old times. Elly was fascinated by Kate's description of Justin Talbott's elegant household, and, in turn, Kate enjoyed hearing Elly's gossip about her boarders and the happenings around Cripple Creek.

It was growing dark and snow was starting to come down in thick flakes when she gave Elly a final hug and headed out the door.

"Are you sure you won't wait until Rory can walk you back?" the Irishwoman called after her anxiously.

"Now, Elly, it's just four blocks to Mr. Talbott's house, and I refuse to take your weary husband back out into the cold after he comes home from work. Thank you for the tea, and for the visit."

She sent Elly a cheerful wave in farewell and turned away. She paused by Elly's gate to look around her. The street looked lovely. Even the roughest tents and shacks appeared softer somehow with a white dusting of snow upon them, and the whole world was hushed and silent.

By the time she reached the front door to Justin's home, her coat and hat were covered with a fine layer of snow. She had just stopped on the doorstep to brush the worst of it off with her mittens when Justin flung the door open.

"Where have you been?" he growled as he pulled her inside and shut the door behind her. "Ben and I were about to start looking for you."

She blinked, surprised by the urgency in his tone. "I appreciate your concern, but mounting a search for me was hardly necessary."

"For heaven's sake, it's dark out, and we could have a real blizzard raging before the night's through. Where in the world were you?"

"I'm not sure it's any of your business, but I was over visiting Mrs. O'Connell," she replied coolly.

"You should have come back an hour ago. Are you such a complete greenhorn that you don't know people get lost and freeze to death in snowstorms like this?"

She stripped off her mittens angrily. "No, Mr. Talbott, I am not a complete greenhorn. I'm quite aware of the dangers of a raging snowstorm, but I hardly consider what's going on outside right now a blizzard." Afraid she might say something more, something she might regret, she looked down and started tugging loose the fastenings on her coat.

There was such a long silence then that she paused to glance up at him. She was surprised to see he was staring at her hands. She looked down and saw what the light from the mercilessly bright electrical chandelier revealed. With her hands so red from the cold, the small white scars she had given herself while ironing stood out vividly.

"What on earth happened to your hands?" he asked in an odd tone.

"Why, I used to take in laundry and ironing after Robert's death to help pay our bills," she answered a little uncertainly. Did the scars seem so unsightly to him? "I grew quite handy at the washing part, but I was always a bit clumsy with the irons. If . . . if the scars bother you, I can try to wear gloves more often," she finished stiffly.

"That won't be necessary," he replied in a curt tone. "Come see me in the library when you are out of those wet things. I think it's time we had a talk."

"Very well, sir," she said, hoping to aggravate him. A real gentleman wouldn't have said anything about the scars on her hands. She saw his brows draw together, but he didn't try to stop her when she brushed by him and marched upstairs.

The more she thought about his insensitivity and the peremptory way he had ordered her to come to the library, the more furious she became. She deliberately took her time once she reached her bedroom. She carefully straightened her new green-and-white winter wool dress and even repinned her hair. All the while she couldn't help wondering what her perplexing employer had on his mind. At last, knowing she could not put off going downstairs any longer, she left the refuge of her bedroom.

When she entered the library Justin was standing by the fireplace staring down into the flames. After she cleared her throat to let him know he had company, he turned about to face her. He didn't smile, but his tone was courteous as he gestured toward the sofa before him and said, "Please come sit by the fire. You may still be chilled from your walk."

"Thank you," she replied as she walked forward and settled herself on the sofa. She made no effort to begin the conversation. This talk was his idea. It seemed only fitting that he start it.

He came to sit beside her and took both of her hands in his own. She longed to jerk her hands from his grasp, but she was afraid she would only seem childish. Now that her skin was warm again, the scars were much less obvious, but she couldn't help being aware of every one as he stared down at them.

"Why didn't you write to me after your father died and inform me of your difficult financial situation? I would have gladly helped both you and Elizabeth."

"But I could never have presumed upon you, after such a short acquaintance—"

"I wish to God now that you had," Justin interrupted her, thrusting her hands away and rising to his feet again. "You silly fool, my entire fortune is based on the money your father lent me. I owe everything I have to Thomas Holden and his generosity. I found my first real strike while I was still living off the grubstake he sent me. The least I could have done for him was pay for your schooling."

He began to pace back and forth in front of the fire, gesturing angrily as he spoke. "If you had gone to college, you could have obtained a good teaching position back east. You never would have found yourself stranded in a costly mining town, waiting tables and doing laundry to make ends meet. And if you hadn't grown tired of such dreary labor, I doubt you would have ended up at the Old Homestead."

"So that's what this is all about," she said wonderingly.

He came to an abrupt stop before her. "You may have no regrets about your ruin, my dear, but I find the issue troubles me greatly. Perhaps it's just because of the affection and loyalty I felt for your father. If only you had the sense to come to me after he died.''

If only you had been here when I did come, she thought to herself. She didn't say the words aloud, for she was incensed that he could possibly blame her for not contacting him during the terrible days after her father's death.

''How could I have conceivably known you would want to help us? I had no idea Papa's loan was the foundation for your fortune. Even if I had, I surely would have been too proud to ask you for anything. I hardly knew you.''

''And look where your foolish pride has landed you.''

''Well, what's done is done, Mr. Talbott.'' She was pleased to hear her voice sound so controlled. ''You needn't feel any regrets on my account, and you needn't feel guilty. As you told me once so succinctly, if you hadn't purchased my services that night, some other man would have taken your place. I was probably destined for ruin, so don't let the matter trouble you any further.''

''Can you honestly feel so little remorse over what has happened?'' he ground out.

''You have only paid for the use of my body. What I feel and think is entirely my own business,'' she said as she rose to her feet. ''Now I would like to know if I should be changing for dinner. Are you planning to eat in tonight?''

He stood very still for several moments. She received the strong impression that he was trying hard to hold his own temper in check. At last he said with equal politeness, ''Under the circumstances, I am tempted to eat at a restaurant this evening. However, I've no wish to drag poor Ben or the horses out on a night like this one. I shall have dinner in my office. You may eat wherever you like.'' With that he turned his back on her and faced the fireplace, her dismissal quite evident. Biting her lip to keep from saying anything else, Kate turned and stalked upstairs to her bedroom.

There she paced back and forth for almost an hour. No matter how much she tried not to let it happen, these altercations with Justin always made her furious. She still couldn't believe that he had the gall to blame her for not coming to him for help after Papa died. She wondered what he would have thought of her had she written a letter requesting his financial aid at that time. She guessed he would have been surprised, and his opinion of both her and Elizabeth would have slipped several notches. But he probably would have helped. She knew that about him now, and the implications of that notion troubled her deeply.

At last she had to admit to herself that she was so upset because Justin had been partially right. If she had swallowed her pride and gone to him sooner, she never would have gotten herself into this fix. It hurt, thinking she might have sold her honor and her future so unnecessarily. And yet, looking back at the course of events over the past two years, she finally came to the conclusion that she would have made all the same choices again. As she stared out her windows at the dark, snowy night, that conclusion gave her comfort of a sort.

She ate dinner that night with Mrs. Parslow, Madame Dupuy, and Ben in the kitchen. She slipped upstairs right afterward, feeling very relieved that she hadn't bumped into Justin. She read in her bedroom after dinner, trying not to listen for the sound of her employer's footsteps coming up the stairs. Could he possibly want her to come to his room tonight after the row they just had? Toward the end of their discussion, he had appeared more interested in throttling her than making love to her. Cheered by that recollection, Kate decided she probably would be free of his attentions for this evening at least. She went ahead and readied herself for bed.

Because her own nightgowns were so worn, she had started wearing the most modest of the elaborate creations Pearl had ordered for her. The gown she put on tonight was made of sheer white lawn that felt sinfully smooth against her skin. The matching peignoir was equally sheer and trimmed with cascades of soft Brussels lace.

She was sitting at her dressing table brushing out her hair when Justin flung the door open and stood on the threshold glowering at her.

"Why the hell aren't you in my bed?"

Chapter Twelve

She put the brush down carefully on the dressing table before turning around on the chair to face him. She considered complaining about the way he continually forgot to knock on her door. From the glittering look in his eyes, she guessed her complaint wouldn't make much of an impression right now.

"You did not make it clear earlier whether or not you wanted me to join you this evening." She chose her words with cool precision. "And I certainly did not want to enter your room without your permission."

"In the future, you can expect to sleep in my bedchamber unless I inform you otherwise." He strode into the room and came to stand beside her chair. He was dressed again in the handsome blue satin dressing gown that made his eyes seem the rich color of indigo. His cheeks and jaw were shadowed by a day's growth of beard. Drops of water still clung to the black, curling hair by his temples, as if he had just splashed his face with water.

He must have come up the stairs without her hearing him. She was very aware of the intense way he was studying her. If only she had changed into one of her old, modest nightgowns. What she had on was far too revealing. Then again, her heavy winter coat would have been too revealing when Justin Talbott was standing this close to her.

"Is this another one of Pearl's purchases?" he asked abruptly.

She could only nod in reply as she gazed up at him, for that smoldering look was back in his eyes.

"Her taste in lingerie far surpasses her taste in evening gowns," he murmured as he moved to stand behind her. He picked up a long strand of her hair and wound it between his fingers. In a deceptively casual voice he ordered, "Turn around and face the mirror."

Slowly she did as he asked. As soon as she was facing the mirror once more, she looked into it and saw he was still watching her, his face taut, his eyes hooded. "Give me your hairbrush."

She was annoyed when her hand trembled as she silently picked up the silver brush and placed it in his hands. What on earth did he intend to do to her now? Not for the first time she found herself wishing Pearl had been able to teach her more about the intimate love games men and women played with each other. Once again the helpless feeling stole over her that she was playing one of those dangerous games with Justin now. And it was a contest in which he made up the rules and altered them at his whim.

Yet his game began in a most pleasant and unthreatening way. He took the brush and began to stroke her hair. He started at the top of her head and brought the brush downward in slow, gentle movements. She fought the urge to close her eyes and give herself up to the relaxing feeling, the soft bristles of the brush massaging her scalp. It had been years since Elizabeth had last brushed her hair for her. And yet there was a world of difference between having her hair brushed by Elizabeth and having Justin perform the same service. This fact was brought home most clearly when he stepped closer to her, and she could feel his warm, hard thigh pressing against her side.

He is seducing me again, she thought to herself bemusedly. How can a man seduce a woman just by brushing her hair? Already her blood was racing and that queer warmth was beginning to grow in the pit of her stomach. As he leaned forward to brush a golden stream of her hair that had flowed forward over her shoulder and down into her lap, she was aware of his warm breath on her cheek. His tangy cedar scent mixed with the lilac fragrance of her perfume in a most unlikely but heady combination. When he reached across her and brought the brush down her front, his arm grazed her right breast. She bit her lip as she hardened, aching for more of his touch.

He stroked the brush downward again, and this time its

bristles lightly touched the tip of her left breast. She closed her eyes, knowing he was watching her all the time in the mirror. She heard the whisper of cloth as his arm moved again. This time when the brush came down, it caressed her breast again and gently trailed across her lap and upper thigh. Stunned by the flood of intense feeling this light touch produced, she opened her eyes again. His burning gaze captured hers in the mirror. It was no use. There was no way she could hide the desire he had aroused in her so easily.

Wordlessly he placed the silver brush on the table before her. He urged her to her feet with his hands on her arms. After sliding the peignoir off her shoulders, he picked her up and carried her to the bed. Moments after he had deposited her there, he was stripping out of his own clothing. The strength of her own passion made her bold, and so she watched as he turned toward her, the last of his clothing falling to the floor. She blushed when she realized he was fully aroused already. Could brushing her hair have been an equally seductive experience for him, or was it her wearing the nightgown shrewd Pearl had chosen?

Kate forgot all about these puzzling questions when he came to lie beside her and promptly hiked her nightgown up about her hips. It was then that she saw he was breathing hard, and the tension in his body matched her own. He threw one leg across her as he began to kiss her face and neck and suckle at her breasts through the thin fabric of her nightgown. A wordless sound of male satisfaction escaped him when his hand trailed lower and found she was more than ready for him.

He took her with a speed and frenzy that made her forget any of the times he had made love to her before. There was only this instant, only this fiery, delirious present in which their bodies strained together, building and driving toward release. The climax they finally reached was cataclysmic for both of them. Afterward they lay joined for a long time while their pounding pulses and their ragged breathing slowed. Finally he withdrew and came to lie beside her. It seemed the most natural thing in the world when they pulled the covers up over themselves, he curled himself around her, and once again they fell asleep in each other's arms.

*   *   *

The next morning when Kate awoke she was hardly surprised to find that Justin was gone. Madame Dupuy told her he often ate breakfast at six o'clock in the morning and was at work in his office by seven. After Kate slipped on her nightgown and robe, she peeked out through the frosty windows and saw it was going to be another cold, snowy day. She frowned as she went to draw her bath. She wanted to go for a long walk this afternoon, but Justin had made such a fuss yesterday, she didn't particularly feel like riling him again. At least not so soon, she told herself with a small smile.

She studied most of the morning again. After lunch she donned her housecleaning clothes, but this time she purposely did not tie her kerchief over her hair. She wasn't about to give Justin Talbott any ideas about calling her a wench or carrying her off again.

She found Mrs. Parslow working at the desk in a little alcove off the kitchen. The widow was frowning at the haphazard household accounts her predecessor had left. When Kate asked to be assigned a chore, Mrs. Parslow looked up from the pile of papers before her with a weary smile.

"I've been meaning to give Mr. Talbott's office a thorough cleaning. Lord knows the place needs it. I'd be grateful indeed if you could start in there."

"Are you sure he won't mind? He was quite adamant about my not disturbing him when he was working."

"I'm quite sure Mr. Talbott won't mind because he's out for the afternoon," Mrs. Parslow reassured her. "Besides, it would be a good thing if you did disturb him back there once in a while. Mr. Talbott works even harder than my dear William used to. I was forever having to remind that man that even our good Lord rested on the seventh day, but I doubt Mr. Talbott would appreciate my telling him so."

Kate was still smiling over that comment when she went to Justin's office, armed with a feather duster and a broom. She pulled one of the large double doors open and stopped short on the threshold. There were piles of papers and folders and books everywhere! She could hardly see the floor or furniture in Justin's office. The large room before her looked as if a cyclone had hit it.

Could this be the way he always kept his working space? Gradually she came to the conclusion that the chaos in this room was indeed no accident. There was too much dust accumulated on the pile of papers nearest her feet. Whoever would have thought the precise, driven Mr. Talbott could be so disorganized?

She made a conscious effort to see beyond the clutter to the room itself. The office was a large, airy space lined with tall windows along the three outer walls. Each window was trimmed with elegantly carved walnut molding that matched the great double doors beside her. An enormous fireplace crowned with an elaborate walnut mantel took up much of the far wall. Above it hung a splendid oil painting of a mountain range. From the painting's intense colors and dramatic lighting, she guessed it might be by the famous artist Albert Bierstadt. She spotted two wing-back chairs covered with piles of papers, and a sofa buried under a similar load that faced the fireplace. The left wall, beneath the windows, was lined with a long row of oak file cabinets. A huge rolltop desk relatively free from clutter sat beneath the windows on the right side of the room and faced the fireplace as well.

How could she possibly clean this? she wondered dazedly. She was still standing in the doorway, trying to decide if she could just shift stacks of papers around and sweep a few feet of floor at a time, when Justin opened the outside door in the far corner of the room. He came in and was just shaking the snow off his top hat when he noticed her standing in the doorway.

"Why, good afternoon, Miss Holden," he said with a dry smile as he hung the hat on the brass coat rack beside him, "and welcome to my office."

"How in the world am I supposed to clean this?" she burst out as she gestured toward the sea of papers flooding the room.

"You aren't supposed to clean it," he replied sharply as he shrugged out of his overcoat. "I've told you before, I don't want you to be doing servant's labor while you are under my roof."

"I enjoy doing some housework from time to time. On a snowy day like today I'd go mad if I didn't do something active. And clearly this room needs cleaning." She saw his dark brows draw together, but before he could voice a protest, she said hastily, "Please, before you decide to be stubborn about this, just think for a moment. How is poor Mrs. Parslow ever supposed to clean in here when she can hardly walk across the room without stepping on papers?"

"Is it that bad?" He looked around him as if he were seeing the room for the first time.

She bit back a disbelieving laugh. "It looks like it's been blizzarding paper indoors for weeks. How do you ever find things?"

"I have my systems," he said, rubbing one of his sideburns.

"Have you ever tried hiring a clerk to help you?"

"Yes, I have, Miss Holden, on numerous occasions and, for your information, I always end up firing 'em. They hover and fuss and talk when I'm not in the mood for it. I'm a man who likes to work alone, and that's that."

"I see. Well, would you consider letting me do some filing for you on a temporary basis?"

He opened his mouth, and she held up her hand to forestall whatever scathing comment he was about to make. "Before you object to my proposal out of hand, you should know I used to help keep Papa's office from looking like this. Left to his own devices, that dear man would have buried himself under snowdrifts of paper. I promise not to hover or fuss, and the moment I do you can order me out of here. There's no avoiding the fact that neither Mrs. Parslow nor I can clean this place in its current state."

"Why, Kate Holden, what a bossy little baggage you are turning out to be." He seemed to be amused rather than irritated by her bluntness. "The problem is, if I let you organize all this to your heart's content, I'll never be able to find anything again."

"Not if we devise a sensible system right at the start. If you could write out a set of logical categories you want the papers filed under, I will put them where you can find them again."

"Very well, we can give your little experiment a try, but I warn you, I have a great deal to get done this afternoon. If I find you're bothering me I'll push you out the door so fast your lovely head will spin."

"Fair enough. Now if you could make up that list for me, we can both get to work."

His black brows rose at her brisk tone, and she thought he was going to make fun of her again, but instead he settled himself behind his desk and promptly wrote out a long list of file names for her. Those would cover most of his more recent business interests, he explained. She could find files for the rest over there, he said with a vague gesture toward the tall wooden cabinets lining the West side of the room. As soon as he gave her the list, he pulled a stack of papers toward him and started reading.

She shook her head at him in exasperation. It would have been nice if he could have bothered to tell her where to find a pen and ink for her own use, not to mention some new files. Determined not to bother or fuss, she decided to go foraging for herself. Fortunately, after some prowling about, she discovered a smaller desk in a corner under a small mountain of papers. She guessed one of his unfortunate former secretaries must have used it once, for it was well supplied with pens and ink and fine stationery. Some more quiet excavating turned up several boxes of empty files. Properly equipped at last, she set to work.

And fascinating work it was. Time and time again she caught herself reading intriguing documents in their entirety rather than just skimming them to learn their subject matter. She was amazed by the breadth and range of Justin's investments. She discovered her employer owned ranches and banks throughout the West. He had even purchased a restaurant called the Wagon Wheel in Deadwood, South Dakota, and he seemed to have won a hotel in Nevada in a poker game.

She was highly amused by the scrawled grubstake agreements she found on scraps of paper tucked away in the oddest places. Justin had given money to over thirty prospectors just in the course of this last year. Kate guessed he had given these funds away more out of kindness than any real expectation that he would eventually share in the prospectors' finds. When Justin wanted to find gold, he was quite capable of locating it himself.

The majority of the papers she filed, however, concerned mines. The paperwork each one generated was appalling. Most of the stacks of papers piled about his office consisted of hundreds of assay reports. As she sorted through these reports, she came to realize that each tunnel in a mine was sampled carefully on a regular basis. The reports seemed to determine which direction the mine managers told the miners to drill and blast.

Time after time she almost blurted out questions to Justin about intriguing terms she didn't recognize, but she always managed to restrain herself. She guessed he had meant his threat earlier, and she didn't want to give him any excuse to shove her out the door. She was, however, storing up a wealth of questions to ask him sometime soon.

Justin looked up from the last report on his desk three hours later to find his erstwhile secretary sitting on the rug before the fire, a pile of assay reports in her lap. After a quick scan of the room he had to admit that she had made good progress in the past few hours. He could actually see the floor and the furniture in one quarter of his office now. True to her promise, she hadn't bothered him once. He had never thought he could get any work done while she bustled about and plagued him with questions, but she had been as quiet as a mouse.

He smiled as he went back to watching her. Her delicate brows were drawn together in fierce concentration while she read through a summary analysis written by one of his mine superintendents. He tried clearing his throat a few times to draw her attention, but she never once looked up.

"I thought you were supposed to be filing those papers, not reading them," he said when it became obvious a less subtle approach wasn't going to work.

She started at the sound of his voice. She flashed him a guilty look and quickly put the pile of reports away from her. "I'm sorry, I didn't mean to pry into your affairs. It's just that I find these so fascinating."

He looked at her in amused disbelief. "I'm sure most women your age would find summaries of assay reports fascinating."

She pushed a lock of hair back from her face and ignored his sarcasm. "It's like reading a new language about a different world. I begin to see why you like geology so much. It's frustrating, though, because there are lots of terms I don't understand. What on earth is a 'winze'? It's a wonderful word. It sounds like a bizarre species of animal, but it's obviously a mine tunnel of some sort."

He leaned back in his desk chair. "Indeed, a winze is a passage miners drill downward, either following a vein or to connect two different levels of a mine together."

"I guessed that a raise must be just the opposite, but what then is a stope? It sounds like your mines are full of them."

Smiling at her serious air, he proceeded to give her a thorough explanation of stoping, which led him into a more general explanation of hard-rock mining techniques. She listened with her head propped on her hands, her green eyes alight with interest. When he finished she peppered him with more questions. Answering each one in turn, he was impressed by how much she had figured out on her own. He wondered when he had ever known a female with such a restless, inquiring intellect. Perhaps it was due in part to the unconventional way her father had raised her. Yet he doubted her sister Elizabeth possessed such a curious mind. Once again he told himself it was a terrible shame Kate had never gone to college. He was beginning to think she could have become the professor she had once longed to be.

Suddenly, in the midst of asking him a question about the chemical processes involved in assaying rock samples, she seemed to remember herself. "I should let you go back to work now. I'm sorry, I said I wouldn't distract you, and now it seems I've done exactly that."

"You have indeed. I haven't a shred of concentration left, and it's all your fault. Why don't you come over here and see if you can help me find it again."

She looked at him in that skeptical way she had, cocking her head a little to the side, her green eyes wide and wary. "Somehow I doubt that's what you have in mind."

"Ah, you are coming to know me so well. Let me phrase my request differently. *Sit pro ratione voluntas*—let my will serve as reason. It would please me, young Kate, if you came over here." That earned him a speaking glance. But she stood up and came to stand beside him, a rebellious look on her face.

He reached out and pulled her into his lap. Before she could protest, he captured her lips and kissed her long and hard. He felt her initial resistance in the stiffness of her body, and in her refusal to open her lips. Intrigued by the challenge she posed, he quickly set about demolishing her resistance. He curled one hand about the nape of her neck, the other massaging her slim waist. He pressed kisses to the side of her throat and the base of her ear. He slipped his right hand from her waist to cup her breast through her shirtfront. He smiled inwardly when he felt her tremble in reaction. He knew the moment she gave in, for she tipped her head back and wrapped her arms about his neck. The surge of satisfaction he felt soon gave way to a jolt of pure desire when she tugged his head down to her own and kissed his lips with the innocent enthusiasm that he found so arousing.

When he caught a whiff of the lilac scent she wore, sweet, sensual memories from the night before came rushing back to taunt him. As she returned his kiss wholeheartedly, he pulled her skirt and petticoats up to caress her soft calves and thighs through the thin material of her drawers. Lost in the delicious taste of her, he let his hand range higher. The warmth and dampness he discovered there proved to be his undoing. He had meant simply to steal a few kisses, but the pleasant, light interlude he intended was flaring too swiftly into something much more urgent.

Groaning aloud, he stood up from the chair and placed her on the desk before him. Ignoring the growing dismay and surprise he saw in her green eyes, he dipped his head and captured her lips with his own. At the same time he reached down and pulled her skirts and petticoats up until they frothed about her waist and spilled across the desk. He spread her legs wide and came to stand between them, kissing her so fiercely she had no chance or breath to voice a protest. When he pulled her full against him so that he could feel her warmth against his loins, she moaned helplessly and clung to his shoulders.

As he began to move against her, he fumbled at the buttons on her blouse. A part of him was aghast at his fervent clumsiness. Usually he prided himself on his finesse and skill at lovemaking. This slip of a girl drove him beyond control, beyond calculated, practiced seduction to a dark, burning place where all he knew and felt was his need to possess her. The last few buttons gave way, and he pushed the garment off her shoulders hastily. His body tightened even further when he saw the dusky areola of her breasts through the sheer fabric of her chemise.

Unwilling to deal with another set of buttons, yet greedy and eager to taste her, he simply tugged her chemise up over her breasts and bent his head to kiss and fondle where he willed. He was vaguely aware that her hands were clasped about the back of his neck, urging him on now. When he drew back and saw her lovely white breasts, their rosy peaks puckered and tight from his attentions, he knew he couldn't wait to take her upstairs. Swiftly he freed himself from his trousers. When he couldn't find the fastenings to her drawers quickly enough, he yanked the garment open, ignoring the sound of tearing fabric. He buried himself inside her, pulling her close with his hands on her hips.

As he thrust faster and deeper, she learned quickly to match his movements in this new position. Although it was hard for him to wait, he forced himself to hold on until she was poised on the edge. He felt the moment she began to crest, for her hands tightened on his shoulders, and a shuddering sob escaped her. He drove deeply one last time and let the pulsations of her body send him over the top, riding wave upon wave of intense, voluptuous pleasure.

When it was over she slumped against him, her face hidden against his collarbone. Gently he straightened her clothing and rebuttoned her blouse, for she seemed too dazed at first to be able to do anything for herself. When they both were presentable again he kissed the top of her head and swept her into his arms. This last action finally precipitated a rise out of her about the time they were passing through his office doors.

"Why do you keep carrying me places?" she asked in a muffled voice because her face was still partially hidden in his shoulder. "It's most undignified. Whatever will Mrs. Parslow think if she sees us again?"

"Our sturdy widow would probably think I was being romantic and dashing. I overheard her say something of the sort just the other day to Madame Dupuy. To answer your first question, I seem to like toting you around." He grinned down at her as they started up the stairs. "In fact it pleases me to carry you, so I'm afraid there's nothing more to be said on the subject."

"Only this," she retorted after a few moments, raising her head to look him squarely in the eye, "you are the most peculiar gentleman I have ever met."

He was in too good a mood to take offense at what he knew she had meant to be a crushing set-down. Her comment was both amusing and quite possibly true. When he started down the hall toward his bedroom, she asked quietly if she might take a bath first. Because that seemed like a reasonable request, he deposited her in front of the bathroom door. Briefly he considered the notion of joining her, but he decided he had shocked young Kate enough for one day.

Before he left her he told her to join him in his bedroom in an hour, wearing her hair down and the tantalizing nightgown he had found her in the night before. Whistling to himself, he went back downstairs to make certain their meal was delivered promptly at seven. He had enjoyed their picnic before the fire so much two evenings ago, he wanted to repeat the experience if he could.

Both Kate and their meal arrived at the same moment. Kate looked fresh and well scrubbed and delectable in the fetching lingerie Pearl had ordered for her. As Mrs. Parslow laid the meal out for them on the table before the fire, Kate's cheeks bloomed bright pink. He guessed she was embarrassed to be seen with him while she was in such deshabille. After the housekeeper left them to their privacy, Kate's blush eventually faded. Unlike the other evening, however, she made little effort to contribute to the conversation while they ate. She listened to his stories politely enough, but the spontaneous gaiety and charm she had brought to their supper two nights ago was missing. Much of the time she stared into the fire, a pensive, troubled look on her lovely face.

"You are a quiet miss this evening." He voiced this observation while she was toying with the exquisite cherries jubilee Madame Dupuy had concocted.

She glanced up at once, that wary look he disliked very evident in her gaze. "I'm sorry, I'm afraid I haven't been good company this evening. I shall try to be more entertaining."

"Indeed, you should. In France the greatest of the demi-mondaines used to discuss philosophy and politics with their gentleman patrons. Perhaps we should talk about Rousseau, John Locke, and the Enlightenment."

She smiled briefly at his jest before the serious look in her green eyes returned. She seemed to make her mind up about something. She sat up straighter in her chair and turned to face him more directly.

"Justin, may I ask you a question? I'm afraid it may make you angry, but there is something I would like very much to understand."

"Ask away, and I promise I shall do my best to keep my ferocious temper in check."

She looked down at her hands and blushed rosily even before she began speaking. "It has to do with intimate relations between men and women, and more particularly, between us. I'm still new to all this, and there are things I simply do not understand." She paused and gripped her knees. "Oh, dear, I can't think of any other way to ask this, except to be direct. Today in your office, were you trying to punish me? I know you are still angry with me for . . . for choosing to work at the Old Homestead. Were you thinking of that this afternoon?"

He stared at her blankly. It never had occurred to him that she might interpret his actions in such a way. Part of him was still furious with her, but when he made love to her today in his office, punishing her had been the farthest thing from his mind.

"Kate," he said after several moments, "I'm glad you asked me this. I forget what an innocent you still are in many ways. I'm only angry at myself for not anticipating this misunderstanding."

He ran a hand through his hair and sighed as he chose his words carefully. "I didn't mean for this afternoon to degrade either of us. In fact I never meant to have things go so far in the first place. It's a testimony to the dramatic effect you have on me, little scholar, that I couldn't wait to take you upstairs. Since you asked, there is something I would like you to think about. In our society people today, and upper-class women in particular, have been taught to view sex as something disgusting and intolerable. I think this is both an absurd and unhealthy way to view a pleasurable act that is as natural as life itself.

"As I told you before, people have been making love at all sorts of times in all sorts of places besides the perfect sanctity of their bedrooms for thousands of years. Our society has things badly mixed and twisted. Just think of what the Greeks and Romans wrote about this subject. Their joyous and uninhibited views on lovemaking were much more wholesome than our own."

"So," she said slowly, meeting his gaze for the first time, "if you did marry, and you felt so inclined, you would enjoy conjugal relations with your wife anyplace in your home that so inspired you?"

His lips twitched at her quaint phrasing, but he managed not to smile outright. "I believe I would, at that," he admitted, even while a part of him wondered wildly if he could possibly find a proper woman who would consent to making love in the places he had already taken Kate. Because he felt he had made progress in changing the warped view of sex that had been instilled in her, he decided not to spoil his efforts by telling her the whole truth.

"Does this make the matter more clear to you, my girl?"

"Indeed, it does. Thank you for taking the time to explain it to me," she said seriously.

"Good, because I am no longer in the mood to converse with you."

"Not even about the Enlightenment and the natural rights of man?" she asked as she tilted her head a little to the side, the teasing light back in her green eyes.

"There's only one natural rite I'm interested in at the present moment." He smiled at his own double entendre and rose to his feet. She followed his example, but she hesitated before the fire, shooting him another curious look between those dark lashes of hers.

"I can see a second question brewing in that active mind of yours, my golden girl." He sighed aloud. "Spit it out and be done with it, so that I can get on with some of those rites I had in mind."

She crossed her arms and looked him up and down as if he were some sort of scientific oddity. "It's only this. Are all men as enthusiastic about exercising, um, this particular natural right as you seem to be?''

He couldn't hold in his laughter this time. Luckily she didn't seem offended by his outburst. She simply stood there looking grave and patient. ''I doubt the married sort are,'' he managed to explain at last. ''It's only the occasional bachelor like myself, blessed by the company of such a uniquely beautiful mistress, who can be encouraged and bestirred to such appetites. And that was meant to be a compliment,'' he growled as an afterthought.

''I shall take it as a compliment, sir, although I still have my doubts about your taste and judgment in these matters.''

''Then I shall simply have to show you again how completely and totally desirable I find you, young Kate.'' He caught her hand and drew her toward the bed. There he proceeded to show her exactly how he felt with considerable energy, enthusiasm, and thoroughness.

Chapter Thirteen

Kate arrived on the threshold of Justin's office the next afternoon wearing a simple, businesslike shirtwaist and skirt, and a rather apprehensive expression. After he greeted her with a smile and urged her to come into his office, she stayed right where she was on the doorstep.

"I've come to continue with your filing," she said simply, "and that is all I'm here to do."

There was no mistaking what she was referring to. Justin sighed as he pushed his chair back from his desk. "I thought we cleared this matter up during our little talk last night," he said as he frowned at her.

The frown didn't seem to daunt her at all. "We did, but I still want to make it clear to you that I am here to do your filing, not . . . not to repeat that other." This time she started to blush, but she held his gaze just the same.

He considered reminding her about the main purpose of her stay under his roof, but he decided to be charitable and not state the matter so baldly.

"You didn't seem to mind it too much at the time," he said mildly instead. That comment seemed to make her just as angry, for her green eyes began to flash, and she looked ready to stamp her foot at him. "That's not the issue here. I should like to do a good job on your filing, and I can't do that if I think you may be about to pounce on me at any moment."

"I don't believe I pounced on you yesterday." He leaned back in his chair and clasped his hands behind his head, beginning to enjoy himself now. "I may have grabbed you a bit, right there at the start, but I don't think any objective observer of the incident would have termed how I handled you a 'pounce.'"

"Thank heavens there wasn't anyone here to see us, and you know very well what I mean. Now, Justin Talbott, you stop your teasing, and promise me you will leave me alone."

"I suppose I do know, at that." He unclasped his hands and leaned forward in his chair. "Very well, I can't promise not to touch you, but I will promise not to let matters get out of hand the way they did yesterday. Since that is the best bargain you will be able to strike with me today, young woman, I advise you to settle for it."

With that he drew a large pile of papers toward him and pretended to start reading. He was very aware, however, of the way she was watching him suspiciously from the doorway. At last she straightened her shoulders and marched forward into the room. His golden girl had gumption, he had to grant her that. Smiling to himself, he turned his attention to the papers in front of him.

Once again he doubted he would get much work done with her bustling about his office, particularly with such delicious memories of what had happened on this very desk to distract him. Once again, however, he was agreeably surprised. She set about her work so quietly and unobtrusively, he soon forgot she was in the room. As the cold snow swirled down outside, the fireplace and the woodstove near his desk kept the office cozy and warm. It was growing dark outside when he at last looked up from his desk and found her perched on a stool across the office, busily filing a stack of papers she had placed on the top of one of the oak cabinets.

Her back was partially turned toward him. When she leaned over to slip a file into the back of the open drawer, she afforded him a tantalizing glimpse of a trim ankle and her charming backside. He grimaced at his body's predictable reaction and wondered wryly just when she would stop having this effect on him. He assumed having her as often as he wished would soon ease his need for her as it had the other beautiful women to whom he had been attracted. He sternly ignored the little voice in the back of his mind arguing that so far every time he had made love to young Kate had only made him want her more.

So she didn't want him pouncing on her, eh? Pushing his chair back, he decided the opportunity was simply too good to resist. Silently he stole across the room until he was standing directly behind her. He let go an Indian war whoop at the same time he grabbed her waist and swung her high off the ladder. She gave a little shriek, and the papers and file she had been holding went flying.

"Now that," he informed her with a smug smile, "was a true pounce."

"Justin Talbott, you are a low-down, mean, lying polecat! You almost scared me to death. Put me down this instant."

He tilted his head back and gave a shout of laughter. Although he did put her down, he kept his arms securely wrapped around her shoulders. "Kate Holden, wherever did you learn such language?"

"Well, we did hear some colorful phrases at the Golden Spike from time to time," she allowed with a small smile, "but I know you've heard plenty worse. Now, Mr. Talbott, you know you promised me you wouldn't pounce."

"Miss Holden, I only promised not to let matters get out of hand."

"But . . ."

Before she could say any more, he leaned down and kissed her soundly. Once again she resisted him until he brought her body full against his own. When she finally gave in, it was with a little sigh. Then she opened her lips and gave him full access to her sweetness.

Groaning inwardly, he raised his head and ignored the sharp pull of desire he felt in his loins. "Now, just to show you that I can keep my word when I've a mind to, I'm going to let you go." Even though it was the last thing in the world he wanted to do right now, he told himself silently.

She just stood there in the circle of his arms, looking up at him out of dreamy green eyes.

"Kate, if you don't get out of here in three seconds, you are going to see a repeat of yesterday afternoon." That threat got through to her. Her eyes widened, and she was scurrying toward the entry to the office before the three seconds he had counted had passed.

"Wait just a moment, Miss Holden," he called out before she vanished through the doors. She hesitated there on the threshold, looking like a young doe poised for flight.

"I wanted to say two things to you, and then you can make good your escape. First of all, I wanted to thank you for your efforts in here today. You are making real progress. Second, we'll be having dinner in the dining room this evening at seven, and I'd like you to wear the green bengaline gown Madame Sophie just sent over." That last order earned him an irritated glance, just as he had known it would, and then she slipped away. Smiling to himself, Justin strolled to the library to read a newspaper before going upstairs to change.

Dinner that night was an entertaining affair. When he first saw Kate coming down the stairs, he wondered how he would manage to keep his hands off her until the meal was over. Far more tastefully fashioned than the loud green dress Pearl had provided, Madame Sophie's smashing gown brought out the remarkable jade color of Kate's eyes, and its flowing lines emphasized her willowy figure. He caught tantalizing glimpses of her white skin through the clusters of lace on her shoulders. Because Madame Sophie's dress left more to the imagination, he found it much more alluring.

He was soon distracted from his body's needs, however, by the new set of questions Kate had for him about mining affairs. She started baraging him with her queries over hors d'oeuvres and kept him talking all throughout dinner. From the time her brother-in-law had spent in the mines, she was very aware of the three great issues the miners cared about: hours, wages, and safety. She was determined to know just where he stood on these issues.

"To be competitive with my fellow mine owners, Miss Holden, I cannot deviate too greatly from the standard industry hours and wages."

"Surely you realize that your men will be much more productive if their morale is high and if they aren't exhausted from overwork."

"I do pay my miners better and allow them longer breaks than most owners in the district. I also insist that my mine managers adhere to a system of rigorous safety regulations and inspections. My mines are operated with tighter safeguards than almost any others in the West," he admitted proudly.

From the topic of labor relations Kate then moved on to

more technical aspects of mining. He had to grant that her powers of concentration were extraordinary. For once he found a way to make them work in his favor. He got her so busy trying to understand the intricacies of mining and claim law, she hardly noticed when he drew her from her chair in the dining room and walked her upstairs with him. Once he closed the door to his bedroom behind her, however, he cut her next question off with a firm kiss and carried her to bed. There he put her powers of concentration to a different and much more pleasant use.

The next three days and nights passed in much the same agreeable manner. The cold, snowy weather continued, but it was always warm and snug in his office with the fire crackling away on the hearth and frost forming on the windowpanes. Justin found he looked forward to the moment when Kate would arrive on his doorstep in the afternoons, ready to continue with her secretarial chores. To his surprise he didn't grow restless the way he often did when winter storms kept him cooped up in Cripple Creek. He didn't even mind the fact that he had to postpone an important trip to Leadville because the passes were closed to rail travel. For the moment he found himself thoroughly entertained by his new mistress. With uncharacteristic self-indulgence he decided to revel in her company, for he was certain the novelty and appeal of spending time with her were going to wear off shortly.

By the time the weather cleared and the sun peeked out of the clouds for the first time in five days, Cripple Creek had been buried under three feet of snow. But the drifts of paper in Justin's office were gone, due to Kate's industry, and the place was sparkling clean. As he strolled into his office the morning the weather cleared, it occurred to him that he did like being able to see his furniture and his rug for a change. Kate had worked hard, and her labors in his office had been well beyond the scope of what he had originally hired her to do. After settling himself at his desk, he decided that he owed her a treat of some sort.

He rose to his feet again and began pacing up and down the length of the office, something he could do now without fear of tripping over piles of paper, thanks to Kate. He could give her a pretty trinket, but he already knew enough about her to guess a piece of jewelry might not please her as much as a less expensive gift.

As he walked past the northern windows, he spotted some boys gleefully sledding down a hill across the street from his home. While he paused for several moments to watch their fun, an idea of what he could give Kate took shape in his mind. From the sounds of things, she hadn't had much time to play these past two years, and the expedition he had in mind would allow her to do just that. It would also solve his second concern quite nicely. Now that she was through tidying up his office, he was very aware of the fact that Kate would have no reason to seek him out. And for today, at least, he wasn't ready to give up spending his afternoons with her. Smiling to himself, Justin ignored the stack of reports on his desk and went off to find Ben and Madame Dupuy.

When he entered Kate's bedroom just before noon, Justin was surprised to find her at her desk, books and papers spread out all about her. So this was how she spent her mornings. For once she didn't take him to task for not knocking first. Instead she sent him a distracted look and asked him immediately, "You wouldn't happen to remember what the fourth principle part of *iacio* is, would you?"

"I believe it is *iactus*, if my memory serves me well."

"Of course, that's right. Thank you very much." She sent him a vague smile and hastily scribbled something on the paper before her. He stood in the doorway for several moments, simply enjoying the sight of her. She wore her luxuriant golden hair tied back with a blue ribbon. With her simple white blouse and skirt, she looked more like a schoolgirl than ever.

He was amused when she continued with her writing, seemingly oblivious to his presence. He wasn't used to being ignored by females, and certainly not by a slip of a girl who seemed to be more enthralled with her Latin translations than with him.

At last he was forced to clear his throat and say, "Miss Holden, I'm obliged to point out to you that I'm not just lingering here to fill up space in your doorway. Do you suppose

I could have a few moments of your time? If it wouldn't be too inconvenient for you, of course.''

She looked up at him at once, her cheeks coloring. She shut the book in front of her on the desk with a snap. "I'm sorry. Papa always said I was lost to the world once I got my nose in a book. What is it that you want?''

He just looked at her, one eyebrow raised until she realized the double entendre in her own words.

"But you can't possibly want that," she almost wailed as she glanced down at herself. "I'm not wearing my kerchief, and I'm not wearing Pearl's nightgown. I'm just sitting here studying. How could you find me the least bit appealing?''

Intrigued by her seemingly irrelevant mention of a kerchief, he strolled into the room. "I'm beginning to believe you could wear a flour sack and I could still find you desirable. But I wish you would enlighten me, my dear. What in the world does your wearing or not wearing your kerchief have to do with my amorous appetites?''

"You said I looked like a wench when I wore it," she admitted as she stared at her lap, her blush deepening.

"Ah, now I understand. You are afraid I'm going to act the part of the pirate again. You needn't look so alarmed, my golden girl. I am here to carry you off, but not to my bedroom. I have something more platonic in mind.''

"You do?" She glanced up at last, looking so hopeful that he almost laughed.

"If you are disappointed, we can delay the outing I had planned, and we could indulge ourselves in other delightful pursuits first.''

"Oh, no, I'm not the least bit disappointed," she assured him hastily.

"I could take your attitude as an insult to my skill, you know," he said with an amused glance at the ceiling, and then he decided he had teased her enough. "But I've decided that I won't, at least not this time. Dress in your warmest wool skirt and jacket, and I expect to see you downstairs in fifteen minutes.''

"And if it takes me longer?" she asked him daringly.

"You'd better hope it doesn't, young woman, or I will be forced to come upstairs and help you finish changing myself.

And if that happens, we may find ourselves indulging in those pursuits I mentioned after all.''

"You can count on my being downstairs in fifteen minutes." She was already rising from her chair as Justin headed for the door, chuckling under his breath.

Kate was as good as her word. She arrived in the front hall with a full minute to spare, clad in a charming blue-and-green plaid wool winter suit, a jaunty little cap, and a blue wool coat to match, all provided by Madame Sophie. Once Justin was certain Kate was also wearing a warm wool scarf and mittens, he escorted her out the front door. She paused on the second step and clapped her hands in delight when she saw that Ben was waiting on the street with the grays hitched to a graceful black sleigh.

"Oh, Justin, what fun! A sleigh ride sounds like a wonderful idea."

"I'm glad the notion pleases you, and you'll find that we have a few more surprises in store for you before the day's over." When they reached the street he handed her up into the sleigh and laid the warm buffalo robe across her lap. Just after he had finished settling himself beside Kate, Mrs. Parslow came bustling out to the sleigh and handed Justin a mysterious, bulky package.

"I found them, sir," she said with a wide smile, "just where you thought they would be. You two have a wonderful afternoon."

"Thank you, Mrs. Parslow. We shall do our best. Ben, let's be off," Justin called out to his coachman. With that Ben twitched the reins over the horses' backs, and the grays started off at a brisk trot, the bells on their harnesses chiming merrily.

It was a perfect day for a sleigh ride. The Colorado weather had made one of those quick turnabouts for which it was justly famous. After five days of cold and blowing snow, now the sun was shining brightly in a cloudless blue sky. All of Cripple Creek looked quaint and clean with so much of its dirt and roughness hidden under three feet of snow. Kate watched folk all over town in the process of digging out, clearing their walks, porches, and doorways of drifts. As they left town behind them, she smiled to herself in delight when she noticed the way the sun was making diamondlike reflections dance on the surface of the crystalline snow.

She turned to glance at Justin curiously from time to time. Although he was quiet, he did not seem to be brooding or angry. In fact he appeared to be enjoying himself just as much as she was, watching the snowy countryside gliding past them and smiling at her reactions to the sights they passed. He had seemed altogether different to her these past five days, much more like the gentle, teasing Justin she had met in her father's garden. He could be such good company and so tremendously charming when he put his mind to it. Her heart twisted when she thought how sad it was that he couldn't be like this all the time.

She knew, though, that events and people had marked and changed him forever. The ruthless man who had purchased her body and taunted her with her ruin was still here. Instinctively she understood he was treating this time with her like a brief holiday. She guessed his careless mood could end at any moment, and so she was careful not to let her guard down with him. It was hard, though, for a silly and naive part of her wanted to simply enjoy being with him.

They followed the Mount Pisgah road and turned off it just before they passed the cemetery. Whatever this new route was they were following, she knew some important mines must lie along it, for the road had already been plowed. It went twisting and winding its way over the shoulder of a small mountain. When they reached the top, the view was breathtaking. Rugged Pikes Peak wore a brilliant white blanket of snow, and the Sangre de Cristos to the south sported similar coverings.

Ben urged the grays onward until they reached a spot just over the ridge where the fierce winds had scoured most of the grass free of snow. There, in a little depression, lay a smooth, round pond that was completely frozen over and blown free of drifts. Next to it rose some small aspens and a large rock outcropping.

"Look at that pond. What a perfect spot to go skating!" Kate uttered the comment before she could stop herself.

"Miss Holden," Justin said with a wide smile, "that's a splendid idea."

"But we don't have any skates," she said sadly as reality came back to her with a rush.

His only response was to lean across the seat and hand her the bulky package Mrs. Parslow had given him. Kate stared down at the package in her hands for several moments before she realized what it must contain. She had brought her old skates with her all the way from Boston. Mrs. Parslow must have found them in the bottom of her wardrobe.

"Justin Talbott, you are a clever, scheming devil," Kate said admiringly. "You even had Mrs. Parslow in on this, didn't you?"

"The good woman was happy to help. She is also very grateful for the transformation you wrought in my office. Now she can actually clean it from time to time without having to worry about breaking her neck tripping over my papers."

"It wasn't anything, I mean, you needn't have gone to all this trouble to thank me. . . ." She was nonplussed by the warm look lighting his beautiful blue eyes.

"Ah, but it was no trouble at all. Besides, I didn't arrange this expedition just for you, young woman. I woke up this morning with a sudden urge to go skating myself."

"You're going to skate, too?"

"I'll have you know, Miss Holden, that I was one of the fastest skaters on Mr. Brown's pond when I was a boy." He leaned over and produced a set of skates, which he began strapping onto the bottom of his boots.

Hurriedly following his example, she smiled to herself. She could just picture him when he was a skinny boy of twelve or thirteen, with a head full of black curls, racing about a pond with a pack of other lads. That mental picture triggered fond memories of her own childhood.

With a toss of her head, she informed him, "I should warn you that I was the fastest skater, boy or girl, on Dary Lake near Papa's farm."

"So the challenge is met, Miss Holden. After you." He gestured grandly toward the sleigh door that Ben was holding open for her now.

"Mr. Gallagher, are you going to join us?" she asked brightly as he helped her out of the sleigh.

"Not on your life, missee. I'm a-gonna sit over here and

laugh my belly sore at you two. Besides, one of us needs to stay healthy in case I have to carry the boss off the ice with a busted ankle or two.''

''Your confidence in my abilities is overwhelming, Ben,'' Justin commented as he stepped down from the sleigh. Ben just winked at Kate and turned away.

Justin proved to be just as good a skater as he boasted, and despite Ben's predictions, no one ended up with a broken ankle. When they stepped out onto the ice, Justin caught Kate's hands and pulled her along with him. For a time they skated side by side, holding each other's hands. Kate was impressed with how easily they kept stride together gliding over the ice. But then they drifted apart. Kate wanted to try some tricks, and Justin said he wanted to watch her. To her amusement, though, he actually began skating faster and faster around the outer edges of the pond while she worked on her twirls and skating backward in the center.

When Justin wasn't looking her way, she caught up some snow and made a snowball, which she hid behind her back. With a dazzling smile she skated up and let fly with her snowball when she was only ten feet away from him. She let go a delighted peal of laughter when her shot clipped the top of his elegant hat and sent it sailing off his head. His look of total astonishment made her laugh again when she should have been making good her escape. From his surprised reaction, she couldn't help but wonder when the last time was that anyone had dared throw a snowball at Justin Talbott.

His expression of amazement soon turned to fierce amusement. ''*Nemo me impune lacessit*—no one provokes me with impunity, Miss Holden,'' he threatened and started toward her.

To her credit, she made almost a full lap about the pond before he finally caught her. Ignoring her giggling pleas for mercy, he picked her up and dropped her in the closest snowdrift. Pretending that she was winded and couldn't get back on her feet, she held her hand up for his help. When he took her hand and leaned over her, she pulled backward as hard as she could. To her delight he landed in the snowdrift right beside her.

''You little minx,'' he said disgustedly as he rolled over on his side to look at her. "Have you no respect for my age and dignity?"

"Mr. Talbott, why must you persist in seeing yourself as a doddering old man?"

"Because, Miss Holden, I am well on my way to becoming middle-aged. You just don't have the sense to realize it. Now, my golden girl, what you just did demonstrates once again that no female is to be trusted. I'm afraid I'm going to have to pay you back with proper chastisement."

She eyed him warily. "Just what sort of chastisement did you have in mind?"

"One I'm going to enjoy a great deal, and one you probably won't mind too much once I get on with it."

"You can't mean to kiss me here." Her voice rose indignantly. "We're all covered with snow."

"Whose fault is that, might I ask?" he said as he leaned toward her, that warm light that did such strange things to her pulse flaring in his eyes.

"Mine, I suppose." She faltered as he drew closer. It just wasn't fair for a man to be so handsome. Even lying in a snowdrift he looked magnificent to her, his raven hair tousled by the wind, the tips of his long, black eyelashes wet with melting snowflakes. His warm lips closed over her own, and she forgot all about the fact that she was sitting in a cold snowdrift on the edge of a mountain pond. His kiss brought back such vivid, sensual memories of the recent nights they had spent together, nights during which he had taught her more and more about her own body and lovemaking, an art at which he was truly a master.

Her eyes were closed, and she was leaning into the kiss when Justin suddenly pulled away from her.

"I congratulate you, young woman. For once you've chosen a place where I cannot allow my baser instincts free rein."

Still caught up in the heat of his kiss, she just looked at him blankly. With a low laugh he rose to his feet and hauled her up to join him. They both spent several moments brushing the cold, dry snow from their coats.

"Since I cannot satisfy my appetite for you, I will have to settle for the picnic Madame Dupuy made up for us."

"You brought a picnic along, too?"

"An old man like me needs regular sustenance, you know."

She looked longingly at the long, perfect snowbank they were gliding past. Making up her mind, she dug her skates into the ice and came to a quick stop.

"Justin, did you ever make snow angels when you were a boy?"

"No, I don't think I ever did." He slowed and glanced back over his shoulder at her.

"Well, that's a shame. You're going to think I'm quite absurd, but then again, you probably believe that already. Do not be alarmed—this is not a faint." With that she grinned at him and purposely fell back into the snowdrift, her arms outstretched. As he skated closer to watch her, she moved her arms back and forth vigorously, making the wings to her snow angel.

"If you think I'm going to help you out of there now, you can think again. You've already taught me the cost of acting chivalrously."

"I don't need an old man's help," she informed him cheekily while she tried to climb out of the snowbank. Despite his pledge to the contrary, he caught her arm when her skates threatened to slip out from underneath her.

After she regained her balance again, she pointed to the silhouette her body had formed in the snow. "Now look, there's a perfect snow angel."

"Hmm, I think I see one right in front of me." He barely glanced at her angel. She looked up to find he was watching her with that hungry look again.

"You said you wanted to eat Madame Dupuy's picnic," she reminded him right as he was reaching out to clasp her shoulders. With a merry laugh, she ducked under his arm before he could catch hold of her and sprinted toward the far side of the pond. A moment later she heard the rasp of his skates as he started after her. Laughing and goading each other on, they raced across to the place where Ben was laying out their picnic in the shelter of the rock outcropping.

Justin reached the edge of the pond just ahead of her. With a smug look over his own victory, he handed her off the ice with a flourish and helped her over to Ben's wool blanket. After they unstrapped their skates from their boots, they set to

work on the feast Madame Dupuy had concocted for them.
And what a feast it was.

There were luscious finger sandwiches, pastries, and cold
roast pheasant. The feast even included hot cream of mush-
room soup. Ben and Madame Dupuy had kept it warm by
placing it in a Cornish miner's pail. This device had a candle
in the bottom of it to keep soups and pastries warm all day.
For dessert there were cookies, cherry tarts, and chocolate
éclairs.

Kate teased Justin mercilessly about the fact that he ate four
of those éclairs and looked longingly at the remaining two Ben
and Kate kept for themselves. After they finished eating, Kate
lay back on the blanket and looked up at the deep blue sky
while Ben and Justin discussed Cripple Creek happenings des-
ultorily. She was pleased to hear Justin speak to Ben just as
if he were talking to a friend and equal rather than to a servant.
As a lazy hour passed, they never once grew chilled, for the
rock outcropping stopped the wind, and the winter sun was
warm.

At last Justin sighed and said they needed to head back
because he did have some work he had to complete this afternoon. In little time the remains of Madame Dupuy's picnic
were packed away, and Kate was settled next to Justin again
in the backseat of the sleigh. She enjoyed the return trip to
town, for the light had changed and the scenes they had passed
earlier all looked slightly different now. As the sleigh glided
smoothly over the snowy road, the cool wind rushed past her
face and the sleigh bells jingled.

She smiled when Justin placed an arm around her shoulder
and pulled her snugly against him. It was a novel sensation,
cuddling like this in the daylight. With no one but Ben to see
them, she couldn't summon the energy to object or push Justin
away. She had never felt so warm, safe, and protected.

When they reached Justin's street, she eased away from his
hold and turned to face him. "I want to thank you for today.
I had a wonderful time," she told him shyly.

"It's not over yet, my golden girl. When we return to the
house I want you to rest for a few hours. Then I'm going to
take you out to the finest restaurant in Cripple Creek."

"My goodness." She was left momentarily speechless. He

had never offered to take her out on the town before. It had been ages since she had been to a fine restaurant. Suddenly another thought occurred to her. "I don't suppose you have another office someplace that needs organizing?" she asked him slyly.

He laughed at that and reached over to tug on a lock of her hair, which had long ago escaped her hairpins. "I'm afraid I only have one other office, little scholar, and that one is located in Manhattan. It's presided over by a very organized and efficient manager, a man who would never dream of letting a single piece of paper go unfiled for more than a minute."

When she made a great show of looking disappointed, he leaned closer and assured her in his deep voice, "Never fear; there are always other ways you can please me."

She just looked at him while her cheeks warmed once more. "For your information, sir, I much prefer to do your filing," she told him stiffly.

"Rest assured, Miss Holden, you've made your preference in these matters quite obvious," he told her in a frigid tone. He straightened up and looked forward once again. "I might point out to you, though, a certain hypocrisy inherent in your missish manner. You may say and imply you do not want me, but your body reacts quite differently when you are in my arms."

To Kate's intense relief, the sleigh came to a stop before Justin's house just then. He said nothing more as Ben helped her down out of the sleigh. Justin only spoke to her again after they were both standing in the front hall.

"I expect to see you in the library at eight o'clock. Wear the red velvet gown Madame Sophie delivered yesterday," he ordered and strode down the hall toward his office.

She stared after him for several moments, fighting to keep her simmering temper in check. As she stormed up the stairs she mentally railed at him. She had been so right to think the hard-hearted side of Justin had only gone away for a little while. How dare he say that she was a hypocrite? How dare he imply that she liked what he did to her? She derived a great deal of satisfaction out of slamming her bedroom door shut behind her. Barely pausing to take off her coat and toss it on the bed, she began pacing back and forth across the room.

She hated being his mistress. She hated the spell he could cast so easily over her body and senses. She hated it, too, when he told her what to wear. It made her feel like some sort of oversize doll.

She suddenly stopped her wild pacing and sank down on the little window seat. She had to face the truth. A part of her knew she was so furious because Justin had echoed one of her secret fears. In all honesty, she realized what he had said was true. She was a hypocrite. God help her, no matter how she fought it, she did enjoy Justin's touch. Again she had to ask herself, was she a wanton because a caress from him could make her head swim and her body long for more?

Perhaps, if she were stronger, she could resist the sensual temptation of his lovemaking. Perhaps, too, she was not entirely to blame for her body's reaction to him. Justin Talbott was a worldly, sophisticated man with a great deal of experience in pleasuring women. Her best and wisest course from now on would be to be more honest with both herself and him. She was hardly going to encourage his attentions, but she would no longer pretend that they revolted her. She could see now that her own "missish manner," as he called it, had ignited both his anger and his scorn.

She still had the ordeal of dinner to face this evening. The more she thought about it, the more she realized people at the restaurant were going to whisper and wonder about the young woman who was rich Mr. Talbott's companion for the evening. Many would probably guess exactly what she was. She clung to the comforting notion that there was little chance she would encounter any of her Cripple Creek acquaintances tonight. None of them were affluent enough to patronize the expensive kind of place Justin was going to take her. Even if no one recognized her, it was still going to be a long and difficult evening. She would simply have to hold her head high and ignore the stares and whispers.

Kate flung herself down on the bed, hoping to elude her fears about the coming evening by falling asleep. Spending the day out-of-doors must have tired her out, for she did soon fall into a sound slumber. She rose just in time to wash and dress.

Once again Madame Sophie had proven her skill and taste

as a dress designer. The deep, wine red color of the velvet made Kate's eyes look very green, and the lines of the dress somehow managed to make her seem more generously endowed than she actually was. Kate grimaced at herself in the mirror as she left the room. Considering her new occupation, there was a certain ironic appropriateness in her wearing the color red.

When she arrived in the library, she had to admit Justin looked incredibly distinguished in his dark evening clothes. The moment he saw her standing in the doorway to the study, he looked her up and down, his face expressionless. Slowly he raised his drink to her in a wordless toast. Then he put his drink aside and strode to stand before her. In a courtly gesture he performed with great grace, he raised her hand and brushed the back of her white glove with his lips.

"I know no man this evening at the Clarendon will have a more lovely dinner companion," he said simply.

Kate shook her head inwardly as he placed her new black velvet evening cape about her shoulders. She should have guessed Justin was going to take her there, for the Clarendon Hotel did indeed have the finest restaurant in Cripple Creek. Only the very richest of the town's Upper Ten could afford to patronize such an expensive establishment.

On the way to the hotel Justin kept up a constant stream of small talk. Clearly he was bent on pretending the angry moment in the sleigh had never happened. After deliberating for a time, she decided to follow his lead. The evening was going to be difficult enough without open hostilities continuing between them.

The most challenging moment came when she had to enter the restaurant on Justin's arm. She knew it was not just her imagination. Almost everyone, patrons and staff alike, watched them walk across the dining room. Justin Talbott was the sort of man who attracted attention wherever he went. His size alone would have drawn notice, but with his darkly handsome looks and the arrogant way he carried himself, he drew everyone's gaze. Kate knew she was receiving many a speculative and curious look, but she could only do as she had promised herself earlier. She held her head high and told herself what these people thought and wondered about her didn't matter.

Once the headwaiter seated them at a very private table in the far corner of the room, she began to relax a little. She liked the decor and ambiance of the restaurant immensely. It was a simple, elegant place, with white linen tablecloths, lovely, gold-edged china, and fresh orchids on every table. A violinist played softly in the background. It reminded her of the fine places Papa used to take her and Elizabeth in the old days. Kate soon discovered the food and service were equally exquisite.

She also found herself relaxing because Justin was making a particular effort to be charming and entertaining. When she commented on the polished appearance of the restaurant's patrons, he gave her a wry smile.

"Don't be fooled by appearances. There are plenty of rough-and-ready characters present here this evening. Those two fellows over there are Jimmie Burns and Jimmy Doyle. They were Irish firemen over in Colorado Springs before they struck it rich. And the dashing-looking gentleman with the gray hair to our right used to be known as Lightning Al Handy. He had quite a reputation as a hired gun before he turned to mining."

Thanks to Justin's amusing anecdotes, the meal went by swiftly. When they finished their dessert, she hardly minded the trip back across the room. She had drunk a glass of white wine with dinner, and the spirits had helped her lose the last of her self-consciousness.

They were standing on the boardwalk before the restaurant, waiting for Ben to bring the carriage around, when a young man walking past them halted dead in his tracks and stared at Kate.

"Kate Holden, is that you? Good lord, you look positively smashing. I'm so glad to see you again." Emboldened by his surprise and his very real pleasure at seeing her, Geoffrey Cooper stepped forward and caught her hands in his own.

"It's good to see you, too, Geoffrey," she managed to reply, even though a part of her was dying inside. It was wonderful to see his kindly face again, but she was terrified that he would find out what she was now. She was only too aware of Justin standing beside her, a black scowl growing on his face as he listened to their interchange. Desperately she tried to ignore Justin and to focus on what Geoffrey was saying.

"I thought you had moved away. Are you here visiting?" Geoffrey asked.

"I'm just here for a few months. . . ." She faltered, for she had been totally unprepared to answer such a question, and she was too rattled to think up a fib with Justin listening to her every word.

"Actually, she's living under my protection, young sir," Justin broke in, his voice as stern and cold as Kate had ever heard it. "I'll thank you to let go of my mistress's hands now. Come along, Kate. I don't want to keep the horses standing in this weather."

And then Justin had her by the elbow and was thrusting her firmly toward the waiting carriage. When she reached the top step she glanced over her shoulder. In the remorseless light from a nearby street lamp, she could clearly see Geoffrey's shock and dismay. Ben closed the door of the carriage, and Justin told him to take them home as quickly as possible.

"That was unspeakable." She turned on Justin the moment the carriage rolled forward. "I don't believe I've ever been so humiliated in all my life."

"If you elect to stay in your current profession for any length of time, I expect you will have to face more incidents like this one," he replied in a coldly indifferent tone.

"But why did you have to go out of your way to tell him? Do you hate me so much?"

Even in the dim light she could see the bored look he gave her. "You are overreacting, my dear. Of course I don't hate you, but I also will not tolerate my mistress holding hands with or smiling at other men who desire her. I'm paying you too generously to allow you to spread your favors around."

She stared back at him, so angry she could hardly stutter out her reply. "For your information, Geoffrey Cooper is a dear friend of mine. He gave up his room for Elizabeth and Robert when we first came to the district so that they could stay in the same boardinghouse with me."

"You may see him as a friend, but I'm sure the young fellow wants you desperately."

"How can you say such an awful thing?" Even as she flung the question at Justin, she was remembering the fervent way Geoffrey had embraced her after they spent Independence Day together. Could Justin possibly be right?

"I can say such a thing easily, young Kate, for I have experienced more of the world than you have, and I have seen a great deal more of human nature. I know lust when I see it, and I'm willing to wager your Geoffrey Cooper would give everything he owns to be in my place this evening."

"Your mind is both despicable and depraved. Geoffrey is a decent, kind man. He would never resort to paying a woman for her favors."

"Ah, if you felt that way about him, why didn't you persuade him to marry you?"

"I think he wanted to," she was stung into replying, "but I made certain that he didn't propose. I didn't love him."

"Then you were a fool. He looked affluent enough to give you a reasonably comfortable life. But perhaps you were after bigger fish, eh? Or perhaps marriage to an earnest young fellow like him seemed dull and boring compared to entertaining fine gentlemen at the elegant Old Homestead."

She was silent for several moments, afraid that if she spoke at once, her voice might give away the hurt she was feeling. It would be far better to give him back scorn rather than to allow him to see the way his cruelty could wound her.

"I suppose you are right after all. Being a kept woman, even to an older, debauched man like yourself, is certainly far easier than the drudgery of keeping house and bearing children."

She realized at once she had gone too far, but there was no catching the words back once they were said. She caught a glimpse of his face from the light of a passing street lamp. His eyes were cold and his face was very still.

"Indeed, Daisy, I believe I have made your job far too easy for you up until now. I think it's about time you started earning your keep. When we return to my home, I expect you to perform like a mistress for this debauched old man."

Chapter Fourteen

After Justin made his pronouncement, the rest of their carriage ride was very quiet. Kate felt her stomach tie itself into tighter and tighter knots the closer they drew to his home. After they descended from the carriage, Justin escorted her up the walk wordlessly. He opened the front door for her and took her evening cape with such studied politeness that his actions seemed like an insult. She hesitated briefly in the front hall, wondering if he wanted to stop for a brandy in the library first. She would have been relieved to have even a few moments' delay before going upstairs with him.

"No, my dear Daisy," he said, seemingly able to read her mind. "I would not like a brandy, or to play poker with you, or to hear you play the piano. I would like to retire upstairs with you immediately."

She winced at this blatant reminder of that first night at the Old Homestead when she had likewise wanted to delay the inevitable. Very well, she would not try to postpone what was to come any longer. As she turned and walked up the stairs in front of Justin, she kept a picture in her mind of Elizabeth, looking happy and healthy. Somehow she would find the courage to be what Justin wanted her to be tonight. He was angry enough with her to terminate their agreement if she didn't finally begin to behave like a mistress.

When they reached his bedroom he switched on the overhead electric chandelier, shut the door behind them, and went to one of the large chairs before the fire. He flung himself down in it and leaned back with his hands clasped behind his head. He watched her as she lingered by the door, trying to nerve herself to move forward into the room.

"Daisy, I don't see how you can perform your duties this

evening if you hang back by the doorway like some innocent, blushing virgin. Although we both know you can still blush, you are hardly innocent or a virgin.''

That was only too true, thanks in large part to his own actions during the past weeks. Even though she longed to fling this retort at him, she refrained. A mistress would never fight with her patron. Instead she took a deep breath and asked him in as steady a voice as she could manage, ''Wouldn't you like to change first?''

He raised a dark eyebrow at her. ''I don't feel the least bit interested in going to bed yet, my dear. For your information, it's your duty to make me want to go to bed. For that matter, it's your duty to make me want you.''

She looked at him helplessly. How could she possibly do that? She wasn't wearing the nightgown that always seemed to have such a dramatic effect on him. Obviously it was time to start remembering what Pearl had taught her. Frantically Kate searched her mind for any tidbit that might help her succeed in the challenge before her: seducing a worldly and experienced man.

Pearl had said with certain gentlemen the mood of a room was important. The madam instructed all of her girls to keep the wicks in their lamps turned down low. A darker room was far more romantic than a glaringly bright one. Acting on this inspiration, Kate walked to the bedside table. She was aware of Justin's gaze following her every movement as she bent over and lit the kerosene lamp. She turned the wick down low and returned to the door, where she switched off the overhead chandelier.

Now, with just the light from the lamp and the flickering flames in the fireplace, the room did seem much more intimate. Her mouth went dry as she peeked at Justin from under her eyelashes. Any room seemed much smaller with him lounging in the midst of it.

Afraid he might accuse her of dawdling again, she racked her brain for more ideas. Pearl had also said different men could be aroused by different things. What particular weaknesses had Justin demonstrated to her in the past? Ah, from the time of their first stroll together in the aspen grove, he had always seemed fascinated by her hair. Before she could lose her nerve, she walked toward him slowly. She stopped when she was only a few steps away from his chair. Forcing herself to meet his eyes, she reached up and deliberately began removing hairpins. She watched his gaze range up and down her insultingly and then fasten on her chest. All of a sudden she was very aware of the way her breasts were pressing against the dress bodice as she raised her arms. Here was another weapon she could use in the battle to arouse him.

When she sensed her chignon was about to come loose, she shook her head back and forth. Her hair came tumbling down about her shoulders. Justin watched it fall, and his gaze darkened. To her amazement she felt an answering flame kindle in the pit of her stomach. Trying to ignore the sensation, she stepped forward until she was standing almost between his knees. She turned about and knelt gracefully with her back turned toward him.

"Would you unhook my dress, please?" As she asked the question, she gathered her hair up and flicked it to the side, where it went cascading down her shoulder and fell across his thigh. She smiled grimly to herself when out of the corner of her eye she saw him reach out and caress the hair that had spilled across his leg. He caught his hand back. After a few moments she felt him undoing the hooks on her dress one by one.

Now for one of the hardest parts of all. Pearl had said many men preferred to watch a woman undress. Each of the girls at the Old Homestead had a screen in her room behind which she could disrobe, but the canny madam had warned Kate there were many clients with whom she should not be so retiring. From the way Justin had lingered over undressing her in the past, she decided to gamble he was one of the gentlemen to whom Pearl had been referring.

Taking a deep breath, Kate rose to her feet, her petticoats rustling softly. She moved back and turned around to face him once more. This time, no matter how hard she tried, she could not meet his gaze as she let the gown slip from her shoulders. When it had collapsed in a shimmering burgundy circle about her feet, she undid her petticoats, too, and let them fall to the ground in a white ring inside the burgundy. Then she stepped out of both. Second nature had her picking up the dress and petticoats and draping them carefully over the chair next to Justin. As she moved past him, she saw he was smiling sardonically at her actions. Ah, so one was not supposed to take the time to be neat in the midst of a seduction.

Blushing at her mistake, she decided to make the smile disappear from his face as quickly as possible. She blessed the surge of temper she felt at that moment. Perhaps anger would get her through the rest of this ordeal. She would give anything to humble Justin by making him want her the way she had been made to want him in the past.

When she was standing before him once more, she raised her hands and began undoing the buttons to her chemise. She noticed a muscle was jumping in his cheek, but his eyes were still unreadable. When the last button was undone she pulled the garment free of her drawers, but she couldn't quite make herself take it off completely. Instead she let it hang open as she knelt before him and leaned forward to undo his tie. Stealing a glance at his face, she noted with satisfaction that he was staring at the open gap in her chemise. Once again a pulse of treacherous warmth shot through her. Sternly she told herself her job tonight was to pleasure him. Why was her own body reacting to the things she was doing to arouse his desires?

After she had pulled his tie free, she also undid his stiff collar. Moving even closer to start on the buttons of his shirt, she let herself lean against his legs. She realized her mistake almost at once. She could feel the warmth of him against her sides, and the flame in the pit of her stomach intensified. His shirt was cool and smooth beneath her hands, and the musky male scent of him was all around her now.

She smiled again when she noticed his hands clenching and unclenching by his sides, but he never once reached out to touch her. Instead he let her pull his shirt open. She allowed her hands the pleasure of exploring and touching where she willed. His skin was warm and smooth beneath her fingers, the hair of his chest silky soft. Acting on instinct, she kissed the places she had just touched. She paused when she discovered his heart was racing beneath her lips. She glanced up at him in surprise. Could she have already been far more successful in her task than she realized? Nervously she wet her lips and wished he would give her some more overt sign of what he was feeling, and then she was overwhelmed by the sign she had been hoping for.

With a groan he lunged toward her. His hands closed about her shoulders and dragged her forward until she was crushed against his chest. His thighs closed until she was pinned between his legs. And then he was kissing her everywhere, her face, her lips, the side of her neck. The fire that had been slumbering inside her leaped high, fanned by the winds of his own passion.

After he raked his hands through her hair, he pushed her back a little and tugged the chemise from her shoulders. When his hands claimed her breasts for the first time, she moaned aloud and pressed closer to him shamelessly. His usual skill seemed to have deserted him. This time he did not tease or play; this time he was consuming her. Yet she found his urgency far more arousing than his controlled and skillful lovemaking.

He cupped his hands beneath her buttocks and lifted her higher until she was straddling his lap. She moaned again when she felt the heat of his hard arousal between her legs. He dipped his head and began to kiss her breasts so fiercely that he made her gasp. Slowly, and then with greater urgency, he began to rock against her, until the sensitive area between her thighs was throbbing. Vaguely she was aware of his undoing her drawers and yanking them downward. He tugged at his own trousers, and then she felt his hard male part moving against her most sensitive place. Suddenly wave after wave of exquisite sensation burst through her. She closed her eyes and clung helplessly to his shoulders.

She would have collapsed against him after this first release, but he lifted her, shifted his weight, and thrust deep inside her. The tension in her body began to build all over again. With his hands on her hips, he showed her how to match his movements. Again the voluptuous, fiery pleasure kindled within her. Once she had learned this new rhythm, his hands left her hips to range across her back and sides. He caressed her hair, which hung like a bright shimmering curtain about her shoulders and trailed across his chest and belly.

Of one accord they quickened their pace. He reached up

and claimed her breasts again, teasing their peaks until the tightness inside her was almost unbearable.

"Look at me this time, my golden girl," he ordered her hoarsely as she hovered on the brink.

Her green gaze found and fastened on his brilliant blue eyes. Through the maelstrom of feeling clouding her mind and senses, she still was able to see the desire in his gaze. She was amazed to realize his need was as great as hers, the pleasure he was feeling was as overwhelming as her own. But she was beyond feeling satisfaction or victory over this discovery. There was only the burning passion that blazed upward, whirling them both past thought, past care, past everything but the great, all-consuming joy their bodies gave each other.

When Kate awoke the next morning she found herself alone in Justin's bed once again. She buried her face in a pillow as the events of the evening before came back to her. Her fumbling efforts to seduce him must have been more effective than she had realized. He had made love to her two more times last night before he finally allowed her to fall into an exhausted slumber.

After depositing her clothing in her own room, Kate went to draw her bath. As she watched the steaming hot water fill the tub, she could not help but think about her painful encounter with Geoffrey Cooper last night and what had happened afterward. She still could not believe the casual manner in which Justin had announced that she was his mistress to Geoffrey. His insinuation that she would share her favors with other men also made her furious. Perhaps because he had been so kind for the past five days, she had not been expecting such callousness. With a sigh she climbed into the tub, feeling dull, achy, and miserable inside.

The only good news that morning came when Madame Dupuy brought Kate's breakfast upstairs. The cook casually mentioned the fact that Justin had left early this morning on a business trip to Leadville and would be gone for at least four days. Madame Dupuy seemed to assume that Kate already knew this fact, and Kate said nothing to correct that impression. Still, it irked her to think that Justin hadn't even bothered to inform her that he was going to be out of town.

She also wondered if he was going to see his fiancée. How could he possibly face Miss LaMonte after spending such a wild night with his mistress? As Kate nibbled on her breakfast, she decided she should feel relieved rather than angry. For the next four days she wouldn't have to deal with her unpredictable, unnerving, and infuriating employer.

She threw herself into her studies for the rest of the morning. She was still feeling tired and depressed, however, when she went to the kitchen to have lunch with the others. Taking her meals with the rest of Justin's staff continued to be a treat. With her dry sense of humor, Mrs. Parslow had made mealtimes in the kitchen even more fun.

Madame Dupuy must have noticed that Kate was quieter than usual. When she served them all chocolate-covered cream puffs for dessert, she said to Ben, "I think you should take *la petite* here for a drive this afternoon. Her sparkle, she seems to have lost it, *hein*?"

"Why, I reckon that's a fine idea," Ben replied promptly. "With the boss out of town, I don't want the horses to be getting fat and lazy."

Kate protested their suggestion. With Justin gone, she thought Ben deserved a day off and told him so. He promised her there was nothing that he enjoyed better than taking the horses out. Because she knew this was true, and because Mrs. Parslow added her urgings to the rest, at last Kate gave in. The idea of spending the rest of the afternoon cooped up studying in her room did seem unappealing.

An hour later Kate went outside dressed in the same warm winter suit she had worn yesterday. With great ceremony Ben handed her into the back of the sleigh.

"Where would you like to go this afternoon, missee?" he asked as he gave her the thick buffalo robe to lay across her lap.

"Someplace high, I think. You've spoiled me with all the wonderful views you keep producing like a magician pulling a rabbit out of a hat."

"It's not hard to find pretty places in country like this. I've got just the spot," he assured her as he took his place up front and sent the grays off at a good clip. It was another lovely, sunny Colorado afternoon. The rolling hillsides about the town were still covered with snow, and the sky overhead was a wonderful deep blue.

As the sleigh drew away from Cripple Creek, however, Kate had to admit the ride did not seem as magical to her as it had been yesterday. She refused to believe that the difference might have anything to do with Justin's absence. When the team started pulling the sleigh up a set of switchbacks, she realized they were climbing the hill next to Elk Mountain where Justin believed there was a bonanza waiting to be found.

Ben pulled the horses to a stop when they reached the very top of the mountain. Once again the winds had scoured the brown grass of the summit ridge free of snow. In each direction the view was just as fine as it had been from Elk Mountain. From so high up, the shops and houses of Cripple Creek down below looked like tiny toy figurines.

After Ben helped her out of the sleigh, she thanked him and said simply, "I think I would like to walk a little way by myself."

"All right, but you be careful, missee. It's easy to slip on this frozen grass, and the boss would have my hide if you turned an ankle up here."

Kate doubted the truth of that statement, but all she said in reply was, "I promise I'll be careful, and I won't go very far."

She walked down the ridge until she found a little cleft between some rocks out of the wind. After she settled herself on a flat boulder, she discovered that the winter sun kept her quite warm. From her perch she could look out over the brown ridge toward the snowcapped Sangre de Cristos in the distance. As she stared at the cold, jagged peaks, the pain and humiliation of the past few weeks welled up inside her. Rather than bottle up the feelings yet again, she bowed her head and let the tears come.

It was terrible to think she was turning into a wanton. It was horrible to realize she could never have a decent man for a husband now. But more than these worries, she kept thinking about the awful moment last night when Justin had told Geoffrey Cooper what she had become. Couldn't Justin have guessed she didn't want her former friends to know her new occupation? Couldn't he have shown just a little sensitivity toward her wants and feelings? The fact that he hadn't hurt her deeply.

And yet Justin Talbott should only be able to hurt her if she cared for him, she told herself bluntly. And she had stopped loving him the night he had bought her body at the old Homestead. But had she? Had she truly stopped loving him?

She clenched her hands as the insidious question kept repeating itself in the back of her mind. What if she never had stopped caring for the man? Surely she couldn't be such a fool. She knew he had little respect for her sex. She knew he might never bring himself to truly love or trust a woman again. How could she possibly love a man who cheated openly on his fiancée? How could she possibly love a man who insulted her daily by paying for the use of her body? Of course, she had more pride and common sense than that.

Only partially reassured by her own reasoning, she buried her face in her hands. Clearly it was time she started to make plans for the time when her arrangement with Justin ended. She needed to make sure she had a place to go and a job to immerse herself in when this time was over. Just yesterday she had read in the paper that they needed teachers in the southeastern portion of the state. Perhaps she should start writing letters of inquiry to school boards in that region soon.

"Why is a pretty girl like you crying on a lonely mountaintop when you should be down in town breaking young men's hearts?" A deep voice startled her from her musings.

She glanced up and found a tall, spare old man smiling down at her. She should have been scared or at the very least offended by a strange man being so bold as to address her directly, but there was a friendly look in his light blue eyes that disarmed her at once. He had the brown, weathered face of a man who had spent years out-of-doors in the wind and sun. He wore his white hair, which was still quite thick, down to his shoulders. He was dressed more like a mountain man than a prospector, with a buffalo robe coat, buckskin leggings, and a fur cap with earflaps. He spoke with a slight singsong rhythm to his words, and he pronounced his *W*s with a Germanic *V* sound instead.

"I suppose I'm doing my best to water the grass," she said,

answering his question with a wry smile. Quickly she mopped
her face as best she could with her handkerchief.

"The grass won't mind, and the mountains can be the finest
listeners in the world to a person with heartache."

Surprised by his eloquence, she lowered her handkerchief.
"Sometimes the mountains seem so close, I feel like I could
reach out and touch them. Other times they appear so aloof
and remote they make my concerns seem puny and unimportant in the grand scale of things. But the high peaks are always
beautiful."

"You like this kind of country?" He sat down on a nearby
boulder, not too close to be intrusive.

"I love the Rockies. When I come up to a wild, high place
like this, it makes me wonder what the land was like before
the miners and the settlers came."

"It was grand when we trappers and the Indians had it to
ourselves. We did not change things. The waves of folk who
came after were the ones who built the towns, cut down the
trees, and killed the game." As he spoke, his blue eyes looked
sad and weary.

"Were you a trapper?"

"Ja, I have been a trapper and a buffalo hunter and a
farmer."

"And now you're trying prospecting."

He smiled at her. "I know what you are thinking, young
lady, even though you are too kind to say it. And it is true. It
is foolish for an old man to be chasing dreams of gold, but an
old man can be as foolish as a young one. And I think I have
a good reason for my foolishness. I am tired of rambling about.
I do not want to have to catch my supper. I want to sit by my
cabin fire and tell stories to pretty girls like you. I hope to find
just enough gold to bring me these things.

"Now I've a question for you, young lady. Was it a man
who had you sobbing just now as if your heart were going to
break?"

Somehow she didn't mind him asking the question. Perhaps
it was because she had so few people she could confide in.
Perhaps it was because this sunny spot on the mountainside
felt so comfortable and intimate. Perhaps it was because he

was a stranger, and she saw so much tolerance and understanding in his wise old eyes.

"I'm crying as much over my own folly as anything he's said or done." As she spoke the words, she realized with some surprise that they were true.

"Hmph, I am not sure I can believe that. I will go to town and beat some sense into him for you. I am not surprised Justin Talbott has made you cry." There was a sternness in his face that wasn't there before. She just stared at him in amazement, wondering how he could have possibly known. Was her liaison with Justin such public knowledge?

"I saw you up on Elk Mountain once before," the old man explained. "You were with him then."

"You're not . . . you can't be the Swedish gentleman who owns the south side of Elk Mountain, are you?" A wave of dismay welled up inside her.

"Ja, that is me. My name is Gunnar Carlson. Justin Talbott has been plaguing me for months to sell my claims to him."

"He can be very stubborn when he is after something he wants." She shook her head.

"And now I also know he is cruel or false to a girl who loves him."

Startled by the anger in his tone, she was horrified to think she had helped to poison the old man's opinion of Justin. She knew how much purchasing those claims meant to him.

"It's not like that," she hastened to explain. "I mean, I've gotten myself into this tangle. Justin Talbott has been very generous with me, and more than fair. You mustn't think there is anything dishonest about him. He is a hard man, but I knew that from the start."

"You are quick to defend him. How can a girl in love truly judge her man?"

She drew in a deep breath. It was going to be humiliating to admit the truth, but she knew she couldn't live with herself if anything she had said turned Gunnar Carlson against Justin.

"Mr. Carlson, I . . . I want to be completely honest with you. I'm not in love with Justin Talbott. He is not my sweetheart. He is the man who is keeping me." She saw the old man's brows rise in surprise, but she managed to keep her voice steady.

"This is the first time I have ever been a man's mistress, but I needed the money badly to help someone. I was crying because this situation has been difficult for me. It's not anything Mr. Talbott has done. I think I would have resented any man in his position." Her cheeks were burning now, but she forced herself to meet the old man's gaze.

"Ja, that is human nature," he said slowly after several moments.

"I meant what I said about his being generous. More important, he is a thoroughly honest man. My father loaned him a considerable sum of money years ago when Justin was broke. Justin repaid the interest on that debt exactly on time every year. Two months before my father died, Justin came east to repay the last of the debt. He forced my father to accept from him twice the accumulated interest they had originally agreed upon."

"He was a friend of your family, and yet he uses you now in this way?" the old man asked skeptically.

"It's mostly my fault. I should have gone to him earlier for help. How I came to be his mistress is a long story, but you mustn't think he is taking advantage of me." She twisted her hands in her lap. "Being with him is far easier than working every night in a brothel," she added softly.

"I see," the old man said, rubbing his chin.

"Now it's my turn to ask you a question, sir," she declared, heartened by the fact that he seemed to be listening to her. "Wouldn't you rather have a hard, ruthless, and honest man looking after your interests? When we were up on your mountain last week, Justin said he would like to purchase your claims outright, but failing that, he would be willing to be your partner. He thinks you are sitting on top of one of the richest veins in the district. I believe he has studied enough geology to know what he is talking about. He also has the resources to develop the mine, and to make certain that lawyers and high-graders and claim jumpers don't steal what you have out from under you," she finished earnestly.

"Your papa must have been a lawyer, child," the old Swede said with a dry smile.

"No, but he always said I could argue like one," she admitted with a chuckle.

"Well, I must be getting back." The old man rose to his feet stiffly. "Claim jumpers might be sniffing about my place even now. I will think about what you said. Justin Talbott should have sent a pretty girl to talk to me a long time ago."

"Did you truly get the men he sent to see you drunk?"

"Right under the table," the old man admitted with a wink.

"You, sir, are clearly a man to be reckoned with."

"And you are much stronger than you think, young lady. You were right to take comfort from the mountains. Things may be looking dark for you just now, but if you stand and endure even as the peaks do, life will get better."

"Thank you for your kindness." She found it hard to speak, for her throat had suddenly gone tight.

"It was nothing, *lillan*," he said with a shrug of his shoulders. "You are welcome to visit me at my cabin anytime. I will feed you *pepparkakar*, which are cookies from my homeland." With that promise, he turned about and strode down the ridge toward his mountain.

What a remarkable man, Kate thought as she stood up and started walking back toward the sleigh. She could just imagine him ranging across the West during his trapping days, trading with Indians and fighting grizzly bears. With his stubbornness and his shrewd understanding of human nature, he would make a fine business partner for Justin. She had meant what she had said. Justin would be the perfect person to look out for the old man's interests.

Working her way back up the ridge, she decided that in the long run she probably hadn't hurt Gunnar's opinion of Justin, and she might even have improved it. In the meantime she meant to take Gunnar's advice. She would endure even as the mountains did, and trust tomorrow would be brighter than today. Feeling much happier about herself and the world in general, Kate waved at Ben and ran the last few yards to the sleigh.

Chapter Fifteen

Kate spent much of her time during the next four days writing letters to school boards located in the southern area of the state. She was hoping to obtain a teaching position not far from Colorado Springs so that she could visit Elizabeth frequently. She took great care with her letter to the Pueblo school board, for she thought she had the best chance of finding a position there. In Pueblo the steel industry was booming, and the town was supposed to be growing by leaps and bounds.

On the afternoon of the fifth day Justin returned. He swept into Kate's room, picked her up, and bore her off to his bedchamber. He didn't even pause to say hello. Of course, it was a little hard for him to say anything, Kate decided later when she was trying to be charitable about the incident, because he was too busy kissing her. Acting as if he had been gone for a year instead of a few days, he proceeded to make love to her with a silent, fierce abandon that left her gasping and dazed. If he had spent time with his fiancée in Leadville, Kate wondered how he could possibly return to Cripple Creek and make such passionate love to his mistress.

But she did not ask him about his fiancée, nor did he ever refer to what had happened the night they encountered Geoffrey Cooper. The days and weeks that followed passed quickly for Kate. She usually studied in the mornings and went for walks or drives in the afternoons. At night she and Justin frequently dined in.

Occasionally Justin asked her to act as his hostess at small dinner parties he gave for his gentlemen friends in the district. His guests always treated her with great respect and admiration. Because she read the papers and talked with Justin daily about current events, she was able to hold her own during the lively conversations that took place at these parties.

Justin continued to treat her with a casual politeness and charm that were clearly a part of the wall he had erected between himself and everyone in his life. She never experienced his searing anger again, but she was also careful not to provoke it. Her common sense told her it was better not to break through his emotional barriers. She was afraid that if she ever did get to know the real Justin, he might consume her heart and soul even as he mastered her body during the long, sensual nights they spent together.

Kate awoke one Monday in early February, surprised to realize she had been living under Justin's roof for almost five weeks now. She had yet to hear back from any school districts, but she went to the post office every other day, hoping to receive good news from one of them soon.

That afternoon when she finished with her studies, she was dismayed to discover the past two days of warm sun had melted the snow and made the roads too muddy for her to go walking. Ben was away with Justin on business for the afternoon, and so she could not look forward to a carriage ride. Mrs. Parslow now kept the house in such good order, she rarely had chores for Kate to do. Feeling restless and edgy, Kate wandered downstairs to the music room.

It was there that Justin found her a half hour later, pounding her way through a Mozart sonata. He folded his arms and leaned against the doorway, enjoying the lovely picture she made. The exertion of playing so dramatically had brought roses to her cheeks, and the sun from the nearby window turned her hair shimmering gold.

"I'm not entirely sure that Wolfgang Amadeus meant that to be played fortissimo throughout," he drawled when she finished the piece.

She started in surprise at the sound of his voice, but when she glanced back at him her face was composed. "I'm afraid you're right," she said with a shrug of her shoulders, "but I only know two pieces by Beethoven, and I've played them already."

"Are we in a dark mood today, Miss Holden?" he asked curiously.

"Not exactly." She turned about on the piano bench to face him. One of her feet tapped the floor as she spoke. "I seem to be suffering from a case of the fidgets. It's too muddy out to go walking, and Mrs. Parslow hasn't a thing for me to do. But you're back now."

His brows rose at the eagerness he heard in her voice. He had often noticed she made no effort to seek him out during the day once she had finished organizing his office. In fact the times he had sought her out, she always treated him with that cautious reserve he disliked so. It took time to charm Kate into lowering her guard. The effort was always worthwhile, though, for he enjoyed her quaint, vivacious conversation no end.

"Would you mind if I asked Ben to take me for a quick drive?"

Ah, so that was the reason for her enthusiasm. Unaccountably disappointed, he replied more sharply than he meant, "I'm sorry to dash your hopes, but I'm about to need his services again."

"I understand." She nodded and rose to her feet. She walked swiftly to the window and stood looking out. "I hope your business goes well for you this afternoon," she said in a tone of polite dismissal.

"Thank you, my dear, I'm sure it shall." He moved away from the doorway, intending to go on about his affairs, but something about the way she continued to stand looking out the window pulled at him. She reminded him of a story in a book he had read as a child. The tale was about a beautiful bird that could not sing after it had been placed in a cage. Surprised by his own fancifulness, he thrust the image from his mind, but his concern for her remained.

One very appealing notion of how to cure her restlessness came to mind at once, but he had business he needed to complete this afternoon, and making love to young Kate wasn't going to get his work done. He could always take her with him. She had said once that she would love to see the inside of a mine. He knew few women who would actually be interested in touring a mine, much less be able to cope with the black closeness of narrow tunnels running thousands of feet beneath the ground. His Miss Holden, however, was surely made of sterner stuff. He made up his mind on the spot.

"I have to go meet with the superintendent of the Shiloh at three o'clock. Would you be interested in taking a tour of it when I'm finished?" he asked her nonchalantly.

She spun about to face him. The look on her face told him her answer before she ever said the words aloud. "Oh, Justin, could I truly?"

"Go get a coat, young woman. I need to leave here"—he paused while he consulted his pocket watch—"in five minutes."

"Thank you so much. I'll be right back down." She sent him a dazzling smile, which made him seriously reconsider the decision he had made moments earlier, but she was already bustling away from him through the front parlor.

Shaking his head over such energy and exuberance, he went to the library, intending to look at a newspaper while he waited for her. He settled himself on the settee with yesterday's copy of the *Rocky Mountain News*. Instead of reading, however, he found himself thinking about Kate's excited reaction to his invitation.

He couldn't help comparing her enthusiastic attitude today to her reserved manner last week when he had presented her with a fine string of pearls. At the time she had thanked him and commented politely on the quality of the necklace. Underneath it all, though, he sensed she was somehow angered by his gift. She had reacted much the same way when he had given her a diamond brooch and matching earrings for serving as his hostess.

Was it all an act on her part, pretending that the gifts and clothes meant nothing to her? After all the time he had spent with her, he was uneasily aware that he still didn't understand Kate Holden. The fact that she had chosen to sell herself in the first place meant money and what it could buy must be important to her. All the females he had ever known had put inordinate value on clothing, jewels, and female fripperies. For some obscure reason, Kate Holden had decided to appear uninterested in any of them.

Frowning at his newspaper, he told himself it didn't matter

whether or not he understood her. Kate Holden was proving to be the most enjoyable mistress he had ever kept. Her remarkable beauty continued to delight him, and he was more than pleased with her passionate response to his lovemaking. Perhaps most remarkable of all was the fact that her company had yet to wear on him. Kate knew how and when to be quiet. When he did feel like talking, she was a good listener and an intelligent conversationalist. Her funny way of looking at things made him laugh almost daily.

A feminine cough roused Justin from his musings. He looked up to find Kate standing in the doorway.

"I am sorry to disturb you, Mr. Talbott, but if you wish to be on time for your appointment, I do believe we should have left three minutes ago." Her tone was demure, but he could see the deviltry in her green eyes.

"Indeed, Miss Holden, it's kind of you to be reminding me of the time. Ben and his nags can still get us to the Shiloh by three."

"In that case, I'm sure it will be an interesting ride," she agreed with a grin and spun away toward the front door.

Given just the sort of challenge he relished, Ben sent the horses off at a brisk trot despite the muddy roads. They did reach the Shiloh right at three. Burly Jack Turner came out of the log cabin that served as a mine office to greet them.

The Kentuckian instantly sent his assistant hustling off to make Kate some tea. When the two men presented her with the tea in a battered tin cup, Kate graciously accepted their offering with a smile that made young Thompson blush, and Turner look as if he were going to bust a button or two off the shirt that was already strained across his considerable girth. Kate sat down in the smallest chair in Turner's spartan office and proceeded to listen eagerly to their meeting.

To begin with, Turner briefed Justin on the mine's recent engineering problems. The rock in this area of the district was very porous, and it was a continual battle to keep the lowest levels of the mine free from groundwater. On level ten the men actually wore rubber boots and raincoats and waded about constantly in over a foot of water. Yet they didn't wish to abandon the lower levels completely, for they were following the best-paying vein in the mine down there.

They went on then to discuss recent assay reports and the whole issue of which levels the men should keep working. At one point Turner, who was far better at managing men and equipment than paper, couldn't find a particular report on his cluttered desk. He rose to his feet and bawled for Thompson to find the February first report for the level-five crosscut.

"Excuse me, Mr. Turner, but I believe the level-five crosscut assayed out at twenty ounces per ton before you decided to shut it down three weeks ago," Kate said quietly.

The look on Jack Turner's face was priceless. Justin was startled, too, but his surprise lasted for just a moment. Then he tilted his head back and let go a gust of laughter.

"It was among some papers I filed for Mr. Talbott," she told the stunned mine manager kindly. "You can check the copy of the report here, but I'm quite sure that is the right number."

Young Thompson burst through the door breathlessly a minute later, flourishing the report in his hand. "Here, sir, here's the report. The level-five crosscut—"

"Assayed out at twenty ounces per ton," Justin finished for him.

"Well, yes, sir," Thompson admitted after a few moments, looking rather puzzled.

"We just wanted to make certain Miss Holden here was sure of her numbers. Thank you, Thompson. That will be all."

Looking more perplexed than ever, the young man withdrew. Turning to Kate, Justin said with a wide smile, "Are there any other contributions you would like to make to our discussion at this time, Miss Holden?"

"No, Mr. Talbott, I don't believe there are," she said, keeping her face straight. "I would love to know what you found in that drift down on level ten. I remember the reports on it looked quite promising three weeks ago."

"Indeed, miss, we struck some of the highest-grade ore in the entire Shiloh in that drift," Turner said eagerly.

"That's wonderful news. Please go ahead, gentlemen. I didn't mean to interrupt your proceedings," she said politely.

"Why, thank you, Miss Holden." Justin sent her an ironic look and plunged back into a discussion with Jack Turner over whether or not they should reopen the level-five crosscut. A half hour later they concluded their business.

With an apologetic look at Kate, Turner rose to his feet and said he needed to find some miner's helmets for them before they started their tour. Kate was delighted rather than dismayed to learn about the headgear she was expected to wear underground. Most females, Justin guessed, would have shown much more concern for their vanity and the damage wearing a helmet might do to their coiffure.

"You've confused the hell out of my manager, you know," he told her under his breath as they walked out of the office toward the main shaft of the Shiloh.

"What do you mean?" she asked him curiously.

"When we first arrived here, he believed you were my mistress. Now he's wondering if you could possibly be my clerk. And if you are my clerk, he's probably wondering why I'm too daft to be keeping you as my mistress."

"Well, if that is truly the case, I am sorry to have perplexed him. He is a dear."

Justin stopped dead in his tracks and let go another whoop of laughter. He had heard miners call Jack Turner any number of names over the years. The mine manager expected hard work from his men, even as he expected it from himself. The Kentuckian had a fierce temper that was forever getting him into fistfights, he could swear like a mule skinner, and he could drink anyone but Ben Gallagher under the table. All in all, Justin was quite certain he had never heard anyone call Jack Turner a "dear." Kate just stood there and watched him laugh, obviously trying to hide her exasperation.

"Are you quite through? Mr. Turner is clearly a busy man, and you are keeping him waiting."

"Mr. Turner is on my payroll. I can make the man wait if I've a mind to."

"Perhaps, but it is very rude of you to do so." Her steps slowed as they drew closer to the head frame and cage, vital parts of the hoist system that would lower them down the main shaft into the mine.

"Goodness, the cage is small, isn't it?" she said while she inspected the tall rectangular box suspended from the cable in front of her.

"We don't have to go through with this," he told her

quietly. "Riding down in the cage is only a part of it. The tunnels below us are dark and close. Many men find it too claustrophobic to be able to stay down there for any length of time."

"Nonsense. If your men can ride this contraption up and down twice every day, I should be able to survive one trip. If they can spend most of their waking hours below ground, I ought to be able to cope with one hour. I am a Holden, after all," she said with a toss of her head.

"All I need is for you to get hysterical or faint down there," he replied grimly.

"I can assure you I have never fainted or gotten hysterical," she declared, "although it is very kind of you to be concerned. Or perhaps you are just worried that I may hold up your ore production."

"You are absolutely right. The efficiency of my ore production is all I'm thinking about right now. The health and welfare of one particular headstrong young woman is of no concern to me in the least," he replied dryly.

That sally drew a round of male laughter. Kate glanced about, clearly surprised to see they had drawn quite a crowd. Almost all of the men who worked topside were clustered about them now. Justin didn't have the heart to send them back to their jobs. He understood full well that a visit by any woman at a mine was a rare event, and the appearance of a beautiful one was a miraculous experience not to be missed.

At that moment Turner came bustling up wearing one hard hat on his head and bearing two others in his hands.

"Here's yours, miss." The mine manager held the helmet up with a flourish. Justin wondered where in the world old Jack had managed to find such a clean and relatively small helmet on such short notice.

"Well, clearly I must get rid of this useless hat at once," Kate declared. Seven men stood there and stared as she reached up artlessly and withdrew two long hat pins. A collective sigh escaped the group when she took off her hat and revealed her shining hair, done up in a simple chignon at the back of her head.

"I could hold your hat for you, Miss Holden, if you like," Thompson got out in a rush. "My hands are pretty clean, I reckon." Justin was willing to wager if the blushing young man hadn't come to that conclusion, he never would have been bold enough to make his offer.

"Why, Mr. Thompson, that is most kind of you. Are you sure it won't be too much trouble? I know you are a very busy young man."

"No, it's . . . it's no trouble at all." Thompson turned redder than a sugar beet as he stuttered out his reply. The boy looked rapturous when she handed him her hat. It was a completely feminine affair, trimmed with ribbons, bows, and feathers. The homely young man probably had no notion of how humorous he looked standing there in his ill-fitting jacket holding Kate's light blue hat as if it were the most precious treasure on earth.

In the meantime Turner had given Kate the miner's helmet she was to wear. Her smile grew wider and wider as she turned the headgear over in her hands. She was particularly intrigued with the carbide lantern that was attached above the front brim. After she placed the helmet on her head, she twirled about so that Justin could inspect her.

"What do you think?" she demanded laughingly.

"If the editors at Harper's should see you now, you could start a whole new fashion in women's millinery."

"That was remarkably chivalrous of you," she allowed. "I know I must look quite absurd." Then her impatience got the better of her. "Now you have to put yours on." The ever helpful Thompson stepped forward and offered to hold his employer's top hat as well. Justin smiled inwardly as he handed the boy his hat. He had no doubt Kate's headgear would receive better treatment.

"Mr. Talbott, you look all business now," Kate said with a delighted nod. "I can just imagine you picking away on the Sadie Sue."

"Just for that, little minx, I may make you shovel a ton of ore once we're below ground."

"Just give me a shovel, sir, and tell me what to muck," she replied gaily.

"I thought we'd light all three of the lanterns up here, Mr. Talbott, so's it won't be so dark on the way down for her," Turner said in an anxious aside to him.

"That's a good idea." Justin nodded to his mine manager and unhooked the lantern from his own hard hat. He pushed the lever that allowed water in the lantern to combine with calcium tablets. As soon as he heard the hiss of carbide gas, he deftly shifted the strike lever until a spark from it lit the lantern. Kate watched his every move intently. When he finished lighting his own lantern, he clipped it back onto his hat and reached over and lit Kate's for her as well. Her green eyes grew even wider when she heard her own lantern begin to hiss.

"Now, my dear, we are ready for our tour. After you." He gestured toward the waiting cage. She took one step toward it, stopped, and glanced back over her shoulder at him.

"Will this conveyance be bumpy on the way down?"

Before he could reply, a man stepped forward from the crowd and snatched his battered cap from his head. It was Dirty Dick Jenkinson, the hoist operator. As Justin stared in revolted fascination at the man's greasy, matted hair, he decided the rumor that Dirty Dick hadn't taken a bath in over two years was probably true.

"Miss, we'll lower you down smoother than the fanciest darn hotel lift you ever rode."

"It's true," Turner added reassuringly. "Dirty Dick Jenkinson is one of the most reliable men I've ever had in the hoist house."

"Why, thank you, Mr. Jenkinson. I'm quite sure now that I will ride in your cage most comfortably."

Justin grinned when he heard her say under her breath, "*Mox nox in rem*," a most appropriate Latin phrase. Literally the words meant, "night soon, to the business," but loosely translated the saying implied, "let's get on with things."

With that she stepped forward boldly into the cage. Despite her brave words, she was looking a little pale. Justin quickly followed her into the small space and put a comforting arm about her shoulders. When Turner stepped into the cage as well, the small platform shifted, and Kate clutched at Justin's coat. The mine manager shut the door to the cage carefully. Kate watched curiously as he proceeded to yank several times on a rope hanging right by the door.

"That rings a bell in the hoist house telling Dick we're ready to go down to level one," Justin explained before she could ask.

As the lift slipped down into darkness, Kate gave a little gasp. He felt her step closer to him. He tightened his grip on her shoulder to reassure her. The light from their three lanterns kept the inky blackness from enveloping them completely. Looking through the open sides of the cage, he could see the wooden timbering and escape ladder built on the side of the main shaft sliding past them.

After a few moments Kate asked suddenly, "Did you ever ride an ore bucket up and down one of these shafts?"

"On far too many occasions. Many miners have to use open ore buckets until they get the backing to put in more sophisticated equipment. This a luxurious way to travel down into a mine, Mr. Turner and his men will tell you."

"It's safer, too, miss," Turner added. "It's way too easy for a chunk of ore or a drill bit to go a-plummetin' down this shaft. Now we have a nice, strong metal roof over our heads. The boss here was one of the first owners in the district to make sure all his mines had these covered cages. A mucker got killed over in Victor just three months ago when a big piece of ore came down the shaft and smashed his head in."

Justin winced at Turner's graphic phrasing, but Kate didn't seem the least bit fazed by it. In fact, she was already asking them both another question.

"It feels so cool and damp. Is the temperature always like this underground?"

"Now that can be a queer thing, miss," Turner answered her question this time. "Usually it's cool like this, but different levels of the same mine can have very different temperatures. Over in the lower levels of the Ajax mine, it gets up to seventy degrees. The men there work in their shirtsleeves all day long. Well, here we are. Jenkinson stopped us nice and easy just like he promised. Welcome to level one of the Shiloh."

Turner unlatched the door and helped Kate out of the cage with a gentlemanly flourish that had Justin smiling inwardly. Kate stood in the middle of the tunnel, twisting her head from side to side. She obviously was growing used to the way she could direct the halo of light created by her lantern. She hardly noticed when Turner pulled the rope, signaling that Jenkinson could put the cage back to work. Moments later it disappeared soundlessly down the main shaft on its way to the lower levels.

"Oh, Justin, this is just wonderful. I can promise you now that I won't faint and I won't get claustrophobia. I'm going to be far too busy learning everything I can down here."

"There was some question in your mind about your having claustrophobia?" he asked with a raised brow. The tunnel she was standing in was no more than four feet wide, and barely six feet in height.

"Well, I'm not particularly fond of being shut in dark closets," she admitted with a sheepish smile.

"Now she tells me." Justin shook his head.

"You need to watch your step here, miss," the mine manager said anxiously. "The timbers and tram rails are slick from all the moisture we have seeping through the rock." Turner led the way down the tunnel. Justin came up and took Kate's elbow. Her dainty boots hardly constituted good footwear for walking along slippery cart ties.

"How do the ore carts get pushed from the place the men are blasting to here?" she asked the mine manager.

"Large mines will use mules to tram the carts along. None of our tunnels are long enough yet to need them. Manpower works well enough for us at the moment," Turner replied.

As they walked along, Turner paused from time to time to show Kate interesting mineral deposits and various winzes and raises along their route. She was amazed by the first stope they passed. Although Justin had already explained to her the stoping process, she listened politely as Turner explained it to her again. When the miners discovered a valuable drift, a large body of ore bearing rock, it was often most economically feasible for them to tunnel under the drift and mine upward into that mass. That way the miners could use gravity to help them with their task. They built wooden chutes so that the ore they blasted loose fell down directly into mine carts.

Stoping often produced large open areas inside of mountains. As Kate peered up into the jagged cleft above their heads that stretched away into blackness, Turner told her they had drilled and blasted this stope up almost two hundred feet before the vein they were mining played out.

"I never realized miners must have a good head for heights. You just don't think of them working up on narrow platforms a hundred feet above the tunnel floor," Kate said wonderingly.

"Miners follow the veins wherever they run. Over at that Comstock mine in Nevada, they're just about stoping out the whole inside of a mountain. Ah, I can hear the fellows working up ahead."

Once they proceeded around a bend in the tunnel, they did indeed find a crew of three miners drilling into a rock face at the end of the crosscut. The men stopped when they saw their manager and their mine owner approaching. The astonishment on their faces was obvious when they realized they also had a woman visitor. Some miners thought women below ground brought bad luck. Justin hoped this crew at least would manage to hide their feelings on that topic. His concern proved unfounded just moments later.

After staring at the men intently, Kate suddenly stepped forward with her hand extended to the tallest of the three. "Hello, Mr. Johnson, it's a pleasure to see you again."

"Well, if it isn't purty little Miss Holden." The miner's dirty face lit up with a wide smile. "It's real nice to see you, too. I won't be shaking your hand, though, because my old paw would just get that dainty glove of yourn all grimy. Hey, fellas, this here is Miss Holden. She wrote some letters fer me when I was laid up in the hospital with that broke arm and leg."

The men on the shift clustered around after sending a wary glance or two Justin's way. Sandy Johnson promptly introduced her to his partners, Pete Roeder and Stumpy Smith.

"I can see you gentlemen have been drilling. Could you tell me a little bit about your equipment and your job here?" Kate asked brightly when the introductions were finished.

"You just bet. This here dee-vice is called a pneumatic drill. That means air pressure powers it. Now you probably know we're making holes we can tamp the dynamite into. In the old days my pa and his partner had to do this job by hand, with a big ol' sledgehammer called a double jack. One man held the drill bit and turned it while the other swung the jack. Took real trust holding on to that bit and hoping you'd still have your hands when your partner was done a-swinging, more than I have in these fellows here, that's for sure."

Johnson grinned at his fellow miners and then continued on with his explanation. "Once we got our pattern drilled, we pack the dynamite in real cautious-like with a wooden tamper. Again, this job today is a lot safer than it used to be. That old-time dynamite was mighty persnickety. You had to keep it at just the right temperature, or kabloom! Still do, for that matter, but at least the stuff don't blow up if you look at it crossways.

"We set the fuses so that the shots fire one after t'other. After we light that fuse, we'll hustle ourselves around a corner, 'cause the blast waves travel straight, you see. And we want to count real careful when the shots are going off. If we drilled an eight-hole pattern, we wait to hear the shots go: boom, boom, boom, right on up to eight. It's not much fun if we lose count and number eight goes off right about the time we decide to come around the corner. That happened to Stumpy here, which is why the man can't hear so good anymore."

"And it's terribly dangerous if one doesn't fire, isn't it?"

"Yep. The fella that packed in a dud is the poor cuss who gets to pick it out again, with no company around him in case it goes off in his face."

"What happens after all the dynamite has gone off?"

"Then we get to muck up the mess and shovel it into the ore carts. That can be upwards of two or three tons of ore. Then we tram it out to the shaft, where the cage lifts it up to the surface. About that time our shift's usually over. We pick up our drill bits so the boys up top can sharpen 'em for tomorrow, and then we go home."

"Well, gentlemen, thank you for your time. Kate, we mustn't keep them from their work any longer." Justin knew she was bursting with questions she wanted to ask, but the men did have work to finish before their shift was over, and he didn't want them hurrying. He made a mental note to tell Turner later to make certain each of these men received a bonus.

Kate started to protest, but he squeezed her arm gently. When she glanced up and saw the serious look in his eye, she quickly followed his lead. "Thank you, gentlemen. You did a fine job of explaining your business to me."

"Me and the fellows shore enjoyed having such a pretty visitor. Now, you keep a sharp eye out for Tommyknockers on the way out of here. One of those little rascals hid my lunch pail just last shift.''

Kate obviously knew that Tommyknockers were mischievous little elves the miners believed lived down in these mines, for she gave a laugh and glanced at her feet. ''I thought I felt someone tugging at my hem just a few minutes ago. That explains it. You gentlemen take care of yourselves.''

''We always do, miss.''

With that, Justin took Kate's arm again and escorted her back toward the main shaft. During the ride back up to the surface, she peppered Turner with the questions she had probably wanted to ask the drilling crew. When they returned topside, Kate was visibly pleased when Turner presented her with a couple of good ore samples. After examining the dull gray pieces carefully, she pointed out as diplomatically as she could that she couldn't find anything in them remotely resembling a speck of gold. Turner laughed and explained that in the Cripple Creek area gold was usually found in sylvanite tellurides. He told her to try putting her gray samples on the stove when she returned home, and beads of gold would bubble to the surface. Kate smiled and promised she would do exactly that.

Thompson appeared then bearing their hats. Kate reluctantly exchanged her miner's helmet for her frilly hat. She thanked both Turner and Thompson for their time and the tour until both men were blushing and beaming. Several of the topside crew escorted them to the carriage. Kate called farewells and waved at them gaily until the landau drew away from the mine site.

''Thank you, Justin, that was just fascinating,'' she said as she finally stopped waving and sank back against the carriage seat. Her green eyes sparkled like emeralds, and her cheeks were flushed with excitement. An overwhelming desire to kiss her rose in him, but he was afraid he would start something he could not decently finish in a carriage during daylight hours. Instead he decided to concentrate on giving her a coherent reply.

''You're most welcome, little scholar. It was entertaining seeing my business through your eyes. I'm not sure, however, that many young women would have found these past few hours fascinating. Nor do I think they could have borne the rigors of walking about five hundred feet beneath the earth so staunchly.''

She wrinkled her nose at him. "Is that a way of insinuating that I'm odd?''

"I daresay you are unusual, but I meant it as a compliment.''

"Thank you, I think,'' she said after a few moments. She fell quiet after that, staring out the carriage window, obviously contemplating the afternoon's experiences.

"What are you thinking, my dear, with that pensive look on your face?'' he asked at last.

She sighed and continued to look out the window. "Only that I understand so much better now what Robert's days were like when he was working as a mucker. Mining is such a hard and dangerous way to make a living. Those men in your employ will drill and blast and strain their backs to bring thousands of dollars of gold to the surface for you. Yet none of them will ever strike it rich themselves. They will spend the rest of their lives earning little more than three dollars a day.''

"It's true,'' he replied gravely. "The majority of them will never find a bonanza of their own. I would like to ask you this, however. Do you think their lives and work here are any worse than those of factory workers back east? There men and women have to work equally long hours doing tedious, repetitive work using dangerous machines. At least these men can take pride in what they do and the expertise that they possess.''

"It just doesn't seem fair.''

"It isn't, but that is often the way of things in this world.''

She was silent for a time, perhaps digesting his words or thinking more about her tour of the mine. When they reached the outskirts of Cripple Creek, he said quietly, "You never told me that you used to help out at the miners' hospital. Why don't you go there anymore?''

"Because,'' she said, raising her green eyes to meet his, "I didn't think the staff would want me there now.'' The bitterness in her voice surprised him. The reproach he saw in her gaze made him look away.

He decided to leave the matter at that for the moment, but the events of the day and Miss Holden herself had given him much to think about.

Chapter Sixteen

It was Friday evening of the sixth week Kate had spent in Justin Talbott's household. She was sitting on the sofa in the library, feeling even less charitably inclined toward her employer than usual. He had told her to dress for dinner and to be ready to leave the house at seven-thirty. Now it was eight-thirty, and there was still no sign of Justin or Ben. Kate got to her feet and began prowling about the room. She had to admit it wasn't like Justin to keep her waiting. Occasionally he had been a few minutes late, but in general Justin was as punctual as his office had been messy.

By nine o'clock she was beginning to wonder if something might have happened to hold them up. She knew he had gone to look at a claim he was interested in purchasing, and he had taken two of his bright young mining engineers with him. If he knew he was going to be this late returning home, it seemed odd that he hadn't thought to send someone with a message. At nine-thirty Mrs. Parslow came to find her.

"I think you should come have a bowl of soup with us in the kitchen. I'm sure we will hear something from Mr. Talbott soon," the housekeeper declared as she led Kate back to the kitchen.

Mrs. Parslow and Madame Dupuy proceeded to make much of her appearance, telling her how lovely she looked in a golden faille gown created by Madame Sophie. Kate smiled and thanked them and did her best to eat her soup, but all the while she listened for the sound of the carriage pulling up and the front door opening.

Just before ten, they heard the team pull around to the back. Kate was already on her feet when Ben Gallagher opened the back door. The grim look on his face made her blood run cold.

249

As she sat down again, her legs suddenly too shaky to hold her up, he came straight to her side. He knelt and took her hands in his own.

"There's been an accident, missee. The boss went to look at a claim this afternoon. These two damn tenderfeet had dug it right into the gravelly side of Gold Hill, and the fools didn't know the first thing about timbering it right. The adit came down five minutes after all of 'em went inside. I went and fetched crews from the boss's mines, and they're working as fast as they can to dig him and the rest of them out of there."

"When . . . when did this happen?"

"Right about four o'clock, I reckon. I didn't come before in case we could dig him out quick-like. I knew he'd have my scalp if I got you all worried for nothing. But now it's looking like the boys are goin' to be a while. I can promise you they're working as fast as they can. They like the boss, and they'll surely do their best for him."

Kate barely heard Ben's answer, for she was desperately trying to figure out just how bad the situation was. If the tunnel had collapsed directly on the men, they had probably been crushed instantly or suffocated shortly thereafter. She forced down the cold tide of panic that rose inside her at that thought. She couldn't, she wouldn't accept the possibility that Justin was already dead.

"How long was that adit?"

"Well, the two tinhorns who dug it got caught in there with the boss and his engineers, so we don't know for sure. The fella working the claim next to them believes they had gone back in a good two hundred feet last time he took a look at their diggings."

"So there still could be air in there."

Ben squeezed her hands and looked as if he was immensely proud of her. "That's right, missee, and that's what I want you to keep thinking about."

"Ben, I know his parents are dead, but should we, should we notify Justin's fiancée, do you suppose?"

"His fiancée? Do you mean to tell me that young varmint went and got himself promised to some gal and didn't even tell me?" Ben's blustering outrage at this notion would have made Kate smile if the situation hadn't been so serious.

"Well, I thought he was engaged to Miss LaMonte. At least, everyone about town was saying so a few months back."

Ben's angry expression swiftly changed to one of relieved amusement. "Hell, no, he ain't engaged to her. I hope he has more sense than that. I'll have to quit working for him the day he hitches himself up to that cold fish."

"Justin's not engaged," she repeated wonderingly. Suddenly she felt as if far too much was happening, and she couldn't take it all in at once.

"No, *ma petite*." Madame Dupuy touched her hand gently. "That one, she wanted marriage, but I think she pushed him too hard for it. *Je t'assure*, Monsieur Talbott is not engaged."

"He has gotten himself into a fix, and I need to go back now to help him out of it." Ben let go of Kate's hands and heaved himself to his feet. "I swear I'll send someone over here as soon as we know anything."

"Thank you, Ben. Thank you for coming to tell us."

"Well, I figured sitting around wondering could get worse'n knowing the truth after a time. Now, missee, you keep thinking about all that air he has in there. The boss, he's one of the toughest cusses I've ever met, and one of the luckiest. If any man could come out of a tight spot alive, it'd be him."

"Benjamin, can you not wait for just a moment? I will fix something to eat that you can take with you."

It was the first time Kate had ever heard Madame Dupuy call Ben by his first name. Kate was almost thunderstruck when Ben smiled back at the Frenchwoman tenderly and said, "No, thanks, Louise. Some of the miners' wives fed me already. Course it wasn't anything like your souffler. I'd best be getting back." He nodded to them all and slipped out the door.

There was a long silence in the kitchen then. Kate found herself staring hard at the little indigo flowers printed on Madame Dupuy's tablecloth while the thoughts tumbled around frantically in her mind. He couldn't be dead. He had looked so alive and vital just that afternoon when he stopped by her room to see how her studies were progressing. He was too big, too arrogant, too confident to die, crushed under tons of rock and gravel and dirt.

No, Justin wasn't dead, but it was far too easy to imagine

the black, cold place where he was trapped now. And to think he could be lying there, in that total darkness, badly injured and fighting to breathe. She closed her eyes and swallowed a sob. She felt a gentle hand cover her own. When she looked up the housekeeper was standing by her side.

"Let's go upstairs and get you changed," Mrs. Parslow said in a brisk, no-nonsense tone, even though her eyes looked suspiciously wet. "You'll be much more comfortable while you wait for him to come home."

"That is a good idea." Madame Dupuy was nodding vigorously. "And while you two are upstairs, I will make our *petite* a special posset. It is very good for difficult times like these."

Kate followed the housekeeper upstairs, for she dimly understood that Mrs. Parslow would be happier taking charge and having something to do right now. She let the widow help her out of her gown and into her nightdress and robe. She even allowed the woman to take down her hair and brush it out. It was comforting, having her warm presence nearby while she tried to come to terms with the notion that Justin could be fighting for his life at this very moment.

When Mrs. Parslow asked if she wanted to stay upstairs for a bit, Kate said she would prefer to go down to the kitchen again. As soon as they were seated at the kitchen table, Madame Dupuy served up three of her steaming possets. Kate took a sip of hers and almost choked as the liquid fire burned its way down the back of her throat. She had regained enough of her equilibrium by then to be amused. Madame Dupuy's idea of a posset contained a very liberal dose of Justin's fine French brandy.

Mrs. Parslow pulled out her needlework, and Madame Dupuy brought over several apples and began paring them. The Frenchwoman declared she meant to make apple crepes in the morning, for they were one of Justin's favorite breakfasts. Mrs. Parslow started talking then in a determinedly cheerful tone. She told them about various cave-ins and mining accidents in which some survivors had been dug out in time. Madame Dupuy joined in, too, after a bit.

Kate sighed inwardly as the two became quite caught up in their stories. The ladies meant well, but all she could think of in every case they mentioned were the men who didn't make it, the ones who weren't saved in time and lived their last desperate moments in the frigid darkness, struggling to pull air into their burning lungs.

"If you two don't mind too much, I think I would like to be alone now," she declared when a lull finally came in their storytelling. "I'm going to sit in the library for a little while."

"Of course, dear," Mrs. Parslow said kindly. "We will wait up right here. If you want anything, anything at all, let us know."

"Thank you." Kate rose to her feet and stood looking at them both, Madame Dupuy so round and dark, and Mrs. Parslow, tall, gray, and refined. "You two have been so kind to me from the very first," she said, a little catch in her throat.

"Ah, bah, it has not been so very hard." Madame Dupuy shrugged her shoulders. "I want you to know Monsieur Talbott has been much happier since you came to live with us. You have been good for him, *petite*."

"And you will continue to be," Mrs. Parslow said in her definite fashion. "Now off with you." She made a shooing motion with her hands, and Kate went. She started toward the library, but she changed her mind and walked down the hall toward his office. She hesitated before the walnut doors. She wanted to feel close to him right now, and this was the place he spent most of his waking hours.

Drawing in a deep breath, she opened the right-hand door and stepped inside. She flicked on the overhead light, closed the door behind her, and leaned back against it. Here in his private refuge, she let the first wave of grief take her. She bowed her head and let her tears flow. She told herself it was absurd to act as though he were dead already, but she couldn't seem to help herself. She stood there, the hot tears scalding her cheeks until some of the tightness in her chest eased. That first bit of fierce weeping seemed to steady her. Wrenching out a handkerchief, she wiped her eyes, blew her nose, and walked forward into his sanctuary.

The big room was empty and cold without the usual fire in the fireplace, and without Justin himself. Yet some of his forceful presence and personality seemed to linger. She could just picture him sitting at his desk, sleeves rolled back while he pored over his reports, oblivious to the world while he worked. That at least was something they had in common, she decided wryly.

She went over and sank down in one of the wing-back chairs by the empty fireplace. She had felt so comfortable with him during that magical week they had been snowed in together. That was the easy side of Justin, the charming, humorous part of his personality she found so captivating. Yet she didn't mind the brooding, intense side of him either. She could understand and respect his single-minded ambition, his drive to build something that mattered, for her father had possessed such drive as well. She could hardly feel intimidated by his restless, powerful intellect when it matched her own so perfectly. And beneath it all there was a basic kindness he tried to hide from everyone, the generosity that made him donate the funds for the miners' hospital and grubstake old prospectors who came to him.

She leaned back in the chair wearily and looked up at the glorious painting above the mantelpiece. It was time she faced the truth. There was no way she could ignore what tonight had brought home to her with merciless clarity. She loved Justin Talbott, loved him with all her heart and soul. She had never stopped loving him through everything that had happened between them, and she never would stop loving him.

She knew how he felt about women. How could she love someone who had no respect for her or her gender? Once again she had leaped before looking. This time her recklessness was going to cost her dearly, for she had landed in love with a man who could not or would not love her in return.

She laid her head back against the chair and let a second wave of tears come. She would give anything to see him appear in the doorway right now, alive and unhurt. If only this terrible time were just a dream, a horrible nightmare that would vanish when she awoke. But she knew tonight was no dream, and somewhere she would have to find the strength to get through the long hours of waiting that lay ahead.

If and when he did come home, she would soon have to face another painful challenge. The time was swiftly approaching when she would have to leave his household. It had been a great relief to discover he wasn't engaged, and yet she wasn't foolish enough to dream he would marry her. He had made it clear what he wanted from a marriage, and marrying an ex-prostitute would hardly enhance his social position. She promised herself that if he lived she would simply try to relish this last week with him. But first his men had to dig him out of that dark, cold place he was trapped, and dig him out in time.

At last she wiped her eyes and face with her handkerchief and rose to her feet. The library, too, was filled with Justin's presence and personality, and it was closer to the front door. Quietly she switched off the light and closed his office door behind her.

She was dozing on the library sofa when she heard the sound of the front door opening. She jerked awake at once, the terrible fear that had never left her through the long night still crushing her in its grip. She barely noticed the gray light from early morning seeping in through the curtains. She wanted to stand, but her legs seemed frozen. All she could do was sit and stare at the doorway, and pray.

Moments later he appeared in the hall, filthy, haggard, but very much alive. She must have made some sound or movement, for he turned about and saw her at once. He didn't say a word to her, but he held his arms out. The need she saw in his gaze helped erase the last of her uncertainty. She left the sofa in a rush.

"Oh, Justin," she said brokenly into his muddy shirt, and held him tight.

"Sh, now, none of that," he said in the gentlest tones she had ever heard him speak, and she felt him stroking her hair.

"I'm going to get dirt all over you, but Lord knows it's good just to hold you like this." He sighed as he rested his cheek on the top of her head. They stood there for a long time, simply relishing the real, warm feel of each other.

"Did everyone get out?" she asked after a time. She felt his hold on her tighten briefly.

"No. We lost Torry Simpson." Justin's voice sounded like dull thunder rumbling in his chest. "The poor devil was the last one in the group. He was right under the section that went first. Rob Morrison may lose his leg. He was pinned under one of the timbers until the men dug us out of there."

"And the tenderfeet?"

"Shaken, but alive, and hopefully a great deal wiser about timbering now. They were walking ahead of everyone else when the roof gave way."

She felt him sway in her arms. After what he had been through during the last sixteen hours, he had to be exhausted. She drew in a deep breath and pushed away from him. "Come to the kitchen now, and we'll find you something to eat. Or do you want to wash up first?"

"I'll run upstairs and wash and find something besides these muddy rags to wear before I leave. I would appreciate it if you could find something for me to eat in the meanwhile."

"You're not going out again?" She stared at him in dismay. From the uncompromising set to his jaw, she realized he meant to do exactly that. "Can't you let yourself rest?"

"I have things I need to see to this morning."

"Justin Talbott, there's such a thing as being obsessed, you know." She shook a finger at him. "Your business affairs aren't going to fall apart if you neglect them for one day."

"Kate, it's not just business, not in the sense you mean. Simpson had a family. I need to see them this morning. I want to take care of the funeral arrangements and make sure Mrs. Simpson understands that she can count on me for financial help. There are a few other matters that need tending to as well."

He didn't say it, but she guessed he would make certain Rob Morrison was treated by the finest surgeon in Colorado, even if he had to kidnap one from Denver to see the young man.

"You'll come back this afternoon when you can and get some rest." She crossed her arms and dared him with her eyes to contradict her.

"That I will, and gladly, especially if I find you in my bed when I come home," he said with a smile that made her bones begin to melt.

"I said rest." She tried to sound prim, but her lips betrayed her with a wide smile. Now that he was actually here, now that she knew he was alive and well, a strange hilarity was bubbling up inside her.

"All right then," she said, doing her best to emulate Mrs.

Parslow's most businesslike tones. "Off you go." And she tried to push him toward the stairs.

"In my own good time," she heard him say, and then she was in his arms again, and he was kissing her soundly. She was just getting into the spirit of the thing when he let her go and turned away.

Hands on her hips, she watched him go striding up the stairs, wondering where he found the energy to keep going after all he had been through. Shaking her head, Kate went to share her relief and joy with Mrs. Parslow and Madame Dupuy.

Justin didn't actually return to the house until three o'clock that afternoon. Kate had given some serious thought to waiting for him in his bed as he had implied she should do. At last she decided to settle for the library. She just couldn't make herself change into her nightdress in the middle of the afternoon and go lie down in his bed. It would be so embarrassing if he found her there, and had changed his mind about making love to her in the meantime.

As it turned out, she was heartily glad she had chosen to wait for him in the library. When Justin returned to the house, he found her at once and made the following declaration: "I'm going upstairs to take that rest you recommended, but I'd like to try it alone. You mustn't take it as any sort of reflection on your own appeal, my dear. I'm just too damned tired to do anything but sleep right now."

His tone was light, but there was a set look to his face that made her think his day had not been easy. It must have been hellish, meeting the bereaved widow of his young engineer and spending time with his other engineer with the badly injured leg. She longed to ask him how Rob Morrison was doing, but Justin had already turned about and started up the stairs.

A short time later she went to her own room and lay down for a nap. Because she was worn out after her long, emotional night, she fell asleep quickly. The sound of Justin's quiet footsteps in the hallway woke her around six o'clock. She heard him hesitate briefly in front of her door, but then he went on. She frowned at the ceiling. Did this mean he wanted to eat alone this evening? Usually he told her exactly when they were going to dine and what he wanted her to wear. She got up and dressed in a lovely blue patterned silk tea dress, which seemed like a good compromise between a day dress and a full evening gown.

At last she ventured downstairs to the kitchen, hoping Mrs. Parslow and Madame Dupuy would know what her enigmatic employer's plans were for the evening. She found the two ladies sitting at the table, Mrs. Parslow doing her needlework, and Madame Dupuy reading a newspaper. As soon as she saw Kate, the Frenchwoman smiled and rose to her feet.

"Come sit, *ma petite*, and I will fix a plate for you. Tonight we are having tournedos Charlemagne. Monsieur Talbott said he wanted beef after having to miss his dinner last evening."

"Tournedos Charlemagne sounds delicious," Kate said honestly and went to take her customary place at the table. "Did Mr. Talbott go out for the evening?"

"No, he told us he thought you were sleeping, and that we shouldn't wake you. Instead he said he wished to eat alone in the dining room," Mrs. Parslow explained quietly.

"And then he ate almost nothing of my fine tournedos, or the gâteau chocolat au Grand Marnier I baked for him," Madame Dupuy broke in disgustedly. "After that he went back to his office. He said he was going to work, but I do not think this was so, because he had a bottle of whiskey under his arm. And he said with that black look of his that he did not want anyone disturbing him."

"I suppose that means I'd better not go back there." Kate stared at the plate Madame Dupuy had just placed in front of her. If Justin truly didn't want company, it probably would be best if she didn't bother him. Besides, she had to admit to herself, the thought of facing a drunken Justin was more than a little daunting.

"Monsieur Talbott is the sort of man who feels responsible for people," the cook said as she stirred a pot on her stove. "He'll be taking that young man's death hard, *certainement*."

"I'd say he's already had plenty of time to himself," Mrs. Parslow said meditatively as she continued to work her embroidery. "He shouldn't be allowed to brood about it for too long."

"Ah, so in you ladies' expert opinion, Mr. Talbott could use some company shortly." Kate tilted her head as she eyed the two women.

"It was just a thought, *ma petite*." The Frenchwoman held her palms wide in disclaimer, but she sent Kate an encouraging smile as well.

"I see. Well, thank you for the advice, I think," Kate said grimly as she turned her attention to the food in front of her. It was all very well for them to hint she should go beard the lion in his den, but they weren't going to have to face his displeasure.

She ate mechanically and listened with only half an ear as the two women talked about inconsequential things. She was trying to imagine what Justin Talbott might be like inebriated. Although he often drank a glass of wine before or during dinner, she was quite sure she had never seen her controlled employer truly drunk. She had rarely encountered men under the influence of alcohol in her sheltered life back in Boston, but since coming west she had seen plenty. Some men obviously became happy and mellow under the influence of spirits, and others became belligerent and angry.

She hoped, rather strenuously, that Justin would prove to be one of the former. When she finished her dinner she politely declined Madame Dupuy's offer to serve her some of the chocolate cake. She didn't have any appetite for more food because her stomach was already tightening. Besides, if she was going to defy Justin's orders, she preferred to do it before he made any more inroads on that bottle of scotch he had taken with him. When she rose to her feet, Mrs. Parslow and Madame Dupuy sent her sunny smiles and wished her luck. Hoping the two women were right to think Justin would be better for some company and distraction right now, Kate started off toward his office.

She hesitated for several moments before the great doors. Perhaps it would be best to abide by his wishes and leave him alone tonight. The look she had seen on his face that afternoon, however, still haunted her. Madame Dupuy was right. Justin had to be hurting now. She doubted there was anything she could do to help, but she knew she had to try at least.

Taking a deep breath, she quietly opened the door and

slipped inside. She spotted him almost at once, even though
the only light in the room came from the flickering flames of
the fire. He was sitting in one of the wing-back chairs, his
long legs stretched out in front of him. She moved forward
silently, clinging to the slim hope that the farther she made it
into the room, the greater effort he would have to make to
toss her out of it. As she drew closer, she spared a quick glance
for the whiskey bottle sitting beside him. She was encouraged
to see the bottle was still seven-eighths full. She thought it
would take more liquor than that to get a man of his size
intoxicated, but she couldn't be sure.

She halted several feet from his chair because the rustle of
her skirts had alerted him. When he looked up from the fire,
she saw he had undone his tie, and his shirt was open at the
neck. His hair looked as if he had been running his hands
through it, and one dark, curly lock had fallen down across
his forehead. She ached to be able to reach out and gently tuck
that lock back into place, but she knew it wasn't time yet to
touch him.

"Miss Holden, it's rude not to knock before entering a
room." The precise way he spoke his words reassured her.
Justin Talbott might be on his way to being sauced, but he
was not completely inebriated just yet.

"Of course it is, but then, you never bother to knock on
mine," she reminded him sweetly.

"True enough, but it's my house, and I can do what I want
inside it. And the folk in my employ are supposed to obey my
wishes and my orders. Right now I'm telling you—go away."

"I don't think I'm going to do that just yet," she replied
quietly and took a seat in the chair opposite him. Even though
he was telling her to go, the pain in his eyes made her resolved
to stay.

"I've managed not to say anything particularly hurtful to
you for almost two weeks now, but I cannot promise to rein
in my temper much longer if you insist on remaining in here,"
he growled.

"I knew there was a reason the last few weeks had been a
bit dull around here," she said with a bright smile. "I hope
you haven't done yourself any lasting harm by restraining your
natural inclinations."

He let go an unwilling laugh. "Oh, little scholar, don't make me smile. The way I feel right now, I'd prefer to throttle someone."

"Since murder is a hanging offense in this town, you are getting drunk instead. I suppose that's wise, but you won't be feeling so well in the morning. Nor do I think drink will truly help what's hurting you right now."

"But it will mask it for the moment," he said almost savagely and lunged to his feet to begin pacing back and forth in front of the fire.

"How did your visit with Mrs. Simpson go today?" she asked when it was clear he wasn't going to say anything further.

"How did it go?" He raised one black brow as he mocked her polite tone by echoing it. "It went just swimmingly, thank you. Mrs. Simpson received me in her tiny, perfectly ordered front parlor. She sat there trying to be brave, and all the while she looked as if her world was falling apart, which of course it has. She thanked me most correctly for the financial help I offered her. She even told me how thrilled young Torry had been when he went to work for me."

"He probably was, at that," Kate said softly.

"And look what good it did him." Justin whirled about to face her. "The young fool died chasing my dream, the same dream that kills and maims men every day in these mining camps. You read the papers. You've been to the hospital. You see how they die. Pneumonia, miner's lung, blasting accidents, cave-ins—they endure all that just to wrest gold and silver from the ground. I sometimes wonder if these metals and the men who search for them aren't cursed."

"Was Torry Simpson a mining engineer before you hired him?"

He looked startled by her interruption. "I hired him away from an outfit in California that had no appreciation for the boy's abilities," he replied shortly.

"Then he probably had gold fever long before he ever met you. He would have spent a great deal of his life prowling about in dangerous places below ground, whether or not he worked for you."

"That's a neat piece of logic, my dear, and one that would

have done Socrates proud.'' There was an undercurrent of amusement in his voice. "It doesn't, however, change the fact that Torry Simpson was working for me when he died."

"No, it doesn't, and that is something you have to learn to live with. At least you can take comfort from the knowledge you've done all you can to make your own mines as safe as possible for your men."

"Comfort, eh? I'm not sure that knowledge can give me as much comfort as you could right now."

It took her a few moments to understand his meaning. When she looked up he was watching her with that familiar flame kindling in his eyes. She let go a sigh of relief and rose at once. When she was standing before him, she tilted her head a little to the side and asked, "Are you saying you prefer me to the contents of that whiskey bottle?"

"*Mais oui*, as Madame Dupuy would say. I can spend the night with you and have no hangover in the morning," he said lightly as he reached out with both hands and pulled her closer. His eyes darkened as he gazed at her face. "With you, I can forget myself and a world of worries and pain. Just looking into your sweet green eyes brings me a world of peace."

Surprised by his poetic words, she stood still while he tipped her head up and kissed her gently. He caressed her lips with his own, offering her an exquisite tenderness in his embrace. Moved beyond words by his gentleness, she made no protest when he picked her up and carried her upstairs.

When they reached the privacy of his bedroom, he proceeded to undress her slowly, with a care and a reverence he had never shown her before. He kissed and smoothed her skin as he peeled her layers of clothing away. Then she did the same for him and, already entwined in each other's arms, they slipped under the covers.

They came together with a smile and a sigh. They moved with perfect rhythm, touched with perfect understanding of each other's needs and preferences. They reached their release at the same moment, exquisitely aware of the pleasure each was experiencing. She was still coming back down to earth when he withdrew from her and began, with his hands and lips, to build her toward a second crest that he clearly meant for her to experience on her own. He kissed and massaged her, strummed her nerves and senses like a master musician playing an instrument he had known for a lifetime.

With my body, I thee worship. She felt a pang of sadness when she realized she would never hear him say those words aloud to her. It would have to be enough that for tonight at least, he was acting them out, giving them a fullness of meaning she had never understood before. As he moved over her, kissing, caressing, creating a sweet melody of desire that resonated and filled her body, she knew she would treasure her memories of this night always.

After he played her body to a final crescendo of feeling, she must have dozed for a time, her head resting against his shoulder. When she woke again she could see the shine of his eyes in the darkness. He was wide awake and staring at the ceiling. Guessing there might be one more thing she could do to help him, she tackled the issue head-on.

"What was it like for you down there?"

He sighed and turned over so that he was lying on his side facing her. "It's not the first time I've been caught underground. This was the hardest, though, perhaps because of young Rob. After we discovered there was no way we could get the timber off him, all we could do was sit and wait. I knew he must be bleeding, but I couldn't get to his leg to bandage it. Although we all had carbide lanterns, we decided to turn them off to save air. And so we sat there in the darkness, hoping they'd dig us out before Rob bled to death and before our air ran out.

"Being trapped underground is an interesting business," he continued, his deep voice calm and almost meditative. "I've found different men react so differently in situations like this. One tenderfoot prayed and prayed for God to help us. The younger one cried for his mother."

"And what did you do?"

"I talked with young Rob during the times the boy was conscious. He told me all about his sweetheart and his family back in Pennsylvania."

"And the times he wasn't?" she asked hesitantly.

"I thought about you." He sounded surprised as he said the words. "I thought about the way the sun looks shining on your hair, and the way your eyes darken when I make love to you. I thought of the way your skin feels beneath my hands, and the sound of your laughter.''

''I'm glad,'' she said fiercely into his shoulder. ''All through that night I felt so helpless. I wanted so much to be able to help you.''

''You did, my golden girl, you did.'' He tightened his hold on her. ''Even as you have been helping me tonight.''

She raised herself up on her elbows and kissed him long and deep. It was all the encouragement he needed. Within moments they were moving together again in a joyful affirmation of life and living.

Chapter Seventeen

The next morning when she awoke, Kate was surprised to find a large, warm, male body lying right beside her. Usually Justin rose before dawn and dressed so quietly she never heard him leave. She turned to study him in the early morning light. She smiled when she realized he was taking up three-quarters of the bed, his right arm and right leg thrown possessively across her. He lay facing her, his black hair all tousled. With his features relaxed in sleep he looked much younger. His long lashes spread out like delicate dark fans across his cheek. Even the dark stubble on his face made him look less polished and more approachable.

After contemplating the notion for some time, she decided she liked the sensation of waking up with him. It certainly was a warm and cozy way to begin the day. She started a bit when his eyes suddenly fluttered open.

"Good morning, Miss Holden." He gave her a warm, sleepy smile.

"Good morning, Mr. Talbott. A little slow getting up and about today, are we?"

He rolled over on his back and stretched his arms up over his head. The muscles rippled in his arms and shoulders. It was fascinating watching such a healthy male wake up.

"I've decided to take you up on your suggestion and take a brief holiday from my labors," he declared when he had finished with his stretch.

"That's a fine idea, but what do you plan to do on your holiday, sir? I'm afraid it's snowing outside."

"Ah, then I shall simply have to stay right here in bed with you." He propped himself up on one elbow and smiled at her wickedly.

"That's your idea of a holiday?"

"Hmm. Let me show you just how relaxing and pleasurable a good holiday in bed can be." And he proceeded to do just that.

Around nine o'clock Kate's rumbling stomach finally drove him downstairs to find them both sustenance. He brought up a tray from Madame Dupuy laden with fresh croissants and piping-hot omelettes. It was a novel experience sharing a meal in bed with Justin, but Kate once again decided she liked it, especially when he was in such a relaxed and amusing mood. She couldn't believe it when he told her drolly that he had bought the very claim that had collapsed on him two days earlier.

"That claim almost killed you. Now I know you have a terminal case of gold fever," she informed him disgustedly.

After breakfast Justin insisted that she come take a bath with him. She blushed all over when he suggested the idea. She blushed again when they were standing side by side in the bathroom, and he nonchalantly dropped his dressing gown and stepped into the steaming tub.

She couldn't help but stare at his long, lean body as he lowered himself into the hot water. She still had relatively few chances to study him in the daylight, and this time she was impressed all over again by his magnificent physique. She doubted most men looked so good without their clothing. She had learned by now how he kept himself so fit. Several times a week he went down to a gym on Myers Avenue and boxed, and a serious business it was. She had seen the bruises on his ribs where a sparring partner had caught him a "good'un," as he described it.

Her thoughts came scudding back to the present when she realized Justin was grinning at her. Caught staring, Kate felt her cheeks flood with yet another wave of warmth. She was relieved when he refrained from teasing her. Instead he simply said, "Come sit here, between my knees."

She dropped her robe and got into the tub so quickly that she splashed water over the sides. She was profoundly grateful when he turned her about so that she was facing forward with her back to him. She was sure his other mistresses were quite used to bathing with men, but she was finding it a very unsettling experience.

Once she was sitting with his long, firm legs stretched out on either side of her, he began kissing the back of her neck. At the same time he started to wipe her belly gently with a soft washcloth. As he moved the cloth higher and pulled her firmly back against him, she began to realize bathing might not be the pastime he had in mind at all. It occured to her that it was a good thing he had installed such a large bathtub in his home, and that was her last coherent thought for a very long time.

Much later, after Justin had gone down to his office, she bundled herself up and went to the post office to see if she had received any responses to her inquiries about teaching positions. There were three letters waiting for her. One was a fat missive from Elizabeth, which she tucked into her coat pocket to read later. The other two she tore open at once and read as she walked back to Justin's house. The first was a negative reply to her inquiry about a teaching job in Canon City. The other made her stop dead in her tracks. The school board in Pueblo was seriously interested in hiring her for a position that would open up in March. Their current instructor's mother was in failing health, and he wished to return back east to care for her as soon as a replacement could be found for him.

As she started walking again, Kate quickly reread the letter. She wasn't sure that they were so much impressed with her credentials as they were pleased with the fact she was willing to start work in the middle of the school year. The Mr. Frederick Kimball who had penned the letter made it sound as if the interview they wanted to schedule was mostly a formality. If she wanted the position, they seemed eager to hire her. On the rest of the way home she did some hard thinking.

By the time she had reached Justin's house, she concluded she had no choice in the matter. She needed a place to go when her time in Justin's household ended, and she didn't want to stay in Cripple Creek. It would be too painful to remain here. Surely teaching was a good, productive occupation. She had enjoyed the teaching part of her job as a governess a great deal. In this new position her students would be older and capable of learning more complicated material. Perhaps she could even introduce a few to Latin. Pueblo was only a few hours' train ride from Colorado Springs. She could visit Elizabeth frequently.

In fact, she told herself sternly as she sat down at her desk an hour later, this opening was exactly what she had been looking for. Her eyes burned with unshed tears, though, as she started to write her response to Mr. Kimball's letter. She promised she would be in Pueblo the first week of March to meet with him and the rest of the school board. When she had sealed the letter and put it aside, Kate put her head down on her arms. She wondered dully if she would ever see Justin Talbott again after she left the district.

The following Monday, Justin appeared in the doorway to Kate's bedchamber, his blue eyes blazing with some strong emotion. She looked at him worriedly as he strode forward into her room and stopped right in front of her desk.

"I'm not sure whether I should throttle you or kiss you, Miss Holden," he declared as he looked down at her.

"I'm quite sure I'd rather be kissed then, if it's all the same to you," she said a little breathlessly. "May I ask why I am suddenly a candidate for such dire treatment?"

"You may, but I don't think I'm going to give you an answer, except this. I am going now to have an important business meeting with a friend of yours. I expect I may be gone all afternoon, and perhaps much of this evening. Don't wait up. And now, my dear, I believe I need a kiss for good luck."

Dutifully she stood up, and Justin came around the side of her desk. When he simply stood there, she sighed and stepped forward. She placed her arms around his neck and gave him a quick peck on the cheek. Before she could slip away, his right arm closed around her and pulled her closer. His left hand tilted her chin up gently, and he covered her lips with his own. Within moments his tongue was plundering her mouth. Her pulse was racing and she was out of breath by the time he broke off the kiss and went striding from the room.

Kate looked after him, wondering what friend of hers could possibly have important business dealings with Justin Talbott.

She woke from a sound sleep that night to hear someone fumbling at her doorknob. By the time the door swung fully open, she had the lamp on her bedside table lit. She looked up to see her employer swaying in the doorway, his clothing in wild disarray.

"What on earth happened to you? Are you hurt?" she asked as she scrambled out of bed and reached for her dressing gown.

"Not at all, m'dear. I feel wonderful." He sent her a beatific smile as he propped his back against the doorjamb.

"I see," she said, trying not to laugh as she pulled on her dressing gown, for she did see. Justin was definitely intoxicated. She had thought he was a little under the influence the night after his mining accident, but now she could clearly tell that Justin was "three sheets to the wind," as her seafaring father used to call it.

"Your business deal went well, I take it," she said as she padded over to inspect the damage close up.

"It did indeed, and you, my golden girl, are in large part responsible."

"Could it be you needed an important document at a key moment, a document that you never could have found if it weren't for my filing?"

"What's filing got to do with it?" He blinked at her confusedly. "Charm, beauty, quick wits, and some delectable attributes I probably shouldn't describe in mixed company most likely carried the day."

"Why, Justin Talbott, you flatterer. I think I like you inebriated, even though I don't have the faintest idea what you're talking about."

Just then his shoulders started to slip off the doorjamb. She reached out and steadied him just in time. His legs looked as if they might give way, too, at any moment. She stepped past him long enough to glance down the hallway. The door to his own bedroom looked dauntingly far away. Obviously her bed was a great deal closer. She sighed aloud. In principle, it irked her to invite him into her bed, but the alternative of letting him fall over and sleep all night on the floor of her room didn't seem like a good notion either.

While she had been studying the situation, he had reached out and caught the end of one of her braids and started winding it between his fingers. "Daisy, Daisy, give me your answer, do," he began singing the popular song in a rich baritone, "I'm half crazy, all for the love of you. . . ."

"That's a nice sentiment, sir, but I don't believe it for a moment," she smilingly interrupted him.

Disregarding her comment, he launched into the next phrase of the song, singing even more loudly than before. She tried to tug him inside her room, with little success. He was going to wake Mrs. Parslow and Madame Dupuy at any moment, which was going to be embarrassing for everyone involved. When he next paused to draw breath, Kate taunted him deliberately, "You can't sing and walk to my bed at the same time, can you?"

He shot her an affronted look. He stood up, lurched a bit, and started off toward her bed, hitting the chorus of the song and his stride about the same time. She closed her door hastily and followed him. He fetched up against her bed safely enough, and promptly sat down facing her. She stopped in front of him, trying to decide if she should take his jacket off. Before she could make up her mind, he reached out and pulled her forward until she was standing between his knees. Then, with his arms locked around her waist, he quit singing and nuzzled his face into her bosom instead.

"Sweet Kate, you always smell like lilacs in the spring. Half of me wants you, but the other half wants to fall asleep right now," he said confidingly.

"Why don't you lie back and close your eyes for few moments and see if the sleepy side wins. I'll be here in the morning if the other half is still in the mood."

"Of course I'll want you in the morning. I always want you, woman. Never had a gal I couldn't get enough of. You're the first. It's the damnedest thing." He was almost grumbling as he lay back against her pillows.

"My humblest apologies, sir. I could see how that could be most disconcerting for you. Perhaps I should wear a flour sack over my head from now on."

That sally drew a smile, but his eyes were already closing, and within moments he was sound asleep. She stared at him in amused exasperation. What was she supposed to do with a fully clothed Justin Talbott who was passed out on top of her counterpane? After a few moments she decided she would have to do her best to make him comfortable. Taking his shoes off was easy enough, but after wrestling with his arms and shoulders for several moments, she decided he could darn well sleep in his jacket. The man was heavier than lead. She went down to his bedchamber and brought back the thick satin coverlet that lay across his own bed. After tucking the coverlet around him as best she could, she took off her dressing gown and slipped under the covers.

Before she blew the lamp out, she turned on her side and studied Justin for a long time. She so rarely had a chance like this to look at him. Even in a drunken sleep, he was a handsome, handsome man. Fiercely she tried to memorize every feature of his face, storing up the little details for the terrible gray time that lay ahead. She loved the way his thick ebony hair curled down over his forehead. With a fingertip she lightly traced his black brows. At last she leaned over and pressed a gentle kiss on his cheek. He smiled in his sleep and turned toward her. After blowing out the lamp, she snuggled down under the covers and laid her head on his shoulder.

A rough masculine voice rumbling near her ear woke Kate up the next morning. "I don't suppose I should ask how I ended up here."

After she thought hard for a few moments, the events of the night before came flooding back to her. "You came visiting me last night. Or perhaps I should say, you came serenading me." She propped herself up on one elbow so that she could grin down at him. She understood that hangovers were supposed to be painful affairs, and she was eager to witness one close up. "I had no idea you were such a fine singer," she added gleefully.

"Hmmmph," he said and closed his red-rimmed eyes. After a few moments he opened his eyes again and peered down at his shirt and jacket. "You could have at least undressed me."

"Justin Talbott, do you have any idea how heavy you are?

It was a miracle I got any of you under that spread. And I did get your shoes off at least. How do you feel, by the way?''

''My head's splitting,'' he admitted candidly, ''but in my heart I'm a happy man.''

''Ah, so the dealing went well yesterday. I gathered as much from your, er, high spirits last night.''

''Or the amount I had obviously consumed, you mean.'' He levered himself into a sitting position and rubbed his face with his hands. ''You'd think I'd know better than to do this to myself. I'm going back to sleep in my bed for a few hours,'' he declared as he dropped his hands. ''But at noon I'm taking you out to the finest luncheon we can find in this town. We have some celebrating to do.'' With that he tossed the coverlet back, stood up, and headed for her door.

''Umm, Justin, could I possibly know what it is we are going to be celebrating?'' she said right as he pulled her door open.

''I never got around to telling you last night?'' He glanced back at her over his shoulder. Even with his wrinkled clothes, rumpled hair, and unshaven cheeks, he took her breath away. She forced herself to concentrate on forming a coherent reply.

''You didn't talk a great deal last night. First you were too busy singing, and then you were too busy sleeping.''

''I see.'' Justin raked a hand through his hair and smiled at her crookedly. ''Well, for your information, Gunnar Carlson just sold me a half interest in all his claims up on Elk Mountain. The main reason, he said, that he finally decided to deal with me was a certain sterling character reference given to him by one Kate Holden.''

She was still blinking in astonishment when Justin closed the door quietly behind him.

When he stopped by her bedroom to escort her downstairs just before noon, Justin looked much better for few more hours of sleep. He was impeccably dressed and freshly shaved and combed. As he escorted her through the front door and out to the waiting carriage, Kate decided she almost preferred the ragged man who had sung to her the evening before. Peeking at him through her eyelashes, she couldn't help thinking that an intoxicated Justin Talbott was definitely more approachable than a sober one.

True to his word, Justin took her out to the finest luncheon to be had in Cripple Creek, which was served at the luxurious Wolfe Hotel. When they reached the hotel dining room, she was delighted to see that Gunnar Carlson was there waiting for them. He looked quite dapper in a dark gray suit, and she told him so. The two of them did most of the talking during the meal while Justin looked on tolerantly. The old Swede told Kate wild tales about his trapping days. Justin contributed a story or two toward the end of the luncheon when Kate insisted he tell about his encounters with the Utes near Aspen.

When they rose to leave, Justin and Gunnar began talking business. Kate was pleased to see Justin was obviously going to treat the Swede as a full partner. The two men were still at it when they walked out onto the boardwalk in front of the hotel. She turned toward the street then, content to watch the fascinating parade of folk going past on Bennett Avenue.

She smiled sympathetically when she spotted a young woman walking down the boardwalk with four small children in tow. As the woman drew closer, Kate guessed she was a miner's wife out doing her shopping. The poor woman obviously had her hands full with four children tugging at her skirts. Even as Kate watched, the smallest girl tripped and fell on her knee and began crying. As the young mother bent over to comfort the child, the littlest boy in the family lost hold of a blue ball he had been carrying, and the toy rolled out into the busy street.

With startling quickness the boy darted after it. Kate watched in horror. A team of cantering draft horses pulling an empty freighting wagon headed directly toward the child. Intent on plucking his toy from the mud, the boy was oblivious to the team bearing down on him. Kate took a deep breath. Lifting her skirts, she dashed out after him. Afraid she would lose her nerve if she looked up at the approaching team, she concentrated on keeping her balance in the mud. She had to reach the boy in time. And then he was there in front of her.

Snatching the child up, vaguely she was aware of the driver swearing furiously, the rattle of the horses' harness chains, and the sound of a woman screaming. Kate twisted about and threw the boy toward the side of the muddy street as hard as she could. She took one step toward safety. Something hit her side and shoulder with bruising, numbing force. She felt herself go flying through the air, and blackness claimed her.

Justin was in the midst of wrangling good-naturedly with Gunnar Carlson about where to sink the first shaft on Elk Mountain when a woman's shrill scream made him turn. Gunnar, who was already facing the street, went pale at the same moment and hissed, *"Kara Gud!"* under his breath. Justin caught a flash of blue and gold out in the street, right in the path of a fast-moving freight wagon. Just when he realized with a cold rush of fear that it was Kate out there, he saw her pick a boy up from the mud and throw him to safety.

With hideous clarity, he saw everything that happened after that. Even as Justin took a step forward and shouted at Kate to run, the wagon driver sawed on the reins, trying to force his cantering team to swerve to the side. Kate lunged forward, gaining one precious stride toward safety, and then the horses were on her. That last step kept her from being trampled, but it didn't keep her from being hit. The shoulder of the left lead horse caught her and sent her flying. She landed with a horrible thump, her head and upper body lying on the boardwalk not four strides from where Justin stood.

He was kneeling beside her within moments, desperately searching for a pulse. The tight feeling in his own chest eased just a little when he saw that she was still breathing. Her pulse seemed strong enough, but her face appeared terribly white and still. Gently he smoothed a streak of mud from her cheek.

"Where's the closest doctor?" He glanced about and saw Gunnar was kneeling right next to him.

"There's one just up the street," the old Swede answered hoarsely.

Ignoring the mud on her sodden skirts, Justin lifted Kate gently into his arms. When he was standing again, he forced his way through the little crowd that had already gathered on the boardwalk. He brushed past a sobbing woman who was clutching the muddy little boy in her arms. When Justin reached the doctor's office, Gunnar was before him, opening the door and leading the way inside. Justin spotted the doctor at once. He was standing in the corner of his tiny waiting room, talking with an old prospector.

"This young woman was just hit by a team, and she fell hard on her side and head on the boardwalk," Justin told the physician curtly.

"Bring her into my examining room at once."

Justin glanced over his shoulder. Some of the curious on-lookers had followed them right into the doctor's office.

"Out," he told them with a glare. Most went, and the last few stragglers headed for the door when the tall old Swede advanced on them threateningly. Justin was already following the doctor into the examining room. He settled Kate gently on the bed and refused to leave the room as the physician began his examination. Kate was beginning to stir by the time the man had finished.

"I think your young lady is very lucky," the doctor said in a low voice. "I can't find any broken bones. She has a slight concussion, but that seems to be the worst of it. She'll be sore and stiff for the next few days. I recommend bed rest for the remainder of today and tomorrow, but after that she should get up and move about if she feels like it."

"You're sure there is nothing worse wrong with her?"

"I can ask her when she comes round, but for now I'd say she is mostly suffering from bruises and contusions."

Just then Kate's eyes fluttered open. He watched her frown as she stared up at the unfamiliar ceiling overhead. Before she could become alarmed, he was by her side and taking one of her hands carefully between his own. Her wandering green eyes focused on his face, and then they widened.

"Justin, what's happened? You're filthy. There hasn't been another cave-in, has there?" Her concern for his own welfare sent a peculiar pang shooting through him.

"Sh, now, nothing happened to me." He brushed a strand of golden hair back from her forehead. "It's you we're a bit more worried about right now."

"Me? Oh, now I remember." She closed her eyes again. "Is the little boy all right?"

"From what I saw, the boy needs a good bath in a horse trough, and after that a spanking, but he's just fine, thanks to you."

She opened her eyes again and looked at him uncertainly. "Am I all right?" she asked after a few moments.

"So far as the doctor can tell, you have no broken bones and just a mild concussion."

She let go a sigh of relief. "That is good news. Papa always said we Holdens were made from sturdy stuff." Justin was relieved to see the sparkle was beginning to return to her eyes.

"Oh, Justin, I just remembered, that poor mother. She was probably so frightened. Can you imagine trying to take four small children shopping with you? Something like this probably happens to her every time she comes to Bennett Avenue."

"No, I don't believe I can imagine what it would be like." He didn't try to hold back his smile. "The fact that you are trying to at a time like this might make some folk wonder if your wits are rattled. It tends to convince me, however, that you are completely back to normal."

She sent him an exasperated look. "I'm not out of my head, thank you very much. In fact, I'd like to get up now if I may." The doctor stepped in, introduced himself, and gave her permission to sit up slowly. When that feat had been accomplished, and Kate said she did not feel dizzy or faint, Justin insisted the doctor give her another examination. Kate was blushing by the end of it, but they had established to Justin's satisfaction that Kate had only been bruised in the accident.

A sharp rap came on the door, and Gunnar poked his head inside. "I'm not waiting a moment longer to see if she is well."

Kate peered around Justin and sent Gunnar a smile that had much of her former spirit in it.

"Of course I'm well. I'm as tough as those Rockies you're so fond of, sir."

"Of course you are fine," the old man mimicked her airy tone and rolled his eyes. "How foolish of me to worry, ja? Perhaps I should go see to the shoulder of the poor horse which hit you."

"You might at that. Perhaps I should send some liniment around to his owner."

Gunnar looked at her in mock disgust. "Now I know you were only pretending just to scare us. Talbott, your man is waiting out front with the carriage whenever you are ready to take this silly *flicka* home with you." With that the old Swede withdrew.

While Kate straightened her clothing and hair as best she could, Justin quietly asked Dr. Smith not to give out Kate's name to any of the sundry reporters who would doubtlessly be calling at this office in the next few hours. Justin was sure the newspapers were going to have a field day with the story of the heroic young woman who had just saved a child from being trampled to death on Bennett Avenue. He was also certain, however, that Kate would much prefer not to have her name bandied about, especially in connection with his own. To make certain the doctor honored his request, Justin pressed a fat roll of bills into the physician's hand.

"I can walk, for heaven's sake," Kate protested as Justin came to her side and gathered her into his arms. Ignoring her protest, he carried her out to the carriage. A small cheer went up from the crowd waiting outside the doctor's office when they appeared. Instead of waving to her admirers, Kate buried her face in his shoulder.

With Ben's help, Justin had her settled comfortably in the landau in no time. Gunnar, who was lurking there by the carriage steps, called out that he would be by Justin's house soon to see how Kate was feeling. Before Ben could shut the landau door, Justin told him quietly, "Take us home as smooth as you can, eh?"

"Course I will, boss. I heard what she done. You know, none of the others you've seen, proper or otherwise, can hold a candle to this little gal, and you're a damn fool if you can't see it." With that the coachman stomped forward toward his seat, leaving Justin looking after him in some surprise.

When they returned home, Justin discovered the rest of his staff had grown equally fond of Kate during the relatively short time she had lived with them. Mrs. Parslow turned pale when he walked in the front door bearing Kate in his arms, and Madame Dupuy began muttering and swearing under her breath in French as he explained what had happened down on Bennett Avenue.

Once he deposited Kate in her room, the two women took over and tried to banish him from the bedchamber. He left only after he was certain they would follow the doctor's recommendation and have Kate take a long hot bath to ease her soreness. Justin went straight from her bedroom down to the library and poured himself a generous shot of whiskey. He downed it in a single swallow and decided to pour himself another one.

Now that the worst was past, he felt the reaction set in. He could picture in his mind the accident happening again and again. He saw the team of draft horses thundering down on her. He remembered the strained look on her face as she tried to save herself after throwing the boy out of harm's way. He could see clearly the way she had been tossed through the air, her hat pinwheeling off on a separate flight of its own. Most of all, he could not forget the moment she had fallen on the boardwalk and lay there before him like a broken doll.

Justin sat there in his quiet library for a long time before he got up and went to his office. He doubted it would do any good, but he hoped to banish the haunting images from his mind by burying himself in his work.

Chapter Eighteen

When Kate woke up that evening she found Justin reading in the rocker by her bed. She didn't say anything to him at first. She simply lay there enjoying the way the warm light from the lamp threw interesting shadows across the planes of his face. At last he seemed to feel her gaze upon him, for he glanced up from his reading and saw that her eyes were open.

"How long have you been awake?"

She dodged his question by asking one of her own. "Are you my nurse now?"

He made a wry face. "Perhaps companion is a better word for it. I had to chase your real nurses out of here to make them go get some supper for themselves."

"They both have been so kind to me." She smiled wistfully. She started to shift her shoulders, and she couldn't help wincing when pain burned through her side. Justin was kneeling by the side of her bed in a heartbeat.

"How do you feel?" he asked as he gently smoothed a strand of hair back from her forehead.

"Do you want a brave reply or an honest one?"

"An honest one."

"I feel like I was almost run over by a very large draft horse."

He smiled at that. "If that horse hadn't turned you black and blue, I might have been tempted to take a strap to you myself. You gave us all quite a scare, young woman."

"Turnabout is fair play," she murmured.

"What's that? Oh, you're referring to my little adventure last Friday. It has been an eventful week for both of us, I suppose."

"I think I could do with some peace and quiet for a change.

Justin," she said suddenly in a much more urgent tone, and then she dropped her gaze and plucked at the coverlet.

"What is it, little scholar?"

"It's just, well, I'm sorry that I seem to have gone and gotten myself a bit damaged while I'm still in your employ. I'm sure I'll be up and about again in a few days. What I'm trying to say is, if you want to extend our arrangement for two or three days, or deduct some money from our final settlement, either would be fine with me." She got that last part out in a rush.

"Don't you worry your head about that right now."

"I am going to worry. We have a business deal, and I don't want you to feel like you . . . you aren't getting your money's worth." She hated to phrase the matter so crassly, but she was too tired to think of a more ladylike way to put it.

"I'm hardly going to dock the wages of the heroine of Bennett Avenue, and I don't want to hear anything more about it. Now, would you like to sit up and have a drink of water?"

"I am thirsty," she admitted. He helped her sit up and deftly arranged the pillows so that she could lie back against them comfortably. He poured her a glass of water and even straightened her bedclothes, all with a tender expression on his face she had never seen him wear before. Unnerved and uncertain how to interpret such solicitude, she took refuge in humor.

"You are quite good at this nursing business. Perhaps you could be an orderly at a hospital if you ever tire of being a mining baron."

"I doubt I would be much of a hand at emptying bedpans." He pulled the rocker closer to her bedside and sat down again. After a few minutes he picked up his book, but he left it lying in his lap.

"That was a brave thing you did today," he said abruptly.

"I'm surprised you aren't giving me a lecture on being stupid, foolish, and reckless."

"It would have been foolish if you had not realized the danger when you ran out in front of that team, but you knew exactly what you risked. I saw your face right before the lead horse hit you. I think your father would have been very proud of you today."

Past the sudden tightness in her throat, she managed to say, "Thank you for that." Her gaze fell before the warm light in his eyes. "Tell me about your plans for your new mine," she said softly after a time.

"Are you sure that you wouldn't rather sleep again?"

"Not right now. I feel wide awake. I heard you and Gunnar arguing about where you are planning to sink the first shaft. I would love to know who won that particular round."

That was all it took. He was off and talking. She relaxed against her pillows and watched him, letting his words wash over her. At least she had brought him this. It felt good knowing she had helped him to achieve one of his fondest dreams. Now she could only hope that he would find a rich vein of gold under Elk Mountain. He would be so pleased to have the funds to develop his other mines the way he wished. She wasn't sure he would ever be a completely happy man, but surely tremendous financial success would lay to rest some of the cruel ghosts in his past.

Soon he would become a ghost in her past, one that would haunt her always. Tired, weak, and hurting, she allowed herself to dream that the warm light in his eyes meant something more than simple approval for a courageous act. For just tonight she was going to imagine that Justin truly cared for her and would keep her with him always. Smiling sadly to herself, she dozed off in the midst of his glowing description of the new ore carts he was having shipped to the district from back east.

Kate saw that same warm light in Justin's gaze frequently during the two days that followed. To her considerable surprise he spent just as much time tending to her as did Madame Dupuy and Mrs. Parslow. During the first day after her accident, her trio of stern nurses barely let her step foot out of bed. At first Kate indignantly protested their orders, but the first time she rose to go to the necessary, her sore, bruised body made it very clear they were right. For the rest of that day she meekly stayed in bed.

Mrs. Parslow looked in on her during the morning, Madame Dupuy during the early afternoon, and Justin took over during the later afternoon and evening. Kate was highly amused and

touched when Justin arrived in her room that first day at three
o'clock and promptly offered his services as a reader.

"I would rather work on my translating, if it's all the same
to you," she had replied politely.

"I'm afraid, young woman, that it is not all the same to
me, or to you. The good Dr. Smith said reading would probably give you a headache, and studying your Latin and Greek
surely would. Do you have a novel of some sort you've been
reading on the side?"

"I did just start on Miss Austen's *Pride and Prejudice*,"
she admitted with a small smile. Although Justin grimaced at
this news, he read the novel to her anyway. He was an excellent reader, his deep voice warm and expressive. Still, Kate
found she was concentrating more on the simple pleasure of
being with him rather than the passages he read to her.

The second morning after her accident, Kate insisted on
getting up and wearing a dress instead of her nightgown. She
spent the day quietly, however, for too much movement made
her dizzy, and she still felt very sore. Because she discovered
reading for prolonged periods did make her head ache, she
found herself left with a great deal of time to think about the
puzzling change in Justin's attitude toward her.

This new, tender way he was treating her was most unsettling. Lord knew she was vulnerable enough to him, but this
gentleness he was showing her was simply devastating. And
she couldn't help but wonder about the reason for the change
in him. She knew she was being naive and foolish, but she
couldn't quite squash the notion that occurred to her in the
midst of that first evening while Justin read to her.

Perhaps, just perhaps, her near brush with death had shaken
him just as much as his being caught in the cave-in had shaken
her. Almost losing him had made her realize how much she
loved him. Could the same have happened for Justin? Had her
accident made him realize he cared for her, at least a little?
Most of the time she told herself she was deluded and worse
to even think such a thing, and yet a stubborn part of her kept
hoping.

On the morning of the third day after her accident, Gunnar
Carlson came to visit. He kept Kate entertained for hours with
his stories. That afternoon after her visitor left, she told every-

one she was going on a short walk just to stretch her legs. She did indeed go for her walk, but she headed directly for the train station. No matter what her foolish heart was hoping, her practical side knew it was time to make arrangements for her journey to Pueblo. When she returned to Justin's home, she had her train ticket safely tucked away in her reticule.

That very evening as he ate supper off a tray in her room, Justin brought up the topic of her leaving. "Our time together, little scholar, is fast drawing to a close. In three more days our arrangement ends."

"So it does," she did her best to reply lightly, even though a tide of despair rose in her at the thought.

"I was wondering how you might like to spend our last evening together. Would you prefer to dine out or to attend the theater?"

"If it is truly my choice, I would like to eat in and spend the evening here."

Justin eyed her quizzically. "That is hardly a dramatic finale."

"We should go out then. It doesn't matter to me," she said, looking away from him.

"No, this night I want to abide by your wishes. I will ask our *chère* Madame Dupuy to prepare a particularly delectable feast for the occasion."

"What would you like me to wear?" Kate managed to ask with hardly a tremor in her voice.

"For this special evening, my dear, I leave the choice up to you."

She glanced up at him quickly, wondering if she had imagined the emphasis he had just placed on the word *special*. He looked back at her, smiling that devilish smile of his, his blue eyes inscrutable. Sighing inwardly, she asked him to tell her about his most recent plans for the Elk Mountain claims.

The next two days seemed to speed past all too quickly for Kate. The worst of her soreness eased, and her headaches vanished altogether. Justin continued to act as though she were still convalescing, however, and did nothing more than kiss her lightly on the cheek before she retired to her own room at night. No matter what she hoped and prayed might happen during their last evening together, she knew it was time to begin packing her clothing and her books.

She was still engaged in this task the second afternoon when Justin appeared in her doorway. He crossed his arms, leaned back against the doorjamb, and watched her actions interestedly. When she finally stopped pretending to ignore him and glanced his way, he had an enigmatic smile playing about his lips.

"You seem to have left all the dresses I gave you hanging in that wardrobe, my dear." He straightened up and wandered into her room.

"I can see to those later," she replied shortly. She still planned to keep the promise she had made to herself when Justin had forced her to accept all the clothing Madame Sophie had sewn for her. She would not take a single garment he had paid for out of this house.

"Yet you've packed all your books, and the tired clothing you brought with you. Perhaps you packed the things you cared for first, or perhaps you didn't want to pack your new things just yet and wrinkle them unnecessarily."

"Perhaps so," she echoed him quietly.

"Quite understandable." He gave her another one of his unreadable looks, kissed her on the side of her neck, and strolled from the room.

The morning of her last full day in Justin's home, Kate woke with a heavy heart. By midmorning she had finished the last of her packing. She tried to read her novel, but she had problems concentrating on the story. It was almost a relief when noontime rolled around and she had a good excuse to leave her room and go downstairs. She was surprised and touched when she found Madame Dupuy, Mrs. Parslow, and Ben meant this last luncheon to be an informal farewell party for her. Madame Dupuy served up chicken crepes, one of Kate's favorite dishes, and for dessert there was a wonderful three-tiered chocolate gâteau. Kate went back upstairs, buoyed by the trio's warmth and good wishes.

She spent that afternoon preparing for her last evening with Justin. With rose-scented soap, she washed her hair and dried it carefully before the fire. She spent over an hour curling her tresses and pinning them up in an imitation of an elegant chignon she had seen in the latest edition of *Harper's*. Perhaps it was simply vanity, but she meant to look her best tonight. She hoped there might be times in the future when Justin would glance back and remember her and the way she looked the last evening they spent together.

Pleased that he had left her free to choose, she decided to wear her favorite of the evening gowns Madame Sophie had sewn for her. He had never asked her to wear this particular dress. He had probably overlooked it because its white satin fabric with embroidered gold threads was not as vibrant or flamboyant as the others. Yet to her the gown seemed the most classical and elegant of them all. It fell from a pointed waist in a graceful sweep. The simple long sleeves of the dress came to small points over her wrists. The gown's modest bodice was unadorned except for some tiny gold braiding along the seams. The golden threads in the fabric and braiding shimmered in the lamplight and emphasized the golden sheen of her hair.

As she studied herself in the mirror, she was quite pleased with the overall effect of the gown. Her cheeks, though, looked far too pale. She was hardly going to a funeral this evening, she told herself sternly, and yet a part of her felt as if she were already in mourning. Knowing he hated cosmetics, she pinched some color into her cheeks.

When she swept downstairs at seven o'clock, she found Justin was already waiting for her in the library. He turned about when he heard the swish of her skirts. He opened his mouth to say something, but then he closed it again and simply looked at her. Gratified by his reaction, she stood there and let him gaze his fill. At last he strode forward and took her gloved hand. He bowed low over it in a courtly gesture.

"My dear, you take my breath away," he informed her when he had straightened up again.

"And you look magnificent," she murmured in return. It was true. He always looked wonderful in evening clothes, but tonight he seemed especially splendid. The crisp white of his shirt, waistcoat, and necktie made his eyes look more blue and his tan skin appear the color of teak. The tailored jacket set off his broad shoulders to perfection. There wasn't another man in Cripple Creek who could touch him. For her, there was not another man in the entire world who could compete with him. And she would be leaving him in the morning.

"Hmm, that may be the very first time you've complimented me on anything," he said with a sardonic smile. "I have a feeling this is going to be an eventful and historic night for us. Come and have a seat. Would you like a sherry?"

She nodded and let him fetch her a glass. They talked for a time about happenings in the district, and then Mrs. Parslow came to tell them dinner was ready. They soon discovered that Madame Dupuy had surpassed herself. Her first course consisted of a lobster bisque served with tiny fresh rolls. The soup was followed by oysters baked in puff pastry shells. The main course was roast leg of lamb served with green beans, new potatoes, and puree of parsnips with orange. For her finale, the cook had concocted a *sorbet au citron* served in lovely fluted glasses.

Knowing how hard the Frenchwoman must have worked to create this feast, Kate tried to make herself appreciate the marvelous meal. Unfortunately every time she looked at Justin, she forgot completely about the food before her. All she could think about was the fact that this was the last time she would sit at this table with him. This evening was her last chance to watch him, to enjoy the planes and angles of his rugged, handsome face. This was the last night she would relish the rich timbre of his deep voice. Tonight would be the final time she could touch the beautiful, muscular body she now knew almost as well as her own.

She must have made the appropriate responses to his conversation, but when the meal finally ended and he escorted her back to the library, she hadn't the slightest notion what they had talked about during the past few hours. He settled her on the sofa and went to fetch himself a brandy. When he returned to stand before her, she noticed for the first time that there was a certain eagerness in his gaze and tension in his body. Sternly she made her wandering mind focus on what he was about to say to her.

"My dear, I have a proposal I should like to lay before you," he said with a smile lighting his eyes. "I have enjoyed our little arrangement far more than I expected. Now the time has come for it to end, I find I am loath to let you go. After considering this problem, I believe I have come up with a solution that might suit us both admirably.''

She could only stare at him, her hands clenching in the folds of her dress, her heart beating in fast, painful, hopeful strokes. Could it possibly be that her wildest dreams were about to come true?

''I was hoping you would agree to continue our arrangement indefinitely, at the same rate I have been paying you to date. Either one of us can terminate our agreement when we find it is growing tiresome. I have already spoken to Pearl about this matter, and she agreed that she has no right to any further commission for having introduced us, so to speak. All the money would be paid directly to you henceforth.''

There it was. He had made her a proposal, but it was hardly the one she had been hoping for.

''That is very generous of you both,'' she managed to get out, even though her heart felt as though it were splintering into a thousand pieces. How foolish and stupid she had been to hope. Of course she could never be anything more to him than a pleasant diversion.

''Can I take that as a yes then?'' he said with another heart-stopping smile.

Fiercely she willed her tears back. Afraid he might see the treacherous moisture in her eyes, she stared at her lap as she said stonily, ''You may take that as a perhaps, sir. I had not anticipated this offer, and I had already made other plans.''

''What plans are these? Have you already found yourself a new protector? My God, you move quickly. I was right to think you were a shrewd little baggage.''

''I do not believe my plans are any of your business, sir.'' She blessed the surge of temper that rose inside her at his insulting words. She was much less apt to break down now that she was so infuriated with him.

''You'd be a fool to refuse my offer,'' he told her bluntly. ''I can't believe any man here in the district would be willing to pay what I've been paying you.''

''Nevertheless, the choice is mine,'' she said, meeting his gaze as boldly as she could. ''I should like until tomorrow morning to make up my mind. Now, may we retire upstairs?''

"Is it someone you met at one of my dinner parties?'' He ignored her last suggestion entirely. "I'll be damned if one of my own friends steals you away from me.''

"It is quite safe to say my new employer is no one you know,'' she replied, even as she wondered if she could possibly be hearing jealousy in his tone. How could a man be jealous of his mistress?

"Did he offer you more money?''

Kate just stared at him. She longed to tell him how much she loved him, and how hard it would be to continue under his roof without his returning her love. She knew such a confession would only bring her humiliation, though, and embarrass him as well.

For the sake of her pride, she summoned the strength to say in clipped tones, "Actually, my choice has nothing to do with money. It's an issue of whether or not I wish to remain in your household and continue my association with you.''

"I see,'' he said after several moments, his face growing cold and distant.

"You've made my stay here as pleasant as it could have possibly been under the circumstances,'' she relented enough to admit. "I'm just not certain I wish to remain here any longer.''

"That is your decision, of course. I can see my browbeating you is hardly a diplomatic way to convince you to change your mind.'' A self-deprecating tone crept into his voice. "My bullying and foul temper may well be part of the reason you wish to leave. I know I have not always been kind to you, but I warned you from the start the sort of man I am.''

"And I told you once before, you are not nearly as cold or hard-hearted as you believe,'' she said, meeting his gaze directly. Afraid she might be about to reveal more of her true feelings than she wished, she added quickly, "Please, Justin, it would mean something to me if we did not spoil our last night together with more unpleasantness. Could we go upstairs now?''

"Very well, little scholar, we will do exactly that, and you can give me your final answer tomorrow.''

Touched by the gentleness she heard in his voice, she

swiftly rose to her feet. She turned away and headed for the door while she blinked back a fresh wave of tears. By the time he had caught up with her on the stairs, she had herself well in hand again.

They said nothing more as they climbed the steps together. He took her hand and held it as they walked down the hall to his room. Once they stood inside his chamber, he closed the door behind them and pulled her into his arms. She placed her hands on his shoulders and met his kiss fervently. Within moments passion was flaring between them. Justin molded her body more tightly against his, and she acceded willingly. When she nipped and nibbled at the corners of his mouth, he groaned aloud. Moments later he broke off the kiss and looked down at her.

"If this is a ploy to raise your price, I think it just might work," he informed her between ragged breaths.

"Justin Talbott, it is difficult to kiss a gentleman properly if he insists on clucking like a hen," she replied in a teasing echo of what he had said to her that very first night he kissed her.

"Touché, my dear, touché," he muttered and bent to kiss her again.

Frustrated by the layers of clothing separating them, Kate reached up and pushed his jacket from his shoulders. Even as he pressed warm kisses to the side of her neck, she tugged his white necktie free and sent his waistcoat sliding down to join his evening jacket on the floor. She felt his fingers busy themselves in her hair, and suddenly the chignon she had spent so much time fashioning came loose. She shook her head until her hair fell in shining waves about her shoulders. He plunged his hands into her tresses and smoothed her hair away from her face. She smiled when she saw the burning, hungry look she knew so well come into his eyes.

"Little temptress, I see you are smiling. Perhaps you have finally come to realize what you do to me," he said hoarsely. "Turn around."

Obediently she did as he asked, but of her own accord she moved back until she brushed against him. She was rewarded by his sharp intake of breath. His left hand clamped her against him while his right made quick work of the fastenings to her gown. Soon he was tugging impatiently at the shoulders of the dress. As the bodice fell forward, his warm hands skimmed the satin sleeves down her arms. Moments later the dress collapsed in a shimmering pile on the floor. Her petticoats quickly followed them. When she was clad in only her chemise and drawers, she stepped away from the clothing on the floor and turned to face him.

She watched his face as he reached out and undid the tie to her chemise. A muscle in his jaw twitched as the garment slipped from her shoulders and whispered down about her waist. She closed her eyes briefly as his warm fingers encircled her breasts. He fondled and teased them until she hardened beneath his touch and the hot ache inside her grew almost unbearable. She opened her eyes and moved back from him. She meant to set the pace tonight. When he reached out again to draw her close, she eluded his grip.

When he started to protest, she pressed a finger to his lips and said simply, "It's my turn now."

She stepped forward and slowly undid the buttons to his shirt, enjoying the smell of clean linen mixed with his own male scent and the tang of cedar. He stood still under her touch, his blazing blue eyes watching her every move. When she reached his belt she tugged the shirt free of his trousers and ran her hands up over his smooth stomach and rib cage. She smiled when she heard him inhale sharply and felt his stomach muscles tighten beneath her fingertips. She knew so much more about him now than she had that awful night he had forced her to seduce him. She had learned many of his sensitive places, and those she didn't know she meant to discover tonight.

Her plan for the evening was quite simple. Since she could not say the words aloud, she meant to show him with her hands, her lips, and her body just how much she loved him. She was going to utilize everything she had learned these past two months. Pearl had been her first instructor in theory, but Justin had been her teacher in practice, and she was going to put all their lessons to good use. Night after night in this room and in this bed he had made her breathless and weak. Now she was going to do the same things to him he had done to her. For tonight, for him, she would be bold.

She stood up on tiptoe and pushed the shirt from his shoulders. Purposely she let the tips of her breasts brush against his chest. He made an odd, half-strangled sound in his throat. She kissed the beautiful, flat muscles of his chest, tasting him the way he had tasted her so many times. She licked the smooth skin about his nipples. When she nipped him in the same place, he moaned aloud and picked her up. Kissing her fiercely, he urged her with his hands to wrap her legs around him. Locked together thus, her arms wound tightly about his neck, he carried her to the bed.

He kicked off his shoes and scrambled out of his trousers. They both fell onto the soft feather mattress, Justin on top of her. She just barely had time to tug her drawers down, and then he was thrusting deep inside her. She rose joyously to meet that thrust and the ones which followed it. With her hands and body she met the pace he set and quickened it. Only vaguely was she aware that both of them were breathing now in ragged gasps. There was only the desire to be closer to him, to bring him fully inside her, to drive them both to the edge and over.

It was sweet to know she could bring him to this state, sweet to feel her own body kindle into flame beneath him, sweet to hear her name on his lips as he plunged into her a final time, the muscles in his face, arms, and shoulders tensing as his pleasure crested. The final, greatest sweetness of all came when her body responded to his, convulsing into exquisite spasms, closing about him as his fluid warmth rushed inside her, and she knew she had pleasured him as fully as he had pleasured her.

He collapsed with a muffled groan on top of her, his chest heaving, his face partially buried in the pillow beside her head. At last he withdrew and came to lie on his back beside her.

"Great merciful heavens," he swore when he had gotten his breath back. Kate just smiled at him smugly.

"We should have Madame Dupuy feed you oysters more often, little scholar."

"Mmmm," she replied noncommittally. She bent her head then and began kissing the smooth line of his collarbone. She shifted until her thigh lay across his hips and her hair spilled across his chest.

"I take it we aren't finished yet."

"You did say you wanted this evening to be memorable." She stopped what she was doing long enough to grin at him. "It's a fine thing you go to the gym so often. It's important for a man your age to keep fit and well conditioned."

"I'll show you just how fit I am, little minx," he threatened and started to raise himself up on his elbows.

She pushed him back into the pillows with a merry laugh. "There's time enough to show me your endurance, sir. We've the entire evening ahead of us, after all. In the meantime, however, I've something else in mind."

"You do, eh?"

"Just lie back and relax."

"I'm not sure I like that look in those green eyes of yours, my girl."

"I believe, sir, that you shall like what I have in mind very much."

He glanced at her skeptically, but he did lie back against the pillows just as she had ordered.

"Sweet lord," he swore again sometime later, and that was the last coherent comment he made for a very long time.

When she had finished with him, he insisted on performing the same service for her, until she was writhing and twisting against the sheets. They made love repeatedly after that. Justin seemed bemused, amused, and quite aroused by her new boldness. He allowed her to set the pace and choose their position, only insuring toward the end of each encounter that her experience was as rich and full as his.

Somewhere during the wee hours of the morning, Justin at last fell into an exhausted slumber, a smile playing on his well-formed lips. Kate kept the bedside lamp burning so that she could lie beside him and look her fill.

She dozed a little toward dawn, but she woke instantly the moment she felt him stir beside her. She pretended to be asleep because she could not trust her voice if she tried to speak with him again. Instead she relished the small sounds of him dressing and moving about the room, the soft scrape of the razor against his skin, and the tart scent of his shaving lather.

She forced herself to keep breathing deeply and evenly when she heard his footsteps approaching the bed. The mattress dipped, and she felt his breath warm on her cheek. He smoothed the hair back from the side of her face and gently kissed her cheek. Then he was gone, leaving her more alone than she had ever been in her life before. Only after she heard the door close did she let the tears come.

Chapter Nineteen

Justin stared at the assay report he held in his hands. When he realized this was the third time he had tried to read the first page, he swore under his breath and slammed the report down on the desk. Damn it, she haunted him everywhere, even in here, his most private refuge. He could remember exactly how she looked that afternoon when she had stood in the doorway and laughed at the piles of his papers lying everywhere.

Now, when he looked at the rug before the fireplace where she had sat reading his assay reports or at his file cabinets that she had organized so diligently during those long, snowy afternoons, all he could do was think of Kate. Even his own desk reminded him of her. His body tightened painfully as he remembered what they had done here on the smooth wooden surface before him.

He stood abruptly and went to pace up and down in front of the windows. He was blind to the lovely sunset and melting snowdrifts outside. It had been a long spring. This should have been a good time for him. The Elk Mountain mines were progressing well. The assay reports on shafts one and two were encouraging, and the rich veins they had hit branching off of three were already paying for all of his development costs. Yet he could take little joy in his success, for Kate wasn't here to share in it.

It surprised the hell out of him. He never could have believed a slip of a girl could get under his skin the way she had. There was no use, though, in denying it any longer. His house seemed like a tomb since she had left. He found excuses not to come home, especially at night. To make matters worse, his staff kept shooting him reproachful looks. He knew he deserved them, for his temper had been foul since the afternoon he arrived home and discovered Kate was gone.

He had sent word at once to the Old Homestead. He smiled mirthlessly to himself as he remembered the politely worded note he had received from Pearl that day, the mocking undercurrent in the missive obvious. The madame had regretfully explained that Daisy had already left Cripple Creek seeking employment elsewhere. Before leaving she had made it very clear she did not wish to be contacted again by her former protector.

Furious, he sent Ben to do some discreet checking down on the row. They quickly learned what Pearl had said was true. Telling himself he was well rid of a mistress who could find herself a new protector and fall so quickly into another man's bed, he resolved to drop the matter. Trying to forget her, he had immersed himself in his work and Cripple Creek's glittering social life. He went out to the theater and to parties every evening. He even returned to the Old Homestead once, but he found Lola Livingston's ample charms now seemed coarse and overblown. He left without going upstairs with her, even though he knew Pearl De Vere was watching his departure with an amused, knowing gleam in her eye.

Justin had just finished another round of angry pacing when Ben opened the outside door and stuck his head in. "Thought I'd see if you wanted to come down to Crapper Jack's with me."

"I've got work to do," Justin replied shortly.

Ben glanced from Justin over to his desk and back meaningfully. "Looks like you're gettin' a whole passel of work done."

"I'm not going anywhere if you're going to lecture me again."

"Hell no, there ain't no use in trying to talk to you. I just thought you'd be better off drinking than wearing a trench in that fancy carpet of yourn."

"I suppose you have a point." Justin walked over and grabbed his hat and topcoat from the rack.

"You comin' dressed like that?"

"I don't feel in the mood to go upstairs and change for an evening at Crapper Jack's," Justin replied sarcastically.

"Good. This should get interestin'," Ben said with relish and led the way out the door.

Ben's prediction proved to be correct. Upper Tens were not usually welcome at Crapper Jack's. It was a saloon and brothel that catered to the roughest elements in Cripple Creek, not to mine owners. The moment Justin and Ben stepped inside the dark, smoky, noisy establishment, they attracted the attention of two large, rough-looking mule skinners at the bar. The two rowdies, who obviously had not been in town very long, immediately decided to convince Justin he should take his business elsewhere.

Grinning, Ben took the boss's fancy jacket and stood back to watch. He grunted appreciatively as Justin made short work of both his opponents. He took the first fellow out with a beauty of a right uppercut to the man's jaw. The other proved to be a more canny fighter, but he, too, eventually went down, and took a table with him.

Justin stood over the wreckage, looking hopefully about the crowded bar for more takers. No one else stepped forward, for there was an unholy gleam in the boss's cool blue eyes tonight. Besides, most of the men knew there was something different about Justin Talbott, and those who didn't understood it now.

"Feel better?" Ben asked laconically as Justin flung himself down in a chair next to him, nursing his skinned knuckles.

"It helped."

"Try some of this." Ben poured him a shot of whiskey.

"Dr. Gallagher's remedy for anything that ails one, eh?"

Ben raised his glass and drained it in answer. The two of them sat drinking quietly for almost an hour, ignoring their noisy surroundings. When the level of the bottle between them had sunk to the halfway point, Ben suddenly said, "This ain't a lecture. It's a question. That Pinkerton you hired found anything out yet?"

"I'm beginning to think the man couldn't find his own arse if he looked for it in broad daylight," Justin replied wearily. A month ago he had finally admitted to himself that he wanted to find Kate again. Whatever her new protector was paying, he was willing to double it. But he had to find the girl first to be able to propose a new arrangement to her. And so he had hired a detective, a man named Albert Jones, who had come well recommended.

The devil of it was, it was beginning to look as if he had waited too long and allowed her trail to grow cold. None of the staff at the railroads remembered Kate, and she was the sort of young woman men would have to be blind not to remember. Two of the conductors and one of the ticket sellers on the Cripple Creek end had quit or been transferred recently. The Pinkerton was trying to find them, and he had been questioning railroad workers at all of the major stops along the lines leading from Cripple Creek. Justin thought it most likely Kate had gone to Denver, either to catch a train to another mining town like Leadville or Aspen, or to arrange for transportation back east. He had explained to the Pinkerton that Kate had a sister living somewhere in New England. Jones promised to send out discreet inquiries in the northeast as well.

"What if he don't find her?" Ben interrupted Justin's thoughts abruptly.

"I'm not sure," he replied, swirling his whiskey about in the glass. He couldn't tell Ben, but his blood ran cold at the thought that he might not see her again.

"The damnedest thing is, I know Pearl knows exactly where she is. I can't get the confounded woman to tell me. I even tried bribing her, and that got me shown to the door in five seconds flat. I never got thrown out of a whorehouse before." Justin was too aggrieved to see the humor in his words.

"I reckon she's just trying to look out for the little gal."

"Why the hell does she have to bother?" Justin slammed the glass down so hard on the table that the men embroiled in the poker game the next table over looked up from their cards curiously. "What I have in mind would be beneficial for us both," he continued in a lower voice. "Kate could live like a queen with what I'd be willing to pay her."

"Mebbe gettin' paid ain't enough, least not for a little lady like her," Ben suggested, his one good eye looking down at the table. "You was her first, after all. Maybe she didn't like the business and decided to up and quit it."

"Once a harlot, always a harlot," Justin countered grimly, but the thought of Kate in another man's arms sent pain searing through the heart of him, pain he thought he wasn't capable of feeling anymore.

Ben wisely kept quiet as Justin went back to working on the bottle. Two hours later when he stood up, he could hardly walk. To Justin's disgust, Ben had to help him to the door. As Justin lurched out into the cool night, he damned himself for a fool. Despite all the whiskey he had consumed, the pain was still there.

It was a beautiful, sunny morning in Pueblo. Kate hurried as she walked to the train station from her boardinghouse. She had overslept this morning, and she did not wish to miss the nine-thirty train to Colorado Springs. Her visit every Saturday with Elizabeth was one of the high points of her week.

Kate smiled as she walked past the schoolhouse where she now spent so much of her time. She enjoyed being a school-teacher, and she loved her pupils. It was such a challenge trying to help her students take joy in their learning. She desperately needed that challenge now to keep her mind occupied while she learned to cope with the tearing grief that was her constant companion.

She was beginning to think she would be a teacher for the rest of her life. She liked being near young people, especially since she knew she could never have a family of her own. For a brief time she had wondered if she would bear Justin's child. The prospect had both thrilled and terrified her, but Pearl's vinegar douches must have been effective. She would have only memories of Justin to cherish. Although the practical side of her knew it was probably for the best, the thought that she would never be a mother still made her feel empty and aching inside.

During the train ride north Kate tried to concentrate on her students, but somehow her thoughts kept returning to Justin. Although she felt thoroughly depressed by the time she arrived at the sanatorium, Kate did her best to shake off her dark mood. She found Elizabeth waiting in her room. After she hugged her sister fondly, Kate stepped back to look at her. Elizabeth was still thin, but the color in her cheeks was healthy, and she seemed stronger and more energetic.

"What would you like to do today?" Kate tried to put a cheerful note in her voice.

"Let's go for a stroll in the gardens. It's such a lovely morning, I've been looking forward to going outside," Elizabeth replied promptly.

As they walked through the sunlit gardens, Kate told Elizabeth funny stories about her pupils' high jinks in class this week. At last Elizabeth admitted that she was a little tired and wanted to sit for a while on a bench in the sun. Staring out at the yellow and lavender crocuses that were just beginning to bloom, Kate thought sadly of the garden at Justin's home. During the long hours she had spent cooped up inside her bedroom, she had often imagined how she would plant his gardens if she were the legal mistress of his home. She had been naive to even dream such a dream; she could see that now.

"Kate darling, what is it?" Elizabeth asked suddenly. "I know there's been something horribly wrong for a long time now. Surely you can tell me what it is?"

As she looked into her sister's sympathetic brown eyes, the feelings Kate had been trying to keep in check all morning welled up inside her. "Oh, Elizabeth, I just don't know how I can bear it."

She buried her face in her hands and let the tears come. Elizabeth began to stroke her hair slowly, just the way she had when Kate cried in her lap as a little girl.

"Is it—Does this have something to do with Justin Talbott?" Elizabeth asked gently after several moments.

Kate jerked upright, her face flushing crimson. Could Elizabeth have possibly found out? She couldn't bear it if Elizabeth knew. She could survive leaving Justin, and she could endure losing her honor, but this one thing had kept her going through it all. She had always clung to the knowledge that at least Elizabeth hadn't known the price her little sister had paid to make her well again.

"You needn't look so horrified. I had guessed it a long time ago. After you asked him for money to help me, I wondered if he had tried to see you again. What I want to know is"—here Elizabeth's gentle voice hardened—"did he take advantage of your gratitude?"

She stared back at Elizabeth, overcome with relief that her sister hadn't discovered the whole truth.

"No," she managed to say at last. "I can't honestly say he took advantage of me. I did see him frequently for a time, and I was silly enough to fall in love with him all over again. But he was always quite honest with me about his intentions, and they were never serious. It was all my fault that my idiotic heart wouldn't listen to my head."

"And so you decided to take the job in Pueblo to get away from him."

"I had to, but now I miss him so much. I can't seem to stop thinking about him. I miss the way we used to talk together. He never thought the things I said were odd or queer, and he took my opinions on things seriously. I miss the way he looked, the way he carried himself, and the way he laughed." And the way he touched me when we were together, she admitted silently to herself.

"Dear Kate," Elizabeth said, shaking her head sadly, "you've been so brave since the day my Robert died, and now you have to cope with a broken heart. It seems so unfair. I've often wondered what I would have done if our positions had been reversed. I'm quite sure I couldn't have been as resourceful and competent as you have been."

"You probably would have found better solutions to our problems," Kate replied honestly as she mopped her face with a handkerchief.

"I rather doubt it. Well," Elizabeth said in a lighter tone, "I can't believe Justin Talbott didn't have the sense to fall in love with you. He struck me as a highly intelligent fellow."

Kate smiled weakly at Elizabeth's attempt at humor and decided to follow her lead. "It is hard to believe, isn't it? We could have conjugated Latin verbs together for the rest of our lives."

"Another man will snap you up quick enough," Elizabeth declared. "You just have to pay a little more attention to them. Men like to be flattered, you know."

Kate winced inwardly. There was a time when Elizabeth had seemed like a fount of worldly wisdom about the mysterious male sex. Now Kate felt infinitely older and more experienced than her sister on this particular topic. Somehow she managed to smile and nod as Elizabeth proceeded to give her a lighthearted lecture on various ways she could attract a nice gentleman. Kate was profoundly relieved when their conversation moved on to other subjects.

A short time later they returned indoors, and Kate ate luncheon with Elizabeth in the sanatorium's dining room. When Kate was about to leave to return to Pueblo, Elizabeth caught her hand and squeezed it warmly.

"I know this is a hard time for you, but I know you did the right thing in moving away from Cripple Creek. After I lost Robert I didn't know how I could go on. But I did, simply by taking each day at a time and trying to relish the small joys in my life. Perhaps right now you should try to do the same."

As she took a cab across town to the railroad station, Kate realized her visit with Elizabeth had raised her spirits. It was wonderful to see her sister looking so well, the one good thing that had come of the wreck she had made of her life.

Looking back on it now, Kate knew her decision to go to the Old Homestead had been rash and foolish. If she hadn't panicked, if she had only waited a little longer, she could have gone to Justin in January to ask him for help. Or, if her stubborn pride hadn't gotten in the way, she could have told him the truth that first night he had purchased her services at the Old Homestead. That had probably been her stupidest and most reckless moment of all.

Now the problem she faced was how to get on with the rest of her life. As she boarded the train she decided Elizabeth was right. She would have to concentrate on one day at a time, and relish her joys—her students, her sister, and the beautiful state where she lived. Surely the terrible loneliness in her heart would lessen over time.

Justin was working his way through the payroll accounts from the Sadie Sue when Gunnar Carlson came striding into his office. The old man's cheeks were flushed and his blue eyes sparkled as he slapped a small stack of papers on the desk in front of Justin.

"These are the latest assay reports on the level-four drift and the level-five raise. We were both right about that mountain. You and I are going to be very rich men.''

Justin stared down at the slips of paper before him. The numbers made his head swim. Six hundred ounces to the ton, seven hundred and fifty-five to the ton, eight hundred and seventy to the ton. The new vein they had just discovered might prove to be the richest ever found in the district.

"I think we should celebrate. I'll see you at the Wolfe Hotel at eight, ja?'' the old man suggested eagerly.

"I'll be there,'' Justin said as he continued to gaze at the reports. He didn't even notice when Gunnar left, for he was too busy trying to come to terms with the news.

So it had happened at last. He had finally achieved what he had been driving toward all these years. And yet he felt curiously remote and detached from his moment of triumph. With the kind of wealth the Little Scholar and her sister mines were going to produce, he could have anything he wanted, be anything he wanted. He had always been intrigued with the idea of entering politics. Doors everywhere were going to be open to him now. Why then didn't he feel elated? Why didn't he feel excited, or pleased, or anything besides this dreary numbness?

Because Kate wasn't with him to share it. Even in this she haunted him. Justin shoved the assay reports off the desk violently. He couldn't help but remember her enthusiasm and interest in the Elk Mountain claims from the start. Lord, she had made the whole partnership possible by telling Gunnar what a hard but honest man Justin Talbott was. She had helped to bring him this, and where was she? He had no idea. He didn't even know if she was well or safe or happy.

Justin bowed his head and sat there as the dusk outside deepened into night. It was a long time before he finally went upstairs to change.

Ben's first reaction to the news was less than satisfying. When informed his employer now owned one of the richest mines in Cripple Creek and possibly in the world, he raised one eyebrow and said shortly, "Nice work, boss. Can I have a raise?''

Ben must have been more impressed than he had let on, for when Gunnar and Justin came out of the Wolfe Hotel after their dinner, he suggested they go down to the row. Justin was hardly surprised when Ben and Gunnar both made a beeline to Crapper Jack's. He started to follow them inside the saloon, but a sudden restlessness made him turn away from the door.

As he started to stride on down the street, he tensed when he saw a slim girl walking along the boardwalk ahead of him. The light from the window of the neighboring saloon shone off her golden hair. Before he could stop himself Justin was running after her, his blood pounding in his ears. Even as he reached for her shoulder, he realized she wasn't Kate.

The young prostitute drew back from him at first, obviously startled. Her eyes widened as she took in his elegant clothes. Within moments she was forcing her lips into a coquettish smile.

"Evening, mister. You looking for some company tonight?"

Justin stared down at her wordlessly. There was a vulnerable look to her that belied her brazen words. Despite the heavy rouge on her cheeks and paint on her lips, she was obviously only fifteen or sixteen. Her complexion was still fresh, and without the makeup she would have been very pretty.

As he gazed at her he tried to imagine what her life was like, and why she had chosen to become a whore. Perhaps no man had offered for her, or perhaps her husband had already been killed in the mines. If she couldn't be a wife, what else could this girl do? She could be a waitress, or a scullery maid in someone's household. For the first time it dawned on him how few the choices were for women who wanted to support themselves.

He reached into his jacket and pulled out his wallet. He thrust all the money he could find in it, some two hundred dollars, into her hands.

"Take this," he told her gruffly, "and go home to your people. This is no life for a young girl like you."

She looked at the money and then back at him in amazement. Quickly she stuffed the greenbacks into her bodice. "Lord bless you, mister," she said, tears welling in her blue eyes. "I don't rightly know how I can thank you."

"You can thank me by leaving Myers Avenue at once," he

said, already turning away. He couldn't stand to be near her any longer. He couldn't bear the thought that like her, Kate might be working the row in some other town tonight.

He walked blindly down the street, taking in deep, shuddering breaths. He stopped when he saw the familiar doorway to the most elegant brothel in town. Suddenly he knew what he had to do.

After the butler opened the front door of the Old Homestead, Justin brushed past him into the front parlor. He saw Pearl at once, perched on the knee of a corpulent gentleman.

"I need to talk to you," he told her grimly. He took her wrist and pulled her none too gently to her feet. As Justin started to tow her toward the stairs, Oliver, the large colored man who served as both the Old Homestead's butler and bouncer, stepped forward menacingly.

"It's alright, Oliver." Pearl waved him off, a half smile playing on her lips. She didn't say another word until they were standing inside her room upstairs with the door closed.

"Now, Mr. Talbott, I should like to have my wrist back, and then you can tell me what's on your mind. Although I think I can probably guess. Does this have something to do with Kate?"

He dropped her wrist and began pacing back and forth across the bedroom. "I have to know where she is. I have to know whether she is safe and well."

"I believe we've been through all this before, Mr. Talbott. Kate made it very clear that she did not want you to know where she had gone."

"Dammit, Pearl, I can't go on wondering whether she's out walking the streets. You know as well as anyone what can happen to a young girl in your profession."

"Indeed I do. But I'm surprised to see you are so worked up over this. Could the controlled, ice-cold Mr. Talbott possibly have feelings for his former mistress?"

He gave a short, bitter laugh. He stopped his pacing and went to stand looking out her window into the darkness. "You know what I am. You've probably seen a hundred men like me walk through your doors. I don't think I know how to love anyone anymore. But I know I care deeply about Kate, and I must find out if she is safe or in need."

He drew in a deep breath and turned back to face Pearl. "The detective I hired has run out of leads. I'll not make the mistake of offering you money again. But please, can you give me some clue, some way I can find her?"

"What would you do if you did find her again? I'm not going to tell you anything if you are planning to coerce her into being your mistress again."

"Once that was exactly what I planned to do. Now it is more important to me simply to know that she is happy. I have to know that her new protector or madam"—here he couldn't quite keep the distaste from his tone—"is treating her well."

"Very well, Mr. Talbott, I'm inclined to give you the lead you need, even though it means breaking my word to Kate. First I want you to consider this. The night Kate Holden sold herself to you, she gave up the only world she knew. If you honestly want to make her happy, you'll marry that young woman. You can give her back the world of respectability, and let her have the children she longs to bear and rear."

"For God's sake, Pearl, I could never be a fit husband for her. I'm fifteen years her senior, and I'm too hard and selfish to make her happy."

"You're the only man she would ever marry now. Because she has been a prostitute, she would never let a decent man near her. Yet Kate is the kind of young woman who will be most content married and raising a brood of children of her own. And for some unaccountable reason she is very fond of you. Mr. Talbott, if you just put half the effort you put into finding gold into your marriage, you could make Kate Holden very happy."

He rubbed his jaw. "Very well, I promise to consider what you've just said. Now, how can I find her?"

"Elizabeth Townsend is living in Colorado Springs. I believe if your detective can locate her, she will lead you to Kate."

"Elizabeth is in the Springs, eh? What the hell is she doing over there?"

"I said I would give you a lead. I didn't say I'd hand you Kate on a silver platter."

"What you've given me should be enough." He was

already thinking hard. "Thank you. I'll let you return to your gentlemen downstairs." He turned and went to the door. He paused there with his hand on the doorknob.

"Why?" he asked, glancing back over his shoulder at Pearl.

"Why did I change my mind?" The madam looked at him, all traces of mockery gone from her face for the first time. "Because I've come to believe you are her only chance for happiness, and Kate deserves to be happy. She is a remarkably selfless and brave young woman. Good evening, Mr. Talbott."

Chapter Twenty

"We have found Miss Holden's sister, sir." The Pinkerton detective was clearly pleased and relieved to be able to report substantial progress to his demanding client for a change. "She is a tubercular patient at the Brentwood Sanatorium."

"Miss Holden said nothing to me about her sister suffering a relapse. How long has she been a patient there?" Justin asked frowningly.

"Mrs. Townsend has been a patient at Brentwood since December. One of my men spoke to the doctor here in Cripple Creek who recommended the sanatorium to Miss Holden. He was called to Mrs. O'Connell's boardinghouse to examine Mrs. Townsend three weeks before Christmas. At that time the woman was very ill. The physician informed Miss Holden that her sister needed prompt treatment at an excellent sanatorium if she were to have any chance of surviving.

"When the doctor gave Miss Holden a list of good institutions in the region, she seemed dismayed to learn a year's treatment at these places can cost hundreds of dollars. Yet she also assured the doctor that she would find a way to provide her sister with such care."

Justin felt a horrible presentiment growing in the back of his mind. When Elizabeth fell ill in December, Kate had suddenly been thrust into a position where she needed hundreds of dollars in a hurry. There was only one way a beautiful, penniless young woman could raise that kind of money in Cripple Creek. But Kate had not started working at the Old Homestead until January. After a few moments he guessed what had happened. He was willing to wager anything that softhearted Pearl had loaned Kate the funds to pay for Elizabeth's treatment.

So his golden girl hadn't sold herself to pay for pretty gowns and an easier life. He closed his eyes when he remembered that first night when he accused her of doing exactly that. What wouldn't he give to be able to take those words back now? He opened his eyes again and tried to focus on the Pinkerton's words.

"An orderly at Brentwood said Mrs. Townsend's sister comes to visit her every Saturday. I will have one of my men watch the sanatorium next Saturday. With your permission, he will follow Miss Holden to her home. We should have an address for you within a week."

"You have my permission to have her followed, but no one is to contact her," Justin regained enough wits to say. "Your people have done good work on this, Jones. There will be a bonus for you and for the man who found the doctor when you have that address for me."

"Thank you, sir. I will let you know if there are any new developments in the case." Looking palpably pleased, the Pinkerton turned about and left Justin's office.

The moment the door closed behind Jones, Justin buried his face in his hands. Good God, what a fool, what a blind, stupid fool he had been.

What must it have been like for sensitive, proud, well-bred Kate Holden to set foot inside a place like the Old Homestead, much less agree to sell her virginity there to a stranger? He remembered only too clearly the desperate, resolute look on her pale face that night as she had walked down the stairs and stared out over the heads of the men gathered in Pearl's parlor.

He could only guess at the courage it had taken for her to face that room full of rutting males. It was, he realized suddenly, the same sort of bravery she had demonstrated the afternoon she had run out into the street before the freight wagon to save a little boy's life. That sort of person did not sell her body or her honor simply to buy herself a more luxurious life. How could he have been so criminally blind? How could he not have seen the truth?

Because he hadn't wanted to. He rose to his feet and began to pace about his office. He had wanted to think she was shallow and frivolous. He had wanted to believe she was vain and selfish because then he could keep his barriers safely raised against her. From the start, from the very first time she had made him laugh in her father's garden, he knew instinctively that he was vulnerable to her. He had persisted in seeing her in a certain light to keep a lovely, spirited young woman from stealing his heart. During the two months she had lived under his roof, she had acted bravely and selflessly, and he was the one who had been a shallow, cruel coward.

He winced when he thought of the things he had said to her, and the way he had used her. Why hadn't she told him the truth that first night? Surely she must have known that she could appeal to him for help. Remembering the way he had treated her that evening, he knew exactly why she hadn't said anything. It was pride and stubbornness that had kept her from speaking then. It had prevented her from speaking during the entire time she had lived in his home, and it had prompted her to walk out of his house, leaving a small fortune in gowns and jewelry behind.

Now he realized the most painful truth of all. He loved her, loved with all the caring of which his cynical heart was capable. Yet he had to face the bitter reality that he did not deserve her. A better man would have refrained from taking what he wanted so desperately. A better man would have seen what she was from the start rather than try to make her conform to his warped view of the world.

He smiled painfully when he thought of the jest she had made two years ago, that he could not be either dried up or a husk until he was at least forty. But she was wrong; he had been a dried-up husk, an emotional cripple since his early twenties. It was time, past time that he faced his ghosts.

He closed his eyes and thought back to that terrible night in Boston fifteen years ago when his whole life had started to unravel. After being out late with his friends, he let himself into his family's home quietly to find his parents in the midst of a violent argument. He meant to slip away, but the shocking words they spoke kept him standing in the shadows by the door to the parlor.

"Brian Talbott, you are a weak, pitiful fool," his mother said shrilly. "Didn't you once think of the scandal you would cause? Didn't you once think of me?"

"God help me, I thought only of you, when I should have

been thinking of our son and my family name. Please, Alicia, don't leave us. Think of what it will do to Justin. He worships you.''

"Justin is grown up now. It's time he knew the truth.''

"That his father is a common criminal and his mother is a whore to Marshall Routman? That's a lot for a young man to take in all at once,'' his father retorted bitterly.

Justin winced as her palm cracked across his father's face. "So what if I've already lain with Marshall? It was clear that you would not have enough to keep me. A woman has to plan for her future. Marshall has promised to take care of me, something that you can no longer do. Good night, and good-bye, Brian.''

Justin would never forget the look of despair on his father's face as his mother stormed from the room. The next morning she had gone to her lover. Two days later the story of the embezzlement hit the papers. That night his father shot himself.

Dazed and reeling, Justin had gone to seek comfort from Lavinia. They had been friends since childhood. They had always understood that they would marry when they were old enough. Before starting his third year of college, he had formally proposed and she had accepted. They had abided by their parents' wishes not to marry until Justin obtained his degree.

She received him in the parlor with both her parents present. He stood there like some stunned, mute animal while Mr. Westford delivered a final blow. "Because of the scandal attached to your name,'' the man had declared ponderously, "and the fact that you are penniless, we cannot allow our daughter to marry you.''

"Lavinia,'' he tried just once, "is this truly what you want?''

She looked at him pleadingly, her pretty brown eyes filling with tears. "I do not want to lose you, Justin, but how would you keep me?''

Her words, a fateful echo of his mother's spiteful ones, had burned in his memory since that day. He had come to think all women wanted only comfort and security from men. The females who had betrayed him made him believe all their gender were venal, frivolous creatures. He had forgotten the warm, caring women in his life, women like his father's mother, Grandmother Talbott, a dear and stubborn lady who had been faithful to her husband through good times and bad.

Suddenly Justin left his office and strode upstairs. He turned on the electric chandelier in his bedroom and went to stand before one of the lovely watercolors Grandmother Talbott had painted. For the first time in years, he thought of what she had told him at his father's funeral.

Justin, my boy, it probably feels like your heart is being torn into a thousand pieces right now. Remember, though, hearts can heal. It only takes time. I fear these terrible happenings may harden you, but do not shut out all feeling, for then you will shut out all joy.

He had disregarded her wise words completely, perhaps because he had received too many blows in too short a time. He had not let his heart heal. Instead he had tried to shield himself against all emotional attachments. He was amazed his ability to care and feel for others had not atrophied completely by the time Kate Holden had erupted into his life.

During the short time she had lived with him, his golden girl had stolen inside his heart and healed it for him. She had shown him her gender was capable of great courage, love, and self-sacrifice. As he gazed at the delicate landscape, full of such serene color and tranquillity, the thought occurred to him: If a man could heal, surely he could also change. If hard work and determination could make him rich, perhaps, with time, the same resolve could transform him into a decent husband.

But did he want Kate back for just for his own selfish reasons? Did a man like him deserve such a sweet, sensitive young woman? Aching and uncertain, he paced his bedroom long into the night.

It was another sunny spring morning in Colorado Springs. Kate was just starting up the steps to the Brentwood Sanatorium when she heard a deep voice say, "Hello, Kate."

She whirled about. "Justin," she said breathlessly. "What . . . what in the world are you doing here?"

Even as she asked the question she stared at him, drinking in every detail of his appearance. His jaw was just as strong as she remembered, his lips as elegant, and his cheekbones as rugged. His eyes were the same beautiful rich indigo color that haunted her dreams. When she looked closer, though, she noticed a certain tiredness around those eyes, and his face was leaner. It gave her a pang to think managing his new mines was making him drive himself even harder.

"I've come to have a quick word with you, if I may."

Even as she registered the uncharacteristically humble tone in his voice, alarm bells were sounding in her head. Several thoughts swirled through her mind at once. She mustn't allow herself to spend time alone with him. It was such sweet torment just looking at him. She was afraid her composure might dissolve completely at any moment. Why on earth was he here?

"I am afraid Elizabeth will be expecting me. I should not keep her waiting," she said falteringly.

"I understand your concern. I promise to take just a few minutes of your time. It might relieve you to know I took the liberty of visiting with Elizabeth a half hour ago. She knows I was planning to waylay you briefly."

"Oh, Justin." Kate stared at him, terrible dismay welling inside her. "You didn't tell her . . . you didn't say anything about what happened between us, did you?"

"No," he assured her hastily. "I guessed you had kept it from her. I told her merely that I wanted to talk with you."

"I see." She couldn't think of a rational reason to refuse his request. If she stood here much longer on these steps, the staff of the sanatorium might notice Elizabeth Townsend's sister was behaving peculiarly. Brentwood was a genteel institution, and she doubted its directors would take kindly to a vulgar scene taking place on their premises.

"Well, if you've come all the way from Cripple Creek, I suppose I can spare you a few minutes."

She saw his mouth tighten at her less than gracious tone, and she braced herself to receive a scathing retort. Instead he simply nodded and suggested that they walk around to the gardens behind the sanatorium. She fell into step beside him, trying not to notice the way he naturally shortened his stride to match hers.

Surely she was strong enough to survive a short talk with

him, she kept telling herself. But as they walked along together, how she longed to reach out and touch him just once. He was intoxicatingly large and male and vital beside her, and she had been away from him for so long.

"How did you find me?" she asked instead to distract herself.

"I had to hire a small army of detectives to locate you. It took the Pinkertons some time, but they came through in the end."

She darted a quick look at him, not sure whether she should feel furious or flattered he had gone to so much trouble to find her. Whatever he had to say to her must be important to him.

"Congratulations on your bonanza," she said after an awkward pause. "You must be very pleased with your success."

"Gunnar is a happy man these days, and I . . . I seem to have gotten what I deserved," he replied cryptically.

Before she could ask him what he meant, he paused and gestured toward a stone bench. They were in the gardens now, and he had led her to a quiet corner between two large ash trees. Of course, he had to choose her favorite spot in the garden for this interview.

"Would you like to have a seat?"

"I prefer to stand, thank you very much," she replied firmly. The last thing she wanted was to sit while he remained looming over her.

"Very well." He paused and cleared his throat.

All at once it dawned on her. He was nervous. Poised, confident Justin Talbott was actually nervous. She had never seen him at a loss for words before. Wonderingly she watched as he squared his shoulders, clasped his hands behind his back, and looked at her, his blue eyes dark and serious.

"First of all, I came here today to apologize to you. I will not ask for your forgiveness because I do not believe that I deserve it. In the process of locating you, my detectives also discovered a great deal about your personal affairs. I now know why you chose to go to the Old Homestead. I know you wanted to give your sister this." He gestured toward the well-kept gardens and the elegant building behind them.

"I know you were trying to save her life by providing for her the very best treatment and care you could. There was

only one way you could do it. That night at the Old Homestead
I accused you of being shallow and venal. I now understand
that you are exactly the opposite. You are the most courageous, selfless woman I have ever known.''

Her cheeks began to flame. ''Justin, there's no need for you
to say these things. It's all over and done now.''

''There's no need? I have insulted and used you in every
way imaginable, and you say there's no need for me to apologize?'' His voice roughened, and suddenly he swung away
from her.

When he turned back his voice was calm again, but she had
gotten a glimpse of the volcanic emotions he was fighting to
contain. ''For me there is every need, even though I know my
saying the words will hardly absolve me of my guilt. Dear
God, I know there is nothing I can do to change what I took
from you, but still I have to say this.

''I am so sorry, and I shall be sorry until the day I die. I
had no excuse for not seeing what you were from the start. I
was a blind, stubborn idiot to think you were like the other
women I had known in my life. Again, I do not expect you
to forgive me, but I do want you to know I regret every cruel
thing I ever said to you. I regret having treated you so cal-
lously, and I regret more than you will ever know having taken
your innocence.''

He paused and drew in a deep breath. ''Kate, I have come
here today to ask if you will do me the honor of becoming
my wife.''

''Justin, you can't be serious. . . .''

''I've never been more serious in my life. Marriage is the
only form of restitution I can offer you. If you marry me, our
relationship will take whatever form you wish. It can be a
marriage of convenience if you so choose. You would have
the protection of my name, but you could go your way and
live your life as you please. With the wealth my mines are
producing now, I can provide you with a fine house anywhere
you would like to live. You could be certain that Elizabeth
would always be well cared for. Genteel society would receive
you once more.

''There could be a final benefit from this arrangement.'' He
paused here, and his voice softened. ''I know you care for

children, and I believe you hoped to have sons and daughters of your own someday. I would be honored to be a father to your children, but I swear the issue of whether we ever enjoy marital relations would be entirely up to you. I understand you may well hate me now, and the idea of marriage to me may seem completely abhorrent. I hope, for your own sake, you can employ your considerable intellect to see past your loathing to understand the benefits in what I am offering you.''

"I could never hate you, Justin," she said quietly.

"Then"—he paused and cleared his throat again—"perhaps you could agree to marry me." He wasn't looking at her now. Instead he was staring intently at the grass near her feet.

"It would never work," she said helplessly. "What if someone found out what I had been and exposed me? You could lose all the position and standing you have fought so hard to regain for yourself. I couldn't bear it if you came to regret marrying me."

"I could never regret marrying you," he said in a low voice. "That I know is an impossibility." He looked up then, and the world of tenderness she saw in his glorious blue eyes stole her breath away.

"I should have mentioned a final reason I hoped you might agree to become my wife," he said slowly, "but I thought it the least important of them all. Little scholar, you have taught this bitter heart of mine how to love again. Since you walked out of my house, my life has been gray and dreary. I have missed my golden girl so very much, for she gave me the precious gifts of laughter and joy, and then she took them away with her.

"I am telling you this not to sway you, but so that you may know I am making these pledges in good faith. I will spend the rest of my life trying to make amends for what I have done to you. I know I do not deserve to be your husband. I understand the offer of my love cannot mean much, coming from a man like me. I realize I have used and hurt you in so many ways. Yet I have to ask you again, will you marry me? I cannot bear to think of the future you are facing now. I want so much to know at the end of every day that you are well, safe, and happy."

She closed her eyes. She could withstand anything, except

the sight of this proud man discounting his love as if it were tarnished and unworthy. Perhaps she was mad, but she did not have the strength to deny him. These past few months had been too bleak and hard. He had said she was brave, but she was not courageous enough to face a life without him. Right there and then she promised herself he never would have cause to regret marrying her. She would do everything she could to fill his life with joy and love.

"I accept your offer, but only if you will agree to be my husband in every sense of the word."

He just looked at her, his face strained and pale. "Kate, my dear girl, are you certain? I am fifteen years older than you. My life until now has been lived quite selfishly. I am hardly a blushing bridegroom, and you already know what it can be like to live with me."

"And just now I thought you were trying to convince me of all the reasons why I should marry you. Men can be such illogical creatures." She was laughing now through her tears.

"Indeed we are." His tense features relaxed into the sardonic smile she knew so well. "Darling Kate, it will be hellish, but I will keep away from you if you wish."

"I am not the least bit interested in a marriage of convenience. I expect being married to you will be all sorts of things—frustrating, exciting, maddening, but it will rarely be convenient."

"You mean, despite all my good resolutions, you will allow me to be my former irascible, irritating, arrogant self?"

"Of course. That is the man I love, after all," she told him simply.

The smile fled his face. He looked stunned. Hope and fear began to war in his expression. The fear made her heart twist for this remarkable man who had gone far too long without a woman's love.

"*Facta nonverba*—actions speak louder than words," she murmured and stepped forward. She raised her hands and placed them on his shoulders. She stood on tiptoe and kissed him full on the lips. Moments later his arms encircled her, and he pulled her firmly against him.

"I don't understand how this could be so," he said wonderingly and framed her face with his hands. "After all that's happened between us, you should loathe me rather than love me. But if you will give your heart into my keeping, I swear you won't regret it.''

"Justin, a man cannot kiss a woman properly when he insists on clucking on like a hen."

The laughter in his eyes made her heart warm. "You've surely turned into a bold piece while you've been away from me, Miss Holden.'' He bent his head to do as she bid him.

''That is much more like it,'' Kate said contentedly a long time later.

Author's Note

Dear Readers,

Cripple Creek still stands beneath the rugged western spires of Pike's Peak. These days, the town's inhabitants are enjoying a second goldrush. People come from all over to gamble in Cripple Creek's casinos. If you wander beyond the outskirts of the picturesque town, beyond the bustle of folk on Bennett Avenue and the clanging of the slot machines, you can still get a feeling for the old mining days. The hillsides are pockmarked with tailing piles where thousands of men labored to find their dreams of gold.

My thanks to the owners of the Old Homestead for the excellent tours they have given of their establishment over the years. I apologize for taking some liberties with the Old Homestead's history. The elegant building I described was actually built after the fire which destroyed much of Cripple Creek in 1896.

The story of Pearl DeVere haunts me to this day. She truly was a madam at the Old Homestead. She died on June 5, 1897, of an overdose of morphine. Some claim she purposely committed suicide after a fight with her lover. Others believe she was simply restless after throwing a large party and took the morphine to help her sleep. Pearl's family refused to claim her body when they saw her occupation listed on her death certificate. The townsfolk of Cripple Creek rallied and gave her a grand funeral. The Elks Club band, mounted policemen, hundreds of onlookers, and buggies full of girls from "the row" escorted Pearl's body to Mt. Pisgah Cemetery. On the way back from the cemetery, the band reportedly played "Hot Time in the Old Town Tonight."

I hope you have enjoyed reading *Golden Dreams* as much as I enjoyed writing it. I would love to hear from my readers. You may write to me at 162 S. Rancho Sante Fe Rd. E-90290, Encinitas, CA 92024. In the meantime, I hope that all your golden dreams come true!

Sincerely,
Anna DeForest

WINDS ACROSS TEXAS
Susan Tanner
Bestselling Author of *Exiled Heart*

The Comanches name her Fierce Tongue; Texans call her a white squaw. Once the captive of a great warrior, Katherine Bellamy finds herself shunned by decent society, yet unable to return to the Indians who have accepted her as their own.

Slade is a hard-riding, hard-hitting lawman, out to avenge the deaths of his wife and son. Blinded by anger and bitterness, he will do anything, use anyone to have his revenge.

Both Katherine and Slade see in the other a means to escape misery, but they never expect to fall in love. Yet as the sultry desert breezes caress their yearning bodies, neither can deny the sweet, soaring ecstasy of their reckless desire.

_3582-0 $4.99 US/$5.99 CAN